I0452447

Once Upon A Time In Texas

By Tom Roush

PART 1

"Texas has yet to learn submission to any oppression, come from what source it may." – Sam Houston, 1861

Chapter 1

The eastern sky turned purple and blue until the morning sun broke over Florida's east coast. Icicles that had accumulated overnight distorted the early light as they began to melt. As the sun rose over the sea, water droplets collected on the tips of the icy fingers clinging to the massive scaffolding on Pad 39A.

Even before sunrise, Kennedy Space Center was a hive of activity. Shuttle launches were a 24-hour business, but this troublesome mission had kept the center busier than usual. The day before, the crew had been strapped into the shuttle, ready to rocket into space—only to have the mission scrubbed at the last minute due to trouble with a hatch handle. There were checklists within checklists, and many things could go wrong. But as the sun rose over the ice, and the ground crew moved across the catwalks inspecting for cold-weather damage, nothing appeared obviously out of the ordinary. The weather was bright and clear. They looked up into a crystal sky over the dark blue Atlantic. As far as they could tell, it was a go.

While the launch countdown began in Florida, it was still pitch-dark in Houston. From the tip of the San Jacinto Monument—dedicated to Texas independence—a lone raven could see the horizon shifting hues. But at Johnson Space Center, no one was watching the sky. Members of the shuttle team were pulling into the parking lot, bundling up for the walk to Mission Control. It was cold for muggy, buggy Houston—but they'd be inside for the next few days anyway. The city's volatile weather didn't matter inside Mission Control.

A few miles away, north along a highway he once drove twice daily, Bob Buckhorn opened his eyes. He was several miles—and four years—from Mission Control now. His wife snored beside him, but his bones told him it was time to get up. He had nowhere to go, but Bob had been an early riser for decades—rising to walk a patrol in Korea, to inspect a section of drill pipe in West Texas, to comfort a crying child in Deer Park, or to make it to NASA's Johnson Space Center in Clear Lake. His best years had been spent at NASA. Now he still rose early, but he no longer went to NASA—or anywhere else.

3

He stood and pulled on a dirty robe he'd left on the floor the night before. He had been wearing it for days, and his wife, Carol, had long since stopped caring what he wore.

Bob made his way downstairs, sleepwalked into the kitchen, and hit the button on the coffee maker. While waiting, he drifted into the living room and turned on the television. There, he saw the news out of Cape Canaveral.

"What the hell?" he muttered.

On screen was the orbiter—massive, ungainly, and impossibly complex. It had consumed his final years at NASA, but Bob's eyes were on the people. The crowd gathered for the launch was bundled against the cold. Reporters exhaled plumes of steam as they gushed about the impending launch and the historic Teacher in Space flying aboard Challenger. It was plainly freezing at the Cape.

After a blank moment, he returned to the kitchen and poured a cup of coffee. Before taking a sip, he paused and lowered his head. The very sight of the shuttle had pulled him down. Above the coffee maker sat a bottle of vodka. Bob grabbed it and the highball glass from the day before. He splashed in a slug, drank it, then poured another. A third shot went into the coffee.

In the darkness of early morning, his long, aimless day had begun. He was 52, he thought—and his often-difficult life already felt over.

* * *

Jack was pulled back to consciousness by the pressure on his bladder. As he came to, he noticed his mouth was dry, his hips ached from sleeping on a hard floor, and then his pounding head took over. He tried to push away the pain but couldn't ignore the full bladder.

The deep, sonorous voice of a radio broadcaster penetrated his mind. It was the morning news roundup, and Jack caught the part about the freezing weather. He suddenly realized that, in addition to a full bladder, numb hips, burning nose, dry mouth, and pounding head—he was cold.

The newsman read a chirpy account of the *Challenger*, which was set to launch. Jack thought of his dad's friends down at Johnson Space Center. They weren't the hearty astronauts of old. Most of them were aging, ragged hippies who had studied math back in the day. When Jack met them, they seemed to expect questions about the space shuttle, smiling and waiting for him to breathlessly ask how he could grow up and be one of them.

But Jack had no desire to work at NASA. He didn't know a single person who wanted to be an astronaut—and he lived in Space City. His friends all thought space was vast, stupid, and a complete waste of money.

He opened both eyes and gently turned his head.

Clutter was everywhere. Beer bottles littered every surface. The floor was a mosaic of clothes, ashtrays full of cigarette butts, and sleeping bodies. Several male forms lay sprawled across the carpet—two with cowboy hats covering their faces. The others were female, with long manes of black hair, heavy hips, and fingernails painted flat black.

Jack grabbed a dirty couch cushion near his head and pulled himself to a sitting position. Sleeping on the couch was the one guy he knew: Miggie. An older Mexican man with long black hair, Miggie lay with his tattooed arms crossed tightly over his chest. Jack's leather jacket was draped over Miggie's feet. Jack carefully lifted it off and pulled it on as he stood.

He stepped over the two sleeping women on the floor and opened the front door.

He winced at the cold and stepped onto the tiny porch. Trucks were scattered across the gravel lot nearby. The voices of cowboys carried on the frigid air as they walked toward the rodeo ring. On the ground lay a flotilla of red Solo cups, wooden corn dog sticks, wrappers, firecracker wadding, and a sea of cigarette butts.

Jack unzipped his pants and dug around. He held onto the doorknob and released a strong stream of hot urine onto the ground. As his mind began to refocus on the previous night, his heart sank—thinking about all the drugs they'd done and all the money he hadn't collected.

"Buckhorn, there's a goddamn bathroom in that thing! Put your dick away, son!"

Jack's stream stopped mid-air. It hurt, and he winced, then looked up. There, in the window of the adjacent trailer, was the old, grizzled face of the rodeo organizer. He knew Owen Williams from back when he was still rodeoing. Williams was a mean SOB who carried a pistol—and had used it. He'd shot several people and killed one. Nobody struck back, because there weren't many rodeo organizers left where a cowboy not headed for the big leagues could still make a couple thousand dollars.

Jack tucked himself away and waved with his free hand at Owen through the dirty trailer screen. Williams had liver spots on his face and a bulbous red nose from years of drinking. His gray hair hung over his ears, and his black mustache clung stubbornly to the memory of a violent youth.

"Good morning, Mr. Williams," Jack muttered, turning to go back inside.

"Take your drugs and get the fuck out of my rodeo," Williams barked, leaning over his sink with his face pressed to the screen. "You hear me?"

"Yes, sir," Jack said.

He immediately regretted not denying he'd been dealing—at least perfunctorily. Owen knew his dad somehow, though Jack couldn't remember how. Maybe they talked about Korea. If so, that meant they were both Marines—and that wasn't good.

If Owen Williams knew he was dealing drugs, *everyone* knew.

Jack went back inside and kicked one of Miggie's boots hanging off the edge of the couch.

"Migs, wake up," he said urgently.

Miggie hadn't survived this long living the way he did by being a heavy sleeper. He felt the kick and heard the edge in Jack's voice, so he opened one eye.

"Hey, we did all the blow. *All* of it. I need some money for that much," Jack said.

Miggie closed his eye again.

"I paid for the strippers," he muttered, adjusting his arms. The cold inside the trailer was finally registering.

Jack looked down at the two women curled up on the floor. They were fully dressed. In no way did they resemble strippers.

"These aren't strippers," Jack said. "They *work* here. That's… eh… what's her name. That's the other one," he added, pointing at the slumbering mounds. "Come on, Migs. I can't give away that much coke."

After a sigh, Miggie reached into his back pocket and pulled cut his wallet. He handed it to Jack. Jack opened the thin old thing and saw a few twenties. He took them out—$120 total. His face fell even further.

"Jesus God. Fucking broke-ass cowboys," he muttered, dropping the wallet on the coffee table.

* * *

While Bob watched the news about the shuttle launch, he heard feet hit the floor overhead. A few minutes later, a toilet flushed—he knew Carol would be the first one down. Sure enough, seconds later, she descended the stairs in slippers and a thick pink robe with her initials, *CB*, monogrammed across the chest.

"It's freezing in here," she said as she passed without looking at him.

Bob kept his eyes on the television. He recognized most of what he saw—from the techies walking the inspection decks, to the steam spewing from the base of the orbiter, to the static shot showing the hatch where the astronauts would board. Ice clung to the scaffolding that held the orbiter in place. Cutaways to the crowd and journalists showed everyone bundled in heavy coats.

He finished his vodka-laced coffee and headed back into the kitchen. Carol stood at the stove smoking a cigarette. She looked at him as if she were looking through him. He reached up to the high shelf for the vodka bottle.

"Already?" she said, blowing a plume of smoke from her nose.

"Early bird gets the worm, darling," Bob replied, not looking at her. He opened the Bloody Mary mix sitting on the counter, poured in a dose, added a generous shot of vodka, and stirred the drink with his finger as he walked back to the TV.

Bob dropped onto the couch.

"Lord, help us. The space plane," he muttered.

Josie Buckhorn bounded down the stairs next. He was all skin and bones, with shaggy, light-colored hair. He'd only recently become a teenager, but puberty hadn't yet filled out his frame.

7

"Good morning, Dad," Josie said.

"Good morning," Bob replied. "Want to watch the shuttle launch and see how NASA handles risk?"

"Why?" Josie asked, already heading into the kitchen. Bob heard Carol ask what he wanted for breakfast. With Josie, her voice was light and airy.

A moment later, Jennifer Buckhorn came down the stairs. Several thin bracelets jangled on her wrist as she walked, making a soft tinkling sound. Her hair was a tangled mess, and her ripped jeans and torn T-shirt were clearly last night's pajamas.

"Good morning, Daddy," she said.

"Good morning, Miss Bedhead," Bob replied. "Would you like to know how the properties of metal are affected by the cold?"

"No thank you," she said, brushing past him.

Bob wasn't surprised his kids weren't interested in the shuttle. None of them had ever shown much curiosity about science—or about his work at NASA—even when he was still employed.

After a moment, he set down his drink and retrieved the phone from the bookcase.

Chapter 2

Too many pine trees mean pine straw rains down and covers
everything. What is covered in pine needles stays shaded and when it
gets wet, it stays wet. Then, mold grows under it, and more pine straw
piles on top, and then everything smells wet, even when the weather is
dry. Domingo's backyard had eight pine trees that had been raining
down straw long before there was a house on the lot.

Before Houston covered the marshland, fires would come through.
Lightning started a fire, or the Akokisa would hunt with fires and drive
the animal life out of the underbrush. Later, the Anglo settlers used fire
and axes to clear land, and they hated pine trees as much as most kids
who had to rake up pine needles. The Anglos burned the pine trees, but
as ranch lands around Houston grew smaller, the forests were allowed
to grow wild again until the suburbs came through. By that time, trees
stood for something again, things like beauty, shade, and comfort,
even if they covered everything in a brown gauze that made everything
damp.

Domingo Ruiz never went into his backyard, so he barely noticed
how the pine straw accumulated. He didn't care if it was wet or dry
because he didn't care about his backyard. Domingo didn't care about
much except money, and he cared about money because it bought him
what he truly cared about—women. Domingo loved women and sex,
and he liked sex dirty and rough. Domingo was a pig of a man in
nearly every way, but his sex life pushed the boundaries beyond what
was legal in his native land of Mexico or his adopted land in the
United States. Because no normal woman would do what he liked, he
had to pay for sex but even then, no woman would do what he wanted
for hours, so he could never pay the same woman twice.

Domingo was that much of a pig.

Given how his thoughts were bent, he never even looked out the
glass door to his backyard unless something brought his attention to it,
like someone tapping on the glass. He looked up from his newspaper
and saw Jack Buckhorn standing at his back door.

Jack had approached the back door and took a breath. He knew
what he had done was wrong, and he knew Domingo would call him
on it. But he did it anyway. Jack snorted the coke he was supposed to

sell because, in the end, he wanted to have a good time and be popular. Neither man, Jack nor Domingo, was in it just for the money. Neither man had defined a larger purpose in life that would preclude doing drugs. Neither man was a drug visionary.

But now, Jack had to face Domingo, and he didn't hesitate. Jack could see Domingo inside at a tiny table drinking coffee and smoking. He had no idea what the rest of the house looked like, not even the bathrooms, and Domingo was always at the same table, doing the same things.

Domingo unlocked the back door and slid it open. Jack held out some cash. Domingo took it and fanned it enough with one hand to find out how much it was.

"What the fuck?" Domingo said. His heavy accent made 'fuck' sound like 'fook.' "I gave you real drugs. This is bullshit. This isn't enough."

Domingo backed away and Jack stepped into the small, spartan dining room. Domingo threw the money on the table and sat back down. He instinctively lit another cigarette. Jack stared at the paltry stack of bills on the table and then at the floor. He said nothing about the extra $40 in his pocket.

"Had to take what I could get," Jack said. Then he looked further down at his boots.

Domingo shook his head. He knew Jack did as much as he sold, but Domingo had no intention of ever passing drugs and taking cash from anyone ever again. He had been in jail in Mexico and in the US. He needed idiots like Jack.

"Puta Madre . . . come back in an hour," Domingo said. He said it fast without looking up. No need to tip Jack off about what was coming.

Jack nodded and turned. This was the problem; disappointing Domingo was never that painful. Dealing with Domingo's feeble disappointment was mildly annoying. Jack had as much respect for Domingo as a drug supplier as Domingo had for Jack as a drug pusher. It was their deal.

Jack fought his way between the fence and the overgrown holly bushes that ran along the side of Domingo's house. The holly brush scratched at Jack's arms, but he pushed past them and walked toward his truck parked at the moldy curb. Across the street, Marco looked up and raised his chin at Jack. Jack dropped his own slightly. They had seen each other. This was the body language of people who had known each other for a long time. Marco was washing his old Mustang in the cold, and Jack knew he would spend the next hour waxing it.

Jack drove down two houses and stopped, trotted up to the front door of the two-story brick house across the street, and disappeared inside.

* * *

Bob looked over at the door when he heard a key turn in the lock. Jack entered and smiled. It was the only smile Bob would see all day.

"Jackie boy!" he said. "Come watch the shuttle launch with me! It's icy cold and this could be interesting."

"Good morning, Dad," Jack replied. He wondered if his dad was already drunk. Without acknowledging the invitation, he headed up the stairs.

Jack turned on the landing halfway up and saw his brother Josie peeking through a crack in the door to their sister's room.

Jack quietly walked up to Josie and pushed the door wide open.

"Whatcha looking at, perv? Huh?" Jack cackled. He saw Jennifer, in her panties, turn from her dressing mirror and cover her chest, even though she was wearing a bra.

"Ugh! Get out of here, creeps!" she yelled, throwing a round brush at them both.

Jennifer Buckhorn had doubts and secrets. She had long, nearly black hair, dark eyebrows, and a slight but pleasant olive tint to her skin. She was well-proportioned and thin. But in her heart, she still believed she'd be more attractive if her skin were lighter, if she were ten pounds thinner—and if all of it came off her waist and went to her ass. She used the mirrors in her bathroom to study her body from all angles. Her dominant concern was hair. She didn't want any body hair that was abnormal, and she kept a collection of razors and creams in case a follicle went rogue.

She was still fourteen when *Like a Virgin* was released, and the video and music were everywhere. The song floated out of a record

11

store at the mall. Going to the Town & Country Mall was the best part of her week, and she was there with her mother and Marco's foster sister, Shannon, when she first saw the video for *Like a Virgin* playing on a TV in the window. She let the images wash over her and light up her imagination. She saw, in a glance, what she wanted to look like—and in Madonna's facial expressions and body language, who she wanted to be.

Shannon was already going Goth, and Jennifer detested the Goth aesthetic. She didn't want anything to do with boys, and certainly not look like one. Shannon had laughed at her that day, and that moment marked the beginning of the end of their friendship. Jennifer went into the store and bought the record.

"It's a joke. Don't you get it?" Shannon had said. "She's a whore, not a virgin. *Like* a virgin means she's a total whore. God!"

But Jennifer didn't see it that way—and she never invited Shannon anywhere again. After that day, Jennifer did everything she could to co-opt Madonna's aesthetic, to move, act, and think like her idol.

She quickly learned that the best way to know if her Madonna metamorphosis was working was to observe her brothers. Jack was older, and her emerging sexuality brought out his protective side. That same year, he told her that if any guy touched her, all she had to do was tell him and he'd beat the shit out of the guy.

Within a year, Josie had started to stare at her.

But when she was trying to get things done, her brothers were annoying—and when her door burst open, she knew exactly what had just happened.

"Now you can see better!" Jack said. Josie tried to wriggle out of his grasp.

"Out! I'm going to call Daddy! Out! *Out!*" she shouted.

There was never any point in waiting for her brothers to do what she asked, so she crossed to the door, pushed them into the hallway, and slammed it shut.

* * *

Jack knew about Jennifer's hirsutism, and he was silent about it. Josie didn't know. Jack had seen her crying about the tiny hairs on her chin when she was twelve, and Bob had told him that he was never, *ever*, to speak to anyone about it—and never to make a joke, either.

Bob had been the one to take Jennifer to the doctor. Carol was afraid of hospitals, and Bob knew that if she went instead, Jennifer would be frightened too—and Carol wouldn't understand or remember anything the doctor said. Bob was there as the doctor examined Jennifer from head to toe and explained, in detail, how her body hair would grow abnormally thick in private areas. The whole experience was painfully embarrassing for Jennifer. She stared at the floor through most of it.

On the way home, Bob stopped at the pharmacy and left Jennifer in the car. He bought disposable razors, blades, creams—everything the doctor had recommended. Jennifer stared straight ahead when he got back into the car with the bag of supplies.

"You're a beautiful girl, and you can easily take care of this," he said. "It's best that you learn to do it yourself. Your mother won't be much help."

She looked down at her feet, and a tear slid down her cheek.

"I want to be normal," she said. "First it was on my legs. Now it's on my face."

"You're not normal, baby—in all the best ways," he said. Despite his own austere upbringing, he knew what to say to a daughter who didn't feel loved or beautiful.

"Everything you need is in this bag," he said. "They make disposable razors now, so just throw away the ones you use when they get dull or start to rust. When you run out, put the empty bag in my sock drawer, and I'll get more. Anything else you need, write me a note. No one needs to know. You're going to grow into a beautiful woman."

In the five years that followed, she had grown into a beautiful girl, but she shaved constantly and never knew what body hair was normal and what was an endocrine abnormality. She never spoke to any other girls about it. Her dad continued to buy her razors and creams, sometimes leaving new products in her bathroom for her to try. They never spoke about it again.

Jack noticed when she started to develop an obsession with Madonna, and he figured it was tied to her wanting to look as feminine as possible. Bob thought the same but said nothing. Carol bought the makeup, rings, and clothes—and said nothing.

As Jennifer grew older and taller, she filled out in the hips and chest, and she mastered the art of keeping any unwanted hair removed or perfectly hidden. But she was constantly vigilant, and her fears drove her to spend hours with mirrors, inspecting her body, and with magazines, studying Madonna.

* * *

In the hallway, Jack let Josie go and gave him a playful shove. Josie tried to look angry, but he was laughing. The two boys were nearly eight years apart—practically different generations. Jack never thought about that, but Josie did. Jack teased him constantly, and always had, but when Jack was around, Josie was happier.

"Druggie loser," Josie hurled at Jack. "Where have you been?"

"At least I'm not a loser who's hot for his sister," Jack said. "You whack off to Jennifer?"

"I can hear you guys! Gross! Go away!" Jennifer yelled through the door.

They retreated to their respective bedrooms, but Josie paused at his.

"Seriously, where have you been?" Josie asked. "Dad was worried about you. No one knew anything."

"I was just with friends," Jack said. "I'll talk to him."

"You better do it soon. He'll be drunk and asleep again by lunch," Josie said.

Jack sat on his bed with a hand mirror—stolen from Jennifer—resting in his lap. He'd saved one small baggie of coke from Miggie and now poured it onto the mirror, using a playing card to line it up. His room hadn't changed since the days he'd just hoped his acne wouldn't get any worse: same furniture, same posters, same collection of rodeo trophies. He glanced around at it all for a moment, then rolled up a twenty and snorted the last of the coke.

He slid the mirror under the end table and leaned back, letting the drug wash through him.

After the initial rush wore off, Jack came down the stairs and saw his dad holding the phone, watching the *Challenger* launch prep.

14

"Kinda early for the Bloody Marys," Jack said.

"This is my drug of choice, and I'm pacing myself," Bob replied sardonically. "Where have you been?"

Jack refused to react to the comment or answer the question—but he thought about Owen Williams. Had Owen called his dad? He stopped and watched the *Challenger* countdown for a moment. *Just launch the damn thing already*, he thought. Wasn't the whole point of a spaceplane that space travel was supposed to be routine?

Carol walked through and patted Jack on the back.

"Good morning, baby," she chirped. "There are extra pancakes on the stove."

"Thanks," Jack mumbled.

* * *

Jack sat at the kitchen counter thinking about Domingo. He thought about how much money he might have made if he stopped giving away so much product, and then he thought about the pancakes he was wolfing down. *This is why I still live with my parents*, he thought. Life was good here.

It had been three years since he'd graduated—barely—from high school. His dad had ridden him hard about college, about somehow getting into A&M, but Jack resisted every push in that direction. He hated school. He hated sitting. He hated studying. He didn't like to read. He had strong feelings about the things he hated and was mostly indifferent to the things he liked. When he graduated, he had a girlfriend and had been sexual with her, but sex didn't drive him the way it seemed to drive others. It had been plentiful at the rodeos, where he was often the star. He did it, it was good, and then he moved on.

Drugs—specifically coke—had flipped a switch in him. He thought about coke more than he thought about sex. Since the first time he did it, at seventeen, the organizing principle of his life had been to make sure coke was available. Staying at his parents' house had served that purpose—and now, three years had passed. His dad was an unemployed alcoholic. His mother was turning into something he didn't recognize. His sister, once a skinny, shy girl who barely spoke,

15

had bloomed into a Madonna clone. Josie was still oddly unformed. The family was breaking apart, but the home base still served his needs—so he used it for what it was worth.

Jennifer walked into the kitchen and took some tape out of a drawer. She applied the tape to the arm of her red glasses.

"What happened to your glasses?" Jack asked. He instinctively protected his little sister ever since Bob had made it his duty. When she was born, Bob told him protecting her was his job. Back then, Bob had been skinny and commanded attention.

"Shannon broke them," she said. "We were in the bathroom at school. She was trying to steal them from me, and when I wouldn't give them up, she tried to snatch them, and they broke."

"Shannon? Your friend?" Jack asked.

"Yes, *Shannon*," Jennifer said as she put the damaged glasses on. "She's a bitch. We're not friends anymore."

"I'll take care of her," Jack said.

In a way, Jack was glad for the excuse to go see Marco—he needed to anyway. Marco was a friend, but Jack didn't enjoy hanging out with him anymore. Marco was odd and needy—maybe because he was adopted, or mixed race, or because he lived in a family where no one was related and everyone looked different. Jack wouldn't visit him casually, but he did have a reason now, and Jennifer had handed him a quick excuse. Marco was also his connection to Shannon, if he ever needed to reach her.

Jack walked past his dad and out the door toward Marco, who was still outside polishing the Mustang. A handful of middle schoolers waited at the end of the driveway for the bus. The boys tossed a football back and forth while the girls huddled in small groups, snickering.

Marco's sister Shannon sat bundled in a coat, filing her nails. She and Marco were stark opposites: Marco had olive skin and curly, almost kinky hair, while Shannon was ghostly pale and blonde, her fine hair cut into a sharp bob. Marco was wearing shorts despite the cold. She was wrapped in a matching wool coat and cap.

The middle school boys stopped throwing the football when they saw Jack's face. Something was going down.

"Bro, what's up? My man!" Marco said with a big smile.

Jack pointed at Shannon. He wasn't smiling.

"That little cunt broke my sister's glasses, that's what's up," Jack said. Marco's smile faded.

Shannon lifted her face from her nails.

"Hey, you little skank," Marco snapped. "Did you break Jennifer's glasses?"

"I didn't touch that Madonna-wannabe twat!" Shannon shot back.

Marco turned to Jack.

"You sure?" he asked.

"Yes," Jack said.

"Don't touch her again. Got it?" Marco said, pointing at Shannon.

Shannon rolled her eyes. She knew Jack. She knew Marco. And she *really* knew Jennifer. She knew nothing was ever what it seemed. Jack and Marco had been in trouble plenty, and she'd heard her foster parents lecture Marco over and over about being a follower and getting into messes.

"Idiots," she muttered as she stood up to go inside. She slammed the door behind her.

Jack looked at the boys with the football, who were staring.

"What are you pukes looking at? Throw the ball some more," he barked, and the boys turned away.

Marco stepped in closer and nodded toward Domingo's house.

"Everything okay over there? Yeah?" he asked.

Jack lowered his voice.

"Got to go see him later."

"Cut me in, brother!" Marco said, flashing a grin. He smelled easy dope coming—dope he didn't have to work for. Jack always did the legwork.

"Yeah, I need help. He gives me a little more each time," Jack said. He also thought maybe if Marco was with him, he wouldn't give away so much.

"I feel ya," Marco said. "All the help you need. Sorry about Shannon. She's a little bitch. Even the 'rents hate her."

"No problem. Thanks for taking care of it," Jack said. He clapped Marco on the back. "Be ready."

Jack waved at the middle school boys and walked back toward his house. As he passed, one of the boys threw the football and hit him in the back. Jack wheeled around.

"Who did it?" he yelled, but the boys scattered, laughing as they ran. Just then the bus came around the corner at the end of the block. The girls got up, and the boys knew they were saved. Jack threw the ball high into a big oak tree. It stuck.

"I'm going to find out which one of you did it!" he shouted, and kept walking.

After Jack left, Marco looked across the street at Domingo's house. A little shiver ran through him. He was glad Jack dealt with Domingo. He'd met the man once—five years ago—when Domingo was backing out of the driveway and Marco was on his skateboard. Domingo rolled down the window, yelled something in Spanish, then made a weird sound and drove off.

* * *

Jack came through the front door as Jennifer and Josie were putting on their jackets for school.

"What did you do?" Jennifer asked.

"I handled it," Jack said bluntly.

She picked up her school bags and glanced in the hallway mirror.

"She's such a little bitch," Jennifer sneered. "Her friends are gross too. Marco's the only normal one."

"Stay away from her," Jack said. "And try not to be so weird."

He looked at Josie, up and down. Josie had his pack on and knew an insult was coming.

"You too," Jack said. "I left behind a good rep at that school. Don't screw it up."

"Your rep as a rodeo clown," Josie said.

Jack punched him in the arm—hard.

"Oww!" Josie yelped. It hurt, and he didn't want to smile. Still, he couldn't help it. Any attention from Jack made him happy.

Carol walked past.

"Get going! You're going to be late!" she said as she passed. She was dressed and headed out.

18

Carol went back upstairs as Jennifer and Josie left, and suddenly Jack found himself alone in the living room with his dad. Bob's eyes were locked on the TV.

"Sit down," Bob said. "This could be interesting."

Jack sat across from him and began to watch the *Challenger* coverage too. The countdown graphic showed the launch was getting closer.

"Arnold Aldrich, please," Bob said. Jack noticed for the first time that his dad was holding the phone.

"What are you doing?" he asked.

"I'm calling Arnold. Look at that thing," Bob said, pointing at the TV.

"What?"

"It's freezing in Florida. The whole package has been in a deep freeze," Bob said. "I've been watching this for an hour, and it looks like they've made no preparation for the cold."

Jack stared at the images of the spaceplane. It looked as awkward and ugly as ever. Nothing was different. What new crazy was his dad onto now? And why now—when the kids needed him, when it was clear Mom was pulling away, becoming someone else?

"So, you're calling to tell them it's too cold? Really? From here, in our living room, watching TV, you know what they should do?" Jack said, shaking his head. "They're not going to listen to you. Hang up before you get anyone."

Bob looked over at Jack. He knew how fundamentally uninterested Jack was in science or actual learning. It frustrated him. He knew doing things that mattered wasn't just profitable—it was fun. But what he'd learned in the oil patch, at school, and at NASA had failed to translate to Jack or any of the kids. Bob was self-made. His kids were unmade.

"Complex systems have a lot of moving parts," Bob said. "If you subject the whole system to a variable that's never been tested, the probability of an untested outcome is very high. This is an uncontrolled experiment in the making."

"Dad," Jack said. He didn't want to see his father embarrass himself. "Just hang up."

Bob kept his eyes on the screen.

19

After another moment of watching him, Jack decided it was best not to watch this stupid scene play out any further. Who gave a shit about the Challenger? Or the space program? Or NASA—or the USA, for that matter? There were more important things to care about.

The adult world, for a while now, had seemed to Jack like a colossal waste of human energy. He hadn't seen his parents do anything worth emulating. They never went anywhere. They didn't have friends. NASA was the only reason Bob had *ever* had friends. Jack knew he had an uncle somewhere, but never met him. He had cousins in Mexico he'd never meet. His entire impression of adult life had been shaped by his parents, his teachers, and his coaches. The other adults he'd known were at the rodeo—a place of perpetual danger and indulgence. If the contest for his future was between his parents' barren social life and the rodeo, then the rodeo won.

Like most kids his age, the only political entity he wouldn't mock was Texas.

He jumped up and headed upstairs.

Chapter 3

In 1892, a mouthy yank from Illinois started his own town in the Houston area on open land north of the shipyards. Simeon Henry West had already been in politics in Illinois, but he was determined to make a start in Texas and the land south of downtown and north of the water was as good as any. He declared, by his own authority, the town of Deer Park and the next year built a hotel. The name came from his regular sightings of deer roaming the area. He invited every able-bodied person he met on his travels to come to Deer Park, and a few did. Soon, there was a railway station.

Deer Park was entirely the creation of Simeon Henry West, or perhaps someone he spoke to through his spirit guide. West ardently believed that everyone had a spirit guide and that through his, a spirit woman named Pansy, he could talk to the beyond. West did not attempt to hide Pansy or his belief in her.

In 1931, Deer Park High School was established. Less than 20 years later, Bucky, and then Bob, attended Deer Park High School, which still met in a series of one room buildings. Jennifer knew her dad had gone to the same school, but she never asked any questions about Bob's high school experience. She drove into the parking lot in her tiny Pinto, passing the giant plywood deer antlers at the gate. She hated the school mascot and never heard anyone say anything good about it. Everyone in Deer Park hunted and owned a gun. They mostly hunted deer.

She was a Lady Deer on the track team, and while she liked to run, she had made the track team more of a habit than a passion. As a runner, she knew what she could do moderately well, and she stuck to that. It was good enough for her.

Josie stared out the window, glassy-eyed, as Jennifer drove to her senior parking spot. He hated school, and he thought of what it was going to be like next year when Jennifer was gone, but he still wasn't old enough to drive. He'd be back on the bus, and he'd rather take a shot to the nuts every morning and evening than ride the bus twice a day. Next year was going to suck and suck hard.

As she reached into the back seat to get her bag, Jennifer noticed the boy's track team was already out running sprints. Morning sessions were entirely voluntary, and not managed by the coaching staff, but plenty of the track stars on the team did it.

At the head of the 100-meter spirit pack was David. She paused her gaze upon him. He was slim, most of the way to skinny, and delicately built like a ballet dancer. His longish blond hair floated behind him as he turned the corner and pumped his arms. When he finished in front of the crew, he turned, and she could see his smile. Instantly, he was surrounded by the other guys on the team. One of them smacked him right on the butt. Right before she turned away, she saw him 'high five' a husky girl who finished two spots behind him. She was tougher looking, with short hair, thick hips, and strong legs. She was the only girl out there.

"Don't forget, you take the bus home today," she said to Josie.

Josie rolled his eyes; already he was being shunted to the bus. His worst nightmare was coming true. The bus was loud, smelly, and more than a little dangerous, and it took too long to get home. He always had to pee when he got on the bus.

"Why?" he demanded. "I hate the bus. Everyone on it smells weird. I'll wait for you."

"It's Tuesday; I have track practice," she said as she got out of the car. "You can wait, but it's going to be a while."

"You do that during school," he protested as he got out as well.

"It's PE during school. It's track practice after school," she said. "We're going into the season."

Josie looked over at the track. David was closest to the fence.

"What a bunch of faggots," he sneered.

"You're a faggot," she said as she turned away and headed to the senior homeroom.

Deer Park High required everyone to have an identity. A crazy quilt of human types walked the halls—talking, sulking, laughing, alternately touching and avoiding one another. The halls were a space for unguarded mingling in a way the locker rooms, classrooms, bathrooms, and cafeteria were not. *Everyone has to be here, so we're all going to get along*—that was the unspoken Mayflower Compact between the cliques. The warfare common in other spaces was suspended between classes, at least in the halls.

Jennifer walked through the halls untouchable in her Madonna looks. It only worked because she really did look a lot like Madonna. She inhabited it completely. Her hair was dyed blonde from its naturally dark hue, and the roots violently showed. Her makeup swooped back from the eyes at just the right angle. Her camisole top over her tiny t-shirt fit perfectly. It looked like underwear, but it wasn't. Her teachers couldn't restrict her.

As she passed the classrooms on the way to homeroom, she saw all the TVs were tuned in to the *Challenger* launch. Houston was a company town, and launches were always a big deal, but this one was special in the hearts of the teachers who controlled the TVs.

She was looking at the TV in the science room when she was elbowed in the shoulder by Shannon who was going the other way.

"Oh, excuse me!" Shannon said as she turned around to walk backward.

Jennifer threw a glare her way.

"Troll," she hissed. She turned her head away so she would be sure to see nothing Shannon did.

"Cunt," Shannon said as she flipped two birds.

* * *

Jack lay on his bed thinking about Domingo. He couldn't go on doing what he was doing indefinitely, that was the thought that kept coming back around, but he didn't want to stop. Drugs made his life more interesting. Instead of going down to Domingo's this morning, he thought about calling Regina, his last girlfriend. It had been months since he had last talked to her, and it would be kind of odd to call her out of the blue and ask her if she wanted to go do something, like a movie. Regina never mentioned getting engaged or married, or having kids, but he knew what she had in mind for their future. After he was in his last rodeo, the one where he was injured, and after he met Domingo, his time had been taken up and he stopped calling Regina. She was too proud and had too many options to call him.

He thought about her often, but he knew he had made a choice: he let her go. He let go of the pursuit of any activity that would have linked him to a career or a family of his own. He knew what he had done was wrong, but he could not, and he would not change direction. If he changed, he would confront a whole phalanx of other issues and emotions, and as long as he had his drugs and his old bedroom, neither he nor his parents had to address anything. They could all go along for a while longer like they were.

He sat up and pulled on his boots.

When he came downstairs, Bob was still on the couch, the phone to his ear. The launch was going forward.

"They didn't take your advice"? Jack said.

Bob spoke without looking away from the screen.

"I couldn't get anyone," he said flatly. "They're all in mission control."

Jack rolled his eyes and went out the back door. He looked behind him to make sure his dad hadn't followed, then he crossed to the fence and jumped up a bit so he could see into the neighbor's backyard. He saw nothing, so he put both hands along the top and hoisted himself over.

Jack crossed the neighbor's backyard quickly. The house and yard were immaculate. Jack knew the people who lived there. The husband, Freddy, worked downtown, and left early in the morning. His wife was Chinese, and she never came outside.

After he married, Freddy got a big dog that would stand in the backyard and bark day and night. Carol called the police about it, and they warned the Chinese wife as best they could, given her limited English, that she had to stop the dog from barking. The dog retreated inside with her.

The big dog saw Jack crossing the back yard and it barked furiously and got dog slobber all over the sliding glass door. It was a Labrador/German shepherd mix, and its ears pointed up as it bared his teeth at Jack. In a fleeting instance, Jack saw a tiny female hand pull the dog back by a collar and the curtain over the sliding back door fell back into place.

Jack hopped the fence on the other side of the yard and landed in Domingo's backyard and crossed to the back door. He peered inside and then gently knocked. After a moment, Domingo appeared at the door and unlocked it. He turned, making Jack open the door himself.

24

Domingo lived a spartan existence. He had little furniture, and the walls were bare. There was a tiny Virgin of Guadalupe statue on the kitchen counter, and dirty dishes stacked up beside it. Domingo smoked continuously, and the house smelled of stale cigarettes. In the background, Jack could smell chorizo as well. As far as he could tell, Domingo lived off tobacco, chorizo, and Tecate beer. Beer cans were overflowing from a cardboard box in the kitchen.

Domingo was always twitchy and untrusting. When Jack entered, Domingo sat back down at a tiny breakfast table where the cash Jack had given him earlier was in a small pile. Domingo spoke with a heavy Spanish accent.

"You are a shitty drug dealer," he said, nodding at the paltry pile of cash.

That comment hung in the air and Jack didn't dispute it.

"There should be more," Domingo continued. "You're selling too cheap or doing too much. I think you do too much. You're a cokehead like your customers, but you have all the coke."

Jack tried to hold Domingo's glare but could not. He looked down and shrugged.

"I have to let people sample, and I have to party some with them," Jack offered. "So, they trust me. It's just part of doing business."

"I sell this shit a long time, didn't do it with my customers," Domingo growled, but then he calmed as quickly as he was angry.

"But I know where you live, if you fuck me, I can get to you, so I don't worry about you," he said calmly.

Jack didn't laugh or say anything, but he didn't fear Domingo. That lack of fear, however, was about to be replaced with a real reason to fear.

"Your good day has come," Domingo started. "You can go down to pick up the next shipment."

Jack's head snapped up. Domingo was looking at a newspaper and flicking his cigarette into the full ashtray on the table.

"Take your negro friend and meet at the Matamoros Cathedral," Domingo continued. "These fucking guys, they know what you look like."

Wait, what? Jack thought. *How do they know what I look like?*

"Wait . . . what?" Jack articulated. "You want me to drive down to Mexico and bring drugs across the border?"

"Yes, Puto. I want you to drive down to Mexico and bring drugs across the border," Domingo mocked him. "How the fuck do you think the drugs get here? It will be okay. I've been doing it but now I can't."

There was a long pause. Jack waited for an explanation of the change. Domingo did not offer it.

"Why not?" Jack finally asked.

"Why do you care, Puto?" Domingo asked. "The coke gets here, and people bring it. People like me, and people like you. It's no big deal."

"But I want to know why aren't you going? "Jack asked again.

Domingo sighed.

"I have a doctor's appointment," he offered.

Jack swallowed hard. His throat hurt.

"A . . . a doctor's appointment?" he repeated as a question. "Can't it wait?"

"No, Puto, it can't wait. This doctor's appointment is important and getting the drugs is important, so you go," Domingo said.

There was another long pause. Jack's mind was spinning. Domingo saw his workforce slipping away from him.

"Look," Domingo said, "I might have cancer."

He let the C-word linger in the air. It was the ultimate excuse. Cancer cut through all reasoning and all recriminations. Jack could not refute it.

"So," Domingo continued, "you go to Matamoros. It's all arranged. They'll make sure you get back across the border. We do this before, many times."

"Wow . . . I'm sorry." was all Jack could think to say at the moment.

"Tell your friend," Domingo said. "They are looking for two of you. They don't like dealers who work alone."

Jack was stunned so he turned to leave.

"Wait, Puto, you don't know when you're going," Domingo said. "You need to be in front of the Cathedral tomorrow morning at seven. Got it? Park at the bridge and walk over. Go to the big cathedral, in

Plaza Hidalgo. Don't be fucking late; these are serious guys, cabron. They don't fuck around."

Jack nodded.

"And don't dress like Americans either," Domingo said.

"What do you mean," Jack asked. "What do we wear?"

"Shoes you can walk a long way," Domingo said. "And nothing with the fucking USA flag, or a football team, or a college. You get fucking killed before you get the drugs or after."

None of these instructions helped.

"Cathedral, seven tomorrow morning, got it," Jack mumbled and left.

This new assignment did not thrill Jack. It scared him and the shock of realizing that he was going to have to do something dangerous to get his high was sobering. As he walked out of Domingo's back door, he thought of several things he had heard through the years, about paying the piper. But by the time he had walked around all the overgrown bushes along the side of Domingo's house and started across the street to talk to Marco, the idea that this was a huge opportunity, a sort of promotion, had taken hold and begun to crowd those other voices out. The messages conflicted, but Jack had learned to let cognitive dissonance lay nicely in his head.

Marco was still out in the driveway, putting wax on the Mustang, when he saw Jack round the edge of Domingo's house. He could spend hours cleaning that old car—then go back over spots he'd already done. The gleaming Mustang brought him a great deal of pleasure, even though he didn't drive it much. The car was clean, but unsound. The transmission was on the verge of failing, the door locks didn't work, and the headlights only worked intermittently. Marco didn't have the money to fix any of it, and he didn't know how to do the work himself. His dad did, but he was always at work—or too tired. So Marco cleaned the Mustang, because that was something he knew how to do well. He liked the way he thought he looked out there, polishing it in the driveway, and he was willing to do it even in the cold.

"Bro, what's the word?" Marco said with a big smile as Jack reached the bottom of the driveway. Getting high was now on the horizon. He'd have a clean car, and he'd be coked up.

27

Jack looked around furtively.

"He wants us to go down to Matamoros and do a pickup," Jack said.

Marco's smile faded instantly. He did not consider this good news. A knot developed in Marco's stomach immediately. This was seriously illegal shit and not just illicit fun. He had only been to Matamoros once with his dad a long time ago to go fishing, and he had gotten sick. He had no good memories and had never heard of anything good happening in Matamoros. Matamoros was where you went to get sick, drunk, beat up, or killed, or some combination of bad outcomes.

"What the fuck?" Marco said. "Are you being serious? Dude, no."

"Look, man," Jack continued, "he's got cancer. If we want to keep doing this, we have to go get the stuff. He says it's all arranged; we meet them, and they help us get back over the border. They do it all the time."

"That's . . . so not cool," was all Marco could muster. "And not smart."

In Jack, fear always showed up as anger. He recalled the many times his dad had told him not to show fear even when he felt it. Jack wrestled up to his senior year, and Bob came to every match. Once, when Jack was still a freshman and Bob still worked for NASA, Bob walked onto the mat in his dress shoes to talk to him. The coach, the ref, and several other parents were yelling at him to get off the mat, but Bob coolly walked over and leaned in to whisper to Jack.

"This sorry SOB isn't to know if you are scared or tired," Bob said. "Most people give up too early."

Jack never forgot that. And he found it to be true; Jack kept going when he was completely exhausted, but sometimes he'd say "All day! All day!" to his opponent and he could see them looking for a way to stop the match. He'd provide them with a way out by beating them. It had worked.

"I cut you in on everything else. Don't puss out on me now," Jack said. He ignored the knot in his stomach. "It's going to be fine. He wouldn't send us if it wasn't okay. We leave tonight. I'll pick you up at nine. Be ready."

Jack walked back towards his house. Marco swallowed hard, then started rolling up the hose. He was done washing the old Mustang, maybe forever, he thought.

Chapter 4

Bob Buckhorn didn't think of himself as a Texan until later in his life. In fact, he didn't think of himself as being from any culture. He didn't think about his life that way.

Now that he was unemployed, and he had time to think, he grew to know himself better. He had never taken that time.

Bob was born to Texas, where the weather is often miserable. The high deserts of West Texas, the parts above the massive rift called the Llano Estacado, push dry air, either hot or cold, towards the water-soaked air that blows in from the Gulf of Mexico which makes the area of south and east Texas volatile from a weather perspective. The weather affects the emotions of the people who live there. It affected Bob's parents. They had lived uncertain, itinerate lives. His mom barely spoke in order not to engage in the banality of weather chat. She had her own miseries to address and shared nothing. His dad dealt with the harsh weather and angry Texas culture by never being home except to bathe and sleep. It affected Bob in ways he didn't understand. Texas weather was a hidden driver of the culture.

In 1932, his dad had disappeared again, presumably to look for work, and so Bob had been born at home since his mother had no way to get to a hospital. She was attended to by midwives while Bob's older brother Bucky stood outside the bedroom door. The birth had gone well, and later, one of the midwives opened the door wide enough for Bucky to look in. What he saw shocked him, and he never forgot it. Bucky had vaguely thought he was getting a brother who could be his playmate, and alleviate his constant aching loneliness, but when he saw the creature his mother had brought forth, he knew he would continue to be alone.

Weeks later, Bob's dad came home, still unemployed. He brought a few newspapers with him, and Bob's mother read them and noted that she had given birth on the same day Charles Lindbergh's baby had been kidnapped. Weeks later, she heard on the radio that the Lindbergh baby had been killed. She looked outside to where she had left Bob with Bucky but only saw Bob lying on his back and crying in the sun.

In time, Bob's dad found work and sent money home, but he was rarely around. Bob's mother kept watch on the boys, which was difficult. Bucky wandered off as soon as the sun rose, and Bob often tried to follow him, but Bucky would throw rocks at Bob until he turned back. Eventually, Bob lost interest in Bucky, and they barely spoke. As soon as he was able, Bucky joined the Navy and disappeared.

Bob was emotionally tuned to the dangers around him, and he had, as many boys of his kind did, a keenly attuned sense of bullshit. He disliked all types of pretenses. At his home, a sort of brutal truth reigned. The few words his mother spoke were all literal.

He was a middling student, often terrible, but liked doing things and learning by experimentation. His chemistry set was his favorite toy, but his mother had taken it away from him when he burned a square pattern on her kitchen table. She told him to just go aside and play, which he did.

His home had no TV, or even a radio, and few books. It was outside where he learned about the world, sometimes by playing with the cattle on the neighbor's ranch. He'd go under the fence wire and see how close he could get to the big bull before it chased him and then he'd roll under the long strand of barbed wire to safety and frustrate the bull who could never get a horn in him. His friends would watch from the fence line. The girls watched most intently, and he noticed that. The girls, so creamy and alluring in their dresses and ringlets, so full of mystery and magic, wanted to see a boy do something dirty and crazy. He liked teasing the bull and running. He knew it was time to drop and start rolling when he could hear the heavy bull hooves close behind him, and he had to be sure he was near the fence when it happened.

One time, he heard the hooves, and he heard the crazed bull breathing, so he started to roll even though he was still ten yards from the fence. The bull lowered his head and used his big snotty nose to push Bob under the fence, but not before getting a pointy horn into Bob's left buttock. He felt the sharp stab in his backside and limped home instead of going to school. His mother demanded that he undress so she could apply a dirty towel to the puncture wound. He was embarrassed at having to be nude in front of his mother and humiliated

31

when she wrote a note to his teacher explaining what had happened and asking that he be allowed to stand at the back of the class, rather than sit.

When he returned home from school, his brother Bucky had heard the story from his mother, and he swatted Bob on the backside right after Bob walked inside.

"Daddy's not here, so I guess I have to punish you for going near that damned bull," Bucky said. Bob's backside hurt from the blow, and he spun to face Bucky who was trying to hit him with his palm again. Bucky was bigger, but he couldn't secure Bob well enough to hit him again on the bottom, and they began to punch each other. Bucky hit hard, but Bob wouldn't submit. He fought and scratched until their mother spoke up.

"Bucky, enough!" she commanded.

Bucky stopped, which allowed Bob to strike one more blow to Bucky's ear.

"If you ever hit me again," Bob said, seething in anger, "I'll come to you in your sleep and cut your goddamned head off."

Bucky and their mother froze and stared at Bob's red, angry face.

"As I live and breathe, I'll do it," he finished. "As I live and breathe."

After that day, he and Bucky never spoke again. Two years went by with no words between the brothers. It wasn't long before Bucky joined the Navy and left home. Bob found out from his mother Bucky was gone.

Over his high school years, romantic relationships came and went with regularity. For most women, Bob was not a good long-term investment. He was from a poor family and didn't have a car. He was, he knew, powerless, and power was their organizing idea. Only stupid women liked weak men, and Bob detested stupidity in a woman as much as he hated weak men. He knew his brother was mean and ornery, but Bucky wasn't weak.

His first inkling of the power of the Texas mythos and his place in it came when he joined the Marines and was sent to Korea. In the early days, everything about the war seemed endemic and native to his upbringing. Marine life was rigorous, but not that hard. Sleeping cold or hot wasn't that different from what he was used to since his family

32

didn't have an air conditioner, and they only ran the heater for a few days each year. The war involved the possibility of lightning death, but that was part of a normal campfire tale in Texas. The Comanche would swoop down upon the Anglo-Texan settlers and murder them without remorse. What worse did the Chinese have to offer? Soon, he would find out.

He survived the combat portion of the war after many horrible sights. Early in his first deployment, an artillery shell hit his company tent and killed most of the men inside. Only the wet ground and the cook stove saved Bob from being blown apart. The ringing in his ears lasted several days but the sight of his shredded fellow Marines lasted the rest of his life. He saw two men turned inside out by the force and shrapnel of Chinese artillery. Everything left of the men in the higher bunks was bloody flesh, except the hands and boots.

He saw many dead Koreans, mostly refugees. There were dead children. His platoon was ambushed along the roads every time they traveled on them. The men around him were shot and killed, always in an ambush.

On the long and dispiriting pull back from the Yalu River, Bob and two other men rushed a Chinese position only to find three skinny Chinese soldiers holding up their hands in surrender. The tiny soldiers wore only sandals and shorts. Bob's Gunny, the one they called Gunny Gung Ho, shot those men though they had their hands in the air. After the first two were shot in the chest, the third one folded his hands in prayer, but Gunny Gung Ho shot him in the top of the head right through his cheap helmet.

After a short rest in Japan, Bob was assigned to a Marine artillery battalion on his second tour. His unit fired thousands of artillery rounds north. It was, his men joked, better to give than to receive. Nevertheless, they often received incoming rounds, and so Bob and his men dug foxholes everywhere, so they'd always be close to one. Inevitably, a Chinese round landed in a foxhole where three men were crouched over. By this time, Bob's platoon was made up of mostly new Marines, and the end of the war was near. He did not want the new men to see what was left of the three dead Marines, knowing they might reach the end of the war and never have to carry around such sights, so he and two of the older guys, plus two Korean civilians, separated as much of the remains from the dirt as they could, put them in body bags, and sealed them up.

He never fired a shot in this third deployment. He spent the last eighteen months of the war as a guard for the diplomats at Panmunjom. The North Korean delegation came and went each day, and at night, the two sides would shell each other and then come back for more talk in the morning. Bob was safe at the diplomatic shelters at night, far from the action. The other guards talked about how they wanted to shoot the North Koreans when they showed up for more meaningless chatter, and it was entirely possible since each man carried a rifle and a sidearm. The North Koreans showed no fear, and the Chinese infiltrators still came in the night, sometimes creeping into the camps and getting inside the tents where soldiers slept. Throats were cut. The infiltrators would be shot on sight if they were caught. Bob had seen one who survived a shooting, and he was left to die on the barbed wire fence that surrounded the camp. The man had a bullet hole in the center of his back, and he moaned all day, but no one moved to help him. Bob thought he should go to the wire and put another bullet in the man, but no one moved to help or hurt; they just let time do the work. Shooting the dying Chinese soldier wasn't going to get done. The dying man wasn't in uniform, and the North Korean negotiators weren't in uniform either. Technically, they weren't supposed to shoot anyone out of uniform.

Overall, Bob had spent three years and eight months in Korea. He had seen nearly all the war. Everything he did was far less interesting after that experience, except in his NASA years.

Chapter 5

Since there was no TV in the girls' locker room, it was the only place Jennifer, and all the other girls, could go to get away from the *Challenger* broadcast. After a full morning of watching TV in all her classes, Jennifer had seen more than enough. She was not interested in a teacher from space any more than she was a teacher in the classroom. She wondered who thought up the ridiculous idea that kids would be interested in being taught a lesson from space. A teacher in space was still just a teacher on TV.

While she brushed out her hair, she watched several other girls behind her in the mirror. Most girls sat on the benches and changed their clothes, but near the shower entrance, three girls were doing pushups. It was a contest to see who could do the most.

Jennifer could see the top of the head of the one that moved the smoothest and would probably win. Lisa had cropped hair parted right down the middle and feathered across the sides. If her hair was longer, it would be like Farrah Fawcett's feathered masterpiece, but Lisa didn't look like Fawcett at all. Her shoulders were broad and strong, and her legs were brawny and short. She pumped out the pushups and when the other two girls stopped, she jumped up and raised her fists in victory. Lisa had a wide mouth and a big, broad nose, and she wore no makeup, but her thick eyebrows didn't need much. Her face was in sharp relief regardless.

The other two girls stood slowly. Marie Mendoza was sickly looking and thin, with braided hair that made two ponytails down the back. Her white scalp showed through her hair where the braids had been pulled too tight. Jennifer thought of a comment Jack had made once when she wore her hair like that. He called it 'bridle hair' and he didn't mean bride as in a wedding. He meant bridle, as in what goes in the mouth of a horse to steer it. She didn't get it then, it was when she was eleven, but now she did.

Vonda Purdue was the other girl, and she was the star of the team since she could do pretty much anything. She had braided hair as well, but her scalp was as dark as her skin, and nothing showed through. Vonda wanted to win everything and the push-up contest loss to Lisa wasn't sitting well with her. She turned and limped away.

After washing off most of her makeup with a damp cloth, Jennifer undressed down to her bra and panties and took out her running shorts. They were white and clean, but she checked them for stains anyway, then she pulled them on and took out her team shirt. 'Lady Deer' was printed across the front with the antlers outline. She pulled her hair back with a simple band and watched Lisa and Marie wrestle as she put on her shoes. Lisa's locker room antics had been going on for years, and Jennifer used to hate being around it, but for a fleeting moment, she thought that she might miss them one day since they were both seniors. Lisa had never tried to involve Jennifer in her locker room activities. Lisa was a girl jock, not a bully.

Within ten minutes, all the girls were running warm-up laps around the track. The sun was high and bright, but the day was still cold. A few girls wore outerwear, but Jennifer wore only her team T-shirt. She loved the chilly air and the feeling of the sun on her skin without the summer bugs and sweat.

The only reason she stayed on the track team was that she loved the feeling of running. She didn't like the team, the girls, the coaches, thought the team's name and emblem was pathetic, and she didn't care if the team won or lost, but she genuinely did love to run. She didn't mind being tired. She loved the feeling of her blood pumping, her breath deepening, her legs pounding, and the trickle of sweat running down her back. She loved that she could do this at school, in the middle of the day. After school was okay with her because it put off getting home where she spent most of her time in her room. With barely any effort, she was also good at track and placed in everything she did, and occasionally, she'd win.

As she rounded for her third lap, she saw David stretching and getting ready to practice the pole vault. The boys started a half hour earlier and he was warmed up and ready to go. David was thin and delicate and had blond hair that hung down past the top of his jersey. She was looking at his legs when she saw that he was smiling at her. She looked away, giving him nothing.

As she came around for her fourth lap, she saw that Vonda was sitting down and looking even more miserable than usual. Vonda was a serious girl who was built strong and thick. She had been that way when she was in first grade and played with the boys on the playground. Jennifer had known her then and was afraid of her. They had spoken but only in passing. Jennifer knew the neighborhood where Vonda lived, but it was all black and Jennifer had never been there. Vonda was a mental mystery to her, but not a physical mystery to anyone. Vonda could do everything well, and she was fast, especially for her size.

But now, one of the trainers that the school used only during the track season was holding Vonda's ankle and straightening out her leg. This made Vonda wince. Jennifer studied Vonda's face as she passed, and then she heard the bark of the coach ahead of her.

"Buckhorn, get over here," yelled Coach Wilson. Wilson was a former NCAA women's track star who still wore knee socks and had thick hair that was kinky and brown. The late sixties had been good for Mary Wilson. She still had powerful leg muscles that showed through with every step. Her skin was like polished leather.

Jennifer slowed and noted that Wilson was flanked by Lisa, Marie, and worse still, Coach Johnson. Johnson was the offensive line coach on the football team in the fall and the head track coach in the spring. Like Coach Wilson, he had been an extraordinarily successful athlete during the sixties and saw no reason to change his wardrobe. He wore a grey tracksuit that somehow was already showing sweat stains under the arms despite the cold. His mustache was the stuff of legend, and he had recently had his afro cut back, but it was shaped like a helmet on his head. The other legend was the bulge in the pants. It was cultivated somehow. Every kid in the school speculated about it endlessly. Johnson had a reputation for entering the girl's locker room unannounced, which was one of the reasons the girls never took off their underwear at their locker. Lisa was one of the other reasons.

"Buckhorn, it's your lucky day," Coach Wilson said.

Jennifer didn't feel lucky. She could sense everything she liked about running about to slip away.

"Buckhorn, Vonda is out, maybe for the rest of the season and so we need you to step up to the hurdles and the high jump," Wilson stated.

It was as bad as she had feared. Hurdles took a lot of training, and she was not that good at it. It was more of a sprint event, and the hurdles took the joy of running down to a set of annoying hiccups.

Miss a hurdle and you plant on your knees or hands or face. She was not interested. Further, she knew that training for those positions would require longer practice and for her to come to school with less make-up. No way.

"I haven't done those events since sophomore year," she said and started to run away. "Find someone else."

Wilson put her arm out and blocked Jennifer's path. This was new. Wilson was not the touchy kind, and she was a little too chirpy as well.

"Hold on, Ace," Coach Wilson said. "We have a shot at state this year, and we got to have someone in every position. We need bench depth. You're who we got. We need you to step up to the plate and find that championship spirit."

Jennifer knew she did not have a championship spirit and didn't want one. She noticed the intense interest Lisa was showing.

"I'm a senior," she said flatly. "I run my sprints and the relay and that's it."

Coach Johnson shifted his weight from one leg to the other. He moved his clipboard to the other hand.

"Girl, I coached your brother," he began. "He had a lot of heart, but not that much talent. But I told him, heart was what mattered most."

"You got that right, coach," Coach Wilson agreed.

Jennifer leveled a steely eye on Johnson. Jack really liked Coach Johnson, and he played football every year of high school. He played football even when he had a fractured arm from rodeoing. He played football even when football and wrestling overlapped, and he had to go to both practices. "You have real talent. Look at those long arms and legs," Johnson continued. "You can win these events. You move like an athlete."

Another black mark in Jennifer's mind. She had no desire to move like an athlete.

"Now," Johnson continued, "you're a senior and if you want your PE credits, you have to pass. Know what I'm saying? And if you want to pass, you have to be a team player. Know what I'm saying? A team player does what the team needs. This team needs you to do hurdles and high jumps, maybe the long jumps too, and we need to know you'll put your heart and soul into it. So, are you with us, Champ?

"I can't replace Vonda," Jennifer said. She knew she was going to have to do what they wanted but was setting the expectations to where they needed to be.

"Vonda didn't make this team, and the team isn't Vonda," Johnson said. "She's just a team player. Lisa's the captain, she'll get you where you need to be."

Jennifer cut her eyes to Lisa and saw Lisa's cheesy wink. There was no way out of this shit assignment.

* * *

Bob stayed in the Marines for a couple of more years after he could have mustered out. He was stationed at Camp Pendleton, and Bob liked California. A couple of months after returning from Korea, he bought a car and traveled around the state when he wasn't assigned a duty. He traveled with some buddies, and then he had a girlfriend named Barbara, and they went camping in the places she said he should see.

The state was beautiful. It *was* golden. Compared to Texas, which was mostly flat and either hot or cold, California was a gem to be experienced in a light pullover with the top down. His Morris Minor was a convertible, and the rag top leaked, but he kept it down most of the time. The rag top flapped at high speed and made a noise so loud that he couldn't carry on a conversation with Barbara, but he kept it down and she learned to hold her hair down with a scarf she kept in the glove box.

Barbara was from San Clemente. She was a golden California girl with blonde hair and rich parents. Her dad worked in aircraft design and was a mean SOB, and Bob knew the man looked down on him for being from Texas and for being a Marine. The man had been at Pearl Harbor, and he looked down on Korean War veterans too.

Barbara had been there that day, and she saw the Japanese planes flying over their house. She thought it was an airshow at first. Her dad had been a flight instructor, and he tried to get to the base during the raid but was stuck on the road and the whole affair happened while he was in traffic.

39

Stuck in traffic during the critical moment in American military history; that's some tale of war glory, Bob thought but kept his mouth shut around her dad. Guys like her dad were common in Korea. They'd drop in for medal ceremonies and then go back to the officer's clubs in Pusan. They were soft around the middle and weak, but they saw themselves as heroic and it was best to let them go on thinking that. Barbara worshipped her dad.

Bob and Barbara traveled when he had the liberty to go. They went camping in Kern County over the Easter weekend and Bob saw the row upon row of pump jacks around Edwards Air Force base. He stopped the car and stared at them for a while. He hadn't been home in five years at that point, and the pump jacks, the 'nodding donkeys,' as his older brother Bucky called them, reminded him of Texas.

"They're kind of beautiful," he said. She seemed distracted and said nothing.

That night, he found out why she had said nothing. He was fishing in the cooler for another beer when she started crying, and he knew she was pregnant. She confirmed and screwed her lovely face into a painful knot.

"We'll get married, and it will be okay," he said. "Married Marines get higher pay, anyway."

This didn't comfort her, so they decided to drive back to San Clemente the next morning. She got out of the car quickly and ran inside. Her ponytail swished back and forth as she ran.

Grass Week followed. He rose early to check out his weapons for the day. The new Marines watched him, and he gave them tips on how to handle the heavier guns. Bob was the only man in his unit who had fired an M1917 Browning in combat, and his Gunny asked him to show the other men the best way to sit and aim. The Browning was to be fired in bursts, and so Bob taught them the way he was taught: a burst was to be as long as it took to yell "Die, motherfucker, die!"

After Grass Week, he called her, and her mother said she wasn't home. After two weeks, he stopped by her house, since he knew she was home, and she came out. She looked thinner and waxy. They sat in his car in her driveway, and she told him she had an abortion.

"You did that without me? You didn't need my agreement or anything?" he asked incredulously. He had thought about the baby all through Grass Week. In the eastern hills at Camp Pendleton, he had become a dad in his mind, and now, it was all gone.

"It was the right thing to do," she said robotically. "My parents thought so, too."

"Did you forge my name or something?" he asked. He was sure she would need his permission. Later, he would realize how incredibly naïve he had been. Of course, she didn't need his permission. She didn't even have to tell him. Women had been getting rid of babies for centuries, and the men didn't know they ever existed. Killing babies was the darkest part of girl magic.

There in her driveway, she didn't look magic. Her ponytail hung limply off the back of her head, and he ceased to have feelings for her at that moment.

He left the Marines and the Golden State months later. His life as a dad and husband and son-in-law all died on her driveway. He never told anyone that when he counted his children, he always included that baby. He imagined it was a boy. In the brief period after she told him she was pregnant until she told him about the abortion, he had imagined a whole future in California, with her, with his son, surfing and hiking and going to Yosemite. He had picked up a newspaper and was looking at houses that would be in good school districts and have room to expand. He almost called his mother to tell her, but then he thought about taking his pregnant wife home and surprising his mother that way, but then he remembered how his mother was and decided it would be best to only tell her about her grandson after the boy was born. He thought about telling his brother but didn't know how to reach him, and he never thought about telling his dad. But he knew he'd be a better dad than his dad had been. He'd buy the boy manly toys and maybe buy a dune buggy. He'd teach the boy to shoot, and maybe, how to tease bulls and survive. Eventually, they'd move to the mountains, which he loved, or the desert, which he also loved. All of California was physically different and better than the flat, hot, muggy, hurricane-prone land of his birth.

But it was not to be. Two potential Californians died in that abortion clinic, and one Texan survived.

* * *

After some peppy talk from Lisa, Jennifer walked over to the other side of the track where the hurdles had been set up. Lisa was annoyingly enthusiastic and that only made things worse.

"You'll see, you'll see," Lisa said as she crossed the field. "We're going to kick some ass this year and take state. I know it, okay? I can feel it in my bones."

Jennifer glanced down the field at David, who was talking to his friends. She had no desire to know about Lisa's bones.

But she knew hurdles and had enjoyed them at one time and now, she thought about finding a way to enjoy them again. She didn't like the way they broke her rhythm, but she knew that hurdles were a special kind of rhythm, harder to find but exhilarating if the beat could be located. She lined up in front of the hurdles and tried to remember what her coaches had told her.

"Okay, okay, we're going to just find out where we are," Lisa said. "I've seen you do this. That's why I wanted you. You're good. Leg strength and reach is what it takes."

Jennifer glanced over. She knew that was supposed to be flattery, but Lisa had just implicated herself in bringing on this misery. Lisa had requested Jennifer for an event she hadn't done in two years.

"Okay, hot stuff, let's just stay in sync and do this together," Lisa said. "Nice and easy and close, okay? Easy and close, no problem."

Lisa nodded to Marie, who raised one hand and put a whistle in her mouth. Jennifer lowered her head and tried to remember all her techniques and patterns.

Marie blew the whistle and lowered her arm. Heads turned to watch. Lisa started fast, Jennifer a tiny beat behind.

Jennifer clipped the top of the first hurdle with her back foot, but her front foot cleared. The muscle memory was still there. She remembered each step and was surprised at how far she was clearing each hurdle. Jump and then one, two three, four, and jump. The pattern fell into place. It felt good. Lisa's stronger shorter legs still cleared the hurdles ahead of Jennifer, but Jennifer's legs were letting go, and she was closing the gap. By the fifth hurdle, her longer legs had taken her past Lisa. She remembered what to do with her arms. At the eighth hurdle, Jennifer was half a hurdle ahead of Lisa.

When they reached the final hurdle, Jennifer let her front leg relax just enough to clip the white bar. The hurdle clattered over in front of her, and she tripped as she tried to step over it. Her hands dug into the track, and she felt a hot sting first in her hands and then her knees. The thrill was gone, and a hot flash of anger spread over her. She looked up to see if David was watching, and he was looking right at her.

"Fucking pathetic" she heard Marie mumble.

"Shut up!" Lisa barked at Marie as she slowed and turned. "What was my time?"

"17.5," Marie reported.

Lisa circled to Jennifer and took her hand to bring her up. A tiny blood trickle headed down Jennifer's knee.

"You were ahead of me, OK, and my time was 17.5. So, you're like 17.2, and that's a great time!" Lisa said. "And don't listen to that cunt."

"Which one?" Jennifer asked as she cut a glance at Marie who was walking over to Coach Wilson in the middle of the field.

Lisa laughed at that. It was funny.

"So, hey, you've kept most of your technique," she said. "We have plenty to work with, yup."

Lisa brushed the sand off the scratch on Jennifer's knee and stood. She instinctively wiped her hand on her shorts. Jennifer just stared at the blood until Lisa noticed.

"Oh, sorry," she said, embarrassed. "I guess I shouldn't have done that.'

"Don't let Coach Johnson see it," Jennifer said. "He'll say something about being on the rag. No way he lets that go without comment."

Lisa laughed again, naturally. Suddenly, she realized Jennifer wasn't just the Madonna clone everyone said she was. She was funny. She could be charming in a discreet way.

"He's a fucking pig in all ways," Lisa said. "Always has been, too."

"Dark meat," Jennifer said, which caused Lisa to belly laugh again.

"Oh my God, you are bad!" she said. "Where are you going?'

"To see how much high jump I still have in me," Jennifer said without turning.

Chapter 6

When Bob returned to Texas in 1955, he stayed at his parents' house, but his mom told him he had two weeks to find a job, or he would just have to leave. It was near Christmas, and Bob had not been home in five years. His mother told him his dad had died while he was gone. Something had happened up in Lubbock, but she was evasive on the details, and so he stopped asking questions.

His brother Bucky came back from West Texas on the eighth day, and they went out for beers at the racetrack in Pasadena. Bucky was now a large, heavy man, and he got in fights all the time. He was drummed out of the Navy for excessive fighting, but not before earning many commendations for his war service. He was awarded the Distinguished Service Cross, which he wore the day he came home in October of 1947. After that, had been a policeman for a couple of years, but he got into trouble for using his pistol too often, and so finally, he went out to West Texas to manage oilfield operations. But Bob was grown now, and a combat veteran himself, with his own service medals, and so things were different. Over beers and smokes, Bucky told Bob where to go and what to bring, and in eight more days, Bob was hearing from the other roughnecks how not to get his hands cut off on a drilling rig.

"You have to suppress the impulse to reach out and grab things that won't do what you want," a big roughneck said to him. "You'll pull it back a few fingers short if you pull it back at all. And I don't want to have to take your fingers to the hospital. I hate doing that shit. I've seen a whole bunch of fingers not connected to a hand."

There were many Marines out in the oilfield, and Bob got along well enough with them, but he found out they hated Bucky, so they tended not to invite Bob to anything after work. Bucky had a whole bunch of ways to dock their pay, and they thought it was all horseshit, but Bucky was a supervisor, and he was big and mean, so the only thing they could do was move to another outfit, which they often did. After a few weeks, Bob moved to another outfit as well, but Bucky didn't care.

It was out in the oil patch that Bob began to notice the finer details of the things around him. He'd watch the drill pipe lift high in the air and then watch the roughnecks struggle to make the connections. He'd watch the drill cuttings pour out of the shakers, and he'd walk into the shack where the mud loggers sat. They tested the cuttings every hour and the displaced rock and liquid that came up out of the ground told them where the drill bit was.

"When the cuttings start having more oil in them," one of the mud loggers told him, "we know we're getting close."

When the well was drilled, if they found oil, they'd case the whole stack in concrete, and Bob worked the mixer. He saw how little things, including minor variations in the air temperature, affected how well and how fast the mixer could move. He asked a lot of questions, and if the other men had anything to share, they would. Often, they said they did things because that was the way they learned it, and that was all they knew. Sometimes, they made improvements to the processes, but improvements had to be kept secret because nothing outside the procedure was approved. They improvised better methods informally based on trial and error and the better processes were rarely institutionalized, certainly not across the whole industry.

On his way home for Thanksgiving, he stopped by the pad site where Bucky was working and saw a pile of books and drawings on the floor in the corner of Bucky's company man trailer. There were drawings of the pad site, details of the permitting process, and some manuals for the gear that was on the site, including the massive top drive motor at the apex of the tower. He asked Bucky if he could take the manuals with him back to Houston.

"What the fuck for?" Bucky said, but Bob knew that meant yes.

Over the next week, he read every chart and manual, and he went to the Pasadena public library and found some books on petroleum engineering which he checked out. They were all written by teachers at Texas A&M.

That winter was harsh. By the first of January, there were few days above 35 degrees, and a few that were well below freezing.

Everything behaved differently in the cold, and not just the people. Bob had seen this same phenomenon in Korea. The men dressed for the cold, but all the coats and gloves and thick shoes numbed the men to the tiny warnings of disaster and signs of danger. No one could feel the tiny vibrational signals that came through the machinery, and they couldn't hear either. Being warm inside their thick jackets also gave them a false sense of security. What would keep them warm wouldn't keep them from getting their hand cut off, and Bob heard Bucky tell the men that, but Bob saw the different behavior. The cold was not safe, but it was numbing. Even in Korea, men worried less about getting killed in the cold. The cold either makes them want to die or they feel like they're part ways there already. The cold, unlike wind or rain, was tricky and it increased risks without triggering the appropriate alarm.

Consequently, there were more accidents in the cold. Most were falls as men slipped on the wet or frozen railings and platforms. A man reached out for a section of pipe that was swinging back and forth, exactly as he was not supposed to do, and while he didn't lose any fingers, his arm was broken and hanging at an odd angle when he came down off the drill floor. He was trying not to cry out in pain, but he was hurting badly. In Korea, Bob had seen men shot who barely flinched, but a crushed arm was terribly painful. That guy never returned.

Before going out back west, Bob checked out all the books his library card would allow on drilling, physics, and basic mechanics.

* * *

Carol thought about Bob and his drinking all the way from Deer Park to the Galleria. She drove the Mercedes Bob had bought her for her thirty-fifth birthday, and she loved that car. She did not ask how much it cost or how it was paid for because Bob took care of all the household finances and always had. Carol had no experience of handling money. Her dad had done it for her, then her first husband, then her mom, and then Bob. She grew up with little of it. Whatever Bob gave her, she took, and whatever money he gave her to manage the home, she used without ever asking for more. He always gave her more than she needed anyway.

Bob's drinking made her mad. It had formerly made her sad, but that sadness had started to turn to anger at the end of the first year of him being home all day. Bob had always been a drinker but rarely drunk. She knew many alcoholics when she was growing up, and Bob

46

hadn't been one. He drank daily, but so did everyone they knew. Why had it gotten so bad? And how was he still paying for things? She asked once if they were OK financially, but he said, "We have savings." When he didn't volunteer any more information, she thought it better for both that she didn't ask any more questions. They talked less and less anyway. Now, they rarely spoke at all.

Everyone in the house knew the two adults present no longer loved each other, and she worried about the effect this loveless household was having on her kids, mostly Josie. She worried less about Jennifer, who was old enough to work. Carol had started working at twelve, and she thought that Jennifer and Jack should have jobs already.

She had concluded that the reason she was so mad at Bob was that his unemployment and daily drinking had caused her to think about her life in Mexico more often. There were always men around drinking where she grew up. They weren't former engineers at a prestigious and historic space program, but they acted like her husband in several ways. They started the day quietly, but then they'd ramped up the drunk talk, and finally, they would fall asleep and snore in the middle of the day. By the afternoon, they were surly and erratic, and the day would conclude with more drinks, self-important declarations, and then, more snoring.

She avoided those men, and there were many of them in her tiny town. Her dad drank, but he also worked at a cement factory, and he would drink beer when he got home, and fall into an exhausted sleep. Her sisters didn't drink, and neither did her mother. They went to the cathedral constantly during the day and spoke of their prayers to the Virgin. There were crops to bring in around the village, and she saw many men there, and they would drink in the afternoon. She started to bring in crops regularly about the same time her body began to change. She could suddenly feel eyes upon her. It was appalling. It was then that she noticed that drunk men spoke more freely to her, and they would sometimes reach out to touch her. They slurred their words, and made strange, disgusting, slithering noises. Drink made everything she feared about men much worse.

When she was fourteen, her mother pulled her aside and had a very blunt and graphic conversation with her about men, what they wanted, what they liked, and how she was going to get married soon. She

47

recoiled at the memory and hated that it had all come true. Her first husband had been exactly as her mother told her he would be. He demanded grunting, rough sex every day. He pulled her hair and yanked her head back and forth. Carol had no intention of ever having the same kind of conversation with Jennifer. Jennifer seemed so knowing already anyway. Carol thought she must have learned a lot from Madonna.

Josie was sweet and young, and somehow, Carol knew that Josie was carrying the emotional load for the family, but she didn't know what she could do about it. Nothing in her past prepared her for her present. No memory from Mexico corresponded with her current situation. Even had she been able to talk to her mother about her situation, her mother would have had no advice other than to be quiet and obedient to her husband.

Thinking about Bob's drinking and unemployment made her want to smoke, and finally, she gave in and lit up a Virginia Slim. She cracked the window to keep the car from smelling like her cigarettes, and the frigid air sharpened her thoughts further. Hope that the problems in her home would work itself out was long gone. The decision to change her life was there but she had nothing, no idea, of what she'd do next. Bob had always provided and fathered and been a good husband, but now, that was gone, and she didn't know him anymore, and she didn't love him at all. He had gotten old very quickly after he stopped working.

As she got closer to where she was going, she finished up the Virginia Slim and tossed it out the window. She opened the windows and let the smoke out of the car and then pulled a tiny stick of gum from her purse. Her driver's license was at the bottom of the bag, and she picked it up and looked at it while she unwrapped the gum. There it was on the Texas Driver's license: Carol Buckhorn. She had no middle name anymore. It was a solid American name and a massive distance from Karola Hidalgo Navarro Jimenez. She gazed at it for a moment then tucked it back in the bag. She looked in the review mirror and shaped her light hair before applying a little bit of lip gloss. Then, she tested a smile on herself. It was game time.

* * *

The Tree Hugger was busy. Health food was new to Houston so there wasn't a lot of competition in the health food marketplace. Every table was full when Carol entered, and she could smell the lattes. After a short head turn, she saw a hand waving.

There were hugs all around when she arrived at the table. First was Sofia, another Mexican who never talked about Mexico. Sofia sometimes put on a fake Spanish accent which only Carol noticed. Her Spanish had no touch of Spain, but her English did. Next to Sofia was Karen. Carol lightly hugged her and briefly smelled her bad breath. Karen's teeth were tiny compared to the size of her mouth and her smile was dominated by her vein-covered gums. Next Carol hugged a light-skinned black woman named Lulu and beside her was a shy nebbish man named Pete. Finally, she reached Dave who had been saving a seat for her next to him.

As she sat, Dave's eyes lingered on her in a way everyone could notice. Had he known his attraction to her was obvious, he wouldn't have cared. His ogling of Carol was the only socially unconscious thing at the table. Everyone at the table was a decades-long counterculture adherent, socially conscious, and dressed in soft organic kinds of cotton that fit loosely. Karen wore tie-died sweatpants she had dyed herself. Only Carol stood out for not wearing the uniform pieces. She didn't like the hippie aesthetic and didn't try to imitate it.

"So sorry I'm late," Carol said as she put her purse on the floor. Her Gucci purse was not appropriate, she thought as she set it out of sight. "I was getting the kids out and Bob's no help at all."

"It's okay. We've just been gossiping," Sofia volunteered. "This is Pete's wife's last shuttle launch. They're getting transferred to JPL!"

"Oh, Pete, I'm so sorry," Carol said. "Please don't leave us."

Pete smiled ruefully. He was hostage to his wife's career.

"We hope we don't have to move again," Pete said with a shrug. He had a neat beard and thinning hair. "That's space life. But you're all welcome to visit!"

"Oh, that would be wonderful!" Carol added enthusiastically. "You'll love it there. When Bob was at NASA, we went so many times, and I'd spend all day with the kids at Disneyland. We're sad to see you go but jealous of that California weather!"

"Of course, you'll all be welcome to visit any time," Pete added.

Dave had been waiting for this announcement to pass and for Carol to react to it so he could seize the moment and start the meeting. Tall and blond, Dave had grown accustomed to being the center of attention and these meetings were not different. He was from California and didn't want to talk about the weather there, which was a Texas obsession. His abruptness was noticed but never commented on by the group.

"Okay! So, this march isn't going to organize itself," he said but that was all he got out of his mouth before the waitress arrived. She spoke to Carol.

"Can I get you anything?" she asked.

Dave almost answered the waitress for Carol but stopped himself just as his mouth was opening.

"Has everyone ordered?" Carol asked the group.

"No, of course not," Karen said. "We wouldn't start without you!"

Carol turned to the waitress.

"Just a latte please with extra cream," she said.

Dave spoke to the waitress as well.

"And then give us about fifteen minutes and we'll be ready to order then," he commanded.

The waitress nodded and walked away. Dave spoke quickly lest another subject arise that would cut into the meeting time.

"Now that Carol is here, shall we get started?" he said.

To appease him, everyone settled down and their serious faces took over. Dave began speaking and he didn't stop for the next half hour. The group was raising money and 'awareness' for the Great Peace March for Global Nuclear Disarmament that was pending, and there was a lot of work to be done that Dave, the one that would be marching, could not do himself.

"This is serious business," he said gravely when he had finished his long monologue about what needed to be done. "The world hangs in the balance."

Carol noted how his eyes seemed to grow a deeper blue when he was serious. He was, as she said to Sofia, *"Kennedy-esque"*.

Chapter 7

In the spring of 1958, Bob drove from Midland to College Station and picked up the application to go to college at A&M. He had been thinking about it while he waited in the cold for things to happen, and he knew life in the oil patch would turn him into a smaller version of Bucky in time. Bucky was perfectly suited to managing workers in the oilfield, and his way was the only way.

At A&M, he walked around the campus and walked through a few of the buildings where classes were held, and he liked what he saw. In March, his birthday passed, and he turned 26, and he knew he'd be older than the average student there, but that was fine with him. In the male students he saw the kind of immaturity that the Marines beat out of such young men. In the women, he saw educated young mothers waiting to happen. In the library, he saw worlds waiting to open for him. Bob hungered to learn, and he was going to get fed.

In the early summer, Bob received a letter at his mother's house that stated he was accepted to attend if he came by the school and took a test and scored high enough. He told Bucky about it, and Bucky scowled.

"You're going there for the pussy, is all," he said.

While he didn't expect Bucky to be positive, Bob was pissed that Bucky couldn't see a motive beyond pussy. He didn't see Bucky for the rest of the summer but expected he'd see him at Thanksgiving. From his mother, he learned that Bucky had moved to Venezuela. He called a friend from the oil patch and was told that three men had died on a pad site where Bucky was the company man, and it was attributed to an undetected poison gas release. After being crushed or burned, being poisoned by hydrogen sulfide gas was the most common way to die in upstream oil and gas. Poison gas sensors were mandatory at all drilling sites, but they were unreliable, and Bucky had never made sure they were in place and properly powered. When several men were overcome with the gas and died, someone had to take the fall, and it was Bucky.

Bob was heartbroken that Bucky had left the country without saying anything. He had hoped to finally have a real relationship with this thick-skinned brother. They had only recently had the most significant conversation of their lives, where Bucky had called him "brother."

It was a few months before Bucky left the country that Bob saw him in Odessa. Bucky was crossing the street and headed into a diner as Bob was driving by, so he followed his brother in and sat down at the bar next to him. He had questions he wanted to ask, and he knew, rightly so as things worked out, that he might lose Bucky from his life for a long time, possibly forever.

From another Marine, Bob heard that Bucky had claimed to have been in the Marines in World War II. Bob was sure that Bucky had been in the Navy and had been in the Navy even before the war started. But one day, as he and another guy were working the cement mixer, the man said "Your brother is the most unfriendly Marine I ever met. And he's a mean son of a bitch."

"Bucky was in the Navy, not the Marines," Bob said.

"That so?" the man said. "He told a bunch of us that he was in the Marines and was at all the bad spots. Palau, Iwo, Oki. Should have known that was bullshit."

Bob hadn't known Bucky to be a liar. Surely Bucky hadn't embellished his war record. Bob was fifteen when Bucky came home from the Navy, and Bucky was wearing a bunch of ribbons and medals which he gave to his mom. Bucky was a war hero; Bob was sure of it.

After a few minutes of pleasantries, as pleasant as things could be with Bucky, Bob brought up the war.

"You were in the Navy during the war, right?" Bob asked.

"Yep," Bucky said.

"I met some guy who was confused. He said you said you were in the Marines," Bob continued. "Seemed really adamant about it."

"Well, that guy is a dumb son of a bitch," Bucky said calmly. "I was with the Marines once they started island hopping. I was a fire controller. An NGLO. I was on the radio with the ships, telling them where to drop ordnance. We'd get up close, figure out where the Japs were and call in the fire."

Bob was satisfied that Bucky was telling the truth. The man had misunderstood.

"They put me in a Marine uniform so I wouldn't stand out and get shot," Bucky continued.

"You were in all those island-hopping battles? Iwo Jima? Okinawa?" Bob asked.

Bucky turned and looked Bob in the eye.

"And Guadalcanal. Other places," he said. "If Navy ships were shelling, I was there. I would have been in the homeland invasion if we hadn't dropped the two big bombs on them."

"I heard it was bad in those fights," Bob said.

Bucky went back to his food.

"I heard Korea was bad," he said.

"It was," Bob confirmed as he looked down at his hands. "When we got pushed back from the Chinese border, it was rough going. Ambushes, wave attacks, snipers, you name it. Lots of dead."

"Well," Bucky said, "then you've been there. The Japanese fought the same way. They would never give up. You had to kill every last one of them. And they didn't die easy. They wanted to take as many of us with them as they could. I saw a Jap hit with a flame thrower, and he still charged forward. Crazy bastards."

"You ever think about it?" Bob asked.

"Some days, I don't think of anything else," Bucky said. "You?"

"Same," Bob said.

There was a long pause.

"Well, looking back is a bad habit," Bucky said. "What else you want to know? You didn't follow me in here because you were hungry. You ain't eating what you ordered."

"Do you know how dad was killed?" Bob asked. "Mom said it was some kind of accident, but she didn't know much. She told me that he was killed in an accident, but it didn't seem like she believed it."

"He was in Lubbock, and he was murdered," Bucky volunteered as he was taking money out of his wallet. "When I was with the police, I drove out there and asked around. I found a cop that worked the scene. Daddy had been selling suits out of his car. He knew suits and always wore one. In 1943, most of the men who might have needed a suit were in a uniform, but that's all he knew, and that son of a bitch couldn't ever keep a job to save his life."

Bucky dropped the money for lunch on the counter and stood.

"He got in an argument with the man that owned the suit store over money, they got in a fight, and that man stabbed him in the neck,"

Bucky said. "Daddy was unarmed, and the police thought it was murder, but the guy that ran the store was in with the local bigwigs, so they didn't charge him. Case closed."

"That's terrible," Bob said.

"Lots of things are terrible, little brother, as you well know," Bucky said as he backed towards the door. "No looking back. What's coming for you comes from the front, not the back."

With that, Bucky was gone. Bob ordered a piece of pie and determined that Bucky was right; there was no point in looking back or talking further about what had happened in Korea, or anywhere else. At least Bucky had finally referred to him directly as his brother.

A few weeks later, Bucky left the country without telling him or his mother. She found out months later when he sent a letter saying he had gotten married.

* * *

College surpassed Bob's grand expectations. He'd go to class from morning to evening, often sitting in classes he wasn't registered for. He declared his major in mechanical engineering and declined the offer to fast-track in petroleum engineering. He had seen enough of the oil patch.

After a year, he was running short of money, so he took a job driving a truck on the weekends and over the breaks. On the weekends, he'd drive up to Dallas on Saturday afternoon and park the truck at a warehouse. He'd study until late at night and then drop off to sleep on one of the dirty couches in the driver's lounge. In the morning, the truck would be loaded, and he'd drive back to College Station. From the time he left until the time he returned, there were only eleven hours on most weekends, and he was sure to study because he had no place to go and no way to get there when he was in Dallas.

He dropped the keys off in the drop box one Sunday and saw a note tacked to the message board. It read 'B Buckhorn, call Mr. Kershaw in the morning.' He called Mr. Kershaw and was offered a job over the Christmas break driving to Mexico to pick up avocados. The pay was far higher than driving to Dallas, and he still had a turnaround period where he could study.

The next Friday, he showed up at the warehouse ready to drive to Mexico. Mr. Kershaw saw the books he was carrying.

"What are those for?" he asked. Mr. Kershaw looked and talked a lot like Bucky.

"It's so I can study on the turnaround," he said. "They'll let me sleep in the warehouse, right?"

Kershaw smiled.

"They'll let you sleep in the warehouse with the pigs," he said.

The drive to Mexico was rough. He drove an old Ford from before the war with no passenger seat and a plywood bed. The farm-to-market roads down to the Mexican border were pothole-rich and drainage-poor. The truck guzzled the gas and so he had to stop every chance he had since he wasn't sure when he'd reach the next station, and the old truck had no gauge. By midnight, he still wasn't at the border, so he pulled over, climbed in the back, and slept for a couple of hours.

At the Mexican border in Reynosa, he bought a map that showed him where he was going. Thankfully, it was only 120 miles in, at San Fernando.

The last few miles of road were tough on the truck, and he had to go slow to avoid breaking the old beater apart. The many donkey-powered carts on the road slowed him down as well, but finally, in the afternoon, he reached San Fernando and asked for directions to the warehouse. In broken English, he was told he was close, and when he reached the warehouse, he discovered that Mr. Kershaw had not been kidding; it was mostly occupied by pigs. The avocados were stacked everywhere, but the pigs were kept inside, out of the sun.

Bob climbed down painfully from the truck and smiled at the many leather-colored men that surrounded him, all asking questions in Spanish. He walked into the warehouse and saw a makeshift kitchen and a couch. This was what he had to work with. He went back to the truck, handed the keys to the man he thought was in charge, took out his books, and went to the couch for a long nap.

He woke to the sound of popping grease and the smell of carnitas. Through half-closed eyes, he saw a girl with a long black braid down her back standing at a table. From behind, she cut a sensual figure. She was wearing men's pants and was well-proportioned throughout. When she turned, he saw her face. She was a beautiful young woman, with a long straight nose and a full chin. Her face was streaked with sweat and dirt. When he sat up, she looked over at him. He smiled at her, but she looked away.

Finally, he stood and stretched, then he walked closer. He knew a few Spanish words and phrases and the one he needed now was easy to recall.

"Como te llamos?" he asked.

Without looking up from her little pan, she whispered, "Karola."

He tried to talk to Karola for the rest of the time he was at the warehouse, but she didn't look much at him or answer his questions beyond a few simple responses. She said she didn't speak English, but she slipped in a few words now and then and when he ate with the other men, he caught her looking at him. She disappeared for several hours, but when he woke in the morning, she was back, cooking breakfast. The warehouse, he discovered, belonged to her uncle, she was divorced, and the avocados all came from her home state of Michoacan.

He had brought a Spanish English dictionary, and he used it to write out questions for her. She laughed at his faulty grammar, and he saw her teeth and noted how she pushed her hair back. She was shy, but she knew she was beautiful, and she could not hide her interest in him. He detected early on a certain internal injury to Karola, and had no idea how that pain would manifest itself in his life eventually.

When the truck was loaded for the return trip, he put his books inside, except for the dictionary, which he left for her. In it, he tucked a note that stated, in poorly structured Spanish, that he hoped she would learn a few more English words by the time he came back in a month.

Back in College Station, he told Mr. Kershaw that he wanted a regular route to San Fernando, not Dallas.

Bob had the phone to his ear and his Bloody Mary in the other hand when it was time to give up. Whatever he was going to say to whomever he could get on the phone was too late when the *Challenger* fired off the main engines and STS-51-L couldn't be called back.

"Liftoff! We have liftoff of the twenty-fifth space shuttle mission, and it has cleared the tower!" the flight director called.

Bob gritted his teeth at the sound of the narrator's cheesy declarations. Even the flight directors had been drafted into the show. There was no reason to call out the number of space missions except to further the narrative that space flight was routine. Very few things captured the serious nature of space flight quite like the formerly stoic voice of a flight controller keeping words to a minimum on launch. They had been converted into carnival barkers.

For the next seventy-three seconds, Bob watched the image on his screen without moving. For one minute and thirteen seconds, his eyes didn't blink or move from the screen. A drink was poised in one hand and the phone was in the other.

For the first few seconds, he was caught up in the preposterous majesty of it all. The orbiter was a massive fireball with a machine on top. It was as if humans had enslaved the primal forces of nature and put their engineering in the master position. Nature in its chemical fury was below the fat and demanding orbiter, pushing the agenda of humanity into the stars in the same way that fire had warmed them so they could tell their stories in the dark. Fire had cooked the food, and burned alive their enemies, and now, fire would carry them to the stars or at least to the edge of the stars. Space was so empty fire wouldn't burn there. That alone represented a huge barrier to making space a new frontier.

The big orbiter rolled over and began to move away as it moved up. The solid rocket boosters burned bright and strong, and the space plane rode helplessly along, strapped to the big external tank that was fueling the shuttle engines.

For a moment, Bob thought back to the jokes he and others had made about the shuttle design and how little like an airplane it was. The entire contraption was shaped like an airplane but no other plane in the world had an external tank that was jettisoned after a brief time and then went fuel-free for the rest of its time aloft. The shuttle was designed like a conventional rocket in all ways except for the time that it was a glider on reentry. The wings allowed for the big hunk of metal to be 'flown' for the period from entering the atmosphere to the landing, but it was being guided by the pilot towards a runway with no propulsion, and thus far, after many close calls, the shuttle had not missed a runway. If that had happened, the nature of the space plane would be plain to all. It couldn't fly, wave off, or circle back around. It would find another place to land or crash. A shuttle had never tried to land on an American interstate highway, but that was not out of the realm of possibility. Bob mentioned to another engineer that a shuttle landing on an American roadway was an inevitability one day unless they stayed lucky or designed a way to actually fly the damn thing, and that guy said "Bob, you don't have to give voice to every thought you have, you know?"

The flight controller kept calling out the statistics as if they were meaningful to the public. Another aspect of the packaging and selling of NASA was the inclusion of the public in measures they didn't understand and were less likely than ever to either know, use, or care. The public didn't travel in nautical miles, and yet the flight controller declared the shuttle altitude was "four point three nautical miles" downrange in a normal voice which would have been appropriate in a car commercial. Four point three nautical miles, three point four cubic centimeters, one point five APR . . . The statistics people didn't know, or use, had permeated society and given the appearance of precision that Bob knew wasn't there.

The price of American commercial and cultural success in every endeavor of human life was ignorance of how things worked. Normal things carry on in the background and few are supposed to know or care about what makes them function. That's the purpose of normalizing activities and NASA had, incredibly, declared space travel as normal.

Bob was aware and deeply lamented that his kids could not perform the most basic math calculations even with a pencil and paper, and they couldn't repair anything that was broken. Jack was recklessly brave and tough, and Bob had praised him for those qualities, but Jack was not curious about how anything worked. Jennifer had been a precious angel as a girl and Carol had dressed her in bows and ribbons and lace, and Bob had praised this as well, but Jennifer was also not interested in the function of things. He could tell her curiosity was entirely social. She cared about people, mostly herself, and about other people, she only cared about what they thought of her. It was what it was. Josie was formless thus far, and Bob knew that he had largely ignored the boy in a way he had not with Jack. Josie was a mystery to himself, and Bob noticed that something persistent occupied Josie's thoughts and prevented him from really seeing the world. Josie rarely asked any questions about anything. A lack of curiosity was inimical to a healthy life as far as Bob was concerned, and only a denial of obvious things was more dangerous.

While Bob was thinking about Josie, it happened. After a short flash, the space shuttle *Challenger* exploded.

In a moment, in the way that the real world of things and forces and chemistry works, it was all over. Design demands and physical reality met, and the tension was suddenly resolved. Politics met physics. Career bets had been placed, and those bets didn't pay off. Infamy replaced fame. Ambition had been body-checked by a catastrophic failure carried live on TV around the world. Nature, still red in tooth and claw, burst through. The face of death flickered on screen for an instant. If there was a God, he just bashed man's shitty space plane into a literal million pieces.

An explosion that Bob could tell in an instant was not the shuttle itself overtook the entire package, and it blew, without any kind of rising mushroom cloud, into many pieces. The big solid rocket boosters, delinked from the external tank and unguided, did what uncontrolled forces do; they spun off in aimless spirals. The rest of the orbiter did what heavy and disassociated objects do, which was to fall back to Earth.

"Oh, my God!" Bob heard over the phone. He had been on hold, but someone had taken the line off hold, and he heard a female voice for just a moment before the line went dead.

"Flight controllers looking carefully at the situation," Bob heard. He stood and put the phone back in its cradle. "Obviously, a major malfunction," he heard the flight controller say.

At this, Bob laughed. It was so perfect. Were any truer words ever spoken? The emphasis should have been on obviously because the obvious was the part no one ever noticed until it was obvious that it was too late. The *Challenger* was gone.

Bob went to the kitchen and put his drink in the sink. He stared into the backyard and saw a faint reflection of himself in the window. The shock of witnessing a shuttle crew die violently as well as seeing a part of his life work fail suddenly caught up with him. His emotions swirled as he steadied himself with a hand on the countertop. Something had exploded in him, and it was something he hadn't suspect was there. He had been, for years, a high-ranking engineer at NASA, responsible for the orbiter. What was he supposed to do now?

Chapter 8

Deer Park had no deer in it. Not anymore. If the area contained any deer, the people of Deer Park would have shot those deer to extinction in a week or so. Bob had left Deer Park a couple of times in his life, once to join the Marines and once to work in West Texas, but he had come back.

Bob liked Deer Park and had no feelings about the other neighborhoods around Houston. He didn't have much feeling about Deer Park, and its claims to being the 'Birthplace of Texas,' and he could barely recount the story himself. There was something about a cabin and Sam Houston. Bob wasn't sure which Buckhorn came to Deer Park first. They hadn't been one of the "Original 300" Texas settlers. Bob went to school with their descendants, and he thought they didn't look as sturdy as their forebears must have been. He also thought it effete to indicate special heritage in a place like Texas.

Bob knew his family had moved to Texas from Boston at some point in the late 19th Century, and the Buckhorns had been Dutch, but his dad had passed on little family lore. Bob knew none of his relatives of that name. The past was dead, but his future wasn't looking rosy either and that made the pit of his stomach hurt. He had never worried about his future any more than he thought of his or anyone else's past, but now, he was frozen in time. After leaving NASA, Bob was lost for the first time in his life.

Since he had more time and sat alone in the backyard at night, he thought about his younger years in Deep Park. From his backyard, he could see the top of the massive San Jacinto monolith. Traffic backed up near the house on San Jacinto Day as the faithful flocked to the giant monument to the battle that saved Texas from being Mexican.

In high school, Bob went drinking at the monolith, and he had thrown up there as well as been in his first fight over a girl. It was there that Bob saw another man's blood for the first time. He saw some of his own there as well. He saw a man stabbed there. He saw some sexual encounters in the cars around the monument that had probably been a little less than consensual. He saw real blood and death in Korea, and his most vivid memory from West Texas was a crushed, misshapen arm.

His time at A&M passed quickly, and his relationship with Karola grew with each drive to Mexico. He met her family, but she kept him from spending too much time with any of them. Early on, he detected in her a distinct dislike of her own family and a keen sense of being made for something better. He knew she saw him as her best chance to leave. He also knew she was trying to get pregnant. After he graduated from A&M, they had a small wedding in Mexico, and then another at the courthouse in Deer Park. Bob invited no one to the ceremony, not even his mother, and when she asked why he invited no one, he said simply "There just isn't anyone to invite. I haven't lived here in a long time."

"No friends, from school?" she asked.

"No, not really," he said. "No one has kept in touch."

But her comment cut him. He hadn't thought much about not having any close friends, but it was true; he didn't. He never kept in touch with anyone after he met them. He didn't know how to reach anyone he knew in the Marines, West Texas, or even A&M. Bob knew he liked people, and engaged with them, but he was austere regarding human relationships. He suspected that one of the reasons he and Karola had gotten along so easily was that she was the same way. It was harder to be a woman, and a Mexican, and be a true loner, but she was a part of the same non-tribe of non-relators.

It was only a few months after graduation that he took the offer from NASA, and he bought a house in Deer Park because it was close enough without being too close to the water and Deer Park was building new, nice houses.

Bob was tremendously happy in the period just after they were married. He marveled at how well his life had turned out. Before he had completed his first year at NASA, he was a new dad. Jack was an active smiling baby and Bob delighted in the boy when he got home from work. Karola seemed happy and she dropped the baby weight immediately. She took pride in her appearance and would walk around the neighborhood in her jeans when Bob came home. She cooked American food most of the time, but Bob told her he wanted her to keep making her Mexican dishes, which he loved. She was never an enthusiastic lover, but she was tolerant, and he was gentle with her. By her breathing, he knew she derived some pleasure from their erotic life, but he never asked her to do anything specific. When he asked her if she wanted him to "do anything different" in the bedroom, she replied, "I want you to never talk about it."

One day, Bob came home from work, picked up Jack, and went outside for a while. From the kitchen window, she watched him take Jack's tiny hand and touch it to trees and grass. Bob talked to the infant patiently. She could see his delight, and so was surprised when he said, just after they sat down to eat, "My mother died yesterday."

She had met his mother only twice. After they were married, Bob took her by to meet his mother, but he had warned that she had "a clouded mind" and probably wouldn't talk much. They stopped by the old house, and his mother sat quietly while Bob talked about Karola's life in Mexico. She never asked any questions. A neighbor had moved in, Mrs. Boutwell, and she spoke chirpily now and again, but Bob's mother mostly just stared. When they dropped by again to show the infant Jack to his grandmother, the house was starting to smell of urine, and Bob's mother was no longer present in her own body.

The Saturday after Bob announced her death, they went to the Methodist church where she had been a member, and she lay in an open casket in the sanctuary. Mrs. Boutwell was there, and her daughter. There were three other people present, but Bob didn't know them. They introduced themselves as friends from the church. The pastor came in and delivered a sermon unrelated to his mother, and in no time, it was over. Karola saw Bob pay a man who had waited in the lobby, and they left. Jack had slept through the entire thing.

"Who was that man?" she asked.

"He's from the funeral home," Bob said.

"What do you pay him for?" she asked.

"He's going to have her cremated," Bob said.

Karola had seen many dead bodies in Mexico. She had seen her relatives, killed by cancer, heart attacks, or strokes. She had seen the bodies of her cousins killed in car wrecks. She had seen dead bodies in the streets the day after a shootout. One of her aunts was murdered by her husband and he had cut her face, but Karola had still seen her in her coffin and kissed her cut-up dead face. In every instance, the church had been full, the dead remembered, the crowd marched to the cemetery, and wailing was heard as the body was lowered into the ground.

The death of Bob's mother revealed to her what she already knew. She saw that Bob was mostly alone. He had no family really, except an absent brother. He had a couple of cousins somewhere, but they didn't communicate. Bob was alone and he carried on in the way the Anglos did, which was practical and robotic in the face of death. The Mexicans claimed that Americans were cold, and lacked culture, which was most evident in the bland food they ate. Karola saw this in the way they went their way early in life, and now she had seen how they barely mourned their dead. Given that she so wanted to put her painful Mexican past behind her, this quality in the Anglo-American cultural constellation offered her a real benefit. To be a real American, she needed to let go and not feel guilty about anything. The coming years would be mostly about letting go of any tradition that tied her to a past, on either side of the border, which defined her. She determined to redefine herself long before she knew what that definition would be. She would become Carol Buckhorn, American.

* * *

Bob's first duties at NASA were assignments as a junior engineer. The NASA management was already seeking graduates from A&M and scores of other schools, and getting a job there was as easy as going to a seminar one of his teachers recommended and filling out some paperwork. It was like going to A&M, getting through Marine boot camp, and working in the oil patch. For Bob, most things were not difficult. He just followed the damn directions. The war would have been easier had it had an orderly process, but it didn't. Bob craved order, and he often picked up after his children before Carol could get to the messes they left behind.

His practicality and age made him stand out from the new employees. The agency made a big show of stating they had hired the best young engineers in the nation because the *Apollo* program was going to demand a lot of them. In some cases that turned out to be true, but in other cases, they hired engineers and had them do secretary work. This was his first glimpse into the way the government worked.

At first, he had the job of carrying drawings around and keeping the different document drafts straight. He did it so well that he was promoted far beyond what his bachelor's degree and oil patch résumé should have allowed. He was invited to design meetings, where he asked a lot of questions. The guys in the middle layer of power liked him. These were the men who made things happen, and they saw in Bob someone who could hold a lot of detail in his head. After two years of steady work, he was being asked to weigh in on everything— from engine design to pressure testing to sealants. Many of the other engineers idolized Marines, combat veterans, and native Texans. Bob took them to the rodeo, the gun range, and hunting. He brought them to strip clubs and paid their tabs when they got too drunk to do it themselves. He took care of them, and it was easy. All Bob had to do was not get drunk—and that made him the genius of the lot.

He also quickly figured out that the men in the most commanding positions of power were weak men, as far as he was concerned. He met George Abbey and all the men who were Air Force veterans. These men didn't seem to care for Marines or A&M, and it was clear to Bob that he would never make it to the top of the power structure. Most of his friends knew they wouldn't either, but they all drank to excess, were close friends, and made the *Apollo* program take steady steps forward.

Even though he knew his career was capped, the next few years were the best years of Bob's work life, which complemented his bliss at home. The *Apollo* program was his life's calling, and his home was vibrant and full of life. He had a family, and he had friends. It was blissful.

And then, one bright shining day, just six days after Jennifer was born, humans walked on the moon. Bob had been in his office across the street from Mission Control, and he was watching it live on TV like everyone else. When Armstrong and Aldrin went to sleep, he and his colleagues walked across the street to celebrate with the others. The people, and the room they were in, glowed with pride, wonder, and accomplishment. The champagne flowed. The night was unforgettable. The following days were heavenly, and when the astronauts splashed down and were picked up by the *USS Hornet* a few days later, there were tears and more celebrations. The decisive step in the Kennedy challenge had been taken. Men had gone to the moon and returned alive. The greatest challenge had been met and mastered. Walking on the moon was humanity's penultimate accomplishment, and Bob had been there when it happened. As he watched the return capsule float down out of the sky towards the ocean, he wished he could call Bucky, and share the experience, but he had no idea how to find his brother.

For a few more months, the good feelings continued, but they began to subside as the reality of the actual moon, and not the metaphorical one, settled in. Each moon mission was a marginal decrease in joy and accomplishment after that. Seeing American men play golf on the moon was good for a laugh, but many, including all the men Bob worked with, knew that the image of men hitting golf balls on the moon was a sign of decay. There was no reason to go to the moon to play golf. Kennedy hadn't included golf in his 1962 Rice address.

Going to work entailed having a lot less to do after the final mission in 1972. Josie was born just a few months before the final December landing and on the same day, it was announced that the final three Apollo missions were scrubbed. The atmosphere at NASA palpably changed. The workload decreased and then decreased again. When a few men retired, they weren't replaced, but soon enough, after reassigning everyone, the natural shrinkage at NASA wasn't happening fast enough and there was talk across the Houston campus of 'cutbacks' and everyone knew what this meant. The nice perks went away, and a sort of spartan campus of limits became the norm.

The spaceplane was what everyone who was still at NASA came to work on and Bob did more work than virtually anyone on the mechanical design of the first draft. As the older men left, Bob's workload increased. The first design was more of an *Apollo*-type vehicle that still had disposable parts and would have to be remade after every mission. Matching the design to the mission requirements was an incredible task. All plans were routed through him and his team, but real engineering input became highly political, and Bob was far less able at that game than many of his younger co-workers. His forward progress stopped, and soon enough, he had been at NASA longer in the post-*Apollo* era than the actual *Apollo* era, and it was clear enough that the new guys that came in didn't want to hear any more stories about *Apollo*. Bob dummied up and put in his hours, but that was all. This went on for years, as Jack grew bigger, Jennifer grew hips and hair, and then Josie was born and Karola told him she wanted to be called Carol.

NASA carried forward with designs that had nothing to do with what Bob had developed with his team in Houston, and after the first few shuttle launches, the agency began moving people to Florida or California, and Bob was pretty sure they thought of him as too old to move. He was lumped in with WW2 veterans as an ancient pre-Vietnam war glory hog, a graduate of A&M in the pre-electronics era, and not a Harvard or Yale graduate at all. He was not in any category that was desirable to promote, and not an adept insider at NASA politics. He was just a damned good engineer interested in how things worked.

In his final year, he was the true outlier. A declining share of the people at NASA were military veterans and, except for Bob, there were no combat veterans left. Those who stayed were high-level planners. The new NASA was exclusively from the Air Force if they were military. They had come from the NORAD crowd; they knew all about rockets rather than rifles. No one cared that going to the moon had been for us all. There was far less Kennedy worship in this new NASA. Kennedy was from a rich family of poor origins, he was young and good-looking but also bookish and well-spoken, and for Bob and many others, Kennedy had impeccable war hero credentials. By 1982, the year Arnold Aldrich offered Bob a 'package', and he left, no one cared.

"The hair stood up on the back of my neck," was the most common phrase Bob heard about the Kennedy speech in 1962, but the space shuttle era had no such animating moment. Bob understood the purpose of the *Apollo* missions, and he thought the space plane was going to be far more difficult than anyone let on, and it was going to be pointless. The *Apollo* missions were man's glory, to show it could be done, and the obvious next step was to send people back to the moon and set up a base. They should have made the moon a frontier. The best plan would be to make it a frontier town and call it Fort Kennedy.

But that wasn't the direction they went. He was a great engineer and a good salesman for whatever position he came to, but that was not enough. The package had a severance payout that was generous to say the least. It was so much that Bob didn't tell Carol how much he pocketed.

The money, however, did nothing to ease Bob's sense of loss. He thought NASA had lost its purpose until he lost his job, and then he found he had lost his purpose. The first day he didn't have to go to work was the first day he poured himself a drink before noon.

In six months, Bob Buckhorn had fallen into a pattern of Bloody Mary's in the morning with the news, and vodka tonics in the afternoon, with bouts of sleeping. He knew that Carol didn't know about the money he had put away, and she didn't ask how he was still paying the bills. He needed a job, but not enough to find one. He needed to stop drinking, but not enough to stop.

* * *

Jennifer combed her hair out again in front of her locker mirror. Now, she had to style it without hair spray and that meant piling it up on top of her head and using a scrunchy to gather and hold. She pulled her streaked mane through the scrunchy, then took out her mascara tube and began to apply thick dollops to her eyelashes.

She felt good in a way that surprised her. The effort she was going to have to put forward to make her hurdles in a respectable time was no longer a source of agitation and anger. The sharp brace of pain that came from her skinned knees felt good to her. She was tough again on the track. She had dug down and found grit. She knew that the extra effort would show up in her legs, and she'd look powerful. More than anything, Jennifer liked to feel powerful. She decided that Marie, the coaches, Lisa, or any of the boys would not see her fail.

As she was putting her mascara back in the tube, she became aware that the noise in the room had ramped up. Girls were running back and forth, mostly smiling, but some looked stricken. Several girls entered the locker room from outside and started cheering. Lisa appeared over her shoulder.

"Did you hear?" Lisa said with a huge grin. "They're sending us home!"

Jennifer looked back at her mirror and began to put on lip gloss. "Why?" she asked.

"The stupid space shuttle exploded," Lisa said. "Okay, so, they are suspending school for the rest of the day, maybe tomorrow too."

Jennifer paused mid-gloss. For a moment, she thought of her dad. He hated the space shuttle; she knew enough about his job to know that much. She heard him say it was a bad idea, well executed but would fail one day. "Complexity is the enemy of execution," she'd heard him say. He would know how and why it exploded, and she could ask, but wouldn't. She saw how her mom talked to him, and now, she didn't take him seriously anymore. And besides, if it exploded, it would be over. They wouldn't have to hear about it.

For a fleeting instant, it occurred to her that maybe someone got hurt in the explosion. But probably not.

She stood and pulled her shirt out of the locker and pulled it over her head, careful not to disturb the scrunchy.

"Hey, okay, uh . . ." Lisa said. She stared at Jennifer's chest and had trouble getting the rest of her words out. Jennifer was four inches taller and now she was standing with her shirt over her head "You want to go get a burger? We can hang out, talk about the hurdles, or whatever you want."

Jennifer paused for a fleeting instant but didn't answer. Her mind turned over the many possibilities that this invitation might be about and might be set in motion. Lisa was unattractive to her in nearly every way, but this invitation was a crack in a door she had never even thought to open. As she pulled her shirt down and smoothed it out, she eyed Lisa coolly.

Inexplicably, Lisa's demeanor, typically brash and somehow male, gave way to something else. She smiled softly, which was something Jennifer had never seen her do. For an instant, Lisa was vulnerable.

"We've been in school together since third grade," she said as her chin tilted downward. "Come on. Let's have some fun. No big deal."

Jennifer gathered her bag from the locker and shut it, then deliberately stepped closer before stepping around. Lisa's face tilted downward further which made her look like a supplicant. That sealed it. Whatever the invitation was about, she was game.

"Fine. I'll drive," she said. Lisa's chin popped back up. "But we have to drop off my little brother."

Lisa smiled, big and bright.

"Great! Okay! I'll meet you at the arches," Lisa said, turning to walk away.

Jennifer listened to the radio as she waited for Josie. Every channel was carrying *Challenger* news. It was somber and, in a way, Jennifer knew it should be heartbreaking, but it just wasn't. She knew so many people at NASA who were friends of her dad, or parents of her friends, and they talked of nothing else, ever, so to die doing something NASA thought up seemed like just another day. They were always hyping up the danger of the job to be impressive, and now, the shuttle had helped give them some much-needed danger credibility. Their bluff, if it was a bluff, had been called. What they were doing really *was* dangerous, and now everyone could see it.

Josie appeared at the door and threw his book bag in the back seat as he got in. He was grinning.

"God, what took you so long?" she said as she started the car.

"I had to go all the way back to my locker from fifth period," he said. "This is awesome! Maybe no school for the rest of the week!"

"I wonder what daddy's going to say," she said.

"About what?" Josie asked.

"About the space shuttle, stupid," she replied.

"I thought he hated it," Josie said. "He'll be happy it's gone."

She pulled out of their parking spot and turned towards the grey span that marked the entrance to the football stadium. Josie frowned. What now? Did this involve track practice?

"Where are you going?" he asked.

"We're picking up someone," Jennifer said flatly without giving away anything.

She passed the cars going the other way as she drove towards the arch that read "Deer Park High School." As she drew nearer and slowed, he saw Lisa stand and pick up her big gym bag that doubled as her book bag.

"Jeez, that girl is such a huge lezbo," he said. "She's built like a man, too."

As the words left his mouth, Josie saw Lisa smile and wave at Jennifer, and he realized that's who they were picking up. His brow furrowed and he turned to Jennifer.

"We're giving her a ride?" he asked incredulously.

"She's on the track team," Jennifer said flatly. She was trying not to justify anything in her voice. "We've known each other since third grade."

Jennifer stopped in front of Lisa, who was now beaming with anticipation.

"Get in the back," Jennifer instructed Josie. He exhaled loudly and opened the car door.

"Hi. I'm Lisa," Lisa said as Josie pushed the seat forward and climbed into the back.

"I know who you are," he said bluntly.

Lisa held the gym bag awkwardly, unsure what to do with it. Josie was sitting behind the passenger seat not looking at her.

"Move over so she can put her bag down," Jennifer said. Josie sighed loudly and picked up his own bag and Jennifer's and pushed them onto the floor, then slid over. Lisa threw her bag on the back seat.

"Thanks, dude!" she said and plopped down in the front seat. She glanced back at Josie, but he was looking away. "Okay, okay! Let's go!"

Chapter 9

Lisa gazed at Jennifer, watching every move. Jennifer cooly watched her back. They sat at a booth by the window at the Texas Tavern. At night, the Texas Tavern was full of middle-aged alcoholics who liked to play pool, drink beer, and chase well shots. The paneled walls of the diner had hand-written signs that told the discounting schedule of the booze. Monday was Nickel Beer night. Tuesday was two-for-one shots. Wednesday was Ladies Drink Free night. Thursday was Dollar-a-Holler from six p.m. to nine p.m. Friday through Sunday, everyone paid full price.

During the day, the bar was closed but the kitchen was open and though it still smelled like smoke and stale beer, it was filled with high schoolers. Normally, they drifted in after school ended, but now, the place was filled at noon. The mood around the room was jubilant since school was out. The boys were at the pool table, discreetly passing around tiny bottles of vodka. The two waitresses who worked the Tuesday shift were not prepared for a celebratory deluge of teenagers. They had never been polite and today, they barked orders as they walked.

"Hey! Four to a table!" the heavy one yelled.

The six teenagers at the table did nothing, just glanced up and kept talking.

Lisa sipped a strawberry milkshake through a straw and Jennifer spooned a piece of ice from her water glass into her coffee. She liked coffee cold in the afternoon and wanted the caffeine buzz. She looked around the room and silently surveyed her feelings about being in public with the school's best-known lesbian. She decided she liked it. Lisa gave the people she didn't like something new to talk about. It was an unfamiliar feeling, but she instantly loved it. She couldn't perfectly articulate why this was good, but she suspected it was. Out of the corner of her eye, she saw people looking at her and whispering to each other. They were talking about her, and what they said wasn't important.

"I have to ask you," Lisa began, "what's with the Madonna thing? It's a good look, okay? I'm not knocking it, but, what's up?"

Jennifer flinched a little bit. She didn't want to talk about "the Madonna thing" because she couldn't articulate the attraction, but she wasn't backing down either.

"I don't know why everyone acts like I'm trying to be Madonna," she said, more defensively than she had intended.

"You don't know? Really?" Lisa said with a smile.

"I like her," Jennifer continued. "She has her own style, she makes her own music, she has her own power. She does what she wants. I like that."

"Yeah, I know okay, but," Lisa said, "how are you going to find your own style if you just imitate hers?"

Jennifer laughed, and Lisa's heart skipped a beat.

"I have to start somewhere!" she said. Madonna had offered the only aesthetic she had ever seen that she liked. She certainly couldn't take the lead from her mother who had embraced a sexless suburban Americana. Jennifer was unimpressed with any of the other girls she knew personally, some of whom had such strict dress codes that they seemed to be wearing a uniform. The cheerleaders were literally wearing a uniform, but so were the goth and country girl crowds. Jennifer hated the country look and refused to wear cowboy boots. The models she saw in magazines looked sickly to her. Even the ones that were beautiful only looked beautiful, but they didn't look powerful or exotic. They didn't look like a sexy beast of prey. They looked like they didn't care. They were still, somehow, passive. Madonna looked like she was grabbing at something that was savage and primal. Madonna exuded power. Power was the only word Jennifer could put on what she wanted from her appearance.

"I'll find my own power eventually," she said.

There was a long pause. Lisa sipped her milkshake and weighed her words carefully.

"You know she's gay, right?" Lisa said, dangling the idea out there. She looked closely to gauge Jennifer's reaction.

"She's not gay. She's married," Jennifer replied.

"That doesn't mean anything. It's just Hollywood," Lisa said "Look, I'm gay, okay?"

Jennifer arched one eyebrow.

"Really?" she said. "Who would have known?"

"Yes, I'm gay," Lisa continued. "Shocker. And I get all the gay magazines out of New York. My Aunt Chloe sends them to me. Madonna is in all of them, all the time, and she's gay and all the gays know it."

"Maybe gays really like her," Jennifer observed. "But I don't know why with all the Catholic stuff. Don't gay people hate Catholics?"

"Oh, my God, gays love Catholics," Lisa said with a snort. "They love all the secrets and forbidden stuff and the clothes. I wish my family was Catholic."

"What is your family?" Jennifer asked.

"Jewish," Lisa spat out. "My parents are Reformed, but my grandparents were Orthodox."

"Is that like, full-time and part-time?" Jennifer asked.

"It's more like full-time and unemployed," Lisa observed, "My parents don't do any Jew stuff. They used to, but now they just work all the time. Nothing is kosher in our house."

"My mother is Catholic, or at least she used to be," Jennifer said. "I don't know what my dad is."

"Oh, God," Lisa said. "Thinking about you in a nun's habit . . . so hot. So foxy."

Jennifer unexpectedly blushed.

"You don't think Madonna's gay? No way?" Lisa continued.

"She might be bi," Jennifer guessed. "Like I said, she does what she wants."

"Oh, girl, you have so much to learn. First of all, bi is gay," Lisa declared. "If you go down on other women, you are gay. Gay, gay, gay. If you're a man who sucks dick, you're gay."

"Even if you're a woman who will do stuff with guys?" Jennifer asked.

"Yes," Lisa confirmed. "But she's gay. All gays know other gays, and I'm telling you, she's gay."

"Whatever," Jennifer concluded. "So, you're exclusively gay, right? I mean, that's what people think."

"I don't care what people think," Lisa said. "And yes, I'm exclusively gay. Even if I wasn't gay, guys are gross, you know? Look at them. Why would any woman choose any one of them?"

Both turned to look around the Tavern. In one short sweep, they saw high school boys throwing food and laughing.

"The idea of one of these apes touching me is just so gross," Lisa said. "Okay and putting their thing inside me? No way in this world."

Jennifer laughed. Her brothers were identical to the guys in the Tavern, and she knew just what Lisa was talking about. The boys seemed like they were stuck on some primitive level.

"You'd put one of these creep's dick inside you? That doesn't just gross you out?" Lisa asked.

Jennifer looked around again. Who were these boys? Would she let them touch her?

"With a couple of them, maybe," she said uncertainly.

"You haven't done it yet?" Lisa asked. "Never sucked a dick?"

Jennifer laughed and covered her face with both hands.

"Gross!"

She composed herself, but her neck and chest flushed red. It was funny.

"Not yet," she said.

"Well, who do you like? Who's getting close?" Lisa asked.

"I like David," Jennifer admitted. "He's sweet looking."

Lisa furrowed her brow.

"Who?"

"David," she repeated. "From track."

"Wingate? David Wingate?" she asked.

Jennifer smiled and nodded.

"Jeez, you might as well be gay, he's so . . . womanly," Lisa said.

"He's not womanly. He's cute," Jennifer said.

"He's got long hair and skinny little legs. He's a chick with a dick if he even has one, okay," Lisa replied. "He's very womanly."

"He's got a big bulge. I think that's a . . . a dick," Jennifer said, wincing at her own voice saying the word.

"Yeah, because he's around all those guys all the time. I've never seen him with a girl," Lisa retorted. "Pretty sure that little kike is a homo."

"What about you? Aren't you and Marie a thing? Pretty sure she's Catholic," Jennifer asked, happy to be off the David subject.

Lisa sneered.

"No way," she declared "No way ever. She might as well have a dick, she's so butch."

"That's not what you like?" Jennifer asked.

Lisa leaned in.

"I'm a lesbian, okay?" she said. "See, I like women. I've always liked women since as far back as I can remember. I like women who look and act like women. I know, I know, I'm not real feminine, but I like girly girls."

"Well, who are you with?" Jennifer asked. She kind of knew what was coming.

"I'm not 'with' anybody. I'm a free agent. I want to be able to have sex with who I want. I don't want to be in a relationship. I'm more like Madonna in that way than any of these Ken and Barbie dolls in here," she said.

Lisa looked around the Tavern at all the different couples. Guys had their arms draped protectively over the girls.

Jennifer realized Lisa was right; Madonna was a sexual free agent and that was a big part of her power.

Lunch was pleasant enough, as far as Jennifer was concerned. Lisa was interesting, in a way, but she was not as interesting personally compared to her lesbian status and Jennifer was interested in the status of someone with a potentially sexual outlaw part of her personality. Just having lunch with Lisa brought her new looks and she saw a few raised eyebrows that she had never seen before. Lisa raised her profile, and she liked that.

Jennifer brought Lisa a new level of power and respect too. She was interested in Jennifer, whom she found to be even more sexually intriguing and mysterious than before they had lunch. Lisa liked everything she saw in Jennifer, her manner, her voice, her tone, her ambivalence, her attitude, and her inexperience. The entire package hit every lever in Lisa's personality. She was intoxicated by Jennifer to her bones. She was aroused just sitting next to Jennifer on the car ride back to school. Her stomach hurt with desire.

They didn't speak as Jennifer drove back to school. She drove Lisa to the arches without asking where Lisa had parked, or even if she had a car. Lisa said nothing either. She was going to have to walk to a store and call her mother to come pick her up, but she didn't want to say that. Her parents wouldn't buy her a car until her grades were better, which they never would be.

Lisa sensed that it was a good idea not to reveal her feelings at this point and so she spoke up as soon as the car came to a stop.

"This was fun," she said. "We should do it again. Okay? That was fun."

"Yeah, it was," Jennifer said as she switched the car back to first gear.

But before she could stop herself, Lisa leaned over and kissed Jennifer lightly on the lips. Jennifer kissed her back ever so slightly. Lisa was surprised, but she then got out of the car quickly so she could declare the win.

"Can I call you?" she said as she pulled the seat forward.

"Sure," Jennifer said as if nothing had happened.

Lisa pulled her giant gym bag out of the back seat.

"See ya later, beautiful," she said and shut the door. She didn't wait for a reaction.

Jennifer turned her gaze away. She hid her conflicted feelings and drove away quickly.

* * *

Jack woke with a start. He was dreaming but could not remember what it was about. Whatever it was, it was not good. He rubbed his eyes in the dark and remembered what was happening. It was time to go. Time to go to Mexico and pick up drugs.

Jack entered the kitchen and looked in the refrigerator for something to eat. He didn't want to stop on the way and knew it would be too late to eat by the time they got to Brownsville. He hoped Marco knew to eat because he didn't intend to stop once they were moving. One tank of gas would get them most of the way and they weren't going to stop for anything else.

As he was looking in the refrigerator, Bob exited the pantry with a fresh vodka bottle in his hand.

"Hey, Jackie Boy," Bob said cheerfully.

"Hey, Dad," Jack said wearily. "I guess you were right about the shuttle. Did you ever get anyone on the phone?"

"Nope," Bob said.

Bob poured his glass half full of vodka and then finished filling it with the orange juice that was on the counter. His break from the sauce had only lasted a few hours.

"I was on the blower for two hours, but didn't get through to anyone," he said.

"That sucks," was all Jack could muster. "Do you think it was the cold?"

"Oh, yes," Bob said as he took his first gulp from the fresh glass. "They'll take a while, looking at this or that. But the chances that it *wasn't* the cold are slim. They had checks and balances for everything but freezing weather in Florida."

Bob slurred 'checks and balances' as it came out. Too many consonant sounds made it difficult to talk over the vodka.

"We had redundancies up the waz," he continued. "We had protocols. We had procedures. But as far as I know, they never tested a system that complex, like the solid rocket boosters, in a temperature that low. I'm damn sure of it. Something little went wrong and then something big followed."

Jack pulled out some left-overs and then took a fork out of the drawer. They heard the front door open and close.

"Found yourself a job yet?" Bob asked. He was swaying back and forth though his hand was on the countertop.

"Nope," Jack said through a bite of potato salad. "How about you?"

Bob's unemployment and Jack's unemployment were vastly different, which they both knew, but Bob was too unsteady to go down that rabbit hole.

"Price of oil is still falling," Bob said. "The whole oil patch is in the shitter. I'm too old for West Texas anyway. And NASA . . . they don't need my help, that's for sure. The pain there is just beginning."

"That must be tough," Jack said.

He pointed at the glass in Bob's hand.

"That must really take the edge off," Jack said.

Before Bob could respond, Jennifer entered. She saw Bob and Jack and no dinner being cooked.

"Where's Mom?" she asked, irritated already.

"She went to an organizer," Bob said.

"For what?" Jennifer asked.

"No nukes, I think," Bob said. "She's making the world a better place."

"Is she making dinner?" Jennifer asked, mostly to Jack.

"I don't know," Jack said. "She usually does."

Just then, Josie entered the kitchen. He smiled, seeing for the first time in a while his older brother, sister, and dad in the same place.

"Where's Mom?" he asked.

"She's at an organizer, whatever that means," Jennifer responded.

"Have none of you paid any attention to what your mother does?" Bob slurred. "She has issues she's committed to. She goes to events, and they must be organized."

"She's not the only one with issues," Jennifer said and left.

Jack handed the mac and cheese he was holding to Josie as he passed him.

"Where you headed?" Bob asked.

"Just hanging out with some friends," Jack said as he left.

Josie was confronted with being alone with his dad, which he rarely was. Bob had spent a great deal of time with Jack, and a little less with Jennifer when they were kids. With Josie, he had spent the least amount of time, and though he loved the boy, Josie seemed more wed to his mother than the other two kids. Carol had, until recently, babied Josie, and Josie had let her.

In the earlier periods of their life together, Carol had been neutral on the things he did with Jack. Bob had initiated Jack into everything he loved, which included guns, the outdoors, and mechanical things, and Carol said nothing. When it became clear that Bob intended to do the same with Jennifer, Carol demanded that Jennifer not go hunting or shoot guns, and she took Jennifer with her on shopping trips with such frequency that Jennifer was not interested in camping, and certainly not hunting. Bob was disappointed to find out that neither Jack nor Jennifer was a science kid.

Initially, Carol had dressed Jennifer in brightly colored dresses and put the giant bows favored by Mexicans in her hair, but that had tapered off as Jennifer got older and Carol began shedding her Mexican identity. Just as Jennifer was reaching puberty, Carol stopped directing Jennifer's appearance. Bob noticed when Carol began letting

Jennifer choose her own styles, and when Jennifer began to experiment with more provocative fashions, and passed into her Madonna phase, Carol said nothing. When Bob asked, "Should she go out in public like that?" to his great surprise, Carol shrugged. Jennifer was wearing a bra on the outside of her clothes, and Carol had no opinion.

Carol had doted on Josie in his early years, but in the same way Carol stopped directing Jennifer's feminine path, Bob took less interest in Josie's manly path. Something had changed in both adults. They shifted their attention to their own struggles and fading identities, and Josie was left to raise himself as best he could.

"How was school?" Bob blurted out.

"They let us out early, remember?" Josie said.

Josie put the leftovers down and picked up a bag of potato chips that was on the counter.

"I knew something bad was going to happen," Bob said.

Josie stopped with a chip halfway to his mouth. This was awkward. He didn't believe that his dad knew what was going to happen, but Bob had just said the most significant thing he had ever said to Josie. Josie scrambled for the best response. He cycled through jokes, denying that foreknowledge of the disaster was even possible, mocking his dad the way Jack did, or rolling his eyes and dismissing his dad the way Jennifer did. But he wanted to know.

"How did you know? Why didn't they stop it?" he asked.

"I tried to warn them," Bob squeaked out.

To Josie's horror, it appeared his dad was about to cry. Josie was sorry he asked and did not want to have an awkward emotional encounter. He knew his brother and sister wouldn't put up with it and neither would his mom.

But he was saved by the sound of the front door opening and closing, and his mother's voice speaking to Jennifer.

"Yes, yes, yes," Carol said. "Just give me an hour, okay? I just walked in the door."

"I'll tell you later," Bob said, and Josie took the opportunity to leave. He passed his mother on his way out of the kitchen.

"Hello, baby," she said and kissed him on the check.

Carol entered and tried not to see Bob. He noted her efforts but said nothing. She stared into the refrigerator and after a moment, took out some hamburger meat. She took a pan from the drawer below the oven and then set the flame.

Bob's head was pressed against the cabinet door as he watched her. She had been such a charming girl. He used to watch her and listen to her sing her Mexican songs and prolonged periods of silence would follow. It brought him joy to gaze upon her. He would think about all the girls he didn't marry, and it would make him glad he waited, how lucky he felt he had been to land on this simple but beautiful Mexican girl from peasant stock.

He knew her life had been hard in Mexico, but she had never talked about it in an existential way. Nothing she said alerted him that a shift was coming. She talked about how hard she had to work, and things that pained her, like sore hands and blistered feet, but she didn't know the language of psychotherapy and didn't connect her experience to her current behavior. He knew she had a huge family that had good and bad people in it, and that the bad people often were killed, and sometimes the good people died from violence as well. He was only now starting to suspect her past was driving her present. She thought the same of him.

When she came to Texas, he saw the opening of her mind. It was like a great weight had been lifted off her. She was mostly happy, especially when he went to NASA. His job somehow made her dreams, not his, come true. But in the 18 years he was at NASA, she changed. She ceased to be Mexican at all. She stopped trying to teach the kids Spanish. She put on weight. She changed her hair. She had stopped touching him long before his career ended, and by the time he stopped working at NASA and began drinking, she stopped talking to him. His actions towards her were commensurate. When she stopped being a Mexican girl, and became an American woman, he reached out to touch her less and less. Now, they never touched each other, except fleetingly and by accident.

For a long time, he wrongly thought that her change began with the wives she met at NASA. Somehow, they shamed her. In 1967, as the moon landings grew closer, they had been at a party when the men began to speak about their college alma maters, and the women spoke up as well. When it was Bob's turn, he said he went to Texas A&M, and there was a disapproving pause. The other men had gone full Ivy League. And then their eyes turned to Carol, or Karolita as he still called her, and he felt her clench his hand hard.

"I went to the University of Mexico," she said, as a joke, but no one laughed, and the conversation quickly moved on.

In the car on the way home, she asked, for the first time, what the A and M in A&M stood for. When he told her Agricultural and Mechanical, he knew she heard farming and fixing cars.

"A&M is a good school," he said. "Don't let those desk jockeys rattle you. They've never gotten their hands dirty."

"No, they haven't," she said. "And neither have their wives."

Clearly, dirty hands meant something different to her than they did to him, but he didn't pursue it. He later thought that he shouldn't have let that shame fester.

Had he brought that evening and interaction up, and credited it with her shifting attitudes, however, she would have denied it had any influence. To her, she was changing in a positive direction for positive reasons. She was "growing."

He watched her silently as she went back to the refrigerator. She was going to make hamburgers, a meal she never ate as a girl. She didn't sing when she cooked anymore. American meals were cooked in serious silence.

Suddenly, he found her standing right in front of him and she put her hands on her hips.

"You're in my way," she said a bit too quietly.

Bob moved out of her way, and she opened the cabinet long enough to take out the salt and pepper.

"Did you hear about the shuttle?" he asked.

She didn't answer for a moment. He had the impression she was contemplating if she should speak at all.

"Of course," she finally said. "It's all that's on the news. Reagan pressured them to launch, now he has their blood on his hands."

He laughed.

"All those years at NASA and all the dinners and galas we went to . . ." he said. "You know it doesn't work that way. They have launch criteria. Reagan has nothing to do with it."

She finally stopped and looked at him. She looked particularly unattractive in the fluorescent light.

"Okay, then you tell me," she said. "You worked there. I was just a fixture on your arm. Why did they launch? It was obviously unsafe."

"I don't know," he said. "I would find it hard to believe what happened wasn't related to the cold."

"Those space jockeys just care about their own glory," she opined. "That's what I remember. Now people are dead."

After another awkward moment, Bob left the room. He knew he could no longer even agree with her.

* * *

Bob woke after a drunken nap and saw it was ten o'clock, and the late news was on. He had a drink in his hand, but the ice had melted, and he was hung over. The sound was turned down low, but the news was a summary of the day's events in Florida. Cameras panned over the shocked expressions on the faces of people; those in the reviewing stands at the Cape, kids in classrooms, and the families of the dead.

Josie came down the stairs with the empty potato chip bag. He disappeared into the kitchen and then headed back up.

"Good night, Dad," he said on the stairs.

"Good night, buddy," he said, smiling at Josie as he disappeared. Something had to be done, he thought. The boy was suffering.

Jennifer passed Josie on the stairs. Bob watched her descending and decided not to say anything about the T-shirt she was wearing that was cut off just below the bra line. She said nothing, but he heard her talking to her mother in the kitchen.

"I'm not going out, Mom, I'm going to bed!" she said.

After a moment, Jennifer passed back through and headed up the stairs.

"Good night, sweetheart," he said. She acted like she didn't hear him.

But a moment later, she stuck her head over the banister so she could see him.

"Good night, Daddy. I'm sorry about today. If you had been there, maybe it wouldn't have happened," she said with her long hair hanging over the rail. Before he could respond, she disappeared.

Carol entered the room and turned off the lamp by the couch.

"Turn the TV off when you're done," she said and went upstairs.

The house fell quiet. Bob was alone now, and he felt the death of the day, and he wondered if he had ever met any of the pilots that had died earlier that morning. He didn't remember them, but they looked familiar, and they would now look familiar forever since they would never age. Quietly, he set the glass down and sobbed into his wet hands.

Chapter 10

Jack was good until they passed the exits to Corpus. From Deer Park to Corpus, Marco had been awake and in a good mood. For the first hour, he looked stricken, but Jack made fun of him and broke the bad mood, and Marco was himself for a fleeting time. They talked about girls they had both fucked and joked about being 'tunnel buddies.' Jack knew Marco was lying about at least one of those girls. Marco told Jack details about Shannon he shouldn't know, like how he had found her vibrator under her bed. Jack answered a couple of questions Marco asked about Jennifer, but he loved his sister and wouldn't dish dirt about her. Marco and Shannon were both adopted, and they didn't like each other at all, and so Marco talked at length about how he spied on her when she was in the shower. He painted a detailed verbal picture of Shannon's stark white body and giant nipples and red pubic hair. He had a friend, he told Jack, whose dad worked for the Houston police, and he was trying to get that guy to nab a police camera that he could hide in the bathroom. Jack asked why Marco wanted pictures since he had already seen her naked, and Marco answered, "So I can pass them out!" A tiny box in Jack's mind scribbled a note about Marco's low level of loyalty.

After Corpus, Marco fell into a deep sleep and Jack drove on alone with the windows down.

Finally, with Marco slumbering beside him, he reached Brownsville. Jack pulled his truck into an empty parking lot. He had been to the Texas Southmost College campus in Brownsville twice before to go to parties. It was there that he concluded college was stupid. If he wanted to party, he could do that without living in a shitty dorm room. He wasn't going to A&M like his father clearly wanted if only to thwart his dad's plan to get him to follow in his footsteps. Jack loved his dad, but he had grown up with Bob's stories about war and death and oilfield injuries and A&M, and then the dream job doing the Most Important Thing That Had Ever Been Done, and Jack just didn't want the pressure. He'd rather be his own failure than his father's success.

He parked the truck in the lot for the dorm he had once been in and thought of the girl he met there. He had her phone number but never called her. Too bad; she was attractive, polite, and respectable. But he went back to Deer Park the next morning and found her number in his pocket two days later. As he looked up at the dorm, he thought briefly of going in to see if she still lived there. It had only been two years earlier, but he reminded himself of why he was there, and it wasn't to chase dates that never happened.

The bright lights of the Gateway Bridge crossing station lit the low hanging clouds and made the night glow white. Matamoros had long been a party town for Texans, but fewer people would drive over unless they were Mexicans returning to Mexico. Kidnapping Americans was a growth industry in Matamoros and the Mexican government seemed to have no interest in stopping it. Perhaps the Mexican government had an interest in perpetuating it, and now, taking a car into Matamoros was more of an act of daring, and fewer people wanted to do it. There was still a thriving practice in going over to Matamoros for the day to get drunk on the cheap, and plenty of prostitutes to buy on the cheap, but the stories about the violent death of fun seeking Americans in Matamoros had circulated far and wide. Now, only young men made the trip, and it was never for anything innocent or legitimate. As Matamoros grew more dangerous, the takers for a walk across the Gateway Bridge grew more daring and brazen. The two went hand in hand. Matamoros was a game of survival that only the foolish and daring would attempt.

Marco slumbered on. Jack thought about waking him but didn't. Instead, he had time to his own thoughts, and he had poured over his decisions that led to this trip. It was all justified. Life was good, Domingo stood for an opportunity, and this trip was scary, but it was all going to work out. Tough calls always broke his way. Even rodeoing, in which he had broken both arms and been consigned to a neck brace for three months, had always advanced his lifestyle. This trip was just another step on the path to being rich and having an exciting time. He knew it.

What bothered him was his dad. Bob was now a mystery to Jack after a twenty-one-year father-son friendship that was populated by good times. Bob had taken Jack everywhere he went. He took his son to work and had Jack sleep under his desk when he had to work into the night. Jack knew that to his dad, that period had been the most exciting time in his life. He didn't know his dad's life was only made better by glancing down at his feet and seeing Jack sleep with his little mouth hanging open.

Sometimes, he'd wake Jack in the middle of the night, and they'd go to the training center and get into the pool where the astronauts prepared for days of weightlessness. They ran into Neil Armstrong there one evening. Armstrong was alone and so Bob told Jack to introduce himself. Jack did so and he spoke to Armstrong for about five minutes. Bob just watched and didn't get close enough to hear what was said. He wanted Jack to have that moment for himself. Bob was proud in a way men who thought they were building the foundations of a future civilization were proud. Those men never spoke about creating a civilization, but many, including Bob, believed in it, at least for a few glorious years. The American order, the American civilization, they thought, was the best the world had ever known, and it was going to get better as the rights and privileges of citizenship were realized by more and more people.

Jack thought of those five minutes often. He remembered it well. And what he thought was that nothing he did in his life would ever come close to what Neil Armstrong had done. Humans had been to the moon and the next closest celestial body was Mars, which was far away and at least as barren as the moon. Jack knew in his bones that the moon was it, and that there was no more space glory. His life was going to be very earthbound. The romance and glamour of the space program reflected on Bob, and Jack thought Bob wanted to believe that it would reflect onto his kids, but Jack knew that wasn't true, and he knew Bob knew it too.

After the final *Apollo* mission Bob and Carol went to a gala at a hotel downtown and Carol drove home because Bob was too drunk to drive. Jack was still awake and watching TV when they got home, but his mother sent him to bed and then she paid the babysitter. Bob went into the kitchen and made some coffee. From his room, Jack heard his dad talking loudly and so he snuck down and listened from the living room.

"It's over and it was all for nothing," he heard his dad say. "There's nothing up there. The whole New Frontier ends here on earth."

Bob was upset. He slurred his words and Jack's imagination of what was happening in the next room, he saw Bob crying.

"Why do you care?" he heard his mother say. "You have a great job. The shuttle will keep you there until you retire."

"I didn't know all I had was a job," Bob said miserably. "We believed in what we were doing. We bought it. We believed it. And now, Kennedy is dead. Vietnam is dead. Our kids will grow up to be hippies."

"You're talking crazy," his mother said. Her Mexican accent was still in her voice back then.

"I used to dream that Jack would come to work with me," Jack heard his dad say of him. "That will never happen. Even if it did, it wouldn't be the same. NASA isn't the same. The hippies… they hate what we did. They want to change the world with music and shit, not math, not engineering. They hate the military. They hate that we left an American flag on the moon. If NASA represents the USA and its glory, then they hate NASA. It won't be worth working for in the future."

Jack heard his dad speak of a failed vision for his future and so he knew that his dad thought he was a loser who missed out on glory and would never find anything meaningful to do. It was what Jack believed about himself. Jack grew up in the shadow of both the moon landing and the counterculture summit at Woodstock, two competing but parallel events, and like so many of his age, he didn't see a future of glory for himself anywhere. Everything that followed was a lame substitute. The war in Vietnam ended, and the shuttle took over from the rockets to the moon, and now, everything was nostalgia. The past peaked on the moon and the future peaked in the mud at Woodstock, and the present was just TV and illicit fun. There was absolutely no reason *not* to do drugs.

Before he went upstairs, he heard one more thing. It was his Mexican mother defending the hippies.

"Everyone hates the hippies. I don't know why. Some are my age, and they try to do something good for the world," she said.

"There is a lot about this country that you still don't understand," Jack heard his dad say as he turned to go to his bedroom. He had left from the same bedroom to go on the current drug running mission.

Jack sat in his truck thinking things through and listening to the hot engine ping. The world had changed so much since he was a kid. The music changed. By the time he was old enough to read Rolling Stone magazine, it was full of stories about aging hippies who complained that they didn't trust young people anymore. He could understand why his dad distained them so much. The few kids at his school that embraced the tie dye hippie aesthetic listened to crappy music and didn't play sports. He now understood that his mother was sympathetic to them. He linked, for the first time, his mother to the thing that was only spoken of with undisguised hatred; the counterculture. This, as much as anything else, explained to Jack why his mother and father were drifting apart quickly. The rift had started a long time ago and was getting wider.

As Jack wrapped up his thoughts about this family, he picked up a baseball cap and put it on, then he slid down in the seat. Marco breathed deep and shifted positions. Jack thought he could get at least a couple of hours before it would be time to exit his module and set foot on the moonscape of Mexico to do something daring. Bringing drugs back wouldn't be meaningful, but Neil Armstrong wouldn't dare try it.

* * *

Those two hours turned out to be eighty-five short minutes. The sun rose and the light went under the brim of Jack's hat. He turned his arm and looked at his watch; time to get moving. He slid up in his seat and elbowed Marco. Marco opened his eyes and then shut them again. He had remembered where he was and what he was about to do and wanted to go back to sleep. Then he opened his eyes and sat up straight. He looked at the dorm across the parking lot.

"We were here before," he said.

"Yep," Jack said.

"For a party," Marco remembered.

Jack opened his door and turned in his seat so he could reach for his boots.

"Bro, this is not smart what we're about to do," Marco said. "It's not too late to back out."

89

"Stop being a pussy," Jack replied as he tightened the laces on his boots. "People do this all the time. The drugs we sell had to be brought across the border and all we're doing is going upstream. The river goes to the same place."

Jack got out of the truck and waited for Marco to decide. Marco hesitated, but he had always followed Jack on whatever path Jack took, and he wasn't going to start leading or stop following now.

"Lock the door," Jack said, and then started walking across the parking lot.

Jack walked several paces ahead as he and Marco made their way down International Boulevard toward the bridge. They crossed over Elizabeth Street and began to bump into the throng of women who were crossing the other way. Heavy women in brightly colored dresses walked past them, all headed for the cleaning jobs they held in the city. Only Marco and Jack headed south. They passed the US Border Patrol station on their left and then passed the booth where US and Mexican station agents were sitting down and smoking. It was early enough for them not to pay attention and so Jack and Marco walked right past without any of them even looking up.

They reached the part of the bridge that crossed over the river and looked down. No river was more inappropriately named than the Rio Grande, or Rio Bravo as the Mexicans called it. It was a dirty trash strewn trickle down below. It wasn't big or brave. Most of the trucks on the bridge could have driven right through it.

Jack looked over his shoulder and saw Marco staring at the river below. Since they left the truck, Marco's anxiety had risen and now he looked sick with fear. For Marco, the reality of seeing the armed mustached Mexican border guards had driven home the reality of what they are doing. The river marked the crossing to sure death.

"How in the hell are we going to get back over this bridge with coke?" he said out loud, his voice quivering.

"Would you calm the fuck down?" Jack said. "You look like a nervous drug dealer. If you just chill, we'll be fine. They'll show us where to bring the drugs back in. But don't get all weirded out and look like a fucking dope dealer. Seriously, man. You've got to decide right now. Can you do this? If you can't, turn around."

Marco looked down. He knew he should say no.

"I can do it," he said.

* * *

Matamoros was not a town until 1824. The town wasn't a trading center or jammed border crossing until the Texans declared independence and later, the Americans came with their army to rip the territory away from Mexico in 1846. It had never been an important town in Mexico, and it looked like it. The town was run down with cheap buildings made of concrete block and stucco rather than stone. A tangle of wires ran overhead. Dogs were everywhere. The sound of cheaply made motorcycles reverberated along every street.

Jack and Marco walked silently down the Calle Primera. More crowds of Mexicans walked the other way. These women had broad faces and mahogany skin. None were over five feet tall. Jack and Marco towered over them. The ancient character of Mexico was written into the faces of every man, woman, and child they passed.

After thirty minutes of steady walking and furtive glances over their shoulders, Jack and Marcos reached the pink Our Lady of Refuge Cathedral, known by most as the Matamoras Cathedral. The structure was small by Mexican cathedral standards and the pink stone edifice was an exception to the mostly white buildings up and down the Calle Cinco. Old men sat on benches across the street and kids were running around in the dust of the Plaza Principal Miguel Hidalgo behind them. Miscellaneous urban noise gently floated in from all directions. The air smelled of grilling meat.

The street in front of the cathedral was peaceful, but Marco felt as if he was in a movie, and this was a set up for a massive burst of gunfire or a huge explosion. Jack looked up at the Cathedral and then leaned against the low wall that separated the holy place from the sidewalk.

"I have to take a dump," Marco said miserably. His voice was faltering, and he was starting to mumble.

"We passed several public toilets on the way here," Jack said.

He was irritated with Marco. The gloom and dread were apparent on every facet of Marco's appearance, and it wasn't getting better.

"I didn't have to go then," he said. "I think I might be sick. I think I'm going to shit myself."

"You have to stop this and relax," Jack said. "What we are doing is not that big a deal. Even if we get caught, we'll work it out. I told you already. If you can't do this, start walking back towards the border. I don't need your help that bad."

Marco shook his head.

"I'm not going to do that," was all he said.

A couple of long minutes passed. Jack looked at the men across the street on the lengthy line of benches. All the men seemed to be looking at them, and of course, they would be able to see Marco's agitation. He had not seen anyone in a police uniform since crossing over. Jack glanced down at his feet and noted how he and Marco were the only men wearing anything other than cowboy boots. But they were also the only men taller than five-and-a-quarter feet so regardless of how they dressed, they would have stood out.

"Have you ever heard about brujeria?" Marco suddenly asked. It was more of a statement than a question. "It's like Mexican voodoo. They have witches and shit, and they worship the devil."

Jack turned and glared at Marco who looked like he was about to vomit.

"You're doing this to yourself," Jack said.

"Shannon had a book about it that she got out of the library at school," Marco said.

Marco looked up at Jack and then saw a commotion behind him. Jack noted the new wave of alarm. He turned and saw three young men walking quickly towards them. They walked with purpose and unveiled malice as well.

"Oh, my motherfucking God," was all Marco could manage.

The three young men arrived and stopped in a line a few feet from Jack. They were dressed in the style of young Latin druggies; baggy shorts, uniform white wife beaters, blue bandanas.

After a moment, the largest passed Jack and Marco and flanked them. He crossed his arms.

"Cabron, fucking puto Americans," said one of the druggies. "Dressed like faggots."

"Sorry," Jack said with a scowl. "My mom threw away my cholo costume."

"We aren't fucking cholos," the druggie said. "That's California, faggot."

The druggie reached into his loose front pocket and took out a big pocketknife. He opened it quickly for effect.

From Jack there was no reaction, but Marco bent over.

"Your fucking niggar friend is going to shit his pants," the druggie said.

"He's fine," Jack said without looking. "He drank the water."

"Keep your fucking mouth closed," the druggie said and turned. Everyone followed as he walked past the giant church and turned down a side street.

Behind the cathedral were three scooters. They were white, with tiny seats and long slender tail pipes. The druggies each took one and started them up. The scooters made a high pitch whine. Jack and Marco just stared; scooters were not what they were expecting.

"Look," Marco said. At the back of the lot was a portable toilet.

Marco started running towards the toilet. The biggest druggie quickly closed the gap between them and hit Marco on the back of the head with his fist which caused Marco to fall.

"The fuck," Jack said. "He has to go to the bathroom, jackass!"

"We tell you when to do everything, puto, now get on!" said the druggie, but then Marco ended all conversation. He stood up, pulled his pants down, squatted, and dropped a load right where he was. It made a loud wet sound.

The biggest druggie threw up his hands and turned away. Jack just shook his head. After a moment, Marco stood, pulled up his pants and walked back to the scooters.

"You should have let him go," was all Jack could manage. Marco looked less miserable but more like a zombie.

"Get the fuck on, faggots!" the lead druggie said.

The other two druggies scooted forward on their seats which made a tiny bit of extra seat space. Jack moved first, Marco hung his head even lower and climbed on behind the other. They had to hug the person in front of them to stay on and their feet dangled out to the sides. The druggies revved the tiny engines and started down the crowded streets.

The scooters were far faster than Jack had anticipated, and the drivers whipped through Matamoros traffic like mosquitoes. The many Mexicans on the sidewalks passed in a blur. Marco, he saw, had his eyes closed and he seemed, somehow, calmer.

After a few minutes, the buildings were spaced further apart, and it was clear to Jack that they were leaving the city and going into the countryside. The long road was covered in cracks and weeds grew though. The scooters were pushed to their speed limit along the long straight road. Little cafes and packs of stray dogs passed by in a stream of sights and smells.

When the high whine of the scooters began to fall, Jack knew they were getting close to wherever they were going. Up ahead, he saw a gas station with cars all around. They wound their way between the cars and circled behind the gas station. In the back was a white pick-up truck and three men in boots, and thick jackets.

The druggies stopped at the truck, and Jack and Marco put their feet down and stood. The men in jeans and boots pointed to the back of the truck, and in a drone of scooter noise, the young druggies pulled away.

"Vas a morir, negro!" the druggie said to Marco as he sped away.

It was quiet, except for the men speaking in Spanish to each other. Jack stepped up on the truck tire and climbed into the bed of the truck. Marco followed and sat down beside him, then put his head on his knees and closed his eyes again.

"I took a huge dump in public," he mumbled.

"You sure did," Jack confirmed. "And in the parking lot of a church."

The truck drove further into the country. Most of the greenery gave way to dust and scrub brush and mesquite and some low oak trees. The road dust blew into the truck bed, covering both with a fine mist of flour-like flake. Marco never lifted his head, but he pulled his shirt over his nose.

Jack watched the road and noted the few turns they made. If they had to walk out, he wanted to have some sense of which way to turn. But the roads were long and wound back and forth, so it was difficult in the morning sun to figure out which way they were going. He thought it was south.

94

Chapter 11

As they rode in the back of the truck to meet their fate, Jack thought about his rodeo days, and how he first got into the business. He had always loved the rodeo. Bob had friends at the Houston Livestock Show and Rodeo, and he was on the scholarship committee. Bob was at the Astrodome all day sometimes, and Jack would wander around, looking at the massive cattle and learning about how to take care of horses. The older men liked him, and he was curious back then. At an early age, Jack had his father's engineering heart and a photographic memory for details. The cows and horses smelled like Texas dirt.

Jack liked the girls that hung around the rodeo, and he lost his virginity to a barrel racer at the Fort Bend County Rodeo when he was a freshman in high school. That, more than anything else, sealed his bond to the rodeo. He told no one at first, but then he and his buddies began to keep score. Jack wanted to win at that and everything else at the rodeo. He'd eat more hotdogs than anyone else, drink more beer, and score more girls. His engineering aspirations stopped right there. If Deer Park High School had a rodeo team, he would have been the star. Jack was too small to be a star at football in Texas.

At his first opportunity, he rode a wild horse, and it was a thrill, though he took several shots to the nuts. The laughter and pats on the back made up for the nutting he had received. His dad had many friends with horses, and they took him to their ranches where he learned to ride, to rope reasonably well, and then finally, he rode a bull for the first time at the Montgomery County Rodeo. The sound of the crowd and the taste of the dirt stuck with him for days. He made out with a new girl that night, and he never thought seriously about anything else. He was going to the PBR—the Professional Bull Rider circuit.

But then he met another cowboy with some coke. Michael went to his high school, but Michael was black, and they rarely spoke until they met at the rodeo. Michael shared some coke which they did under the bleachers after the bull rides. He put a baby spoon of coke on the back of Jack's hand, and Jack sniffed it up. The rush was so fast and so strong that he had to sit down.

"You a lightweight, man!" Michael said with a giggle.

From Michael he learned that barrel racers and buckle bunnies and rodeo clowns like cowboys, but they really liked coke more. Cowboys and coke were the perfect combination to be the most popular cowboy at the rodeo, and so when Jack noticed Domingo at a rodeo and recognized him as the odd guy that lived in his neighborhood, it didn't take long for him to notice that Domingo was selling. He knocked on Domingo's front door the next day. Domingo sent him around to the back, and after Jack entered the back door for the first time, Domingo lined out more coke than Jack had ever seen.

Domingo liked the girls at the rodeo, but not the cowboys, or the noise, or the distance he had to travel, and he thought the sheriff deputies at the rodeos were watching him. Domingo didn't dress cowboy or country, and he didn't want to learn. Jack solved a real problem for him by being a cowboy, dressing to fit in, and Jack was willing to sell coke, so he had a supply for himself.

After that first meeting, Jack was set up to sell coke to Michael, who quickly spread the word. The first time Jack went to a rodeo with coke, he sold all he had in a few minutes. He gave the money to Domingo and Domingo told him to raise the price. Jack did that, but it didn't work; he still sold out in a few minutes and people started coming up to him when he first pulled into the parking lot. Jack stopped being a cowboy himself, stopped roping or riding, and he just focused on supplying coke. That had been a little over a year ago. Jack pulled his shirt over his nose and reviewed the year in his mind. It was a natural evolution to head upstream, which is why he wasn't scared. Surely, no one would kill their sales force.

* * *

Jack had closed his eyes and was breathing through his mouth to avoid caking up his nostrils, but then the truck slowed. He looked up to see where they were going, and ahead, was a low two-story house that was a mansion by the standards of the tiny adobe and plywood shacks surrounding it. He saw men with machine guns standing at a cattle grate. Jack recognized the Kalashnikovs; his dad had let him shoot one at the range. A Kalashnikov could pump out lead fast and they were easy to shoot. These were serious killers, Jack knew, and he and Marco needed to say as little as possible to get out alive.

"Wake up," Jack said to Marco. Marco lifted his head and turned to see where they were going. He saw the Kalashnikovs.

"We're so fucking dead," Marco said and put his head down.

"Get up," Jack said as he kicked Marco hard in the side. "Enough of this horseshit. We're going to get the coke and go home."

The swift kick seemed to work; Marco opened his eyes and rolled up to his knees.

The truck came to a stop. The men in the truck spoke to the men with the Kalashnikovs, and then one waved to Jack. It was time to go.

Jack and Marco climbed down from the truck bed and walked towards the house, and Jack began to take in other aspects of the situation. The big house had no foundation and was built on stilts. Under the house was a pen with two pink pigs and a few chickens. He could hear dogs barking furiously from somewhere, but he couldn't see them. Beyond the house were the adobe shacks, and there were women sitting under reed umbrellas in a few places. They had baskets and corn husks at their feet.

A wooden staircase ran up the side of the house and one of the men used the Kalashnikov to point that direction. Jack started up the stairs, but Marco stopped at the base.

"Don't you do it," was all Jack had to say. Marco put a foot on the first stair and then started up.

At the top was a heavy metal door that was rusted around the frame. Jack tried to handle but it was locked. A face appeared at the window to the side. It was another man who looked like the rest; a broad, brown face with patchy facial hair. After a moment, the door opened and the man in the window was standing in front of Jack. He stood back, and Jack, followed by Marco, entered.

It took Jack a moment to adjust to the low light inside. The room was big but smelled of cigarettes and garbage. The floor had dirty white tiles, and the ceiling was water stained and low. There were couches along each wall, and a few paintings, each of the Virgin Mary or Jesus with a beam of light coming out of his sacred heart.

As his eyes adjusted, Jack came to see that there were women sitting on each of the couches. They were all noticeably young, and they looked at Jack and Marco with lazy laconic eyes. They were dressed in tiny shirts and shorts, and most didn't look up from the TV on a stand against the wall. The man with the Kalashnikov sat down by the TV and turned to watch it as well. Jack saw the screen; they were watching a dubbed version of *Rocky 2*.

For a long time, no one said anything. Jack and Marco just stood, looking at the room, and slowly, they too turned their attention to *Rocky 2*. It seemed the natural thing to do. They were so intent on the movie that they didn't notice a heavy Mexican women enter the room. When she struck a match to light a cigarette, Marco saw her, and he elbowed Jack.

She exhaled a rich plume of smoke and stared at Jack and Marco. She was clearly evaluating them.

Finally, she spoke.

"You are the leader," she said to Jack. "Your friend is scared."

Jack glanced at Marco, who was looking at the floor tiles.

"He'll be okay," Jack said. "You can trust him."

Jack regretted the words as they were leaving his mouth, and her snort confirmed his regret.

"Trust," she said. "Sit, por favor."

Jack sat next to one of the girls on the couch nearest to him, but there were no more spaces there, so Marco had to cross the room, to get to a seat.

"My name is Karlotta," she said. "You don't need to know more. I know your names, and where you live. Domingo tells me everything."

She went into the kitchen and called out to someone from the window. Then she took a chair from the dinette table in the kitchen and sat.

"You work for Domingo, not good," she said suddenly. She stabbed the cigarette in their direction as she spoke. "Domingo is a motherfucker. Chingado." She ended the sentence with a spit on the floor. None of the girls even looked away from the TV.

Jack glanced at Marco, and he was no longer looking at the floor. He watched TV with the rest.

Just then, the door opened, and another man came in with two back packs. He dropped one on the floor in front of Jack and one in front of Marco and then he left.

"Look inside," Karlotta said.

Jack leaned forward and pulled the bag to himself. Marco mimicked his moves. Jack unzipped the top of the backpack and pulled the top flap back. Inside, he saw coke in bundles.

"You sell, take the money to Domingo," Carlotta said. "You do good, I kill Domingo, do the business only with you."

A shocked silence gripped Jack and Marco. Only the sound of Rocky's Spanish dub artist filled the silence in the room.

"What if we don't do good?" Jack asked. "That's a lot of coke. We sell little bits at a time to guys in our neighborhood. This is . . . that's a lot of coke."

"That is a problem for Domingo," she said.

Marco finally spoke up. His throat is constricted so he could barely be heard.

"We can't get back over the border with this," he mumbled. "They won't let us walk back with this much coke."

Karlotta didn't understand what Marco said. She turned to Jack.

"He says we won't be able to walk back over the bridge with these on our backs," Jack said. "They'll search us for sure."

Karlotta laughed. Then she started coughing, so her laughter stopped.

"Domingo didn't tell you how you get back? You didn't ask? Americans are so stupid," she sneered. "You don't go with the bridge. Chingado, puta madre. You swim! Like Mexicans!"

As if on cue, Karlotta nodded to the man with the Kalashnikov, and he stood. He went to the door and yelled something down to the men below.

"Go to the window and look," she said to Jack and Marco. "I have a message for that motherfucker."

The window was behind Marco, so he turned and looked out. Jack crossed the room, and the girls on the couches stood as well to get a look.

Below, they saw men directing a girl to the area beside the truck. The girl was blindfolded, and her hands were tied in front of her. She was sickly thin, and she wore nice jeans and high-heeled shoes Blood had dripped from her swollen nose to her white T-shirt. Her body showed no emotion. Her blonde hair was clamped down by the blindfold.

One of the men pulled a revolver from his waistband and before Jack or Marco could blink or look away, he shot the girl in the side of the head. The bullet blew the blindfold off. Blood sprayed all over the bed of the truck. The sound of the shot echoed off the compound walls.

She dropped to the ground and blood pooled quickly on her face and head.

In an instant, everything returned to normal. One of the men grabbed her by the arm and dragged her back towards the house. Her T-shirt soak up blood, and after a moment, a man grabbed her other arm. Her head flopped back and forth. Her lifeless eyes stared up at the sky.

"Her name was Lissie," Karlotta said. Her 's' sounds hissed like a snake. "Tell Domingo, that piece of shit."

Jack sat back down in front of his backpack. A hollow spot had opened inside him, but he showed no emotion. It was too late to panic, and it had happened so quickly that he hadn't had time to build a well of fear. He felt cold, and that was all. He didn't dare look at Marco.

"They will take you to the river soon," Karlotta said as she stood. "You can have one of these girls, if you can get your dicks hard."

She dragged the chair back to the kitchen and left.

Only the sound of '*Rocky 2*' remained. Jack could hear a clock ticking in his mind. He thought about Domingo and his cancer, which was probably a bullshit story. Jack concluded that Domingo was not welcome here and so he sent Jack and Marco. Domingo had lied.

"Me quieres?" Jack heard. It was one of the girls. She was skinny and standing in front of Marco. Her bony frame gave off an adolescent unfinished look and her face was childlike. Marco looked up at the sound of her high girlish voice. Jack saw hope for the first time in Marco. Marco gazed at the girl for a long moment, as if she had appeared in a vision.

"Me quieres?" she said again, to Marco, gesturing at her tiny body.

"Okay," Marco said, swallowing hard. She stuck out her hand and he took it. She led him out of the room like he was blind.

Marco returned to the room a half hour later with the girl. None of the others had offered themselves to Jack. The girl held Marco's frozen hand. After another half hour, the man with the Kalashnikov stood and yelled out of the door, then he said something in Spanish to Jack. It was time to go.

"Marco," he said. Marco looked up and then stood.

"Get the backpack," Jack said calmly, and Marco picked it up. Marco was drained of emotion now, with no look of dread or anything else present.

They were led downstairs where they could hear the rattle of the old truck starting. The same men were waiting, and they directed Jack and Marco to get in the back.

The side of the truck and a part of the truck bed were sprayed with a mist of blood. Jack dropped his backpack in the truck bed and climbed in. Marco looked at the blood.

"Oh, my fucking God," he mumbled, and Jack could see his bottom lip quivering.

"Don't you do it. Shut up and get in," he said.

"We're both so stupid," he said. "Bro, this is your fault."

"Maybe so, but it will be your blood if you don't get in," Jack said.

Marco handed Jack his backpack and climbed in. He slowly lowered himself down into the blood.

* * *

The ride out seemed even longer. The dirt road gave way to other dirt roads that were less dusty. They passed brick and abode buildings, and each had dogs and kids running back and forth in the dusty yards. It was so normal and innocent, and he thought back to less than an hour earlier, when he had witnessed an execution. And now, normal life.

They were near trees again, and so he figured they were near water. Jack watched the villages pass by and sniffed the air, hoping to smell something other than dirt and dust. The little villages and stores and tiny gas stations they passed looked exactly alike.

Marco stared ahead vacantly. He wasn't hiding his face anymore, but there was little to read. Anxiety had given way to fear which had given way to numbness.

"You fucked that girl?" Jack asked.

"Yes," Marco said robotically. "She wanted to come with us."

"What did you say?" Jack asked.

"I said we'd come back for her," Marco said.

Jack looked away. Marco was more than scared; he was a coward. He couldn't control his bowels or his mouth. Everything that had mildly irritated Jack about Marco since they were in kindergarten was now in stark relief. It was all real, everything he had partly suspected. Marco was an empty vessel.

The truck stopped, and they turned around to see why. In the distance was the Rio Grande, with a tall bank of river cane visible on the other side. That was home.

"I guess you know I can't swim," Marco said as he glanced up at the river. Then he looked away.

"The fuck you can't swim," Jack replied as he loosened the straps on his bag. "I've seen you swim."

"I can push myself from one part of the pool to another, but I can't fucking swim across a river," Marco said flatly.

"You're about to learn," Jack said. "But it doesn't look deep enough to even swim in; you can probably just wade across.

"I'm going to drown in that river with a pack of coke on my back," Marco said. His voice was dead of affect and emotion. He had resigned himself to his fate.

"I hope not. They'll make me sell two backpacks of coke," Jack said and stood. He was ready to go home. "You can swim or dog paddle or something for thirty yards to get home."

At the riverbank, several people, mostly young men, walked back and forth to a food truck parked nearby, and then back to the river, and then under some low trees. It was cold, but the sun was high, and the few women gathered near each other. They had their hair covered with bandanas, and they spoke quietly. The men didn't speak at all.

Jack noted the tension as soon as they got out of the truck. There was something pensive about the body language of all those people milling about. They were standing differently in some undetectable way. The men in the truck said nothing; they stopped, waited for Jack and Marco to get out. and left without a word. One of the men looked briefly at them, then down at their blood-stained pants, but then the truck drove away. Jack and Marco were back on their own, but now in quite different circumstances.

The riverbank was sandy and brown, and the river was slow and muddy. It was not far across, and a middle school little leaguer with a good arm might toss a baseball all the way across and hit the stalks of river cane on the other side. There was no fence, no signs, and no obstacles.

Jack walked halfway down the riverbank and sat. He pulled the backpack off his back and set it in front of him. Marco did the same.

As Jack looked around, he started to notice more. They were not dressed like the others, which was obvious enough. The other men who were waiting were much darker than the men who worked for Karlotta. They had more severe faces. They had smaller backpacks, and they had caps. They were dirty already, like they had crossed from the other side recently. The few women waiting were much older, or they looked it. There were no girls and no kids.

Jack hoped to pick up a clue about how the whole operation worked, but there was nothing to guide him. No sign from anyone about the process, or the timing. They seemed to somehow be waiting for the same unnamed moment.

"What's everyone waiting for?" Jack wondered aloud. Marco was staring at the water.

After watching the crowd for a few more minutes, Jack stood. lifted the backpack onto his back, and walked to a young Mexican man who was sitting closer to the bank, and was alone.

"Buenos Dias," he began. He had taken three years of Spanish at Deer Park High but forgotten most of it. "Que es la hora por… la hora por cruzar?

"We wait until dark. If you cross during the day, the Border Patrol can see you," the man said in perfect unaccented English.

"Oh, yeah, that makes sense," Jack said. He started to turn away, but the man seemed friendly enough.

"After we cross, how far from Brownsville are we?" Jack asked.

"Eleven miles north," the man said. "There's a lot of trails, but it's easy to get lost. At night, you can see the city lights against the clouds."

Jack nodded and turned to walk back to Marco.

"That's a lot of coke, cabron," the young man said.

Jack stopped in his tracks.

"You don't know what's in these packs," Jack said. "We buy leather goods, sell them in Houston."

"Yeah, okay," he chuckled. "Leather goods. Whatever you say, cabron."

"And we have guns," Jack said. "Make sure your friends know."

"I hope so, because there's coyotes in this crowd, they have guns, cabron," he said. "And the eggs to use them."

Jack looked at men along the riverbank. They were all looking at him.

"Every swinging Mexican dick here knows what's in those packs. They take it off you on the other side, sell it themselves," he said calmly.

"Where are you from?" Jack asked.

"I grew up in Houston," he said. "Went to Alief, went to TCC, drove a truck. But my parents took me there when I was a baby and so I ain't legal. When I want to go back and forth, I got to cross this river."

"That sucks," Jack said. He knew several guys at Deer Park who were illegal, but they were minors, so they didn't get deported when their parents did.

"What would you do, if you were in my shoes?" Jack asked.

"I wouldn't be in your shoes," the man said. "You got fucking blood on your shoes, bro, and your pants. It ain't yours or his. But you ain't killers, that's for sure. You two idiots are in deep, that's what I think. I wouldn't be in your shoes."

Jack paused. It was true, but his instinct told him not to reveal it.

"We've done this before. We'll be okay," he said without conviction.

"They drown babies, cabron. You think they won't stick a knife in you for those packs?" he said as he turned to look at Jack. "If I was you, I'd get my happy ass across that river right the fuck now. At least on the other side, in the daylight, the Border Patrol is your biggest problem."

"Thanks," Jack said. The message was clear enough and probably right.

He walked back over to Marco.

"Get up. We're going," he said.

"What . . . now?" Marco said in alarm.

"Keep your voice down, and yes, now," Jack said.

"We should wait, go over as a group," Marco said, still not moving. "Then we're less likely to get caught."

Jack picked up Marco's backpack and held it up for him.

"We go over with the group, one of them is going to stick us in the liver when we get on the other side. We've got thousands of dollars' worth of coke on us. They know, every one of them. Now let's go!" Jack hissed.

Marco looked around; suddenly he saw the same thing Jack saw; lots of young men, doleful and unreadable, watching them. Dead eyes looked back at him.

"When we get to the other side, we need to find a place to hide until dark. Can't let any of these wetbacks find us, can't let the Border Patrol find us. And we have to be quiet," Jack said.

"Jesus, look . . . I wasn't kidding. I'm a terrible swimmer. I really, really can't do this," Marco said.

"When we get in the water, just roll over on your back, I'll pull you," Jack said as he pushed Marco's backpack on. "We won't be in the water long. If anyone follows us in, they're going to try to kill us on the other side. When we get there, we're going to haul ass and get as far away as we can as fast as we can."

The boys walked towards the water. Jack looked back; no one was moving to follow.

But then, at the edge of the water, Jack turned around and yelled, so all the men could hear.

"Karlotta, putas!" he called out. "Esta es her drugs! Tu take them from us, esta comprede, and she'll kill every last one of you fucks! Muerte, motherfuckers! Mucho Muerte!"

He made a slash sign across his throat. No one responded in the least.

Chapter 12

Jack and Marco waded into the chilly slow-moving water. When it came to Jack's waist, he lifted his pack into the air.

"Hand me the backpack," Jack said. Marco passed his pack to Jack and Jack held both packs over his head.

"Now lower down. Roll on to your back and push yourself over here," Jack said.

Marco rolled onto his back and Jack grabbed him by the back of his collar. Jack walked until his feet stopped touching the river and then he started kicking. The backpacks were in his right hand and Marco in his left.

Marco watched the guys on the shore. A few had moved and were talking to each other. There was laughter. "Puto," someone yelled out, and there was more laughter, but none followed them into the water.

"Stand up," he heard. Marco reached for the bottom of the river and found it. It was just that easy. He couldn't believe it, but he was across, and it took less than a minute. It was the easiest part of the whole trip.

Jack stood and quickly waded to the shore with the backpacks. He handed Marco his pack and slipped his on. Both looked back to the other side again and saw no one following. One problem solved, at least for a moment.

Passed the thick river cane was more heavy brush with a trail worn through. Jack and Marco walked quickly down the trail and away from the shore. If anyone was going to follow, Jack was determined to be far ahead and have the brush and the noise of heavy feet to help them survive. He picked up a heavy stick with a point and handed it to Marco. When he came across another, he kept it for himself. At least they had something other than their hands to defend themselves.

The narrow trail was worn well enough to follow. Sharp mesquite branches grabbed at their clothes. The path was cluttered with trash left by generations of earlier crossings. They stepped over bottles, cans, clothes, diapers, shoes, underwear, broken glass, fishing rods, coolers, and sometimes, sterno cans, and dead cookfires. Trash was everywhere. The trail crossed what would otherwise have been a landfill.

After a half hour of fast walking away from the water, Jack slowed a bit. He heard Marco panting heavily. He glanced back and saw Marco breathing through a wide-open mouth.

"Ugh, sweet Jesus, it smells like shit everywhere," Marco said between breaths. He was right, it smelled like sewage, and the mud they walked through was likely a mix of mud and human waste.

Jack stopped when he saw a road up ahead. He reached back and touched Marco's arm, and they knelt.

"This has to be the Border Patrol Road," he said. "We need to go back, cover up, and when it gets dark, go north and east."

"Dude," Marco said, and then he stopped. "They shot that girl. Who was she?"

"I don't know or care," Jack said. If it was eleven miles back to Brownsville, he thought, it would take about four hours of walking. Plenty of time if they started at dark, but plenty of time to get killed as others crossed over.

"Please, man. Let's ditch these backpacks and start walking back now," Marco said. "Fuck this."

Jack stood.

"We can't do that, and you know it," he said. "Those people can get to us. We sell what she gave us, never go back. It's the only way. They'll kill Domingo and then come for our families."

"Fuck Domingo." Marco fumed. "He knew what he was getting us in to. And I'm adopted, man. Like I care about my family."

"I'm not adopted, Marco!" he said, his voice tense with anger. "You fucking do what I tell you!"

Jack led and they retreated into the brush. For the next three hours, they walked a zig zag of trails that headed in several directions, but Jack kept the sun to his back and left, so he was sure they were headed north and mostly in the right direction. Finally, Marco was quiet. Jack glanced back at him every few minutes and saw Marco no longer had his mouth hanging open and was calm.

Just as Jack came to believe Marco was doing better, the brush grew thicker, but the smell grew thicker as well. Jack stopped and set his pack down.

"Wait a minute," he said. He looked around. Both saw it at the same time; a corpse moldering in the leaves. It was a man, and he was face down, but his black hair stood out from the fall leaves.

After a horrid moment, Marco broke.

"Fuck this, man! Fuck this!" he said as he dropped his backpack and ran.

Jack knew better than to try to catch him. This was the second dead body they had seen, and this one was close up and a man. Jack wanted to run, but he didn't. He just sat down and pulled his shirt over his mouth. He looked at the man one more time and then turned away. The smell, he thought, would keep others away.

* * *

After a few minutes, Jack heard a truck engine. There was a vehicle coming down the Border Patrol Road. Even this far back into the brush, sound traveled, and things could be heard clearly in the humidity free crisp air. What he heard he could visualize.

The truck noise grew closer and then there was a short 'beep' of the siren. Clearly, they had caught Marco. For a moment, Jack considered if Marco would rat him out and lead the Border Patrol to him. If he heard footsteps, he would just start moving and leave the backpacks and come back for them. The corpse might keep others away long enough for him to return. But he didn't think that would happen. In a way, it was perfect. Marco would lead them away with some lie. This was finally something he knew Marco would inherently get and be good at.

Jack could barely hear voices. It might have been Marco talking, or it might not, but after a few minutes, there were other male voices, and then another vehicle. The voices rose and fell, and then the sound of the engines started back up, and he heard tires on gravel. And then the sounds faded back to the dead quiet around him. Jack sat motionless in the deep brush. He was on his own, but it was probably better that way.

Marco sat shivering in the dark. He was watching the parking lot they had left the previous morning. Jack's truck was at the far end.

People and cars came in and out of the parking lot throughout the afternoon, and he had thought about bumming some money from them so he could get something to eat, but then he decided not to. One of the Border Patrol guys had given him a Three Musketeers bar, and that had gone down well, but what Marco really wanted was a drink, and something stiff. He wasn't going to get it.

After night came, the temperature dropped quickly and he was cold, but again, he didn't want to speak to anyone or attract any attention to himself. He had decided that he'd watch Jack's truck and if nothing moved by morning, he'd call Shannon somehow and get home. He'd say nothing about Jack, possibly not ever, but certainly not to Shannon or anyone in the neighborhood. He knew if Jack didn't come back, Domingo would come to him, and he'd have some harsh things to say, but even with Domingo, who had set the whole shitshow in motion, he intended to stay away and stay quiet. As far as he was concerned, he had cheated death and wasn't going to push his luck again. His drug dealing days were over.

Also, after dark, he started to see men like the ones at the riverbank drift by on the highway. They were all dressed the same and surely, the Border Patrol and everyone else knew who they were. That was the unspoken deal between the Border Patrol and the illegals; if you get to a town or out of our immediate reach, we won't chase you. Everyone knew it.

But Marco stayed at the edge of the parking lot and at the base of a large crepe myrtle. He was out of sight and couldn't be seen by any of the migrants who he saw back in Mexico. He could see them, and he could see the truck, but he was safe for now. His concern was Jack and the cold. These concerns were nothing compared to what he had just been through, and so Marco was happy. He was happy to feel the cold because that was a pain that meant he was alive.

He saw a single migrant man walking across the parking lot which was a bit unusual. They were normally in twos or threes. The man had a hat pulled low and he had a big pack on his back. Marco blew warm air on his freezing hands as he watched the man, but he stopped midbreath as the realized the man had reached Jack's truck. In an instant, he knew it was Jack.

109

Jack arrived at his truck and set the big backpack on the ground. He began to fish for his keys in his dark pants. His shirt, his hat and gloves, everything but his pants and shoes he had picked up on the trails. As he opened the door to the truck, he saw Marco running towards him from a dark corner of the parking lot.

"I threw the Border Patrol off you," Marco said with a broad grim. He was ecstatic to see Jack. "They thought I was alone. I told them I was robbed in Mexico, and they bought it. They gave me a ride here."

Jack threw the pack onto the passenger seat of the truck without a word.

"You switched out the backpacks?" Marco asked.

Still nothing from Jack. He slid into the driver's seat and shut the door. Marco knocked on the passenger side window.

"Come on, man, don't leave me here," Marco pleaded.

Jack hesitated for a moment and then reached over and rolled down the passenger side window.

"You ditched me in the brush," he said. "You can ride back with me, but not in here."

Marco looked at the bed of the truck.

"Come on, I'll freeze to death back there," Marco pleaded.

Jack took off his hat and threw it at Marco. Then he took off his dirty jacket and did the same. Marco looked at them.

"Did these come off that dead guy?" he asked.

"Yes," Jack said as he rolled the window up and started the truck. Marco pulled the extra layers on and climbed into the bed of the truck. A frigid ride back was better than being dead or calling Shannon.

PART 2

"Some folks look at me and see a certain swagger, which in Texas is called 'walking'." – George Bush

Chapter 13

In April of 1836, Sam Houston secured his legend by launching one of the greatest surprise attacks in military history. At the swamps of San Jacinto, while the forces under the command of the Mexican leader and generalissimo, Antonio Lopez De Santa Anna, were settled in for a nap, Houston sent his Anglo-Texans at them and routed the entire Mexican force in less than twenty minutes. Santa Anna ditched his preposterous generalissimo uniform and put on the uniform of a private, but the Texans noticed how their other captives reacted to the sight of the great man. The general was paraded before the triumphant Houston, made to sign a treaty with the Texans that secured Texas independence, and then sent to meet with the American president, Andrew Jackson.

This was the history taught to Bob Buckhorn. The San Jacinto monolith memorialized the place where it all went down. The victory there defined the state that followed. Historical glory, and not misery, was built into the Texan character. It was no accident that Bob and his friends got drunk and entered fights at the foot of the monolith. The victory was very New World, and it occurred while the Old World rotated through its various miseries.

By the time Houston gave the order to attack the dozing Mexicans, Chernobyl had been a hunting village and town on the Eastern European plains for at least five hundred years. It had been a part of the Russian Empire, fought over by the Poles, the Russians, and the Lithuanians, and then it became a part of the Soviet Union. The ground had been trod over by hundreds of warriors, brigands, and thieves. It had always been a hard, unforgiving place to live. The land had seen more war than Texas or Mexico ever would know.

The town was on a long flat plain on the Pripyat River that changed hands multiple times over the centuries, never peacefully. The blood of generations soaked its fertile earth, even before the Jews came. The Jews, of all people, should have known to stay away, but they had limited options, and so Chernobyl became a town with a large Hasidic Jewish population in the 19th century. The rebbe and the synagogue was a common feature of village life until the Nazis arrived in 1941. Their tanks and boots rang the death-knell for the Jews of Chernobyl.

112

Behind the Wehrmacht was the Einsatzgruppen forces that tracked down and murdered Jews. They set upon the Jews of Ukraine with ferocity, and they came to nearby Kyiv and then Chernobyl determined to leave those territories entirely Jew free. They succeeded. The Nazis left millions of their young men, the flower of youthful German manhood, in the fertile soil of Ukraine to rot, but they left the area Judenfrei.

In August of 1972, construction began on a nuclear power station at Chernobyl and in the subsequent years, four nuclear reactors were built there. The Soviets willed them into being and named the new power station after the Soviet founder, Vladimir Lenin.

When Reactor 4 exploded in April of 1986, 150 years after Sam Houston was crowned in glory, and four months after *Challenger* destroyed NASA's reputation for making miracles, the Soviets quickly retreated behind a wall of denials.

The operators in the Chernobyl power station were Soviet to the core. They were men of science, and they were performing a safety test when they initiated the contamination of a huge mass of their homeland. The final desperate step in the poorly designed test was to reassert control over the reactor by inserting massive control rods into the reactor which was supposed to freeze the action in place. If the reaction of atomic forces began to gallop out of control, and the reactions ceased to be under the purview of humans, the SCRAM feature would be triggered by emergency action.

The idea of a SCRAM feature, however, was a human fiction steeped in humanity's overestimation of itself. The word was said to have stood for 'Safety Control Rod Axe Man' and it described the safety system at the first reactor built in Chicago by Leo Szilard, the Eastern European scientist liberated by the Americans and assigned to make the world's most destructive devices. The safety control rod at that reactor hung by a rope, and a man was assigned to stand by it and whack the rope with an axe and cause the rod to fall on the reactor if there was trouble.

The technicians at the Vladimir Lenin Power Plant in Chernobyl believed they had a SCRAM device, known in the Russian system as AZ-5. If translated to English, this title stood for 'emergency protection of the 5th category' but the Russians managed to create an emergency override that did the exact opposite of what it was supposed to do. When the Soviet control room operators punched the safety override, an explosion blew the reactor apart and exposed the reactor core.

Bob saw the first reports about Chernobyl in the newspaper, and he didn't believe the Soviet denials. He read about the investigations into the *Challenger* disaster in the Houston Chronicle daily. He knew already that the cold was the primary driver, from a strictly physics point of view, but behind every human disaster are humans. Human fallibility and delusion were always the primary driver of catastrophe, and he reasoned that human failure was probably at the core of the Chernobyl disaster as well.

At his time at NASA, the engineers all liked each other and worked closely together, so they had as much safety as the missions could allow by sheer cultural force of will. Bob spoke and listened to hours of predictions about 'what happens if' and the men chimed in together. They poured over every step of the *Apollo* missions at length, and there was not a lot of finger-pointing or ass-covering because they were insulated by the Kennedy speech. They had a popular cultural mandate.

The Soviets were driving towards a historical end point and Chernobyl was the greatest evidence of their pending failure to date. In the same period, a series of *Challenger* hearings were carried live on American TV. Bob observed both events unfold, and by late April, on most mornings, he was watching or reading the news with only a cup of coffee in his hand. Events were sobering, literally. He wanted to be awake and clear-thinking when his former friends and distant acquaintances took to the stand and told their part of the *Challenger* story. He knew there would never be public testimony about what happened at Chernobyl.

Bob had sobered up to his family, his marriage, and the world. None of them looked good sober. The reactor core of his household was exposing the fissile material inside. In the weeks before Chernobyl, before Bob had completely sobered up, the lives of his wife and children were driving forward fast, and he was vaguely aware of the impending disaster. He watched with as much detachment as he could manage and waited for the big moment to arrive.

* * *

Spring in Houston is muggy and prone to afternoon rain. The dank air that fled in the winter returned with a vengeance. The heat was coming, and everyone knew it, but the steady rains offered a bit of comfort. The cool weather made its final stand before the heavy-handed heat pushed the mercury up and the Gulf of Mexico, rather than barren West Texas, took over for the following third of a year. Summer was something Texans survived, and spring was just a jumping off point for the ordeal.

At Deer Park High School, spring meant another school year coming to an end and for the seniors, twelve long years of primary education was reaching its wasteful conclusion. Most seniors were determined to take their foot off the accelerator, if they ever had it there, and carry out as much partying as possible. Many were going to work after school, often at the refinery where their dad worked. Some of the students didn't change their behavior as the end drew near, but they were dorks and geeks and other outcasts. Spring Fever was part of the senior rite of passage. You had to get it. Not complaining about the school year and brag about the summer was shameful and so everyone had a big plan to talk about.

Jennifer was not a geek or dork, but she cultivated herself as an outsider. Sometimes when she walked the halls, she saw how many friends the other girls had. She had few, and she had let go of all of them when she made the transition to high school. Shannon had been her best friend for years, but that had ended poorly. And now, it was, of all people, Lisa. Jennifer had watched as so many girlfriends transferred their identity onto a series of boyfriends, and Jennifer still had no interest in doing that. It was on this fact that Lisa pinned her hopes.

Throughout the spring, Lisa had tried to push the envelope of the relationship as far as she could. Jennifer rode the relationship brakes the whole time. When they were alone, Lisa tried to kiss her, but Jennifer kept it light. She resisted Lisa's tongue which Lisa continuously tried to insert into Jennifer's mouth. She flicked Lisa tongue with her own, and it was nice, but it wasn't something she really wanted to experience further. She sometimes felt like she was practicing on Lisa, and she knew Lisa was not practicing on her. Lisa told her things she had done with other lesbians, and Jennifer knew some, perhaps all, of it was an exaggeration. Maybe Lisa read about those things in a magazine. Lisa watched Jennifer's face when she told her about 'fingering,' and 'eating out,' and one time, 'rimming,' but it was only rimming that got a reaction from Jennifer.

"That's gross," Jennifer said, and changed the subject. Lisa, of course, took that to mean that Jennifer didn't find the other stuff to be gross, so she stayed with those stories. She doubled down on how she wanted to 'eat out' Jennifer but Jennifer offered no hope that such an event was forthcoming. There had been no fingering and no eating out. Lisa had kissed Jennifer a lot and touched her breasts, and on a couple of occasions, lightly rubbed Jennifer's crotch when Jennifer was dropping her off.

"Does that make you wet?" Lisa asked. "Please say yes."

"None of your business," was all she got from Jennifer.

What Jennifer liked, more than anything, was how her body was responding to the greater effort she put into track. Lisa was enormously useful in this endeavor, and Lisa physically drove Jennifer to places she had never gone. Her coaches, who were supposed to be driving her, had never given her so much attention or expressed such joy in her performance. Lisa was ecstatic when Jennifer excelled. Lisa was emotional about track, the uniforms, the timers, the times, the lengths, and mostly, she was emotional about winning. Lisa was driven to see Jennifer succeed more than anyone had ever cared about her success. Jennifer responded, and now she could see the extra effort in her body. Her leg muscles stood out. She looked at them while she lay in bed. She stood sideways in front of her mirror and looked at how her stomach was flattening out. She looked at photos of Madonna's body and saw how her own was taking on the same muscular shape. For this reason alone, she thought it was worth allowing Lisa to do what she wanted, up to a point.

Based on her success with the hurdles and long jump, Lisa convinced Coach Wilson to put Jennifer in the 200-meter race. The team had several girls who were excellent in the 200-meter, but Lisa thought Jennifer could be better. Jennifer had less endurance, but she had leg strength. In the short bursts, Jennifer was top notch. And the 200-meter wasn't an endurance race; it was more like a prolonged sprint.

Even in the rain, Jennifer liked doing the 200-meter, and it was a warm drizzle that came down on the team late in the warm and lengthening day. Practices were running long now that the team was going to state.

Jennifer stepped into the blocks and focused. Lisa and Marie were both in the lineup with her. The coaches stacked the 200-meter and used the fastest in the meets. It was important now, late in the season and with a state championship realistically in sight, that they get the best, and so they had a sizable portion of the team in the blocks, ready to see who had the burst of state championship speed.

The boys track team was on the other side of the field, and David glanced up from his warmup to watch the girls. In the past, Jennifer would have noticed if she was being watched, but now, she was too focused, too in the moment, to know who was watching what. That was another precious gift from Lisa.

Coach Wilson blew the whistle, and the 200-meter sprint began. Jennifer made a perfect leap from the blocks. She felt her legs pumping without any input from her mind. She saw Lisa to her left and Lisa was already half a step ahead.

David watched as the girls rounded the top of the track and came to his side of the field. The other boys stopped what they were doing as well to watch the girls pump their legs and arms furiously.

At the front was Lisa, who always ran like a man. Her legs were larger and shorter, but they pumped at the ground and pushed forward with power. A single length behind Lisa was Jennifer. Her legs were longer, and they were starting to lengthen out as they passed the halfway mark. Marie came along behind Jennifer, but she was starting to drift behind. She had neither the strength of Lisa nor the length of Jennifer.

In the final thirty meters, the winner would be decided. Jennifer brought the speed as the finish line grew closer. Her arms pumped and her mouth opened. Lisa was one step ahead, and Marie was two steps behind her. In the final second, Jennifer leapt and leaned in, pushing past Lisa by a fraction.

Lisa was surprised at how closely she lost to Jennifer. Marie was pissed and she turned away and headed back across the field without saying a word. Lisa slowed and crossed to Coach Wilson.

Jennifer stopped suddenly when David stepped in front of her. His hair was wet, as was hers. He held out a towel for her. She took it and wiped her arms and face.

"Nice 200-meter," he said.

"Thanks," Jennifer said as she tried to recover her normal breath.

As Jennifer wiped her arms, she noticed her shirt was wet and nearly see-through.

"It's like a wet t-shirt contest out here," she said.

"Yeah, we kind of noticed," David said. He glanced over at the boys, and they were watching.

She smiled. She didn't want to, but she did. When she was thirteen and started her period, she didn't think she would ever want male attention like that, in an obviously sexual way, but now she wanted it. This was, in an odd way, yet another gift from Lisa. Jennifer had learned to like being desired.

"Pigs," she said. "Filthy pigs, all of you."

She snapped the towel at him and caught him on the neck. The wet towel made a cracking sound.

"Sorry!" Jennifer said.

"Buckhorn! Get over here!" Coach Wilson barked out.

Jennifer threw the towel back at David.

She ran over to Coach Wilson and Lisa. Lisa held an umbrella over Coach Wilson to keep her clipboard dry.

"You're in the 200-meter now, champ," she said. "That puts you as our lead in four events. Winning state can't happen without you. That's the bottom line."

"I know," Jennifer said, unsure where the coach was going.

"If we're counting on you, which we are, you have to get with a few things," Coach Wilson said. "I don't trust you so I'm going to make this clear. You've never been a team player, and you still aren't. What I expect from you is this: don't get injured. Stretch, eat well, get some sleep, don't play around. Injuries are stupidity in practice. Also, don't do drugs. I've lost more championships to potheads than to faster runners. Don't do that to me or yourself. And more than anything, don't get knocked up. I think you know how to prevent that, though I doubt that's going to be a problem."

Jennifer glanced over at Lisa.

"Got it?" Coach Wilson summarized.

The coach looked at Lisa.

"Keep her ready to run, got it? At the least, you can keep her from getting knocked up," the coach said.

"I'll take care of her," Lisa promised.

* * *

Jennifer was combing out her wet hair when Lisa sat beside her and started putting on her shoes. The period after practice always made Lisa chatty and euphoric. She talked aimlessly and chose subjects randomly. Lisa talked endlessly about her family, mostly about how much she hated them. She would lean in and talk about things she wanted to do sexually with Jennifer, but Jennifer would roll her eyes, and that kind of talk would stop.

"Okay, okay, you smoked Marie, and she is pissed," Lisa said. The outcome clearly delighted her.

"I beat her by a cunt hair is all," Jennifer said. She didn't look at Lisa. The comments from the coach were still in her ears.

"Wow. By a cunt hair, huh? Where did you learn that expression?" Lisa asked.

"My brothers," Jennifer said as she switched from brush to mascara wand.

"Yeah, I like it when you're all potty mouth. Anyway, you beat her, and she's pissed," Lisa continued. "She was throwing stuff around in the equipment room. It was hilarious."

"Too bad, so sad," Jennifer said as she layered the mascara back on.

"What did that Jew homo Wingate want? I saw him flirting with you," Lisa asked. She tried to make it sound like a spontaneous question, but Jennifer knew it was not. Lisa had seen it and been thinking about it.

"If he's a homo, why would he flirt with me?" Jennifer asked. She didn't really want to provide any information because she knew Lisa would mentally run with whatever she was given, and it was best not to give her any fuel for speculation.

"He's sexually confused, okay," Lisa declared. "He always has been. His dad is a huge asshole, and he has massive mommy issues."

"So, you're not worried about him knocking me up?" Jennifer asked, glancing sideways over to Lisa.

Lisa smiled. Knocking up was more sex talk, and she was glad she didn't have to initiate it for a change.

"I knew you'd bring that up," she said. "Look, Coach Wilson is just like that. I didn't tell her anything about us. Really, okay, I didn't."

"It doesn't matter," Jennifer said. "I don't care what she says, or anyone else. That bridge is burned."

She striped off her wet shirt and pulled on a dry one. This action made Lisa swallow hard. She looked around to be sure no one was watching, then she leaned over and kissed Jennifer, who lightly kissed her back.

"Hey, can you give me a ride?" Lisa asked. "You know, you can't get pregnant from having a lesbian in your car. It's a known fact."

Jennifer stood and started packing her gym bag.

"Sure," Jennifer said. She had a warm feeling that being lusted after gave her.

The ride to Lisa's house was short and Lisa talked or adjusted the radio the entire way. Lisa could not listen to a full song on any station, even songs she liked. She was continuously turning the radio up or down, adjusting it in the middle of a song, or mimicking the station DJs. She passionately hated the commercials and mocked them all in the most profane way. Any product her parents used or was advertised on the radio, she refused to touch.

"If they run their stupid ads on the radio, I won't buy the product, no matter what it is," she announced.

"Even if it's a concert?" Jennifer inquired.

"There's no one I want to see that badly," Lisa said. "I might go see The Smiths, but they'd never be on the radio."

"Who?" Jennifer asked absently. She had learned to turn Lisa down in her mind when they were in the car.

"Jesus Christ. The Smiths!" Lisa said. "You don't know about The Smiths?"

120

"No," Jennifer said. "What songs do they do?"

"They do…let's see…they do 'What Difference Does It Make' and they do 'How Soon Is Now' and they do 'Heaven Knows I'm Miserable Now' and a bunch of other great ones," Lisa said as she changed the dial again.

"They sound like a ton of fun," Jennifer responded. "Do they do songs about cutting themselves?"

"Yes, they do, and they're great," Lisa said, missing the joke.

Just then, Lisa passed 'Dress You Up' and Jennifer responded with only a second of the sound to tip her.

"Stop! Go back!" she said.

Lisa sneered.

"God, not this song again!" she said. "It's been on forever! I can't believe they're still playing this stupid pop trash. It's pushing out all the good music."

"It's pop and it's fun," Jennifer said defensively. "And I like it."

"Ugh," was all Lisa could manage. "I know I can't talk shit about Madonna around you, okay but Lord help us all, that miserable slut is everywhere, OK, everywhere."

After 'Dress you Up,' Jennifer pulled up in front of Lisa's house. It was larger than Jennifer's house, and the lawn and flower beds were immaculately manicured. A gardener was working on the roses.

After Jennifer stopped, there was an awkward moment and Lisa just stared at her.

"Thanks," she finally said.

"You're welcome," Jennifer said. She had not taken the car out of gear.

She leaned over and kissed Jennifer again with barely a response.

"Listen," Lisa began. "I want to tell you something."

But Jennifer knew where this was going and didn't want to get into a long conversation while her foot held down the clutch.

"No, you don't," she said. "We're friends, maybe a tiny bit more, and that's it. You don't need to tell me anything."

Lisa looked down. Then she leaned over and ran her hand back and forth, very lightly, on Jennifer's crotch.

"I just want you so bad," she breathed. Her words came from deep in her limbic system.

Again, Jennifer didn't stop her, and she didn't respond. She felt it, and she acknowledged to herself that it felt good, but she knew better than to let Lisa see that, even a little bit.

After a moment, Lisa pulled her hand back.

"Okay. Okay, I understand. See you tomorrow," she said. She jumped out of the car, reached into the back seat, grabbed her big gym bag, and shut the door.

Jennifer let off the clutch and pulled away. Lisa turned to look one last time, but Jennifer did not.

Chapter 14

Jennifer drove to her home in peace. After she pulled away from Lisa's house, she turned the radio off and let the wind blow through the car. It was cool, but still dry enough to enjoy the air. That feeling wouldn't last in Houston.

She thought about Lisa, but she also thought about David. Mostly, she thought about what she was going to do next. She knew her body was opening and growing. Everything was working together now. Everything was moving her forward. The track, her legs, her hair, shunning Shannon, liking Madonna, doing her own make-up, but also, it was Lisa, and it was David.

Sometimes, thoughts of the future would creep in, and she would think about how she needed to prepare for college, but she had done the minimum she needed to and that was all she was going to do. Her mind was 100 percent engaged with her body, for the first time, and she wasn't going to let anything else in.

For a moment, she thought of a boy who had called her a werewolf when she was in fifth grade. Her arm hair had grown thicker and darker, but it had happened so slowly that she hadn't really noticed. She had also not noticed that the tiny hairs on her legs were getting a little darker and could been seen. She wore pants most of the time, and by this time, her mother had stopped buying her dresses. Since they'd stopped going to church regularly, she didn't get a new dress, not even on Easter.

But Jennifer had many pairs of shorts, including a couple that were hand-me-downs from Jack. They were just cut offs, but she liked them, and she wore them one day and at first no one noticed that her leg hairs, down around her ankles, were dark and stiff.

But on the bus home, Bobby Thompson noticed, and he told a couple of friends. While Jennifer was reading a book, the word spread. It spread from the boy's side of the bus to the girls, and then Shannon was told to look at Jennifer's ankles. She noticed what everyone else was talking about, and at the next stop, she walked up to Jennifer's seat and pushed her way in. Jennifer looked at her, confused at Shannon's decision to push four girls into a seat, until Shannon leaned in and said, "Everyone's talking about your hairy ankles."

Jennifer did not need to look down towards her feet. The comment clarified for her the picture in her mind of her arms and legs as hairy. She tucked her feet under the seat and hugged the book to her chest. When the bus reached the school, she waited to get up, hoping everyone would pass without looking at her or commenting.

But that mercy was not to be. Bobby Thompson had spoken of nothing else for twenty minutes and each person that passed looked closer at her. And then Bobby passed and said, "Are you a werewolf?"

The laughter was heard up and down the aisle. It wasn't explosive or sustained, but it was there, and Jennifer heard it through her ears and down into her soul. The cut was still there, years later, and it still bled.

She got off the bus last, went directly to the principal's office, said she felt like she was going to throw up, and had the school call her mother. On the phone, she told her mom that she was sick and needed to come home immediately. Carol was irritated; Josie was sick, and she was worried that everyone would be sick soon. But after a long half hour, a half hour during which Jennifer lay down with a blanket over her legs, Carol came to get her. When she got home, she lay in bed and thought about what she needed to do. She rubbed the hairs on her legs, but they wouldn't rub out, and she pulled out most of them, but that hurt, and she knew they'd grow back.

She waited until her dad got home, and when he came to her room to check on her, she told him what happened. Bob was at the peak of his engineering powers then. He smiled, patted her back, and said there was an easy solution that would work 100 percent of the time. He then brought her one of his razors and shaved her leg hair off himself.

Bob didn't think there was any disorder then, and sometimes, when she was ready for bed, he'd drop by her room with the razor and shave around her ankles just to be sure. When she noticed a few dark hairs around her chin a couple of years later is when he took her to an endocrinologist, and the doctor discussed hirsutism. Jennifer was appalled. The doctor happened to be from Syria, and so Jennifer could only stare at his face, which was clean shaven but still marked with the place where his beard started, and she thought her face would one day look the same. The doctor told her it was minor in women and easily addressed with razors, creams, and Nair, a product that literally was a contraction of 'no hair.' Three bottles of Nair were in the original package that Bob bought for her on their way home from that first appointment, and she had used it religiously.

Eight years had passed since that day on the bus, the day Bobby asked if she was a werewolf, and she felt feminine and as hairless and clean as any women should, but she didn't credit that to Nair; she credited Madonna. Madonna was fully feminine, so much so that both boys and girls wanted to be with her. Jennifer felt, for the first time ever, powerful in the way she thought Madonna was, and that feeling was intoxicating. She didn't really have any sexual feelings for Lisa at all, but she had discovered that she genuinely liked Lisa, for reasons that even Lisa didn't like herself, and she was glad they were friends. Lisa, also, made her feel powerful in the way that Bobby Thompson had robbed her of. All the power was back, in spades, and in her body, and she was not ever going to lose it again.

She still had classes with Shannon though they never spoke. Seeing Shannon reminded her of the period when she felt ashamed and invisible. Shannon was difficult not to see since she was constantly changing her hair color and she tried various make up combinations, all extreme. She wore a green army jacket every day for a while, with baggy pants that had probably belonged to Marco.

Months had passed since their brief interaction in the hallway when Shannon entered the girl's bathroom on the second floor and saw Jennifer at the mirror combing out her hair. For the first time in years, they were briefly alone. Shannon smirked and went into a stall. After she sat down and began to pee, Shannon said loudly "How long are you going to keep up this Madonna act?"

"How long are you going to care?" Jennifer responded as she rushed to finish her hair and wash her hands.

Shannon exited the stall and stood at the sink.

"I have to say, it is interesting in a trite, uninteresting kind of way," she said to Jennifer. "Madonna is a narcissistic whore, which you aren't. I know you. You aren't a whore and aren't a narcissist either. Whores are fun, which you aren't, and narcissists are interesting, which you also aren't."

"Thank you, Doctor Joyce Brothers," Jennifer said. "And you don't know me. You don't know my friends, what I do, who I do it with, or why. You don't know shit. You're a poorly dressed little girl destined to work retail."

"Well, I know you aren't a lesbian," Shannon said. "Whatever you're up to with Lisa, it's some sort of sociopathic game you're playing on her. You're using her. I'd warn her, but I kind of want to see how this plays out."

"Shannon," Jennifer said as she backed towards the door, "mind your own business."

Jennifer rode home in silence as she thought that short interaction with Shannon, now months back. She was enjoying the breeze, and the easy feeling of having a car and being able to go anywhere she saw fit. As she reached her street, she saw Jack walking around the side of Domingo's house. He had a backpack on his back, and he crossed Domingo's lawn and headed towards their home. He saw her and suddenly headed down to the side of their house to enter the back yard.

* * *

Carol sat cross-legged on her bed. Speaking with Dave made her giddy and she wanted to sit like a child.

"It's just exciting really," she said, "to walk so far, and to make history. I'd love to go with you."

In the kitchen, Josie made a face upon hearing his mother say such a thing. He held the phone in the kitchen to his ear, but he had his hand over the mouthpiece. He had not met Dave, but he'd listened in on enough of his mother's conversations to know who the man was and who he was to his mother.

"I so, so, so wish you were going," Dave said with a light laugh. Josie instantly thought that Dave was glad his mother wasn't going.

Josie had his back to the back door and didn't see Jack come through the door behind him.

"We could snuggle at night after walking all day," Dave said suggestively.

"Oh, no. Oh, no, no. But I bet you'd like that," Josie heard his mother say gayly.

Josie looked up when he heard the front door open and knew it was Jennifer, but he still hadn't heard Jack creeping up behind him.

126

"I might find a way to like camping if it was for a good cause," Carol said.

"Who you spying on, you little puke?!" Jack yelled into Josie's ear. Carol and Dave heard the sudden third voice on the call loud and clear.

"Oh my God, that's my kids," Carol blurted out. "I have to go."

Josie hung up the phone and clutched his ringing ear.

"God," he swore at Jack. "You're such a putz!"

"What, are you listening to Jennifer's phone calls?" he asked. "Little weirdo. Gross."

"It wasn't Jennifer," Josie said and turned. He was humiliated and wanted to get away.

Josie slammed the phone down and walked out just as Jennifer walked in.

"It was mom? That's even worse!" Jack yelled after Josie.

Jennifer cast a gimlet eye towards Jack and went to the refrigerator.

"What?" he said. "What's up your ass?"

"What's in the backpack?" she asked.

"What backpack?" he responded innocently.

She pulled out a Tab and opened it.

"The one you've apparently hidden in the backyard," she said as she popped the top of the Tab. "The one you got from the neighbor. The one with all the drugs."

"It's not hidden," he said, "and it's just camping gear."

"Right," she said. There had been a time when she believed everything her brother told her. He was heroic, and he delighted in threatening people who might pose any threat to her. She thought he meant it, but now knew he mostly did it for fun.

"If I know you deal drugs then so does everyone else," she said evenly. "It used to be little baggies. Shannon told me everything because Marco tells her everything. You're a total, complete idiot to trust that guy."

Jack tried to hide his irritation, but it didn't work.

"Please don't tell anyone," he said, after an embarrassing moment. "I'm getting out of it, I promise.

"It's backpacks now," she said. "That doesn't look like you're getting out; it looks like you're getting way further in."

"I know how it looks," he said. "Jennifer, I swear, this is the last time. I'm in…it's crazy. The less you know the better, but I swear, this is it, no more after this."

She saw the alarm on his face. It made her more, not less, worried.

"When you go to prison, you're going to break daddy's heart," she said. He looked at the floor. She took a moment to realize he wasn't going to respond, took her Tab, and left.

Jennifer had become ambivalent about her mom long ago, but she loved her dad, and she loved Jack and Josie. The idea of Jack in jail made her anxious and sad, and she didn't want to hurt, so she tried not to think about it anymore and went to take a shower.

* * *

Jack slowly entered his parents' bedroom. Across the room by the big picture window was a display case with pictures of Bob when he was in Korea, some medals, and two pistols. Carol had put several peace signs on top of the case, but it was what it was: a war trophy case.

Jack opened the case quietly and removed one of the pistols; it was an old Army issue Colt 45. Just then he heard the toilet flush and he quickly put the Colt 45 back in place, but before he could leave the room, Bob came out of the bathroom. He was wearing his robe and slippers. Bob saw Jack just as he reached the door.

"Hi, Dad," Jack said.

"What's up Jackie boy?" Bob said calmly.

"Uh, nothing. I was just thinking about your old guns and wondered if you still had them," Jack said.

Bob walked over and looked in the case. He knew the .45 had been moved.

"Yeah, I still have them," he said. "Your mom hates them, puts all this peace shit here like it will get the stink of death off them."

He opened the case and took out the .45.

"Stink of death?" Jack said, walking closer. "You killed people with that gun?"

"Not this one," Bob said. "I bought this one at a pawn shop."

Bob popped the clip out and looked; it was unloaded.

"We used to take this one to the range, remember?"

"Yeah, I remember," Jack said.

"Come look," Bob said as he walked into the closet.

The master bedroom closet was dominated by Carol's clothes. Bob pulled some clothes back and revealed a gray gun case. As Jack watched over his shoulder, Bob spun the combination lock and then opened the case. The inside was perfectly clean and there were two rows of black military rifles glowing against the black interior. Clips and rounds of various ammunition in brightly colored boxes were stacked on the top shelf.

"Holy shit!" Jack said as a smile crept across his face. "Does mom know about this?"

"It's a huge metal box in the middle of her closet; of course, she knows about it," Bob said. "She doesn't know the combination, though. If she did, she'd clean it out by the end of the week."

Jack looked at the row of guns. In the middle was a vicious looking weapon with a barrel that had a perforated tube surrounding it.

"What the hell is that?" Jack asked.

Bob took the heavy weapon out of the case and then pulled out a black ammo carousel. He expertly attached the carousel to the top side of the weapon and then handed the whole thing to Jack.

"This is a Lewis Gun," he said. "The Brits used it in active service for sixty years."

He pointed to the tubing that wrapped the barrel.

"This deflects heat back here, so the barrel won't warp," he said. "The carousel can hold up to ninety-seven rounds which makes it heavy, but if you strap it around your neck, you can hold it up."

"You have ammo for this thing?" Jack asked.

"Sure," Bob said. "You can put regular Mauser rounds through it, and there are boxes right there."

He pointed at the stacks of ammo.

"Bob," they heard Carol yelling.

Carol suddenly appeared at the closet door, dressed in a sweatsuit. She saw Jack holding the giant Lewis gun.

"The bathroom smells like a rotting carcass," she said to Bob. "You have to start eating better."

She paused for a moment, then addressed the guns.

"Why do you have to show those things to our kids, huh? Isn't the world violent enough as it is?" she asked rhetorically.

Bob took the big Lewis from Jack, detached the carousel, and carefully put it back in the rack.

"I'd really like you to get all of those out of this house," she said.

Bob closed the case door.

"I'll get right on that," he said dryly.

Carol stared at them both, and they stared right back for an uncomfortable moment. A contest was being carried on, and Jack thought, just for an instant, that she wanted him to confirm her beliefs. In a fleeting moment of clarity, he realized that his parents might not see the end of the year together.

Finally, she blinked.

"Could you please open the window when you use the bathroom?" she requested. "It's a toxic waste dump in there."

She turned and left. Bob opened the case again and pointed at the weapons as he named them.

"That's an M1," he continued. "That's an M-16. That's an AK. That's a Browning."

He paused and looked at Jack.

"Do you need a gun for something?" he asked.

Jack wanted to ask his dad for help, but he couldn't. He would have so much explaining to do, and he just didn't want to do it. And he knew that if he told his dad, his dad would act, and that would be dangerous for all. The best thing to do was to sell the drugs, give Domingo the money, and then never do it again.

"No," he said, hoping it wasn't a lie. "I just wondered if you still had them. Thanks."

Jack turned and left abruptly. Bob closed the case. He knew Jack was lying, but he knew his window to act had not yet opened.

Chapter 15

Spring wore on and the rain finally came. The rain gave Jack a few peaceful opportunities to think. He lay in his bed listening to the thunder and pondered his path. He longed to go back to the day Domingo told him to go to Mexico, which was the day the *Challenger* exploded. Every time he saw his dad watching the news about *Challenger*, he thought about that day. It was a hinge day for them both. It had been a day of disaster. He knew that day had affected his dad in some way, but he wasn't sure how or why. His dad was changing. Bob rarely had a drink in his hand anymore. He watched the news quietly, and he read the newspaper with a cup of coffee in the morning.

As the summer grew slower, and the spring rains turned to summer deluges, he knew he could be passive no longer.

Jack walked through the kitchen on his way to the backyard, but he stopped when he heard voices in the garage. One was a male voice he didn't recognize. This stopped him in his tracks. He walked over to the door to the garage and listened. He heard his mother's voice which was high and gay and happy.

Jack opened the door and saw that the cars had been moved out to make space on the garage floor. Josie was on his hands and knees on the garage floor with a paintbrush in his hand. He was kneeling on a long roll of paper. Beyond Josie, Carol was talking to Dave. They stood close and were all secret glances and private knowing.

Carol saw Jack standing at the door. He knew his mother wanted to put on a show.

"Oh, honey, I want you to meet someone," she said with a broad grin. "This is my friend Dave. Dave is getting ready to take part in the Peace March. He's going to walk all the way across the country, LA to Washington DC!"

Jack looked closer at the signs Josie was painting. Texans For Peace was painted on part of the banner, and If Not Now, When? marked another.

Jack didn't speak or move from the door, but after an awkward moment, Dave stuck his big hand out and he marched towards Jack.

"Hi, Jack," he said. His big teeth gleamed in the garage light. "Good to meet you."

He shook Jack's hand vigorously.

"Your mom has told me so many nice things about you," Dave said. Up close, Jack could see the crow's feet and jowls. Dave dressed like an old hippie.

"She has?" Jack said absent mindedly.

Carol read Jack in an instant and intervened.

"Of course, I have, baby," said. "I've told him all about your rodeo trophies and what a bright boy you are!"

Jack looked down at Josie, who was miserable. He was made to paint all the slogans because he was the kid with the least power. Josie made a rude gesture to show he thought Carol and Dave were having sex.

"Rodeo," Dave said. "That's great! It looks so...scary!"

"That's why God made tequila," Jack mumbled and retreated into the house.

Jack smiled sympathetically at Josie as he closed the door. In an instant, he saw Josie as a captive of the family's decline.

But, before he could do anything about Josie, he had to do something about his own situation. There was a rodeo in Midland, and he had to move more coke, or the end was upon them all, nukes or not.

* * *

The day after he came back from Mexico, Jack dropped the backpack off with Domingo, who was also horrified at the massive pile of drugs they had to sell. Jack had decided to make the whole thing Domingo's problem and sell exactly as he had.

"Puto, what the fuck!" Domingo had said.

"Yeah, what the fuck," Jack countered as he looked down at the filthy death smelling backpack.

They went back and forth like this for a while, and Jack broke down at one point and started to cry.

"They shot a girl right in front of us!" he said.

"Who?" Domingo asked.

"I don't fucking know! Some poor girl! They shot her in the head and blood spewed out and we had to sit in it," Jack said.

Domingo sat down. Jack glanced up at him and saw something he'd never seen in the reptilian manners of Domingo. He saw sympathy. Jack clued in that this girl was someone he knew.

"What did she look like?" he asked.

"Why do you care?" he asked.

"What did she look like?" Domingo said as he lit another cigarette. His voice was rising in pitch and tone.

"You already have one lit in the kitchen," Jack said.

"Jesus, puto! What did she look like?" Domingo growled.

Jack stopped crying. This was new, and he suddenly had the sense that something important was about to be revealed.

"She had blonde hair. I couldn't tell much more. She had a blind fold on. She was skinny," he said. "She was wearing a t-shirt."

Jack played the entire scene back in his head, but he couldn't remember anymore. Then, it occurred to him. Her name had been spoken.

"Wait, that evil witch said her name," Jack said.

Domingo looked Jack hard in the eye.

"What was it?" he asked.

Jack thought hard, trying to get the soundtrack of the moment to load up in his head but he could only see the image of the girl, her flopping head, and the blood on the T-shirt. He couldn't get the sound of the name to play, but he knew it was there.

"Fuck, I can't remember," he said.

"The negro, he heard it too?" Domingo asked.

"Yes, he saw the whole thing," Jack confirmed.

Domingo jumped up and brought the phone back to Jack.

"Call him," he insisted.

Jack lifted the phone and dialed Marco's number.

"Hello?" he heard. It was Shannon.

"I need to speak to Marco," Jack said.

"Say please," Shannon replied deadpan. Jack saw one of Domingo's fists ball up.

"It's important, Shannon. This is Jack. Put Marco on," he said, trying to stay calm.

"If it's important, you can say pretty please," she said.

"Pretty please, put Marco on, please," he said.

Jack heard the phone hit the table in the hallway.

"It's your boyfriend," she said.

Marco came to the phone.

"Sorry about that. I didn't know it was you," Marco said.

"That girl in Mexico. Do you remember her name?" Jack asked. He saw Domingo lean in to hear better.

"That girl I fucked? Bro, I can't remember. She told me but I don't remember now," Marco said. "Her English sucked. She could have said any name. Anna, maybe? Maria? Anna Maria?"

"Not that one!" Jack said. "The other one. The blonde one. That witch said her name, but I can't remember what she said," Jack said. "Do you remember?"

"Oh, yes, I remember," Marco said. "She said to tell Domingo that it was Lissie. Her name was Lissie."

Domingo put his forehead on the table.

"Why? What's up?" Marco asked.

"I'll call you later," Jack said and hung up. "Okay, asshole. Who was she?"

Domingo said nothing.

"That's why we were down there, wasn't it?" Jack said. He knew it was true and really didn't need Domingo to confirm. "She was a girlfriend or something like that.'

"Yes, something like that," Domingo said. "She was the love of my life."

"Oh, bullshit," Jack said. "You don't have a love of your life. Look at how you live. There has never been a women who's lived in this house."

Domingo took a huge pull from the cigarette.

"She was," he said. "She grew up in my village. I knew her since she was a little girl. I never loved another. When she was old enough, I took care of her. Her family was poor. I saw her when I could, and she fell in love with me. We had not much times together, but they were heaven. We gave each other the peace we never had, or ever will have."

Jack stared at Domingo in disbelief. Who was the poet who had suddenly emerged from under the austere filth of Domingo's life?

"Okay, fine, the love of your life. But you don't have cancer, do you?" Jack asked.

"No," Domingo said. "Karlotta found out about Lissie, and if I went, she would have killed me. She is my wife."

Jack's mouth hung open in disbelief.

"So, you sent us?" Jack asked.

"Yes," Domingo said.

Jack stood. He was pissed, and he was ready to go home.

"Well, we got the drugs up here, and you can fucking sell them yourself," he said. He turned to leave.

"They've seen you, stupid," Domingo said. "Sit down. You want to live, you want to save your family, sit your puto ass down and listen."

Jack sat, but he didn't want to.

"Karlotta is not the big jefe," Domingo said. "She's just in the middle. But she sent all these drugs up here to fuck me. She thinks we can't sell that much, but we have to sell them. She'll tell the real drug dealers, the Sinaloa motherfuckers, that we stole the drugs, and then they'll come up here and kill us. Not just me, but you, the negro, and whoever is around."

Jack stood again. Domingo had put him in an impossible place. Selling that much coke was the kind of thing real dealers did, and they went to jail or got shot. But not selling the drugs was a death sentence as well.

"Sell it yourself!" Jack said and turned to leave.

"You think about it, Jack Buckhorn!' Domingo said. "They know you just like they know me. And you can make a lot of money here!"

Jack stopped and thought hard. He had few choices and the path out of trouble was also the one that had the most money.

"Same deal?" Jack asked. "I keep half of what I sell?"

"Same deal," Domingo said. "Even you can't snort up this much."

Jack added up what he thought he could make. It was enough to change his life forever. He could go to college, take a long vacation, or do whatever he wanted. He was going back to business, and he was going to have to go to a lot of rodeos, but in nine months, he figured he could have it sold.

In the first few weeks, he took just a few baggies of coke with him, and he sold them out cleanly. No partying, no doing it himself. He made more money than he ever had, and he gave it all to Domingo. After he came back from Longview, he handed a pile of cash to Domingo and Domingo gave him half back for himself.

"How do you know how much they expect in total?" he asked Domingo.

"I don't," Domingo said as he counted out the twenties. "I hope it's enough."

"Wait, you don't know? How do you know you have enough to give me half?" Jack asked, incredulous at how loose such a big business was.

"I don't know," he said. "Maybe you should have asked that, stupid."

"Jesus!" Jack said as he put some of his cash into Domingo's pile. "I'll keep 25 percent; you give me another 25 when this shit is over."

And so it went, week after week, with the money coming in at a trickle. Jack went to a few rodeos, and he went down to Galveston to the clubs and sold to college kids. He called a few customers and recruited them to bring him customers, and it worked. He paid a few friends in coke and sold a few more bags. He was busier than he had ever been. It was exhausting, but a lot easier now since he didn't do it himself and he was sleeping better, even if often, it was in his truck.

It was raining when Jack stopped by to get more coke, and Domingo brought out the big backpack and let Jack look inside. Most of the coke was still there.

"You have to move it faster," he said to Jack.

"What's the hurry?" Jack asked. "I sell some every day practically. I'm on the fucking road every weekend. This is work, puto."

"I got a call," Domingo said, looking up and the ceiling. He was genuinely scared.

"From who?" Jack asked.

"From her," Domingo said. They both knew it was Karlotta. "I have to go to Laredo in a month with the money."

Jack swallowed hard.

"How much money?" he asked.

"She didn't say," Domingo answered. "She just said all of it. So, you got to sell more."

Jack thought, almost against his will, of the Midland Rodeo that was coming up. They loved coke in Midland. There were not just cowboys in Midland. There were oilfield workers, and they loved to drink, whore, and do drugs. The only reason he had never tried to sell in Midland was that he was afraid he'd run into someone his dad knew. But now, he had no choice.

* * *

Jack came around from the back of the house and saw Jennifer on the front porch. She had fed the phone line through the window and was talking to someone. She smiled and laughed; Jack paused because he had not seen her smile in so long.

At the street, Carol was holding an umbrella and talking to Dave. Dave was making a habit of dropping by every three or four days.

Jack walked past Carol and Dave and down towards Marco's house.

The same middle school boys seemed to always be in the street when Jack walked down to Marco's house. Jack scowled at them as he crossed the street. He thought about himself just a few years earlier stamping in the puddles and getting covered in mud. It was funny then and it was funny to see the boys doing it now, but he had to scowl at them. They expected it.

"Don't fucking get mud on me!" he growled as he passed.

The boys snickered. Jack was older so he could use the words that were still forbidden to them.

Jack knocked on the front door of Marco's house and then stepped back to watch the boys stamping in the puddles again. He looked back at his home and two members of his failing family. His mom was talking to a man not his dad and his sister was flirting some someone no one knew. It couldn't last much longer.

After a moment, Shannon appeared. She saw it was Jack and sneered long and deeply.

"Where's Marco?" Jack asked.

"You're not in jail yet?" Shannon said, rather than asked.

137

Jack fumed. Her comment was her way to telling him she knew what had gone down in Mexico. Jack knew that Marco made fun of Shannon relentlessly, and he had told Jack that he would fuck Shannon if she would allow it since she wasn't his real sister. Still, even though they were terrible to each other, they talked all the time.

She read his face perfectly. Shannon wasn't an empath by any means, but she could read faces perfectly.

"Hold your water; I'll get him," she said and closed the door.

After a moment, Marco appeared. Jack walked away from the front door so no one could hear them talking.

"What did you say to that little snitch?" he began.

"What are you talking about?" Marco said, playing dumb. He was not good at that game.

Jack started to continue but decided not to. Nothing he could do about it now anyway.

"So…you want to make some money?" he asked. He knew that answer to this question as well.

Marco hung his head. Yes, he wanted to make money, but he knew what that would entail, and he didn't want to draw any closer to what had happened in Mexico.

"All you have to do is help me out," Jack said. "I'm going to Midland for at least a week, maybe more. We have to get rid of the rest of it. I've already sold a lot, but we have to move faster. There's the rodeo, and we'll hit the clubs. We go a week, sell the shit out of some coke, then back. Easy peasy. What we brought back is good shit."

Marco gestured towards Domingo's house.

"What's up with him?" he asked.

"All good," Jack said. "Nothing has changed. But he's getting pressure. We have to move this shit and be done with it forever."

Marco sighed. He was in. He had to be.

"When?" he asked.

"We leave in two hours," Jack said. "And don't ditch me this time, fucker."

"Yeah, man. That was pretty shitty of me," Marco confessed. He would have justified his actions if forced, and he told Shannon he had saved the whole mission by diverting the Border Patrol.

But Jack and Marco were friends, Jack had no one else to turn to, and so they shook hands.

"All good," he said. "Be ready. Keep that yappy sister quiet. Give her this."

Jack took a little baggy out of his pocket and palmed it to Marco. It was a tiny bag he had taken from the backpack.

"She does like her nose candy," Marco said with a smile.

"Make sure it goes up her nose and not yours," Jack said.

He went back to see Domingo who was still at his table with the backpack.

"I'm going to Midland tonight. There's a rodeo, and other places to sell," he said. "Cut me out about a hundred baggies and I think I can move it all."

Domingo stood and handed him the whole backpack.

"Sell it all," he said dramatically.

"Whoa, wait," Jack said. "That's a life sentence worth of coke."

"It's a death sentence, too," Domingo said. "Stay there until you sell it all. Give some of it away like you used to but get rid of it! And if you can't do it, we both need to start running now."

Jack had never seen Domingo like this. He took the backpack, turned, and left.

* * *

Two hours later, Jack was ready to go. He pulled on his jeans and rodeo shirt, then his black boots he had bought with the last prize money he ever collected. His jeans were loose because he had lost so much weight in the past six months, but he didn't have a belt small enough either. His high school graduation picture hung over the mirror and he looked at it, and then at himself. He was aging. He saw an aging scared loser. But there in the corner was the backpack. He brought it in from the backyard when he heard thunder.

He entered the kitchen with the big backpack on his shoulder This backpack had been taken off a dead man, but Jack had forgotten about that part, and he wasn't prepared for his dad, who entered the kitchen from the back yard. Bob had an empty high ball glass in his hand. The drinking he still did, he did in the back yard so Carol couldn't see it.

139

They saw each other at the same time. One had an empty glass, the other a full backpack.

"Where you headed, Jackie Boy?" Bob asked. He was fairly sure he knew there was something forbidden in the pack and that it had come into Jack's possession at a high cost. He had no idea how high it was, but the pack was too dirty and generic to be one Jack would have purchased.

"I'm going camping with Marco for a couple of days," Jack said.

"Great! Where?" Bob asked.

"Midland. I mean, you know, near Midland," Jack said.

"I used to live in Midland. Some campgrounds I might have heard of?" Bob asked. He wanted to see Jack squirm.

"Marco found it. I don't know the name," Jack said. "Looked like you were slowing down on the vodka there for a while."

Bob glanced at Jack sadly. They both had so many things they needed to talk about.

"Yeah, I have, but sometimes, it's just a tough day," Bob said. "One day, I'll be done. I know you have no reason to believe me."

Bob passed Jack and put the glass in the sink. Jack hesitated, and almost started speaking. He wanted to tell his dad that of course he believed him. He believed him and he believed in him. They had been so close and had so many good times, and something had happened. Growing up had happened to Jack, growing older had happened to Bob, and both were influenced by forces well beyond their control. Jack started to speak, but he felt the heavy backpack on his shoulders, and he knew there was nothing more to say. He couldn't tell his dad what was happening, and the man before him, he thought, couldn't do anything about it anyway.

"I believe you," Jack said quietly as he turned towards the door. "See ya later, Dad."

Bob watched Jack slip out the back door. He knew Jack was a tough boy, and a survivor, and somewhere in himself, he knew that Jack would set up the survival conditions for himself as part of a test. He had done it. He had volunteered for dangerous things in Korea. He had taunted bulls when he was a child.

Jack, he figured, was probably doing the same thing. Bob wondered if his dad should have ever advised him or told him to do things differently. It didn't matter, because his dad didn't, and wouldn't have been listened to.

Bob put the vodka back in the cabinet and decided to go to bed early.

Chapter 16

Rodeo is the official sport of the late cowboy profession. Feed lots and barbed wire ended the career of the real cowboy after only twenty-five years on the open range, but the skills a cowboy had to master were so sublime that the men who had used them kept faith long enough to see them translated to a sport.

Of course, the rodeo cowboys added a few things to the palate of dangers, things like riding bulls. Real cowboys had enough risks to worry about without climbing onto the backs of those monsters, but the rodeo cowboys ate regular meals and slept in real beds, often with soft, sweet, hot pink buckle bunnies at their sides. They could afford a little extra risk. The real cowboys slept on the ground, worried about snakes, watched for renegade bands of murderous natives, and were mostly alone. They knew they'd die alone if they weren't careful and might die alone anyway. They had little family to speak of. They weren't a family as a group, not like a sports team. Each man knew they were responsible for their own survival and so they acted like it.

But rodeo is a sport and like all sports, there are feeder leagues, and small-time rodeo is the feeder league for big-time rodeo. They are impromptu affairs, mostly owned and operated by counties, and usually for profit. They attract lots of men and women and kids and plenty of cowboys, good and bad, mostly bad. There is country music and carnival food, thick girls, dirty children, lots of horses and cows, goats and sheep, chickens and turkeys. The 4-H associations use them as showcases for their animal husbandry programs but the rich long ago subverted these events by hiring ringers to coach the kids and shelter them from any real unpleasant work. Rich kids won the 4H trophies.

Jack knew all about how the rodeos were organized and so didn't let his conscience trouble him for selling drugs there. Everyone was in it for something, mostly having a good time and some people liked to have a better time than others. For them, drugs made a difference.

Jack drove out to Midland with Marco sleeping beside him. Nothing new there.

When they reached Midland, Jack tracked down Miggie and arranged to take a nap in the trailer. He and Marco slept late, enduring people coming and going from the trailer. Jack slept with the backpack wrapped in his arms and at one point, turned the zipper to the floor just to be sure no one opened it. It still smelled like river mud and death.

By the afternoon, he and Marco were up, they had filled themselves with corndogs and beer, plus a little coke, and then they went to work.

Jack gave Marco a few bags of coke and sent him on his way. He knew he couldn't carry the backpack into the rodeo, and he couldn't leave it at Miggie's, so he had figured out a way to strap it to the underside of his truck. After he had sent Marco on his way, he wove his way back to the truck, sure that he wasn't being followed, then he tied the backpack to the underside of the truck just behind the front bumper. Even if someone looked under the truck, they wouldn't see the backpack. He could drive away, and the backpack would be secure all the way back to Houston. He had thought about leaving most of the coke back at his parents' house, but he couldn't do that to his dad. And he wanted to see if he could get Miggie to do some sales for him. At the rate they normally moved the drugs, he and Marco would take the rest of the year to sell out, so he lowered the price and word was spreading.

Marco learned the names of most of Jack's friends after a few trips to the rodeo, and those friends only knew Marco in one context: buying coke. Jack figured correctly that Marco didn't need his help finding customers and that he could be trusted to make sales. Marco seemed like, moved like, and had the persona like a drug dealer when he had drugs on him. It was an act he could put on and he did it well. After twenty minutes of walking around, the first cowboy stopped him and leaned in to ask, "Are you carrying?" Marco sold $100 of coke to that guy.

Word spread, and soon he was approached every few minutes. He walked behind bathrooms and into various dark corners and kept an eye out for anyone who was following him. Everyone wanted to buy coke. He saw a cop, but that guy was watching the rodeo. He thought about just giving the guy some coke to keep him uninterested in what was going on since the cop looked just like his customers, but he figured he's best to talk to Jack about that plan first.

Jack kept an eye out for Owen Williams, the only man who didn't seem to want him at the rodeo, but he knew Owen stayed in his trailer or the whatever office he could commandeer, and he also knew Owen was a severe alcoholic. Owen was not hard to avoid since he was often drunk and napping.

Jack also knew the rodeo workers better than Marco did, and so he could focus on those sales. The rodeo clowns were very reliable customers except for the part where they didn't have much money. Every one of them wanted the drugs on credit, and Jack sometimes took that risk, but now, he said no every time. When anyone said, "I'm good for it" Jack saw Karlotta, and the poor girl Lissie, and he'd say, "I'm sure you are but I have to have the money now." They paid up, which he took to mean they always had the money and the request for credit had always been a request for free drugs.

Marco kept an eye out for girls he wanted to fuck and finally convinced two prospects to take him to their car. They snorted coke off a mirror he had snapped out of the frame in the car visor.

"I said god damn!" one of the girls bellowed.

Marco smiled and rubbed her back.

"We're going to be partying later tonight," he said.

"Yeah, we heard," the other girl said as she lowered her face to the mirror in Marco's lap. "At Miggie's. We'll be there. We hear it's going to snow real hard!"

Marco smiled, but something was a bit off. Jack told him they would set up at Maggie's, but that it was to stay way down low, like very quiet. He said he wasn't even going to tell Miggie until the rodeo was almost over. There would be no free coke, no loans, and it wouldn't go on all night. They'd sell some coke and be gone by the time word spread; that was the plan. When Marco asked why they didn't just stay all night and sell as much as they could Jack said, "Because requests for loans will become demands for loans when cowboys get too fucked up."

And now, these two girls were talking about a party.

Jack didn't know news of the party was spreading. He would have been alarmed had he known. He walked around behind a food truck at the end of the carnival and sold some coke to a Mexican guy who gave him two tacos as well as cash.

He ate the tacos as he walked back to the big rodeo ring, but then he saw Owen Williams talking to two cops. This looked bad. He pushed the rest of his taco into his mouth and shifted directions. From behind the edge of a tent, he watched Owen and the cops. They were laughing at something. There was no sense of seriousness or alarm in their demeanor.

After Owen headed back to his trailer, Jack went back into the arena. He saw Marco talking to a couple of girls and bumped into him. Marco followed him to a tiny space behind the bathrooms.

"How's it going?" Jack asked.

"I'm tapped out," Marco said with a smile. "Jesus H, these cowboys love the coco. And there are some fine bitches here, too."

"I'm going to the truck. Give me what you got," Jack said. He was serious and furtive.

Marco took a bundle of cash from his pocket and handed it to Jack. It was an unsorted wad of bills. Jack had asked that Marco keep his cash in good order, but that wasn't going to happen. He started to say something about it, but then he noticed Marco was fidgety and clenching his jaw.

"Are you high?" Jack asked.

"What?" Marco said. He didn't fake incredulity very well.

"Are you high? You're clenching your teeth. Your eyeballs are on fire," Jack stated.

"Couple customers wanted to share with me, that's all," Marco said. "People here are real friendly. I did their coke, nothing was free."

Jack chose not to pursue it further. The money looked right.

"We're going to Migs in about an hour. We sell as much as we can, and then we're going to find a motel," he said. "Some bad mojo around this place, and nothing is safe around Migs. I see Owen and cops everywhere I turn. Keep your shit together. Seriously."

Marco was too high to let Jack harsh his mellow.

"It's all good," Marco said.

"Famous last words," Jack said and headed for the truck.

Jack kept looking for Owen as he headed back to the truck. As he was turning to go to the parking area, he saw that the rodeo was beginning a round of Cowboy Poker. A few of the players were walking out to the middle of the arena, and Jack recognized from the cheap plastic furniture set up in the middle of the dirt that the most foolish and dangerous event in rodeo was about to begin. The event featured members of the audience, mostly very drunk men, and a bull.

Jack stopped at the rail around the ring to watch. Four young men sat at the plastic lawn furniture arrangement and the rodeo clowns stood by to interdict the bull when the players were in trouble. Jack knew which clown was Miggie.

But then Jack was bumped by someone to his left and he thought for a panicked moment that it was Owen or one of the cops. But it wasn't: it was Michael King. Michael was his age, black, tall, rangy, good-looking and he was wearing a red leather jacket and sunglasses.

"Jack Buckhorn!" he said enthusiastically. "My man."

Something inside Jack tensed up. Michael had been a sketchy player back in high school and he cheated at rodeo any time he could, and he had an odd smile on his face. The encounter didn't seem like chance.

They shook hands soul style.

"Michael," Jack said. "You still cowboying around?"

"Yeah, motherfucker! Going to get to the PBR in the fall," Michael said. Jack knew that was not true. "What about you? When am I going to see you back in there?"

"My rodeoing days are over," Jack said plainly. "I just watch now."

"See you at Migs later?" Michael asked. "Always a party at Migs, baby! He says you coming."

"I'll be there," Jack said. He felt his stomach fall. Michael wanted free coke, for sure.

Michael turned to walk away.

Jack looked back at the Cowboy Poker match and saw one of the contestants flipped high in the air by the angry bull. The crowd cheered.

On the way back to the truck, Owen Williams saw him. This was not good. Williams called out to him from a distance.

"Buckhorn, get the fuck out of my rodeo, son!" he yelled.

Jack kept walking, and pretended he didn't hear Owen bleating, but he did.

"I know which truck is yours," he yelled. "If I see it, it's getting towed."

Shit. He needed to get the bag, get to Migs, sell some dope, and leave.

Jack reached the truck and quickly slipped under the front bumper and untied the backpack. He was going to stock up with baggies, but Owen's threat to tow the truck was ringing in his ears. A tow truck driver would be poking around the front bumper, and this wasn't good. Tying it off elsewhere under the truck was not something he wanted to do in the dark.

So, he rolled out from under the truck and looked around. No one was nearby. He lifted the backpack onto his shoulders and headed for Migs. He hoped he'd be back in the truck in maybe two hours. It was time to leave.

By the time he reached Mig's trailer, there was a party. Cowboy Poker was the last event and Migs had not changed out of his clown make up. He was standing in the kitchen mixing drinks when Jack walked in. Marco was beside Migs, and he had his arms around another Latin girl. Two other girls sat on the couch.

Jack said hello and headed for the bedroom. Everyone knew what that meant. Within ten minutes, Jack had set up shop in the bedroom and sold baggies to everyone in the trailer. He heard Marco doing a line in the bathroom with one of the girls.

A steady stream of cowboy riffraff entered Mig's trailer in the next half hour. They formed a line after a few minutes and Jack was selling bags fast. There were requests for credit, along with the usual promise "I'm good for it" but when Jack heard that, he would just pull his hand back. Only one guy, a haggard clown missing a tooth and a brown tooth by the gap, left because he didn't have any money. The rest just pulled cash out of their pants or purse, or in two cases, their bra, and paid up.

As soon as the traffic let up, Jack started putting the rest of the baggies away. All that traffic that fast meant Migs had talked to everyone, and the situation was dangerous. He glanced at the bag as he zipped it up. They had sold a lot, but there was still a sea of baggies tucked inside. He had to pull Marco away, and he knew Marco would beg him to stay a while longer and Jack knew he'd leave Marco if he had to.

Bob opened his eyes early and stared out the window across the room. It was growing light outside. Carol did not stir beside him.

He thought for a bit about his parents, and how little help or instruction he received from his dad. Bob's life had unfolded under his own direction, and, he thought, it had turned out well. He had good instincts, and that had proven to be enough. Bucky had years more experience with their dad, and he'd have asked Bucky for details about the man, but he suspected Bucky would have been evasive, and besides, at this point, Bucky was a myth.

After a few more moments of thought, he rose and went downstairs. The kitchen was dirty, and the trash needed to be taken out. While his coffee brewed, he cleaned up and then he made some eggs.

When he heard feet on the floor above him, he went upstairs and entered the bedroom. Carol was putting on her pink slippers, but she said nothing to him. After he dressed and put on a collared shirt and dress pants, he paused, but she still said nothing to him as she passed on her way into the big closet. The doors to all the kids' rooms were closed as he went downstairs, found his keys, and went out of the garage door.

Traffic was thick as he made his way down Highway 8 and then I-45 toward Johnson Space Center. It had been years since he had made the drive, the same one that he used to do ten, and sometimes fourteen times a week. I-45 was the typical slalom of orange cones and 'slow down' signs.

He parked at a coffee shop across the street from the grand entrance to Johnson Space Center. Cars were backed up and entering the sprawling campus. Bob ordered a coffee and a pancake and ate as he watched cars enter the facility and the parking lot filled up.

After an hour, he paid his bill, walked across the intersection, and up to the big guard shack at the gate. The windows were smoked, but he knew the guards would see him coming when he was still across the street. As he got closer, one of the guards stepped out of the shack, and held his big black hand up.

"No walk-ons at this gate, boss," the man said menacingly. "You need to turn around."

Bob kept walking.

"Hey, Patrick, I heard this is where you can learn to fly that big space plane," Bob said.

The man's face turned from menacing to incredulous as Bob got closer.

"Bob Buckhorn?" he exclaimed! "Christ on a cracker, Dempsey, look what the cat dragged in!"

An even older black man in a uniform stuck his head out.

"Mr. Buckhorn, you back?" Dempsey said respectfully.

"Just for today, Dempsey," Jack said with a big smile.

They entered the guard shack, shook hands and Patrick even hugged Bob. Dempsey kept checking in cars as Bob sat down.

"It's good to see one of the old timers back here," Patrick said as he sat down heavily. "They hire kids now, they look like they're still in high school," he said.

The two men exchanged updates on their lives and families. Bob was as vague about Jack as he was about what he had done in previous years.

"So, what the hell are you doing here," Patrick asked.

"I need to see if you can issue me a visitor's pass, just for the day," Bob said. "I need to track down Aldritch, and I can't get him on the phone. *Challenger* stuff."

Patrick rubbed his balding head.

"I can't give you no visitor's pass," he said. "They don't do it like they used to, with a supply just hanging here for us to give out. They have tracking numbers, and that goes into some damn data log."

"I understand," Bob said. "Any chance you'd let me just go in for a couple of hours?"

"If you don't have no credentials hanging around your neck, you'll stand out like a sore thumb," he said.

Then Patrick pulled his badge from around his neck and handed it to Bob.

"This will get you into anything, and any building," he said. "Bring it back when you're done and don't do anything stupid."

Bob looked at the picture on the badge, where he saw Patrick's stern black face.

"The resemblance is remarkable," he said.

Patrick laughed. Bob had been one of the few *Apollo* men who learned his name and gave him a Christmas gift. Getting Christmas gifts for the guards had been Karolita's idea.

"Da fuck out here," Patrick said and stood. They shook hands and Bob walked through the gate and towards the big, white, featureless buildings across the parking lot.

Bob's mission was simple. He wanted to talk to Arnold Aldrich, the only man he knew from the *Apollo* days that was involved in the *Challenger* mission, and the man he knew would have been in on the launch decision that sent *Challenger* to its doom. As he was sobering up, Bob had thought over what he wanted to ask, and why he wanted to ask, and concluded that he wanted to hear about the launch for himself and settle for good what he felt in his bones. He felt that after the *Apollo* missions, that NASA had been corrupted by its success, that the corruption had driven the design of the orbiter, that the disintegration of NASA's Cold War mission had led to the adaptation of a new, far more political set of missions, and all of these drifting priorities had led not only to the 'Teacher In Space' gimmick, but was probably responsible for the explosion and death of all on board the *Challenger*. Bob wanted to know this because it would allow him to admit that his departure from NASA was a result of the corruption of the agency, and not his personal failing.

He put on a pair of sunglasses he had tucked into his pocket and turned his credentials around backwards, and walked directly to building 4N, the one he knew was dedicated to the Flight Director's office.

Bob entered the building and passed several people on the way to the stairs. He didn't recognize any of them.

On the third floor, he noted the hallway was exactly as he had last seen it. It was the only floor that had a carpeted hall, and therefore was far quieter than the noisy offices on the other floors and virtually every other building at the base. A previous flight controller had the carpet installed, and it was worn through, but never taken up.

As he approached the lobby that was outside Arnold's office, he saw Arnold's secretary heading down the hall in the other direction. It was another stroke of luck since it meant no one was minding

Aldritch's door. Bob rounded the corner, saw the big wooden door with the metal plaque that read Flight Controller and noted it was ajar.

Arnold Aldritch looked up from his desk as Bob entered and took off his sunglasses. What this exact moment was going to be like was something Bob had rehearsed in his head for weeks. He had rehearsed a hostile version, where he was told to leave and then escorted to the gate, and he had rehearsed a cold version where he was merely indulged. He had not rehearsed what happened, which was Aldrich smiling, rising, and extending his hand.

"Bob, Jesus Christ, man, how the hell are ya?" Aldritch said as he came around his desk. Again, to Bob's surprise, Arnold Aldritch shook his hand and then pulled him into an embrace. Bob had not been hugged by a man, or anyone else, in years, and now, back at NASA, he had been hugged twice in the past thirty minutes. He realized that he had not felt the touch of another human being further back than he could remember. He resolved to hug his children more often.

Aldrich stood back and motioned for Bob to sit down on the big leather couch under the window.

"Great to see you Arnold," Bob said. He sat down and Aldritch sat in the giant leather chair across from him.

"It's been a few," Bob said.

Aldritch smiled again, broad and deep.

"Yes, sir," he said. "Quite a few. Lots of water under the bridge since then."

Arnold saw the credentials hanging around Bob's neck.

"You kept your pass?" he said, pointing.

Bob turned the pass around and showed Patrick's scowling photo, which prompted another big smile from Aldritch.

"Patrick, he's a hell of a guy," he said. "Karolita's gifts paid off," he added.

"She goes by Carol now," Bob said.

"She shamed my wife into giving Christmas gifts to all the service people," Arnold said. "How the hell is she?"

For the next few minutes, the two men chatted amiably about their families. Aldritch had kids the same age as Bob, and he was just a few years younger. Arnold wasn't a military man, but he was a damn good engineer, and so both men shared patterns of thought. Catching up was easy and enjoyable for men with so much in common. While they were talking, Bob saw Arnold's secretary return to her desk, hear the voices inside, look in, then gently and mercifully close the door.

It was Aldrich that changed the subject.

"I got your messages, Bob," he said. "I should have called you back. I'm sorry."

"I'm sure the past few weeks have been busy," Bob offered.

"You have no idea," Arnold said aimlessly. "But that wasn't it. I didn't call you back because I knew what you were calling about. That morning, I got your messages. I was right here, and I got the message that you were on the line. I saw the light blinking, and it was you, on hold. I knew it was you and I let that light blink for at least a half hour, then I had to go to flight control. You know what happened next."

Bob was quiet for a moment. If he was booted out right then and there, it would have been worth the trip.

"I was watching it on TV," Bob said.

"You and about a billion other people," Arnold offered. "After it happened, I came back here and closed the door. I should have called you back right then. I thought about it. It would have made me feel a little better, but I just didn't do it. I didn't deserve to feel better."

Bob let that sentiment settle for a moment.

"You know, I must have heard you say a thousand times," Bob said, "that complexity was the enemy of execution. You said that. It's the enemy because complexity reduces the variables that can be tested. But weather is a known variable, and temperature is a common variable to test. I know it was the cold that doomed the orbiter, but how in the hell was it something as simple, as known, as cold weather?"

Aldritch sighed. He was glad his door was closed and for a moment he could say what he thought without thinking about what the evidence would show, or what the implication was going to be for his career, his future, and his family. Bob Buckhorn had been a great guy at NASA, but Bob had never been considered for a leadership role; he was too unpolished. He was too much of a Marine. Bob was smart, personable, intelligent well beyond his training, and the best man to use as a sounding board because Bob wasn't ambitious. Bob could be trusted, but he couldn't be trusted to lead. Leadership at NASA, in the post-*Apollo* age, required sublimating all the other good qualities in a man.

"The solid rocket booster team in Marshall, and the flight team at the Cape all were concerned about the cold on every launch system," Aldritch recalled. "The orbiter itself was tested for every condition, heat and cold, but the solid rocket booster hadn't been tested down to sub-freezing. The whole damn thing was engineered around heat tolerance."

"How low had it been tested for?" Bob asked.

"The lowest launch on record was 53 degrees," Aldritch said, with his eyes cast on the floor.

"Jesus, it got down to 8 degrees that night, and they still launched?" Bob asked incredulously.

"They waited until 11:38 a.m. to launch when it was back up to thirty-six," Aldrich said. "That was the compromise they made."

"Compromise? Between who?" Bob asked.

"The details will be in the official report, but I've seen all the docs," Arnold responded. "The night before, the guys at Thiokol raised the issue of safety and the cold, and there was a conference call with Marshall, KSC, and their team in Utah. Larry Mulloy told me about it, but he didn't tell me all of what they had said. I know now. They said the big O-rings might not seal in the cold, and they pointed out that there had already been breakthroughs at the booster seams before. But the SRB team didn't want a new launch criterion developed right there on the spot, and they said so. Thiokol put the meeting on hold for a while, and when they came back, they said they were a go for launch. Marshall asked for the recommendation in writing, which they got, and at that point, they were going to launch no matter what."

Bob shook his head slightly, and then asked: "Had they ever asked for a recommendation in writing like that before?"

"No," Aldrich said.

After a moment, Aldritch continued: "The flight tempo for the orbiter was entirely unrealistic. It still is. But when you put a man on the moon in under a decade, start to finish, people want more miracles. Corners get cut. There are some risks we've just been willing to take. But putting a civilian on the orbiter was another risk we took, and no one questioned it. A civilian teacher, a woman, what that variable might mean if the whole thing failed, systemically, we're finding out the consequence now in real time. They aren't going to change course, though. The shuttle will fly again. It has to. And no matter what we do, it won't be safe. It won't be like a civilian airliner no matter what we do. That's the lie at the heart of this enterprise, and you and everyone who said or implied that are gone. That explains some of why I didn't call you back."

"I'm sorry, Arnold," Bob offered. "You deserve better."

"I don't think I do," Arnold said. "Bob, I got to get back to work, and you need to give Patrick back his credential before he is forced to take a package. But I'm glad you came by. I want to talk to you some more."

Bob stood and the two men shook hands. A few minutes later, Bob was back on I-45, headed north. The traffic was light and already getting lighter. Bob felt lighter as well. It wasn't that he took any pleasure from hearing that Arnold had intense pain associated with the destruction of the *Challenger*. Arnold had always been a stand-up guy. What made Bob lighter was that he had been at Johnson Space Center, talked to a man who was there for the *Apollo* days, and heard the few unvarnished truth about *Challenger*. In his heart, he could let go.

154

Chapter 17

Marco never tired of the party when he was high. His foster parents were strict, they didn't drink, and they made he and Shannon go to church.

Marco hated every second of church. Mostly he hated the music. His only memory of his dad was of his dad playing the bass. His dad was a musician as well as a drug addict. His dad often talked about music and how it was transformative. Marco remembered that about this dad and little else. He knew his dad loved Miles Davis, Charles Mingus, Count Basie, and Charlie Parker. His dad was smart, but he was indulgent and weak. Music was a drug, and drugs were his drugs, and nothing about kids made music or drugs better and so he just wasn't interested in them. He also loved sex, when he wasn't too high, and he found out that many women, mostly white women, loved to have sex with black musicians as well as get high with them. So, Marco's dad took maximum advantage of that. Marco knew of three that ended up pregnant, but his dad didn't accept paternity of two of them and refused to have anything to do with the kids.

Marco's mom, however, happened to be with him during a period when he was too sick to fuck other women, so he had accepted for a time that he was Marcos's dad and so for seven years, he acted like Marcos' dad, and in this period, Marco developed the only memories he had of his parents. And, in addition to 'black music' as he called it, his dad loved to do drugs, any drugs, but especially coke.

When Marco first tried coke, he knew he would like it, he wanted to like it, and he did. It allowed him to have something in common with his dad. It was Jack who had opened the doorway to coke, which was a door where his dad stood, ready to get high and talk black music. Marco charged through.

Marco grinded his teeth and groping one of the Latin girls when the trailer door opened, and Michael King entered with three enormous black cowboys right behind him. Marco knew who Michael was, but Michael didn't know who Marco was, so he didn't even see Marco standing there. Marco knew what would happen next without any deliberation. He knew Jack was blind to Michael King's true nature, in part because Shannon knew Michael King. Michael had grabbed one of Shannon's breasts when they were in sixth grade. Marco was afraid of Michael King.

The three men with Michael wore biker vests covered in patches. Across the back was a skull and beneath, in block letters, the vests read 'Black Satans.' Even Marco, as high as he was, saw the biker vests to be more than just trouble. This was deadly trouble. These men killed and disposed of bodies.

Marco saw Miggie nod towards the back bedroom. Michael and the black cowboys headed that way. As Marco pulled on his jacket, he wondered if he'd ever see Jack again.

* * *

In the tiny trailer bedroom, Jack was putting away baggies of coke. He had $1500 dollars in his pocket, and he knew Marco should have at least about $700, but there was still a lot of coke in the backpack they had to sell. They had sold plenty but had only managed to turn about a quarter of it into cash.

Just as he was about to lift the backpack onto his back, the door flew open. Jack saw Michael's friendly smile, but right behind him, he saw himself in the mirrored glasses worn by the behemoth that followed.

Michael stepped sideways and the three black cowboys entered, forming a black wall in front of the door.

"Jackie Buckhorn, my man!" Michael said.

Jack had known Michael for a long time, and so he knew what a sincere greeting sounded like. This was not that. He looked past Michael at the nearly identical black cowboys in front of him. They were the same size, wore the same jeans and vests, wore similar sunglasses. Only one was wearing a starched white cowboy hat. All had their stone eyes hidden under identical sunglasses.

"'Sup?" Jack managed.

"My homies here need a hook up, man," Michael said. "How much you got in that backpack?"

"I have a little left," Jack said. He knew all of this was foreplay. "Sell it by the 8 ball."

"How much you got, man?" Michael asked again.

156

"How much you want?" Jack said, and he regretted these words as soon as they left his mouth.

"We want it all, motherfucker," the closest cowboy said. "And we want your skinny white ass out of here."

The smile still hadn't left Michael's face.

"This is what…your territory?" Jack asked. He stopped looking at Michael.

"Yeah, you could say that. Wherever we are is our fucking territory," the black cowboy sneered.

Jack instinctively reached for the backpack and in a flash, the two other black cowboys had pistols in their hands.

"Whoa, okay," Jack said as he pulled his hands back.

"Keep your motherfucking hands out," the cowboy said.

"I don't have a gun," Jack said, and again regretted it as soon as he spoke.

"What kind of drug dealer doesn't have a gun?" the lead black cowboy with the hat said. "Now, listen up. We going to give you $100 for that motherfucking backpack and you're going to get the fuck up out of here."

Jack's mind spun quickly. This was a potential death sentence either way. Michael held out a crisp C-note and waved it back and forth to get Jack's attention.

"I can't take $100 for all this coke," Jack said. He decided right then and there that the death that might come from Karlotta was further away than the death that might come in the next few seconds. "The people I got it from will kill me. Then they'll come for you."

"A gun would be useful right now, wouldn't it? And a crew," the black cowboy said. "You ain't cut out to be no drug dealer, white boy. And the people who gave you the drugs need to rethink their distribution network. Get some motherfucking professionals. You don't make a quality product and hand it off to no toddlers. They ain't going to do shit except cry and shut the fuck up. Now get that $100 and get the fuck going before we take whatever money you already collected and bury your sorry ass under that motherfucking rodeo ring."

In his mind, Jack ticked a moral box; he had warned them. They assumed whoever had provided the drugs was foolish, and not so awash in coke that they could afford to take distribution risks. The big man in front of him was dead wrong. Jack decided it was neither his job nor his obligation to point that out any further. They were going to pay. He knew it; he just didn't know how much *he* would have to pay. He feared that all would pay in the end, as Lissie had.

Jack snatched the $100 from Michael.

"Thanks, friend," Jack said, finally leveling a gaze on Michael. "I know where you live."

"You don't know shit, cracker!" Michael said, amping up the black on a dime. "And that's my $100, homey. They would have just shot yo sorry ass."

It was Michael that Jack felt real anger towards. He knew that if he had a chance and a choice, it would be Michael that would pay.

But now, he had $100, the $1500 in his pocket which they hadn't taken, whatever Marco had, and he wasn't bleeding out in Miggie's trailer. He slid between the big cowboys and left, leaving the dead man's backpack on the bed.

Jack walked into the party in the front room, where all eyes were on him. He suspected Miggie had set him up as well.

"Where's Marco?" he asked.

"He left you, homes," Miggie said, looking right into Jack's eyes. Miggie was an old, broken down, alcoholic drug-addled rodeo clown, and Jack decided then and there that his days of association with derelict old people had just ended.

Jack left the trailer, alive, and changed. Nothing that had happened before had changed him quite like the past two minutes. He knew that he would do whatever was required to survive the last step in this drama and then he would be free.

The walk back to the truck was refreshing. He felt great. The drugs were no longer under his control and therefore, no longer his responsibility. The weather was beautiful. He could smell the cotton candy coming from the carnival. The lights made the low clouds glow green. He was alive and it felt fantastic.

Marco was already sitting in the bed of the truck when Jack arrived. Jack said nothing, fired up the truck, and headed for home.

He stopped for gas in San Antonio. Marco went into the gas station, bought some beer, went to the bathroom and got back in the bed of the truck again without speaking. Jack bought a map of Texas in the station and tore off a piece of it. Using the cashier's pen, he wrote a note to Domingo that read *"The drugs were stolen by other dealers. Marco has the money for what we sold. I'm done, stay away from me."*

When he reached Deer Park, Jack stopped in front of Marco's house. As Marco stood on stiff legs to get out of the bed of the truck, Jack pulled out the cash he had and held it out.

"I'm sending him a note about the drugs. I'm going to tell him you have what cash we took in," Jack said.

"I don't want it," Marco said.

Jack leaned forward and stuffed the cash into Marco's front pocket.

"I don't give two shits what you want," Jack said. "Spend it or throw it away, but I'm telling him you have it, and then I'm out of business. Forever."

With that, Jack walked around the side of Domingo's house and up to the back door. It was early morning. Jack slid the door open and tucked the note in as he slid the door closed again. Domingo couldn't miss it.

When he came back around to the front of the house, Marco was gone. Jack looked down the street at the house that was his home. He was going there and going to bed. The sun was coming up and everything looked beautiful. He was finished with Marco and Domingo, come what may. The mistakes he'd made were in the past and the consequences were in the future. As far as Jack was concerned, it wasn't just the backpack that had been left behind. With any luck he'd never hear about any of it ever again.

Chapter 18

A track competition is unlike other sporting events with a central focus. The entire meet plays out like a process with events occurring across the field at various times which tend to slip as the day wears on. The athletes score as a team but perform as individuals. A team can't win with one star but can win with a few above average standouts. Getting the right performers at the right events is key. Coaching is largely finished by Meet Day; the athletes are on their own. They meet, perform, calculate, and depart.

The Deer Park track team was well-managed with coaches yelling now and again but mostly, they relied on the team stars to keep the other team members focused and in the right place at the right time. What the school didn't know is that Coach Wilson paid the standouts, and they were paid both for doing the job and not talking about it. They paid Lisa double the normal rate of $100 per meet because she kept her teammates in line and she could coach them, manage her events, and she never lost her place or her cool. Lisa was a natural born leader and a track star, and she seemed to be able to know where she was all the time. She knew as much as the coaches in every event, even the ones dominated by the men. Lisa was a standout. She was indispensable and the coaches knew it.

The coaches worried when they saw her interest in Jennifer. Because they thought Jennifer was a cold and sexually immature little bitch, they figured Lisa's attentions would go unreturned, but they had been proven wrong. As far as they could tell, Jennifer and Lisa were an item, and they saw the commitment in Jennifer they had never seen. They credited this entirely to Lisa and sex.

The ride to Clear Lake High School was short and mostly uneventful. The boys sat on the right and the girls on the left, and no one had to be told where to sit, or why. Lisa sat in the back, and everyone knew it. She chose who sat next to her, and it was Jennifer. Jennifer knew sitting in Lisa's back seat would not go unnoticed. She sat next to Lisa on the trip down Red Bluff Road, and she looked out at the farmland passing by. Lisa was napping and had leaned her head on Jennifer. Jennifer watched David, who sat in front. He combed out his long hair and seemed to be constantly rearranging his giant gym bag.

She hoped to catch him looking at her, but he didn't. He was talking to his friend James Miller the whole time, and then James went to sleep as well.

Vonda sat in front of Jennifer, and she had the window down. Chilly air streamed in, and Jennifer was cold, but she said nothing. The cold made the strong whiff of the black hair care products that Vonda used less powerful. When the weather was hot, the smell of Vonda's hair would permeate the whole bus.

Finally, when she knew they were close, Jennifer closed her eyes. She had been to Clear Lake High School many times and knew they had a nice stadium. They were close to NASA and the NASA staff lived in the area. The engineers and aeronautical parents made sure the school had the best of everything. She wondered why her family didn't live in the Clear Lake area, since her dad had worked at NASA. She knew her dad had gone to Deer Park High School, but she also knew he didn't care about the area. He had said so. There was no legacy in Deer Park, just familiarity.

She also wasn't sure how her dad felt about their house. He had done a few home improvement projects over the years, mostly shelves and things her mother wanted, like an organizing system in the pantry and more storage in the garage. Still, the house and the town were not a source of pride or sense of place for anyone in her family. Jack was all about the rodeo, but there were rodeos in Oklahoma and Kansas. The only place her mom hated more than Houston was 'backwards' Mexico. Josie barely knew where he was because he'd never been anywhere else. She had no specific connection to anywhere either. Why did they live where they did? She couldn't say. Her dad should have known, but he probably didn't. She didn't know if they were 'Texas' people or not, but she suspected they were. She intended to find out one day. She knew Farrah Fawcett was a Texan, but that Madonna was not. She liked the idea that 'Texas women' were powerful but she didn't like the idea that they were beneath the cultural power of the men.

When the bus stopped, she opened her eyes. She nudged Lisa. She watched David get off the bus, and in the distance, she saw Clear Lake's beautiful stadium.

* * *

The next two hours were the ones Jennifer disliked the most. There was a lot of pointless waiting around, coaches talking with each other in small huddles, and preparation of the field that should have been done the day before. Lisa was busy, but she hovered around Jennifer whenever she could and made a point of touching her over and over, on the arm, on the hair, on the thigh.

But eventually, they were given ten minutes to dress for the next series of events, and the hurdles were up soon. Jennifer stripped off her tracksuit and slipped on her uncomfortable sports bra. She made sure that she changed her bra when Lisa was occupied.

The next period passed quickly since Jennifer was not thinking of anything but hurdles. The boys' event began, but Jennifer just stretched as she watched the hurdles being put into place. She was unaware of the cheering that came from the stands, until Lisa brought attention to it.

"I'm so glad my mom doesn't give a shit about track," Lisa spat out. Lisa rarely said anything about her parents but every comment she made was negative. She made mention of how annoyingly Jewish they were, and how they 'didn't accept' that she was a lesbian. She hated the food they ate, their friends, their decorating tastes, the books they read, and she spoke often about how ugly their feet were and how their feet made her gag. She said she had to go into her parents' bathroom to get tampons from her mother's inventory and it was always a sickening chore where she would see something that would gross her out. But it was hard for Jennifer to tell what any of this meant because Lisa's comments were usually scant on details.

Nevertheless, Jennifer was silent for a different reason when Lisa spat out her last disdain. She knew her mom didn't care either, and she didn't care about football, rodeo, or even soccer. Jennifer thought about what her mom cared about, and it took her a moment to fill in some boxes. Her mother cared about the environment, natural or organic food, and maybe a few other things. She thought about her mother as she was pushing her feet into the blocks. She had no idea what her mother's feet looked like. She couldn't name a book her mother read even though it seemed like she was talking about books all the time. Her mother cared about her; she knew that for sure. She cared that Jennifer 'had her own power' as she had said many times.

Her mother loved in an abstract way. Her mother loved her as a daughter, and as a female, but Jennifer was unsure if her mother had any feelings about her as an individual. She knew her mother didn't like Madonna and did little to help Jennifer cultivate that aesthetic. Her mother wore no crosses, and she chose clothes that were not form-fitting. She put tampons in Jennifer's bathroom, and they never discussed Jennifer's periods again after an initial conversation.

But then Jennifer thought about her dad and his love. From her dad, she felt adored. She thought he viewed her as a perfect being, and he had no comment on any effort she needed to make to improve or educate herself. She had always felt this way about her dad. His love was different. It was as if it wasn't even coming from him. It was there, without any qualifications. For a moment, she wondered if he had felt that way about her mother at one point. She knew her mother no longer loved him, and she knew, in an unformed way, that his rection to the withdrawal of her love harmed him. She knew she couldn't and shouldn't seek to replace any of that love and that if she did her dad would know better than to try to accept it.

But now, it was time for the hurdles.

Since Jennifer was in the inside lane, Lisa could lean in and speak just to her. Lisa spoke in a calm, almost whispering, cadence with perfect diction and confidence. It was welcome and helpful. Lisa was a wonderful coach; the best Jennifer had ever known.

"Okay, champ," she said pleasantly. "Nice and smooth, okay, just like you trained. There's only you on this track. Just you, baby. Just you. No one else. No one else counts."

Jennifer nodded and pulled back into herself. The other runners took their marks in her peripheral vision, but she only noted it calmly. They didn't matter. They were ghosts now.

There was a moment of PA squeal and then she heard the announcer say "Runners, take your marks."

Lisa ran across to take a position at the finish line. Coach Wilson was there with a few of the other team coaches and a collection of students.

Jennifer put her hands on the track, raised her butt in the air, and waited. A drop of sweat dripped off her nose and hit the track. Everything was silent. She only heard her own breath. Now, there was nothing; just her and 300 meters of track and hurdles.

At the gun, she popped up out of the blocks and started churning. Her long lean front leg swept ahead, and she devoured the first hurdle. It was like it wasn't there or wasn't made of matter. Before she could think, her legs had swept over the next hurdle. The space in between the jumps passed in milliseconds with no thought. Her legs did all the work. She only felt her arms and the delicious pain of her fingernails digging into her own palms.

The turn came but it didn't matter. She moved into a deep rhythm. It was the same but at a slight angle, which almost made it easier. In an instant, she felt something like love. She was thankful for this moment and her own powerful body. The hurdles were objects she flew over on the way to somewhere fantastic, somewhere meaningful.

In the final few steps, she realized she was going to win. She saw no one in her peripheral vision, and she knew she had not touched a single hurdle. At the finish line, she saw Lisa stepping onto the track with both hands raised. She leaned into the finish as she had been told hundreds of times and she imagined the photo of herself there.

Before she had taken six steps after the finish line, Lisa was hugging her and lifting her off the ground.

"You did it! You did it! You did it!" Lisa chanted.

Jennifer smiled. For a moment she wished her father was there. She was a winner.

While she was thinking about this, Lisa kissed her on the lips. It was brief, the brush of lips was less than a second, but it was unmistakable. With everyone watching the winner, Lisa claimed Jennifer as her own with a kiss. Jennifer had a moment, one that seemed longer than it was, to choose a reaction and she did; she smiled and let it pass. The price for the kiss and the reward in attention and discussion was such that she knew not to recoil or push Lisa away. Of course, Lisa, seeing this reaction, grabbed Jennifer around the waist and lifted her back up. After a brief, triumphant moment, she put Jennifer down and then walked to Coach Wilson with Lisa's arm draped over Jennifer's shoulder.

"We knew you'd go do it, killer," Coach Wilson said, and then turned and headed for the other side of the track.

* * *

For the next quarter of an hour, Lisa did not leave Jennifer's side. Their teammates came and went, each offering their own form of congratulations. Jennifer smiled until her cheeks hurt. The kiss was clearly on everyone's mind, and she rightfully thought that it had spread and easily surpassed her hurdles victory as the source of conversation. She knew what it was doing, but she also knew that the hurdles were what had really freed her. The physical thrill had been there for her all along, though she hadn't taken advantage of it. Now, she knew there was a place she could go on her own with her body and mind that no one could touch. If Lisa wanted to cling to that place for a moment, she was fine with that, but she also knew it was all hers. Lisa had enabled it, but it was still hers.

Lisa finally had to leave Jennifer's side to run the final leg of the 400-meter relay. Deer Park was winning the meet, but the relay was still a culminating event, and it held prestige, at least to the runners. It was the only true team event, and they needed the points to clinch the team victory.

Jennifer had pulled her track pants and team jersey over her shorts and t-shirt, and she stood near the finish line for the event. After Lisa left her side, she detected a distinct lack of her teammates coming near her and she wondered if they viewed her as belonging to Lisa now.

The 400 meters was Lisa's favorite event. She ran the anchor leg and there were never any other events going on during the team relays. She would cross in the eye glare of every coach, referee, and player and she usually came in first. As the anchor, she was the last one to take the baton and so it was like she got in the final word, and she liked that. She liked it a lot.

Jennifer stood with the other girls, when suddenly, David Wingate appeared beside her. His long hair hung down the side of his head and covered much of his face. She glanced up and saw his profile.

"Congratulations on the hurdles," he said without looking at her.

165

"Thank you," she said, also not looking his way. She knew mentioning the hurdles first was a way of saying he knew all about the kiss.

"Runners take your marks," came over the address system.

The first runners took to the blocks and nearly everyone, except a few parents in the stands, grew quiet. Lisa was at her spot at the top of the first turn.

The race began with Celia, the Deer Park runner, strong out of the blocks and easily ahead.

David watched the runners without comment, but Jennifer glanced at him as his head turned with the runners. He had fair skin and a faint line of acne along his forehead. His hair was dirty blond and tussled, and he had his hands in the pocket of his jacket.

The first girls reached the transfer box marked in blue lines. The second girls ran up to speed and reached their hands back for the transfer. Celia handed the silver baton off to Vonda, who, even injured, was faster than most girls. She was 25 pounds heavier, but still faster.

Jennifer watched the race intently, but she could feel his gaze upon her neck. The hair on her arms stiffened.

The second handoff went perfectly. Vonda reached the blue transfer zone and gave the baton to Marie. Marie was thinner than the other girls, but still fast.

Lisa took a couple of jumps in place and then came out of the transfer box. In a few seconds, the baton would be hers. The finish was her job. Marie turned the corner and lifted her head up in a final effort. As she came near, Lisa started to run and then she hit speed in the middle of the blue box. Her hand went back, and Marie smacked the baton tightly into her palm. Lisa's hand closed on the baton and then she let her legs go.

"I'm having a party tonight at my house," David said nonchalantly as Lisa came to the final steps of the race and then crossed the finish line a full two seconds before the next runner. "Parents are gone. Lots of private spaces. I hope you come."

Jennifer looked up and saw his smile as he turned and walked away. She knew the timing was entirely deliberate.

* * *

The bus back to Deer Park was loud and half of the kids were standing in the aisles. The coaches sat up front talking to each other, and the boys roamed up and down the aisles stopping to talk to the girls. It was already a party. The coaches had decided not to enforce any of the normal bus rules for the ride home.

Jennifer and Lisa sat in the back seat. Jennifer wore a thick medal around her neck. Lisa had one as well. Lisa was jubilant, chatty, and dominant with all the team, including the boys. She ran up and down the aisle talking and challenging people to different contests and she got into many good-natured disputes. The coaches had suspended the language rule as well so Lisa could yell, "Hey, go fuck yourself!" and laugh with impunity. Then she'd sit back down and try to hold Jennifer's hand. She leaned over to whisper to her every few minutes as well.

When it had quieted down and most of the boys had gone back to their seats, Lisa leaned close to whisper again.

"What did he say to you?" she asked.

"Who?" Jennifer asked though she knew.

"Your boyfriend, okay, jeez," Lisa teased, in a kind of solemn way.

"If you mean David, I've already addressed the boyfriend thing, and if you must know, he told me about the party," she said. She whisked a finger under Lisa's chin. "You love calling him my boyfriend, don't you?

"You going to go?" Lisa asked. Her question was pregnant with anticipation of a whole variety of feelings.

"Of course," Jennifer said. "The whole team is going. I'm sure you're going."

"You want to go together?" Lisa said. "I can wait at the school for you to go home and change."

"You aren't changing?" Jennifer asked?

"I keep clothes at the school," Lisa said.

Jennifer thought the evening over. She knew Lisa had another agenda, which was clear, but she could only speculate what might be in David Wingate's mind.

"I'll meet you there," Jennifer said, and then she watched carefully for the reaction. It was there instantly; Lisa frowned and then got up. She knew what meeting there meant, or at least she thought she did. Jennifer was putting the party on an equal footing. She was her own agent. Tonight, Lisa thought the competition would be decided. She walked up the aisle a few seats and sat down to talk to Vonda. Jennifer turned to look out the window into the darkness, but on the horizon, she could see downtown.

Chapter 19

Jack woke with a start. He had been dreaming, and the dream was not good. He tried to remember what his dream was about, but he couldn't call it back. It was more of a dream about a feeling, and the feeling was doom. It was a dream about being trapped, about facing the consequence of a series of bad decisions. It was a dream about fear, but also it was a dream about inevitability.

But wait, why did he wake? Did he just hear a siren or bell or something? He tried to drive the fog of sleep from his mind and decide if he really had, in this life, heard a bell.

He heard voices in the house, and they were getting louder. It was his mom's voice, and she was raising her voice at something. Suddenly, his door opened. He sat up, in fear, but it was Josie.

"Someone at the door for you, loser," Josie said and turned away.

Jack suddenly came fully awake. No one had come to his door in years.

"Who is it?" he called to Josie.

"Guess you got to get up to see. It's 5 o'clock," Josie called back.

Jack laid back down for a moment. Nothing good was about to happen, and he knew it, but he also knew there was nothing he could do about it. All he could do now was try to keep it away from his family.

Jack came downstairs and saw that Bob had vomited on the living room floor and Carol stood over him.

"Go ahead! Why don't you get down on the floor and roll around in it," she said.

"Why don't you get stuffed," Jack heard his father moan in return. "I'm sick! Can't you see that?"

"'I'm sick! I'm sick, can't you see that?'" she mocked. "I'm sick too; sick of your not working and getting drunk all day."

Jack observed the scene and then went to the door. He opened it just enough to see out; it was Marco. Jack opened the door the rest of the way.

"Domingo wants to see you," Marco said abruptly and turned away.

"How do you even know?" Jack called out.

Marso spoke over his shoulder as he walked away. He didn't want to interact.

"He called me over to his front door and told me," Marco said.

Jack watched Marco walk back to his house, hoping to detect something in his body language. There was nothing but, still, something. Maybe it was good, he thought, and Domingo was going to tell him the issues had been resolved. Maybe he just wanted to know who stole the drugs.

He turned and saw his father holding his head in his hands. Josie was watching the whole scene from the middle of the stairs. This family was coming apart, and it was his job, Jack knew in that instant, to keep them from all getting killed. He couldn't ignore Domingo; that seemed like the most dangerous path.

"Mom," he said, "he sick. Just help him."

"I don't need help," Bob said as he pulled himself up. "And I'm not drunk. I haven't had a drink in three days. That's the longest I've gone in four decades. These are called DTs. Detox. I'll be fine. And I don't want her help."

Jack hesitated but headed back up the stairs.

"You shouldn't watch this," he said as he passed Josie.

* * *

A few minutes later, Jack jumped the fence and landed in Domingo's backyard. In the distance, he heard dogs barking and he noticed the damp. Dampness was so prevalent in Houston that it was generally not worth noting but this was different. He felt a cold hand on his throat, but he knew there was no turning back. As he walked across Domingo's pine straw cover backyard, he thought about what would come of the family if his dad died, and then he was killed. What would Jennifer and Josie do with their lives?

He walked up to the sliding glass door and looked in. Domingo was standing in the kitchen with some sort of rag held to his head. He saw Jack and motioned for him to enter. Jack slid open the door.

As soon as he entered, Jack sensed the bad mojo in the room. The air was filled with nervous tension and an acrid ammonia smell of fear. Domingo was holding a dish towel wrapped around ice to his swollen eyebrow. Before he could ask any questions, Jack saw how it all went down; there were two big, brutal looking men in the room, and they were pressed against the wall so they couldn't be seen from outside.

One of these men was thick and large with red hair. He had all the looks of being Mexican except for his red hair and ice blue eyes. He was wearing a dress shirt and black slacks. If he had a coat and tie, he could have been a banker.

The other man was thinner and taller with dark eyes, like a shark. His hair was slicked back, and his eyebrows grew together. He was wearing a tracksuit.

"Sit down," the red headed one said to Jack.

As instructed, Jack sat gingerly at the dining room table. The two men circled around him. The red-headed one sat down in front of Jack and the other took a position behind him. Jack glanced over his shoulder at the man in the track suit but said nothing.

The red head laid a shiny 9mm pistol on the table for Jack to see. It sat between them, like another person. It was black with a clip that extended beyond the handle. His dad has one just like it, so Jack knew he was looking at a clip that held fifteen rounds.

Against his will, Jack turned his head the other way and looked over to Domingo, who watched without a word.

"Hey! Don't look at him," the red head said as he pounded a palm on the table. "He's not the one with the problem, puto; you are."

Jack looked at the man and gave away nothing. Finally, the reckoning had started, and in some deep part of himself, Jack was glad. He could stop thinking about it now.

"Me and my friend, we get sent to shoot stupid Americans who use the fucking drugs they're supposed to sell. Drug dealers like drugs," he said, and then he watched Jack for a reaction. There was none.

"But now," he continued, "we find you because pendejo says you take the drugs around like its Reese's peanut butter chips and some other drug dealers take it from you, and you let them. You give the fucking drugs to other dealers!"

Another pause. Jack knew there were no good reactions, at least not yet.

"They are your friends? Huh? You deal with them now," Red asked.

"I had never seen them before, except one of them," Jack said, level as he could be. "Not my friends. They were armed. They stole the drugs. I didn't give it to them."

"You go with all those drugs, and you got all the cash, but you got nothing but your dick with you," the red head said, less as a question than a statement.

"I was never given that much to sell," Jack said. At this point, the truth was still the best option. "Normally, I just had a few baggies in my pocket. I sold it to my friends. I didn't need a gun."

The red head cut a look at Domingo, then back to Jack.

"You know who we work for," he asked.

"No, but I guess it's Karlotta," Jack said.

"Karlotta! She's a little fish," Red said. "We work with big guys. Big dicks, big money, big guns."

"You shouldn't be working with me," Jack said. "I never asked for more. Karlotta said she was going to cut him out and deal with us. We didn't want it."

The red head laughed.

"You take the drugs, stupid, you take the responsibility," he said. "You're going to help us get those drugs, maybe you don't get hurt so bad. We let your family live."

Jack flashed anger for a moment, but then put it down.

"My family doesn't know anything, and can't help you," he said. "I'll help you as much as I can. Leave them out of it."

"We get the drugs, they never know about anything," Red said. "But you fuck us, we go straight to your house and kill everyone. Everyone. Old people, babies, dogs, gatos. We don't give a fuck."

"Ok, well, first…" Jack looked at Fernando. "What are your names? Not your real names, I don't care. What do I call you?"

"My friends call me Ivan," the red headed one said. "You call him Fernando."

"Ivan and Fernando," Jack repeated. It comforted him to know their names. "Look, I was doing my job, but it was a lot of coke. I was at a rodeo, and three big men, big black guys, they came in with another guy I knew, and they took the backpack with the drugs. They would have shot me, and still taken the drugs. There was nothing I could do, even if I had a gun."

"You know one of these niggars?" Ivan asked. "The names?"

"I know one of them," Jack said. "Michael King. He was a friend of mine. We rodeoed together in high school."

"This is your fucking friend?" Ivan asked.

"I thought so," Jack said.

"You know where he is?" Ivan continued.

"I know where he used to live," Jack said. A knot developed in his stomach. He knew where Michael's family lived, all of them. He knew the next demand would be to lead these two killers there. But fuck it, Michael's family or his.

Ivan glanced over at Domingo and then at Fernando. Then he stood. He said something to Domingo in Spanish and Domingo nodded.

"Let's go, pendejo," he said to Jack. "We come to clean up your mistakes. You hope your friend is there."

* * *

Ivan led Jack out of the front door of the house. This was the first time Jack had ever seen the front of Domingo's house, and he saw the empty front rooms. They went out of the front door and got into the Ford Bronco at the curb. Ivan told Jack to get in the passenger seat, and Fernando got in behind him. Jack looked at Marco's house and then down to his own to see if anyone was there to witness him leaving. There was no one.

Once in the Bronco, Jack directed Ivan to Michael's house which was just a few blocks south. Michael had lived in that neighborhood since Jack met him in first grade. He had not liked Michael then because Michael was loud. He thought that Michael was always eating something and yelling, which may or may not have been true. When he was in elementary school, he wanted to touch Michael's kinky hair but dared not ask.

It wasn't until middle school that they ever spoke to each other. They often sat together on the bus and played cards. Jack taught Michael how to play poker and he wanted to place a bet so he could take Michael's lunch money. But Michael didn't have any money to stake on a bet.

When both boys reached high school, they played on the same sports teams, where they became uneasy friends. Michael wanted to dominate everything he did, and Jack did as well. They were often pitted against each other by the coaches. In the football games, they worked well together. Michael was a running back and he was fast. Jack was a fullback, and he was strong. Michael would get the ball on the first down and Jack would get it on the third. Michael would get a few yards, and then Jack would get the first down.

They had to block for each other in those days. Michael was a good teammate in Jack's estimation. Jack threw himself at the linemen who would try to catch Michael's feet or jersey as he rounded the corner, and it usually worked. If Michael was going down, it wasn't because Jack missed a block. Michael didn't block as well for Jack, mostly because he just wasn't a good blocker, but he didn't have to be. The defensive players would focus on Michael even when Jack had the ball and in the half second it took for them to realize Michael didn't have the ball, Jack could get two steps forward. Michael was particularly good at faking the hand off, and it was enough.

But then both boys started to rodeo. It was here that Jack had the advantage. He was stronger, and he could handle a rope better. Jack started going to camps to learn more, and Michael had no advantage. Michael had an uncle who was a rodeo cowboy, but he lived in Huntsville and Michael couldn't get up there much. Plus, his uncle wouldn't help him. His uncle had been in jail, and he was bitter. He learned to rodeo in prison, and he did it outside of prison for money. He didn't want Michael to rodeo or be in the country or have anything to do with white people. Michael's mom convinced him to help Michael but only a couple of times.

Still, no matter how many games they played together, or how many rodeos they went to, Jack and Michael could not become close friends. Jack thought Michael was slick and a show boater. Michael relied on his long frame and natural athletic ability, and he made excuses for anything he didn't get. His coaches said the same thing about him. Jack worked harder, and he didn't blame his teammates for anything. Michael thought Jack was another kid from a rich white family that should stay out of his way. Michael King had bullet proof confidence in everything he did, and nothing could shake it.

But all the history between the two of them was about to change permanently. Michael should have known it was coming. The day of reckoning was at hand. Jack held Michael's life in his hands, and he was going to throw it over to save himself.

"Turn here. It's the second house on the left," Jack said.

Ivan turned and then came to a stop. Small houses were lined up a tidy row all the way down the street. There were kids running in different directions. A car drove by as Ivan watched the kids, people, cars, and houses.

After a couple of minutes, Ivan looked over his shoulder at Fernando, and then he opened the driver's side door.

"Don't run," Ivan said to Jack. "We catch you with a bullet."

Ivan and Fernando walked towards Michael's house. The two men seemed to move without anyone noticing even though they were the only two men in sight who weren't black. They walked quickly without looking like they were running or rushing. Nothing they did drew attention.

Jack watched as Ivan stepped up to the front porch of the house, looked around, and then drew the Glock. Fernando put his hand to his waistband. Ivan tried the front door, and it was unlocked. Both men entered the home and closed the door.

Time passed slowly. Jack looked around at the kids playing outside on both sides of the street. These little kids were Michael a few years earlier. Down the block, he saw a woman raking leaves as a man across the street mowed his yard. The sound of the lawnmower worked its way down the street.

Another car passed and Jack heard music coming out of the window. It was all so normal, but Jack knew something not normal was happening just a few yards from all of them. Something was happening that they would all come to know about and remember.

Jack heard a muffled thump. No one else noticed. Jack watched to see if anyone lifted their head. Nothing. No one varied their routine.

Then, there are three more thumps in quick succession. Jack felt his heart pumping wildly. He took a big breath and tried to calm himself. A couple of the kids stopped what they were doing and looked towards Michael's house. They had heard the unusual noise, but they didn't know exactly where it came from, and the lawnmower sound confused everyone's sense of the direction of the thumps.

The three kids convened. One pointed towards Michael's house. They heard it.

"Good," Jack whispered under his breath. Someone would know.

Suddenly, with the kids looking on, Ivan exited the house. Fernando was right behind him. Two of the kids went back to what they were doing, but one, a girl, watched the two men walk down the block. It was weird that no one else noticed them, and no one seemed concerned.

Ivan and Fernando climbed back into the Bronco. Jack just looked at the floorboards. He could feel his life getting shorter.

"Your friend is in Galveston at a rodeo," Ivan said.

He started the car.

"Who told you?" Jack asked.

"His sister," Ivan said without comment or emotion. "Which way to Galveston?"

Jack looked out the window; he knew Michael's sister. She was a nice girl, never in trouble, inside most of the time. Her mother was disabled, so she would surely have been there as well. Only Michael's dad, who was in prison, would still be alive once everything was done. Jack thought back to the first coke he had ever done with Michael. In some macabre way, events were coming full circle.

"Go straight," Jack said. Ivan pulled forward and Jack watched as the little girl who had been watching them turned and ran into her house as fast as she could.

Chapter 20

Jennifer arrived home to find the house mostly dark. Her mother's car wasn't there so she knew her mom was out somewhere.

At the top of the stairs, she saw light coming from Josie's room.

"Where's everybody?" she asked Josie. He was watching a tiny TV and had his feet propped up on the dresser. He sat up when he saw her.

"Dad's asleep, I think, and Mom's probably with that big dork she hangs out with," Josie said. "They got in a big fight, and she left."

"What dork?" Jennifer asked.

"You haven't met Dave? He's some guy she's talking to that's going on some march or something," Josie said.

"What was the fight about?" she asked.

"Dad got sick and threw up and she was yelling at him about it," Josie said. "She says it was because he was drunk, but he said he wasn't drinking. He quit."

Jennifer nodded and started to retreat.

"Hey, want to watch Cosby with me?" he asked.

In a short window of clarity, Jennifer saw Josie for the first time in a long time. Dad was sick, mom was gone, Jack was probably in trouble. Josie had no one.

"Sure, when I get home," she said with a smile that sent a tiny jolt through his stomach. "I have to go to a track party."

He looked back at the TV and so she entered the room and put her hand on his shoulder.

"I won the hurdles today," she said. "I beat every other girl, and we won the overall."

Josie smiled.

"You beat those Clear Lake bitches?" he asked.

"Beat the track shorts off those miserable cunts," Jennifer said.

Josie's smile faded a bit.

"You going to see that lesbo girl tonight?" he asked.

She started to get mad but didn't.

"Yes, she's on the team," Jennifer said as she sat on his bed. "She'll be there. And all the boys."

"If Jack was here, he'd threaten to beat up all of them," Josie observed.

177

"Jack's not here. Will you beat up someone for me if I need you to?" she asked coyly.

Josie knew this was a rare soft opening from her.

"I might take a beating instead of giving one out, but I'd try," he said.

"I know you would, kid," she said as she stood. She leaned down and kissed him on the forehead. "You're just as good as Jack, Josie. In a lot of ways, you're better."

He looked down at the floor. He didn't feel as good as Jack.

* * *

Jennifer went to her room and undressed completely. She looked at her nude body in the mirror and flexed her leg muscles. They made her happy. She turned on her shower and took a tiny pair of scissors to her pubic hair as she waited for the water to warm. There was the chance someone would see down there tonight, and she wanted to be prepared. She took a razor out of her drawer and then took it into the shower with her. She washed her hair and shaved her legs while the conditioner was setting. She shaved her trimmed pubic hair into a upside down pyramid. She had read once that Madonna went to a waxing salon, but she didn't know anywhere in Houston that waxed.

But as she thought about the waxing, she thought about all the things she had not tried. She thought about sex constantly, and she tried for a moment to think of all the things she could let Lisa do that would feel good but that wouldn't expose her to the risks she associated with sex with a boy. She could let Lisa touch her all over, and lick her, which she knew Lisa would do with gleeful abandon, but then she thought about Lisa, and what that would do to her. In that moment, she thought about the power her body held. Finally, she had the power. She had the golden object so many held in esteem. As she rinsed out the conditioner, she felt how much power she had, and she touched herself just to be sure the feeling really did feel like sex. She flexed her legs as she touched herself, and it was good. Even her little brother was entirely hostage now to whatever she had.

And if she had it, she wasn't going to waste it. She would care for it as well as build its reputation. She couldn't be all talk, or all show, and she certainly wasn't going to be the possession of anyone at Deer Lake High School, male or female. They could call her a 'cock tease' or 'carpet muncher' or whatever else they wanted.

After she dried her hair, she looked in the mirror and had to decide how much like Madonna she wanted to look. She started with the eye shadow, which she knew how to do perfectly. But then there was her hair, lips, cheeks, and even her neck to consider, and she thought it would be better, and faster to do the minimum there. Just the eyes were enough. She pulled on a tight bustier bra, slipped on one cross earring, pulled on a black mini skirt, and then decided to wear her converse All Stars. She looked in the mirror and was pleased. It worked; it looked effortless because it was. Finally, she pulled on a red sweatshirt with one shoulder cut out.

She stopped back at Josie's room when she was ready to go. He was laying on his bed now.

"Tell mom or dad, if you see them, that I'm at a track party," she said, leaning in the door.

"Let me see," he said.

She stepped in and spun around.

"They'll all say I'm copying Madonna no matter what I do," she said.

"Who cares what they say," he commented. "You'll be the prettiest one."

"Thank you," she said as she waved a pinky finger at him and left.

* * *

On the way to the party, Jennifer turned the radio back to 93Q. Lisa was always flipping the knobs on her radio, switching back and forth from AM to FM. Sometimes Jennifer turned the dial to KIKK, which Lisa found to be unbelievable. Jennifer had heard Shannon call KIKK 'the KKK station,' and then Lisa called it 'Kike radio' since her Jewish parents liked it, too. Lisa, of course, hated it.

"Most country and western music stars are gay," Lisa declared one day on the way to the Texas Tavern. "The men are all shits. Mark my words; that stupid twat Tammy Wynette and her 'Stand by Your Man' bullshit song will be an even bigger joke one day. Dolly Parton's probably a drug addict. Johnny Cash sucks big George Jones dick. Why do you think the men are all going to prison to do shows? They're gay."

"Oh, my God," Jennifer let out. She couldn't help but laugh at Lisa's serial exaggerations.

"I'm telling you, okay," Lisa said.

Jennifer didn't know if Lisa was joking or just trying to sell the gay to her. Lisa gave her gay magazines she'd order or bought or stolen. Jennifer didn't recall an article about gay country music stars, but she hadn't really read much in them of interest. She noticed they were mostly filled with political articles and news about AIDS. Most of the content was about gay men rather than lesbians. The gay men were hairy and horny, and it seemed to Jennifer that they were determined to make a losing war of fighting AIDS. They referred to 'when I got my diagnosis' as if they owned it. AIDS gave them a way to martyr themselves for being gay and Jennifer could see the martyr in Lisa. Jennifer had no interest in that, but she looked at every page to see what fashions the gays in New York and LA were wearing, and she liked the ads.

At 93Q they played Top 40, and they announced concerts. Jennifer had never been to a huge arena rock show, but she had heard Jack talk about them. He was going to take her to see Aerosmith, but she got the measles and had to stay home. When Jack started to rodeo, he lost interest in arena rock and her mother didn't like how the rock star men were always grabbing their crotches.

"Look at these little boys playing with their things," she said of Rod Stewart when she saw a picture of him in Cosmo grabbing his groin. One of the many reasons Jennifer refused to talk to her mother about sex any more was because her mom was such a nagging puritan about men.

* * *

They rode in silence to Galveston. Jack knew the Galveston Rodeo well and competed in it when he was in high school, but it was mostly a carnival, and the prizes were lame. The cattle show was small as no one wanted to drive down from Dallas or over from San Antonio to

180

show cattle in a tent buffeted by the wind. The whole island was sandy, and the hotels were expensive. The City of Galveston wanted to call it a rodeo, and they re-branded it the Cotton-Picking Rodeo, and they did some rodeo stuff, but mostly they wanted to make money on food and rides, and so they did the minimum cowboy stuff they could get away with. If Michael was at the Cotton-Picking Rodeo, it was to sell drugs.

One step and turn at a time, Jack directed Ivan south. They crossed the causeway over the water onto Galveston Island.

"The fuck," Ivan said. "We're going to the beach?"

"It's Galveston, which is an island," Jack said, unsure if Ivan was joking.

"This road is the only way back?" Ivan asked.

"No," Jack said, "but it's the fastest. One of the other ways has a ferry and you have to wait."

"Fucking shithole," was all Ivan had to say.

Ivan eased through the line of cars moving into the parking lot at the Cotton-Picking Rodeo. Most were trucks and all had people, kids, or dogs crammed in the bed. Windows were down and music drifted across the sand.

In the bed of the truck in front of Ivan, a group of ten teenagers yelled at friends and strangers alike. Each had a can of beer in hand. Most were boys but there were three hardy girls as well. One of the girls stood up. Her long blonde hair blew around her face as she mumbled something loudly and her friends laughed. Suddenly, she threw a beer can at another small group of teens walking across the parking lot and then she fell back down.

A big teen in the parking lot picked up the full can of beer and threw it back, but the truck full of teens moved and Ivan's Bronco took its place. The beer can bounced off the hood of the Bronco, and the teens in the truck burst out laughing.

Fernando opened the door and put a leg out. He had his hand at his waist. Ivan hissed, and Fernando climbed back in. The big teen that threw the can didn't see Fernando and walked closer to the Bronco.

"Sorry, man," he said earnestly. "I was throwing it back at my friends."

Ivan did his best to conceal his accent, and he spoke in an overly friendly manner.

"It's okay, young man. Just be careful next time, okay?" he said.

The teen picked up on the weird accent, threw a polite salute, and turned away.

"I hate this country," Ivan said. "How is this country still number one in anything?"

When they reached the gate, they could see the carnival rides that lit up the night sky. The air was thick with humidity and salt.

"Give me some money," Ivan said to Jack.

All Jack had was the $100 Michael had passed him. Ivan looked at the $100 and started to say something but didn't.

"That will be ten dollars," the parking attendant said.

Ivan handed the attendant the $100.

"Got anything smaller?" the attendant asked.

Ivan turned on his weird American manner and accent again.

"No, I'm sorry, that's all I have," he said.

The attendant counted out $80 in tens, fives and ones, and Ivan handed it to Jack.

"Don't worry, I'll pay you back," he said with a chuckle.

They drove to the parking lot and Ivan backed into a parking place near the exit.

Ivan reached into the glove box and retrieved a box of 9mm rounds. He passed a few to Fernando and reloaded his Glock. He and Fernando applied large noise suppressors to each weapon.

"Okay, pendejo," Ivan said to Jack. "You're going to find your friend and he's going to show us where these niggars are, and then we get the drugs. Then you go away. You get back home by yourself."

"You're going to shoot them?" Jack asked.

"No, we're going to let them fuck us in the ass, like you," Ivan said. He translated the exchange for Fernando, and Fernando laughed. It was the first emotion Fernando had shown.

Jack thought about the situation and how it was likely to play out. Ivan had murdered at least one person an hour before, and he and Fernando were about to kill a few more. Everything Jack did now was life and death. He thought back to Michael and the black cowboys, and then he thought about Miggie.

Jack was sure Miggie had been in on the whole thing. Miggie was a drunk and a loser, and Jack realized he'd been surrounded by losers or killers in every instance when he was selling drugs. Marco, Domingo, Miggie, Michael…they were all pathetic and he had let himself hang out with them, they had screwed him over, and now he had the power of life and death over all of them. Now he was on the side of Karlotta, Ivan, and Fernando. Only Marco had been with him, and Marco was weak and only in it for the drugs. None of them, Jack determined, were anything close to being friends. He knew, in an instant, that he had no friends, and whatever opportunity he had for friends, or even for a girlfriend, he had squandered. He knew he deserved to be where he was.

"They'll use Miggie's trailer. That's what I did," Jack said.

Ivan did not like hearing a new name.

"What the fuck is a Miggie? Nobody said anything about a fucking Miggie!" he said, his voice rising sharply.

"He's one of the rodeo clowns," Jack said. "He's just a guy that let us use his trailer."

"Chingado. Domingo didn't say nothing about a Miggie or a guy with a trailer," Ivan said as he tucked the 9mm away.

"What if they see me coming?" Jack asked. "They'll know something is up."

"We don't give a fuck what they know," Ivan said. "You just point to the guys, and we'll do the negotiations. Fucking Miggie, Chingado. Domingo, ay, mi Dios, stupid. Nothing about Miggie."

"His name is Miguel," Jack said as he stepped out of the truck.

"Then call him Miguel," Ivan said. "Jesus fuck me, Americans."

Ivan and Fernando stayed two steps behind Jack as they crossed the parking lot and then headed towards the line of trailers and campers. The wind was blowing hard, and the air was saturated with the salty smell of the beach.

As they came closer, Jack could see that the trailers were arranged as they always were, with Owen Williams's trailer first, and then Miggie's beside that, and then campers passed that. He thought for a minute that he might point out Owen and say that Owen was Miggie, but that wouldn't get the drugs back. Telling the truth was the only option.

183

When they reached the edge of Owen's trailer, Jack stopped. He heard the rodeo announcer calling rides, which meant Miggie would be at the rodeo, but the lights in the trailer were on.

Jack pointed to Miggie's trailer.

"That's it," Jack said "If they're in there, they'll be alone. Miggie will be at the rodeo right now. The lights are on, and Miggie wouldn't do that. Someone is in there."

Jack backed up a step, ready to run away from what was about to happen.

"You find out who is there," Ivan said. "Go knock."

"If they see me, they'll know something's up," Jack said. "You won't have any element of surprise."

"Puto, just do what I tell you. Go!" Ivan snapped.

Jack walked robotically to the steps of the trailer. He tried to make no sound, and he felt nothing. His actions were on autopilot, and if Ivan had told him to walk in and ask the others to come outside, he would have done it.

He knew it was Michael and the black cowboys in there because they had to be. Miggie didn't have a girlfriend or a family. Jack thought about the crossfire he was exposed to, and which way he would jump when the time came.

After Jack was on the wooden steps, Ivan positioned himself low and nearest the door hinges so that when the door opened, he wouldn't be seen. Fernando ducked down behind him.

Jack heard music inside, and it was coming from the radio. It sounded like KCOH, the black radio station in Houston. Miggie never listened to KCOH. He knew for sure; they were in there, and Miggie was in on it all along.

He thought about how long he had known Miggie, and how much free coke Miggie had taken from him.

Fuck Miggie; Jack thought. He's the one that deserved to die.

Jack knocked on the door and took a full step back so that Ivan and Fernando could fire and not hit him in the back of the head.

After a moment, Michael opened the door. A huge smile crept across his face, and he was all bright white teeth and fake charm.

"Well, if it ain't Jack Buckhorn!" Michael said. "Niggar, you got big balls to show your face here. You should turn your happy ass around."

"Hello, Michael King," Jack said loudly as he stepped back a little further. Michael read his face and gestures perfectly. Michael reached for the doorknob, but Jack kicked the door with his foot and pushed it open enough for Ivan to see Michael.

"Oh, what have you done, motherfucker..." was all Michael got out of his mouth.

Ivan fired from low and the big 9mm made a sinister chirp. The round popped Michael under the chin, blowing out the top of his head in a geyser of blood, bone, and brain. In an instant, Jack's mind snapped a shot of Michael's distorted face as a bullet passed behind it, and he saw blood spray on the door frame.

Ivan and Fernando bolted up the steps and pushed Jack through the door. He fell over the threshold and landed on the floor beside Michael's twitching body. Michael's lifeless eyes stared at the ceiling, but his face was collapsing.

Jack turned his head away and saw one of the black cowboys in the kitchen with a beer in his hand. He frantically tried to find his pistol rather than duck down. When he saw Ivan and Fernando pointing two barrels at him, he raised both hands in the air.

Fernando double tapped him in the chest and forehead. Jack saw him launch backwards and hit the tiny table he and Miggie had sat at the first time Jack ever did drugs in that trailer.

Without hesitation, Ivan and Fernando rushed down the small hallway to the bedroom in the back. Jack heard a short burst of suppressed gunfire and one loud unsuppressed shot. He hoped it was Fernando that took the answering bullet.

But he couldn't get himself to rise and run, not yet. He turned his head back to Michael and could only stare at Michael's distorted face. Michael's eyes were starting to droop shut.

Ivan returned to the room with the backpack. Jack had taken that backpack off a dead man and now Ivan had done the same thing. That backpack was a curse all by itself.

"Get up," Ivan ordered.

Jack stood as Ivan dropped the backpack at his feet.

"How much is missing?" Ivan demanded.

Jack kneeled and looked inside. Most of the coke was gone. Michael and his friends had sold or done at least half of what they'd stolen but Jack didn't think it wise to say so.

"Looks like it's mostly there," he said. "So, we're good?"

When Jack looked up at Ivan, he saw Ivan raising the big pistol. In a reflex, Jack threw the backpack at Ivan and turned for the door. Jack passed the doorframe just as Ivan fired. The bullet missed Jack's ear by a millimeter and Jack heard the next bullet strike Owen's kitchen window.

Jack jumped off the steps and ran instinctively to the corner of the trailer. He rounded the corner as Ivan stepped out onto the steps. Ivan raised the pistol but didn't fire.

Chapter 21

Jennifer had to drive around for a while when she reached David's neighborhood. The big houses didn't have numbers on the curb like they had in her neighborhood.

She rounded a curve flanked by mansions and saw cars parked up and down the street. These were high school kid cars; Mustangs, old Camaros, a lucky Trans Am, a few Volkswagens, and a van. She saw kids walking up the driveway of a big house with no numbers. That was it. She saw Marie's bright yellow Volkswagen in the street and Vonda on the front porch smoking pot. She stopped at the curb and flipped down her mirror so she could finish her makeup.

She had been to parties before, but not as a senior. There had been plenty, and she knew about them, but she hadn't wanted to go. She went to the Noel dance by herself but being there had reminded her of all the social opportunities she had let fade over the years and so she left after an hour. It was hard for her to admit to herself that she liked being alone and didn't feel the same social pulls as other girls. It just seemed unnatural, and she didn't like that about herself, but it was true. She also knew that most of her friends couldn't dance well, and neither could she. Not dancing, given how well Madonna could dance, was unacceptable. She danced in her room but didn't like the way she looked, and she was mortified at the thought that Jack or her dad would see her and laugh.

She kept to herself when she was a freshman and watched as her middle school friends joined groups and found their way. She still had braces for most of that year, and she thought she was fat. And there was the hair she could see on her upper lip. She imagined all the other kids were making fun of her for having a mustache.

She started running track to lose weight, and she did; in her freshman year, she got two inches taller and eighteen pounds lighter. Nothing she had ever done made her happier about herself than dropping those eighteen pounds.

As she touched up her make up and applied a brush to her hair, she thought about how far she had come. When she was thirteen, she tried a few things she had seen in her mother's magazines, but they looked like *Charlie's Angels* hairstyles, and she didn't like it. She had no desire to look like Farah Fawcett.

In the spring of her freshman year, Jack brought one of his barrel racer girlfriends to the house and she had the hair Jennifer wanted. Casey's hair was piled up on her head and looked both made and unmade. When Casey was in the bathroom, Jennifer whispered to Jack, "Ask her how she does that to her hair." When Casey came out of the bathroom, Jack told her to go to Jennifer's bathroom and show her everything that needed to be done. Jennifer was mortified by the request at first, but Casey was kind, and she had everything Jennifer needed in her purse; she had the brushes and hair spray and in thirty minutes she advanced Jennifer's knowledge of contemporary hair techniques to the level of an intermediate. From there, Jennifer had become an expert, and when sophomore year rolled around, everything changed.

That year, she started dating a senior named Eric. Over the summer, she lost more weight, but her breasts doubled in size, and she learned from Casey how to pad a bra in a way that didn't look ridiculous. On the very first day of school, she knew within fifteen minutes that she was in for a completely different experience. Girls approached her and asked her name.

"Jennifer," she said incredulously. "We've been in school together for nine years."

"No way!" one of the girls said. "I never noticed you."

Other girls gathered around and suddenly, Jennifer was popular in a way she didn't ask for or try to be. Shannon, of course, noticed this immediately and even though she and Jennifer had not been close for a while, not since Shannon made fun of Jennifer for liking Madonna, Jennifer could see the turn for the worse. Shannon had barely acknowledged her previously; now Shannon visibly curled up her lips and snarled when Jennifer walked past.

The new status was fun at first, until Jennifer realized how much obligation and energy it took to stay friends with the other girls. Those girls were exhausting.

Eric has pressured her for sex, but she wouldn't give it to him. When they were on her driveway, he put her hand on his groin, but she pulled it back.

When he did it again, she said, "If you don't stop, I'm going to tell Jack."

He released her hand but said defensively, "I'm not afraid of Jack."

"You should be," she replied as she adjusted her clothes and went inside. That was their last date. Later she found out that he told his friends that he had "popped her cherry" but also said that she was "frigid" and a "lousy lay." Just before prom, he told her he wasn't going to go, but he went with his friends, and she saw him there. He didn't speak to her all night. She refused to take his calls after that and then her girlfriends told her what he had been telling the other guys. She thought about telling Jack, but she knew Jack would track him down without hesitation and there was no need to risk Jack's status with the law over Eric.

The experience affected her, however. It made her feel powerless, and she hated that feeling over all others. She came to think that there were various levels of attractiveness; the kind that made you a target, and the kind that made you an object of power and reverence. She wanted to be the second kind, but she didn't know how to do it, and she didn't know any girls who had it either. Most of her girlfriends were under the direction of their boyfriends and had given them the sex they wanted by the middle of their junior year. Jennifer heard all about it and knew that if she dated, it was the same thing as agreeing to have sex. None of her girlfriends who had a boyfriend had held out. She knew what kind of sex it would be; she'd be on bottom. The only person that represented the sexuality she wanted was still Madonna.

The first experience that made her feel the way she wanted to feel was with Lisa. She had barely been sexual with Lisa, but Lisa had been interested in Jennifer having power. Lisa accepted her strong attraction to the Madonna aesthetic without making fun of her. Lisa adored her. Lisa pined for her in a pure way. Lisa took no for an answer. Lisa worshipped the female body and had a female body. Lisa used her female body in a powerful way. Lisa had her own power and didn't apologize or sublimate it.

And yet, it was Lisa who had set her up for this night, the first party she had attended in all the years where she cared about what she looked like, and knew that someone in that house, most likely David, was going to touch her in a sexual way and she was going to touch that person back. After all that had happened, it came to this. This was the first night she cared about in a long time, and she was going in with both guns blazing.

She finished her make-up and applied the last coating of cherry lip gloss. Then she winked at herself; everything had fallen into place. She was a winner in all categories, and it was time to reap the rewards.

As she walked up to the house, the attention began. Vonda was taking another hit from her bong but stopped mid-toke. The girl she was with turned her head to see what Vonda was staring at.

Jennifer mounted the steps without acknowledging Vonda or her friend. She opened the front door and saw a house packed with high school students. It was the Texas Tavern crew but in a luxury home. A group far larger than the track team was there. "Walk Like an Egyptian" was blasting out of a sound system somewhere. Jennifer loved the song. If she wasn't into Madonna, she'd try to look like Susanne Hoffs. A few of the track girls let out a cheer when she entered. Jennifer smiled and curtsied, which got a cheer so loud that Lisa heard it over the music. Jennifer noted that she wasn't the only one dressed to kill. She saw the cheerleaders were present and they had their hair piled up high and the make-up layered on strong.

Lisa made her way to Jennifer and was all smiles. She took Jennifer by the hand and pulled her deeper into the party.

"Oh my God, you look so hot," Lisa said over her shoulder "Oh my God, I'm so wasted already!"

As Lisa dragged her towards the back of the house, Jennifer saw David at the balcony railing on the upper floor. A line of the male track team members stood at the railing, gazing down on the party, whispering to each other. She saw him looking at her and nodded his head just a millimeter. It was enough; he knew, she knew, they knew.

Lisa dragged Jennifer into the big kitchen. It was packed with the track team, the baseball team, a few of the footballers, the cheerleaders, and even a claque of men that Jennifer was sure had already graduated. Lisa dipped a plastic cup into the punch bowl that was on the island and handed it to Jennifer.

"Bottom's up!" Lisa demanded.

Jennifer took a big drink, and Lisa pushed the cup a little higher so that a tiny river or ruby red punch dripped from Jennifer's chin.

"Oh, my God, that's so sexy!" she moaned and leaned in to kiss Jennifer. Jennifer pulled back and laughed the gesture off. Lisa saw her looking around.

"Why do you still care?" Lisa asked, not unkindly.

Jennifer smiled. No one was really paying attention to them, and it didn't matter. She felt freer and more at ease in a crowd than she ever had.

"Show me the outside, okay?" Jennifer requested.

"It's so awesome! The Wingates are rich kikes, and they paid to get a huge pool put in," Lisa said as she grabbed Jennifer's hand.

After threading through more of the crowd, Lisa led Jennifer through the doors that opened to the huge covered back porch. Beyond the porch was a pool lit with blue lights, and kids dangling their feet in the water. The entire yard and porch were packed with more high schoolers, and Jennifer wondered for a moment what percentage of the school was there. She had thought it was a track party, but now it was a gathering bigger than the prom. Whatever happened here, it was, by default, happening at an official school party because officially, so much of the school was there.

In the center of the porch was a beer keg. Marie pumped beers for several other girls. When Jennifer approached the keg with Lisa, heads turned. Jennifer did the social math; these were the non-track lesbians. These were the softball girls.

"Hook us up, bitch," Lisa said to Marie.

Marie smirked and handed two beers over to Lisa, and Lisa handed one to Jennifer. Before any awkwardness could fester between Jennifer and the other gay girls, another line of girls lined up at the keg. Shannon was second in that line, and it took Jennifer a moment to recognize her. Shannon's hair was cut short, and she had died it bright pink.

Jennifer stared at Shannon's pink hair and Shannon noted it.

"Take a picture," Shannon spat out. Marie handed her a beer and she started to turn away.

Lisa picked up immediately on the open hostility that had instantly emerged between Jennifer and Shannon. She didn't like it and the alcohol in her system loosened her tongue.

"Who is this cotton candy cunt?" Lisa said loudly. Shannon turned back. All eyes turned to Jennifer. Jennifer weighed her words for maximum impact.

"Just a former friend," she said without emotion. Lisa absorbed the information.

Shannon knew the spotlight was on her, but she didn't know anything about the track team and didn't play any sports. The details of the setting hadn't registered yet, and she had no knowledge about the ladies assembled on three sides, but she knew Lisa. Lisa had been the bull dike in her classes since fourth grade. Lisa had changed little except gotten bigger.

Shannon was not foolish about these situations. Before she came to be with her current foster family, she lived in homes with all girls, and she knew the look of girls who could fight. They were usually the short, thick ones. It was the girls with thick looking skulls that fought, and they won either outright or by default. They hit hard and could take a punch. At one of the homes, she had seen two big girls get in a fight that lasted for a long time. The dad was at work and the foster mother was too small and afraid to break the girls apart, so the mom just called the police and waited. Shannon had curled up on the bed and used pillows to hide from the fight. By the time the police arrived, both girls were covered in blood.

Lisa was absolutely one of those girls that could fight, and she was surrounded by several others. It disgusted Shannon more than anything else that Jennifer had used her Madonna schtick to attract these dikes, but she knew full well she had just gotten a chit to use when the gossiping started. Her task at hand, one she had developed real expertise over the years of foster care, was to back out without losing too much face or starting a fight. It was not going to be graceful. One line to the jugular was the way to go.

"Still only 'Like a Virgin?'" Shannon said to Jennifer, and then she turned away. She knew it would take Lisa a drunken 'two Mississippi' to get it, and she intended to be gone when it happened.

Marie got it first and burst out laughing. The line was snappy and well placed. Lisa didn't fully register the insult since she hated Madonna and hadn't put the line and the artist together, but she detected Shannon walking away a bit faster than required.

"You better run, skank!" she called out.

Jennifer smiled; it was a perfectly timed response, and it reminded her of the old Shannon she had been friends with, and it further confirmed Jennifer's Madonna-like hold on attention to her sexuality. It was perfect. It was better than any sort of insincere effort on Shannon's part to avoid a fight with contrite talk. Shannon had just cemented in Jennifer's status as the most desirable sexual object among at least twelve other girls, many of whom were physical stars, or girls who tried hard to be sexpots. Jennifer had trumped them all.

"That cunt was a friend of yours?" Lisa said after Shannon and her friends were gone.

"She lives across the street from me," Jennifer said. "You've had classes with her. Her name is Shannon."

"That was Shannon?" Lisa said. "The little foster care ditch rat?"

"Yes," Jennifer said. "I used to think she was a lesbian."

"Lesbians wouldn't have her," Lisa said.

For the next hour, Jennifer and Lisa worked the party together. They spoke to most of the other girls on the track team, all of whom credited the win to Jennifer's hurdle performance. Lisa encouraged this kind of talk and instigated it if no one else brought it up. Jennifer smiled more than she had in many years and felt her face getting tired. Lisa fed her plenty of beer and punch, but Jennifer paced herself and poured most of it out when she went to the bathroom. Lisa drank fast and was starting to slur her words. As her drinking advanced, her language degraded, and she became more physical. It was time to detach.

When Jennifer saw David staring at her, she knew the situation was combustible, but she also knew her course of action. Lisa wasn't paying attention to Jennifer's every cue anymore, so Jennifer could hold David's gaze a bit longer and in the space of a few minutes, the die was cast.

"I'm going to the bathroom," Jennifer said to Lisa who was drunk talking to Marie.

David watched her cross to the hall bathroom. She caught his glance one more time as she shut the door. In the bathroom, she stood at the sink, washed her hands, took out the condom she had brought

193

out from her bra, adjusted the bra a bit since it was tight and cut into the skin under her breasts, tucked the condom back in, and waited.

When she opened the door, she saw that David had not moved. He quickly crossed over to her as he glanced over his shoulder to see if Lisa had popped up. She hadn't.

"Come with me," he said.

She followed him down the hallway and around a corner. There was a door that he opened, and it led to a steep and narrow stairway.

"This is the maid's stairs," he said. "Goes upstairs, but no one can see it. Want to come up?"

Well, she thought, *it doesn't get any clearer than that.*

She nodded, and he smiled, took her hand, and started up the stairs.

Chapter 22

Jack ran towards the rodeo where the crowd and crowd noise offered some protection. When he reached the edge of the crowd he looked back and saw Ivan and Fernando walking towards him. Fernando had the backpack on. They weren't going to run away without cleaning up behind themselves.

Jack weaved into the stream of people walking around the rodeo ring. There were teens moving slowly and laughing at everything. Jack squeezed past. The thronging teens walked closely together, which was good; they didn't know they were providing a flesh wall between him and the two assassins who had killed at least four people in the past ninety minutes.

Jack passed the bull pins. He looked but couldn't see Ivan or Fernando. Much of the crowd had stopped to look at the bulls and they offered some protection, but Jack thought about how much space he needed between himself and the killers. And that was not all; he needed to get home and get his family out of the house, possibly for good.

He saw Ivan's red hair, and then saw the edge of the backpack, and turned to run again. Up ahead, he saw a group of men putting on thick vests. There were the drunk and crazy who were going out to play Cowboy Poker.

"I'm in, I'm in," Jack said to one of the clowns. He recognized the man but couldn't remember his name.

"Not without the waiver, you ain't," the clown said without looking up.

"Miggie has the waiver," Jack said as he glanced behind him.

The clown looked at him and shrugged; paperwork wasn't his problem and mentioning Miggie was good enough for him. He handed Jack a vest and Jack stepped into the ring, the first time in over three years he'd been inside the fence at a rodeo. He wondered for a moment if Ivan and Fernando would shoot him inside the ring while he was in full view of everyone.

Ivan and Fernando saw him and stopped. As Jack buckled the vest, he saw Ivan and Fernando's faces and noted their confusion. This was good; they had not hesitated to kill previously, and now they had paused. He smiled at them and ran for the center of the ring.

"Okay, bring out the sacrifices!" the rodeo announcer said. "Let's hear it for the drunkest men at the rodeo!"

The crowd cheered on what they knew might be injuries to come.

The Cowboy Poker players walked toward the center of the ring where a plastic lawn table had been placed. At the table, Miggie, dressed in his clown gear, was passing out plastic lawn chairs.

"Go to the table and sit down," Miggie repeated to each man as they arrived. "Go to the table and sit down."

Even through his makeup, Jack could see surprise on Miggie's face when he saw Jack.

"Go to the table and sit down," he said to Jack as he handed over the lawn chair. Jack leaned closely.

"Your friends are dead, Migs," he said. "Three bodies are in your trailer. Michael's brains are on your ceiling."

Miggie was old and had survived years in the same dirty oval with giant and angry bulls. He wasn't scared easily, but he knew from experience that drug deals can go wrong, and Jack's news rattled him.

"Too bad," was all he could muster.

Jack took his chair and sat down at the table. Six men in total sat around the white plastic lawn table and each grinned at each other, all except for Jack who was looking back towards the crowd. He saw Ivan and Fernando watching from the fence. Their frustrated faces were easily recognizable from a distance.

Jack glanced over at Miggie, and Miggie had followed his eyeline to the fence.

Miggie leaned in enough to speak to Jack.

"Red hair?" he asked.

"Yes," Jack said. "They want me next, and now, they'll want you too."

Jack looked at Ivan and Fernando, made sure they were paying attention, and gestured with this thumb at Miggie. Miggie saw it and he wheeled backwards. Jack had fucked him.

"You'd best not go home, motherfucker," Jack said. "Not ever."

Jack laughed, since it was the only thing that made sense. For a moment, he looked around at the nutters at the table with him. There

was a huge country ploughboy with a black cowboy hat. He was with a
friend who was thinner and had a blond dirty beard and he wore a
white starched hat that curved at the brim. There was a fat man with
glasses who wore a mechanic's shirt stained with motor oil. He had a
friend as well who wore the same shirt but had a baseball cap with the
STP logo across the front, and a skinny high school student with
inflamed acne and he was wearing a worn FFA jacket. The high school
student laughed nervously, and Jack noted his glassy eyes.

"What the hell are you doing here?" Jack asked the mechanic. This
guy stood out as not being the right type to be at a Cowboy Poker
match.

The man looked away from the crowd and at Jack and gripped his
chair even tighter.

"My god damn girlfriend put me up to this shit," he said. "She
dared me to do this. I'm a fucking idiot; that's why I'm here."

"What about you?" Jack asked the high school student.

"I'm so high," the kid whispered.

Jack looked again at the gate where Ivan and Fernando were still
watching just as the announcer came back on the PA:

"There they are ladies and gentlemen. Give them a big and final
hand," the announcer said.

There was a smattering of scattered applause. The two clowns,
Miggie and the one at the gate, came to the center of the ring.

"Okay, gentlemen, let's explain the rules," the announcer said as
the crowd quieted. His words echoed around the big ring. "The last
man that keeps his butt in a chair wins. It's that simple. If your butt is
in the chair and the chair is on the ground, and there ain't nobody left,
you win a thousand dollars."

The crowd let up a halfhearted cheer.

"And now, let's bring out the bull, Bala De Muerte! That's Bullet
of Death for all you pale faces," the announcer said.

Jack looked around at the others, then he let his head fall.

"Oh, no, not that bull again," he groaned.

The other men perked up, especially the terrified mechanic.

"The fuck you mean? You know that bull?" he asked.

The gate opened at the far end of the ring, and Bala de Muerte
charged out. This bull was big and young with large white horns that

had been blunted off but were still six feet across. He was the same shade of brown as the dirt which made the horns look like they were floating over his dark pig eyes. His black hooves skittered across the sandy dirt, and he clocked the table of men immediately.

The mechanic's eyes grew wide.

"Hell, no!" he said and jumped up and bolted for the fence.

Bala De Muerte saw the sudden move he charged at it. Neither Miggie nor the other clown made a move to deflect the bull, because they could tell the mechanic would make the fence in time.

"Oh, we got a runner already," the announcer said enthusiastically. "He's a oily streak of lightning!"

The mechanic pumped his arms and legs but made the mistake of looking over his shoulder. When he saw the huge bull running towards him, he tripped and fell on his face.

Bala De Muerte closed the gap before Miggie and the other clown could get in the bull's eyeline. The big bull's forehead reached the mechanic just as he staggered to his feet and took a step. The scoop of the bull's head lifted the man and slung him high in the air, so high that he sailed over the fence.

Finally, the crowd engaged. This is what they wanted, and they stood up cheered and stamped their booted feet. A moment later, the mechanic popped up on the fence. Anger and relief were marked on his face, and he looked like he was about to cry. He flipped off the crowd with both hands and turned away.

"He dodged a bullet there, ladies and gentlemen, but it looks like the man hurt his fingers, on both hands!" the announcer offered.

Bala de Muerte began to stalk the ring. He ran along the fence, all the while staring at the table in the middle of the dirt and the two clowns who had fanned out.

"What about this bull?" the skinny guy with the STP cap asked. "What do you know?"

"He's a killer," Jack said. 'He killed a guy in San Antonio two weeks ago."

That report was enough for the skinny guy.

"Fuck this shit," he said as he stood.

His chair flipped backwards, and he bolted for the fence. Bala De Muerte saw him and ran across the ring. The big bull passed within a few feet of the table.

"Somebody heard the dinner bell, and it wasn't the bull!" the announcer said.

The fat guy saw his friend bolt and decided to run in the opposite direction. Both he and his friend made it over the fence before the bull could dig a horn into them.

"This is how you separate the men from the crazy men," the announcer said. "Bala De Muerte taking scalps right here, right now."

Three men still sat at the table. The big man with the black cowboy hat was smiling and drooling a little. The high school student giggled.

"This is just fucking crazy," the big ploughboy said.

Suddenly, Bala De Muerte turned towards the center and accelerated. He charged the group and lowered his massive head.

"May I join you gentlemen?" the announcer said.

The bull brushed past Jack and his massive horns caught the edge of the table. The table flipped into the air and landed several feet away. The bull paused for a moment. His giant muscled body stood at the center of the men. A plume of snot and steam and dirt blew from his huge nostrils. Then he lowered his head and flipped the big guy in black cowboy hat high in the air.

The big guy hung like a rag doll in midair and hit the dirt. His hat landed several feet away. Bala de Muerte dropped his head and drilled his thick forehead into the big guy who tried to grab the horns and push the massive skull away. Jack and the high schooler watched as the bull rag-dolled the man on the ground.

The crowd stood and cheered; this was the action they craved in a gladiator event.

"This is what they call feeding time where I'm from," the announcer intoned.

Miggie grabbed Bala De Muerte by the horns and was able to turn his head while the other clown grabbed the big guy and pulled him up. The big guy stood and limped towards the fence as Bala De Muerte chased Miggie.

As the big guy pulled himself over the fence, everyone had a look at the blood and torn flesh on his back. More cheers went up.

Jack turned his head when he heard the high school kid laughing even harder.

"Hard core," he said.

"Two peas in a crazy pod!" the announcer said. "Give it up for the laziest men in Texas!"

Miggie ran over to Jack and the high schooler.

"Go!" he said. "We can't control him."

But Jack wasn't running. He looked over at the fence but could no longer see Ivan or Fernando at the gate.

"I'm not leaving," Jack said evenly. He was hoping the high schooler would bolt like the rest. "The bull can kill me. I'm okay with it."

"I'm too high to run, man!" the boy said. "This is just trippy."

The clowns formed a wall between the bull and Jack and the high schooler. They began yelling at them to run, but neither man was moving.

"Just stand up," Jack said. "Start walking towards the fence, and I'll keep the bull off you."

"Then you'll win," the boy said. "I'm high but I'm not stupid."

Jack looked around and clocked Fernando and Ivan moving towards where he intended to run. Now was as good as any to take his exit. He suddenly bolted for the side of the fence furthest from Ivan and Fernando.

As soon as he started to run, the high schooler stood and pumped his arm in the air, but that was a mistake; Bala De Muerte didn't see Jack but he saw the boy, so he blew past the clowns and plowed over the kid, knocking him to the ground and began to deliver a mauling.

As Jack ran to the fence, he saw Fernando and Ivan trying to figure out which way around the ring was quicker. Crowds were coming down the aisles to get a closer look at the hideous mauling that was taking place.

When Jack reached the fence, he hauled himself up and took one last look. The boy was on the horns of the bull and Fernando and Ivan were pushing through the crowds. He turned and jumped to the ground and started running for the parking lot.

In the crowded parking lot, Jack weaved between the trucks waiting
to get on the highway. Many of the horse breeders were pulling
elaborate trailers.

Jack ducked behind one of the trailers and saw Ivan and Fernando
enter the parking lot. The mass of cars and trucks and trailers and
people hid him.

He moved up the line towards the highway and found a horse trailer
where the big swinging back door was held shut with a rope. It had a
space big enough for him to slip inside. He gingerly stepped on the
slow-moving trailer and slipped inside. He was looking at the flanks of
two large horses. He kneeled between the animals, and then he laid
down on the metal floor and pushed himself against the wall, where he
scooped up straw to further cover himself.

Through the slits in the medal sides, he saw Ivan and Fernando
running past and trying to see in the trailers, but the truck pulling the
trailer eased slowly onto the highway and accelerated. Ivan and
Fernando fell into the distance. Jack exhaled, but he knew his trouble
was not over. Not by a long shot.

* * *

David took the last two stairs in one step which tugged Jennifer's
arm. He'd been going up and down those same stairs for a decade. His
parents had forbidden him from using the steep maid stairs for the
longest time, but they had also insisted that the maid use the maid
stairs and none other. The maid caught David on the stairs when he
was seven years old, and she had looked the other way. It was not the
last time the maid had allowed him things his parents sought to deny
him.

David led Jennifer down the red carpeted hall past all the other boys
standing along the railing. Most were looking down on the party
below, but a couple saw her pass and nudged the next boy over. Heads
turned, and she saw it. She also noted the red carpet.

At the end of the hall was a tall door, which he opened for her. He
saw the line of boys watching, and he winked at them as he closed the
door.

She looked around at the palatial bedroom. It was clearly the master suite in the house and was dominated by an ornate bed. She let her eyes linger on the abstract patterned art on the walls. The wallpaper was textured, and the curtains ran from floor to ceiling. She had the sense that the room was designed to demonstrate wealth, and it worked. It seemed like a wealthy parlor from a 19th century mansion, but it was in a suburban house in Houston. Jennifer could deduce the emotional and social math that decorated that room.

David went to the tape deck on the dresser and pulled the tape out, and slipped another in.

"I have a treat for you," he said.

The first song started; it was "Get into The Groove."

"I made this mix tape just for you," he said.

"You did?" she said with a smile. He was thinking of her when she was not in his sights.

After letting the music set the mood in the room, David started to dance. She thought it was odd for a moment, but he could dance well. This, she took, as another sign that she was doing the right thing. He danced past her and then around her.

"Come on, girl!" he said to her. She started dancing slightly. They danced for a moment longer and he moved in close and began to grind his hips into hers. She did not resist. Her mind and body swam into an ocean of feelings and sensations and emotions. All of them were good, none said to stop.

Suddenly, the bathroom door opened. Jennifer felt her heart drop in a jolt of fear. In a moment of confusion, she registered James. He held his hands aloft and smiled, which made a portrait of him only in his underwear. Jennifer pushed David back.

"I didn't know anyone else was here!" she said.

David laughed and danced over to James.

"It's just James, baby," he said, delighted. "Look, it's James!"

James laughed and came dancing out of the bathroom. She saw that he was also a good dancer. James had mastered the sensual moves that came from his hips. But up close, she could see his eyes and thought, for the first time, that both he and David were on some kind of drug. A boy dancing in his underwear was not in her experience zone.

Something was different, and for a moment, she thought it was chemical.

"Get into the groove," James sang as he passed by the other direction. David put his arm around her and gently coaxed her away from the wall where she had retreated.

She began to move again but watched with wide eyes. She felt a lightning bolt run through her, the combined effect of the music, the bodies, the booze, the smiles. It was everything she wanted this moment to be, but in her mind, there was only one man. Never had she fantasized of this critical moment with two men. She turned the puzzle over in her mind several times. Was two men in this room at this time good or bad? What would Lisa say? Lisa was constantly talking about complex sexual situations. She constantly criticized the 'normals' and 'breeders.' This situation had already gone off that road. Was this what Madonna, or Lisa, or anyone else whose opinion she valued, think was right?

David came in close and lifted the edge of her red shirt, encouraging her to take it off. She hesitated for a moment, knowing that if she took her shirt off, she'd be signally her interest in what was clearly going to happen next; she was going to make out with two guys at once. How far they would go was yet to be determined.

But she didn't think hard about it; she slowly, with great skill, lifted the shirt and pulled it over her head. James and David began to clap and laugh. They worshipped her, she suddenly thought, the way she wanted to be worshipped. And then, she danced differently, in a way she noticed but didn't control. The energy and sex appeal began to flow through her. Her arms moved differently. Her hips swayed back and forth. Her eyes closed and her chin lifted, and her long flat stomach muscles stretched and tightened, and she knew she was pure sex in that moment.

What happened next, she would barely be able to recall because there were so many inputs and emotional outputs. It took just a few seconds.

James came up behind her and put his big hands on her hips. Then, slowly, David came in front of her, and for a few delicious moments their hips were in sync. She had the thought, gloriously and for a shining moment, that she was in a Madonna music video. David kissed her on the mouth, and she felt his tongue swirl past her teeth. Then James turned her head by her chin, and he kissed her as well. She could taste beer in his mouth and smell the alcohol in his breath. Still, she let his tongue linger in her mouth.

But then, James leaned forward, and he kissed David on the mouth deep and long. Jennifer was an inch away from this obvious display of male sexual affection.

She tried to hide her shock and it worked; James and David focused back on her. David reached around her hips and grabbed her ass. James, who was taller than both, reached around her and grabbed David's ass. Their hips synced up again, but Jennifer could see James's hands working David's rump.

The group slowly rotated with the music until they were all facing each other in a triangle. The music was pumping, deep, rhythmic, sensual, and sexy. Her mind ran in at least two directions; she was able to grow through an experience that Madonna would approve of, and she was in a situation that would cause Jack to burst into great violence.

The threesome swapped another round of kisses, but this time, Jennifer had a harder time hiding her issue with seeing James kiss David. The sight made her want to push away, and she knew for an inkling moment what was going to come next. She might have two guys, but she was not going to watch two boys have sex. No way.

James took Jennifer's hand and placed it on his groin. She felt his erection. She complied and rubbed his stiffy through his jeans. For a moment, the swirl of emotions sped up in a good way and she let herself compare the years of wondering what a penis felt like to the real thing. Eric had not been erect when he did the same thing, and this was different. She was different.

But when she looked down, she saw James reach over and grab David by the groin. David unzipped his jeans and pulled his penis out. It was stiff and tall, and Jennifer saw it clearly. It was just like every picture she had ever seen of a male penis but still the first sight was shocking. It was purple and angry.

Then, slowly, James began to lean down, and it was clear that he was about to put David's penis in his mouth. She looked up at David, and he had his eyes closed.

This was the breaking point. She didn't want to see this.

"Whoa," she said. "Okay, I have to go."

She backed up.

David broke out of his concentration and saw instantly the rejection that had spread across her face. His chance for a score on the night of the party was slipping away.

"Wait…did that make you uncomfortable?" he said as he tucked his penis away. "It's okay. We can just focus on you."

James stood up. The spell was broken for him as well.

"It's okay. It's my fault," she said. "That shouldn't bother me, it doesn't bother Madonna, I've just never seen that before."

James put his hands on hips.

"Don't let the door hit you in the ass on the way out," he sneered.

"Shut up," David snapped at him. This was not good. The ecstasy and mood, so carefully planned for, was rapidly dissipating, and he wanted it back. He smiled and tried to pull Jennifer close.

"Maybe just you and me, huh?" he cooed. "James can just watch, okay?"

Jennifer blocked his advance with her hands. She'd seen what she'd seen.

"Wait, so, you're like…gay?" she asked.

"No! No, it's not like that at all," David said.

"It's not?" James said sarcastically.

"I mean," David said. "It's James! He's like my friend. But he fucks girls all the time. He's like, gay kind of, but I'm not gay. I mean bi or anything like that."

"What about you and that carpet muncher?" James asked.

"Shut up, James!" David bellowed.

It took a moment for Jennifer to get it.

"There's nothing going on there," Jennifer said. She suddenly, in a flash, thought that maybe Lisa had been right all along, and maybe everyone was gay somewhere in their soul. But before she could have any further thoughts, James pushed past her.

"Whatever, I'm gone," he said and headed towards the door.

Jennifer did not want to be alone with David now, and she also headed towards the door. David threw up his hands.

"I've got to go," she said.

"Wait!" David hopelessly pleaded.

James arrived at the door and opened it, then stepped back.

"Ladies first," he smirked.

She stepped through the door just as she realized that she was not wearing a shirt. Only her push-up bra kept her from being topless. As she turned back, James slammed the door shut. She heard the lock click. She checked the knob, it wouldn't turn, and she banged on the door but only heard David yelling at James. Suddenly, the door opened, and James threw her tiny purse at her and slammed the door again.

She picked up her purse. The boys from the team that had watched her pass moments before stared in disbelief at their luck witnessing such an event. They had waited four years for something so clearly socially momentous to occur. All the staring and speculating had paid off. They were smiling and pointing in a way she had not seen since way back when Bobby Thompson called her a werewolf. She knew, in an instant, that these boys would talk, and word would spread. What happened in David's bedroom would be the talk of the party, no matter what she said or did.

She eyed them cooly. These three boys were now howling and cackling and pointing and attracting the attention of those below. Only they could see her, but when she walked down the hall, everyone would see. The pointing and jeering would be intense. She knew it. She took out some lip gloss and applied it slowly. History was about to repeat itself, and this time, she wins.

Suddenly, the bedroom door opened, and David stood there, shirtless, a look of terror on his face, her red shirt in one hand. James was right behind him. The boys from the team froze, sure that something even better was about to happen. He handed the red shirt to her.

"Oh, my God, I'm so sorry," David whispered in her ear. "Please don't tell anyone what happened. Please!"

A great calm seized her. She knew that she was about to receive a notoriety that would give her social power, and she hadn't even had to do what was going to be credited to her. She would be branded a slut, like a virgin but not one, a woman of immense sexual power, and she didn't even have to suck a dick or munch a carpet even once. Without having had any sexual contact with anyone, she was going to be marked as the most sexually experienced girl in the whole school. The girl who was laughed at for being hairy, like a werewolf, or a boy, was to be the most feminine of them all, and it would be confirmed at the top of the stairs in a gay boy's home.

"Okay," she said as she took his hand. "Walk me to the top of the stairs, and never talk about what happened in there. Let them only imagine. If James stays quiet, I'll keep your secret."

The laughter and pointing began as she came into view, towing David behind her. It was a sound of shock and disbelief. The noise morphed into cheering by the time she reached the top of the stairs.

At the top of the grandiose staircase, she paused. The stairs had been made extra wide at the insistence of Mr. Wingate when the house was built and they had added $15,000 to the cost of the house, but he wanted a wide entryway to the living room each morning as he came down, like he was entering a stage for a Hollywood musical. He had demanded an ornate post at the top with a huge, rounded cap, and a top and bottom railing with carved balusters between. The rails were white, but the balusters were glazed in painted gold. Jennifer didn't know that, of course, but she knew the stairs were awesome. The event that would define the evening, and the rest of her time in high school, was going to happen on those very stairs.

She stopped at the post and put her hand on the golden ball that capped the entire structure. Every eye was turned to her. There was laughter and whistling and she knew, she felt, that the laughter and pointing and whistling and whispering and carrying on was complex in its origin but celebratory. Had she not carried the day on the track earlier? Had she not pushed her body and floated over every hurdle with perfection and strength and beauty and grace? Had she not carried on the only lesbian affair at the school that was public enough to even be the subject of whispers, and, on more than one occasion, pointed fingers and muted laughter? She had done all of that, and there was speculation about a lot more. She had a track record and a reputation, and it pleased her greatly. What was happening now was the capstone of her ability to be someone of note, someone worth talking about, or liking, or even hating. That so much of it was imagined made it better.

She stood long at the golden post there, in a skirt but no shirt, and lifted her chin. The longer she stood there, the more the laughs and points tuned into cheers and pumped fists.

David's shirtless appearance prompted even more waves of laughing and pointing. He was unsure what this meant for him, but he had to go along, so he smiled, and sheepishness waved.

As he held her shirt out to her, she took her hand off the golden ball and delivered a perfect middle finger just below his nose. Her fingers were not in a lazy fist; they were arched, and the middle one was painted blood red. She snatched her red shirt back and began carefully walking down the staircase. No stumbling needed to happen here to ruin the moment. At midpoint, she paused and pulled a tiny mirror from her purse. She stopped and looked at herself, then tucked it away. The gesture took the cheers up a notch, and as she was tucking the mirror away, she saw the one face in the assembly not curled into a smile.

Lisa stood at the entry to the kitchen and her mortified expression told the story. But Jennifer saw that she was no longer looking at Jennifer; she was looking up at David. Jennifer turned and looked at David now, and James was now standing at his side. Lisa's dead gaze was up at the two of them, and for a moment Jennifer wished she could tell Jack about how she had managed to be an object of fascination, lust, and derision in the world's most impossible and weirdest four-sided lust triangle.

At the bottom of the stairs, time moved back into regular gear and Jennifer simply turned towards the front door and left.

She was in the driveway before she heard Lisa calling from the front door.

"Hey," Lisa said as she bolted down the front steps. "What happened up there? Did you fuck that guy?"

Jennifer kept walking.

"You're such a whore," Lisa said. "I knew you were nothing. I knew you were an airheaded bimbo!"

"Don't you mean Madonna whore?" Jennifer said without turning.

Jennifer reached the street and walked towards her car. Lisa ran past her and stopped her under the streetlight.

"Don't you do it," she pleaded. Tears formed in her eyes. "Don't you walk away from me. You owe me more than that."

Jennifer was briefly thankful that there would be no witnesses for this part of the drama.

"I was trying to help you, but you're like the rest of them. You're just too chicken shit to be who you are," Lisa sobbed openly.

Jennifer considered seriously what Lisa was saying. She knew it was not fear that stopped her from doing anything with Lisa or with David or James. It was a clear conviction at having seen her alternatives, and she knew, at that moment, that she had engineered the whole thing to get what she needed. Being the object of affection for Lisa, who she rejected, and then David, who she had rejected, had been somehow a part of her plan. She had used their homosexuality to her own selfish and heterosexual means.

"I'm not afraid," she said. "I'm just not who you are, and I won't be. You shouldn't wait around anymore."

"That's just great," Lisa said. "I finally see you with your shirt off outside the locker room, and it's in the street in front of that kike faggot's house. This is why I know there is no God."

"I used you," Jennifer said, and thought instantly of what Shannon had said to her in the bathroom weeks earlier. She knew that Shannon had put those words in her mouth, and that Shannon had been right all along. Jennifer had a sociopathic nature, born of fear and shame. This dark nature was going to be the next stronghold she'd somehow have to overcome. "I used you, and it worked. I shouldn't have, but I did. It's terrible, and you deserve better. I'm sorry."

She walked around Lisa and towards her car.

"Wait," Lisa said without moving. "What do you mean?"

But it didn't matter what she meant because Jennifer was not turning back. It was time to move on.

PART 3

"Tomorrow is the most important thing in life. Comes into us at midnight very clean. It's perfect when it arrives, and it puts itself in our hands. It hopes we've learned something from yesterday." – John Wayne

Chapter 23

Josie came down the stairs to a quiet house. He stopped in front of the TV and observed an image of a smoking building that looked like it had been bombed. The sound was down but the graphics read, *nuclear power station'* and *'Soviet Union'* and *'meltdown.'* It looked bad.

He walked over to the TV and turned up the sound.

"Soviet authorities rarely report on disasters within the Soviet Union, and so experts have confirmed that the scale and scope of the meltdown at Chernobyl is much larger than what was reported," a newscaster intoned. "Photos released show the aftermath of a large explosion that housed the reactor core which has left the core of the reactor exposed to the outside world."

Josie wondered if they might close the school for another week like they had for *Challenger*.

When he entered the kitchen, he saw his dad leaning on the counter and looking at the floor. Bob no longer dressed for the day in pajamas. He had a cup of coffee in one hand and a cigarette in the other.

Josie liked that his dad dressed like he used to, but it had been so long that he couldn't tell if this was a good sign or a bad sign. He passed his dad and pulled a box of cereal out of the pantry, then he got the milk from the refrigerator and a bowl from a drawer and sat down at the table. Bob had not moved or said anything.

Josie broke the silence.

"Are you the way you are because of Vietnam?" he asked.

Bob watched Josie pour the cereal into the bowl and then pour milk over it. This question was the most consequential thing he had ever heard Josie say or ask. It was the only time anyone in the house had asked about what he was going through and why.

"I wasn't in Vietnam," he said.

Josie tipped the bowl up and let cereal and milk dribble into his mouth.

"Mom says you were," Josie said after he brought the bowl down.

Bob was nearly overcome as he stared at Josie. The boy was not even using utensils to eat.

211

"You're mom said I was in Vietnam?" he asked as he took a spoon out of the drawer and set it by Josie.

"She said you were in the Army, and you went to war," Josie said.

"I was in the Marines, and I went to Korea," Bob said. "And yes, there was a war there at the time."

"But not Vietnam?" Josie asked.

"No, but same neighborhood," Bob said with a sad smile. "It was the war before the Vietnam war. We didn't lose in Korea like we did in Vietnam."

"So, we won?" Josie asked through a bite of cereal.

"We tied," Bob said. "But a lot of good men were killed."

"Did you kill anyone?" Josie asked.

Before Bob could speak, Carol entered the kitchen in a hurry. She was dressed for her aerobics class, which meant tights and headband. She saw Bob's long ash fall from his cigarette and hit the floor. Her tolerance for Bob was low and she didn't hide her contempt any longer. She had become even more icy.

"I just cleaned up in here," she said as she grabbed her water bottle from the refrigerator, "and your ashing all over the place."

Carol ripped a piece of paper towel off the roll, but Bob leaned over and picked up the ashes with his fingers.

"I got it," he said as he dropped the ash in the ashtray on the counter.

"Are you ready, honey?" she said to Josie.

He nodded since his mouth was full of cereal. Carol left just as Jennifer entered and poured herself a glass of milk. She was wearing her track uniform which made Bob lift his head and smile.

"Look at you!" Bob said enthusiastically. "You're still doing track?"

"Yes, Daddy, I've been on the track team for four years," she said warily. "There's a meet today."

"Where?" Bob asked.

"Districts," she said, "at Pasadena."

"Pasa 'get down' dena, great!" he said as he stubbed out the cigarette. "I'll take you."

This offer struck Jennifer as odd, and not in a good way.

"That's okay," she said. "Mom's taking him to school so I can drive myself."

Bob's smile didn't wane. The sight of her in her tracksuit had made a little spark in him and he was still enjoying it.

"Ah, got it," he said.

She poured a full glass of milk, drank it all, and then poured another.

"Jack's truck has a flat tire. When's he going to be back?" she said, more as a statement than a question.

Bob was quiet for a moment. He noticed the truck, and Jack's absence, and suspected something was wrong. So did Jennifer, but no one had spoken about it.

"I don't know," he said. "I'm going to ask Marco. He knows something."

"Marco is a little weasel," she said. "Don't believe anything he tells you."

"I know how to deal with weasels," Bob said.

She put the glass in the sink, and started to leave, but stopped.

"He's in trouble," she said, breaking the taboo on discussing anything of importance. "I know it."

Josie's head snapped up.

"Jack's in trouble? For what?" he asked.

"I know," Bob said. "I'm going out looking for him today. Both of you, don't let your imaginations run wild. Jack's a survivor."

A pall hung over the room, until both Jennifer and Josie left.

* * *

Bob walked out of the house and into the sun. It felt good, though there was still a slight chill in the air.

He had a folded-up newspaper in his hand which he threw onto the bench seat of his truck. His Chevy was old and dirty and needed cleaning, but Bob did all the servicing himself. It was deep blue and had a white pinstripe down both sides.

He let the big eight-cylinder engine idle for a moment and dialed the AM radio until he heard a voice. It was a newscast report about

Chernobyl. Weeks of Soviet denials about the severity of the mishap were coming undone.

As he backed down the driveway, he saw Marco come out of the front door of his house and go to his car.

Marco was looking under his front seat for a lighter when he heard an old horn. He looked up and saw Bob Buckhorn at the bottom of his driveway waving at him.

"Hey, Marco," Bob said loudly from the truck. "Come over here."

Marco's alarmed look confirmed to Bob that Marco knew something about Jack's whereabouts and that something was not good.

Marco walked down the driveway.

"Hello, Mr. Buckhorn," he said from a few feet away.

"Where's Jack?" Bob asked. "He hasn't been home for a couple of days."

"I don't know," Marco said. He was glad he didn't have to lie, at least not yet. "I haven't seen him either."

Bob waited a moment and let Marco sweat. Marco's eyes darted around.

"Where do you think he is, if you had to guess?" Bob asked.

"I don't know," Marco said. "He goes to a lot of rodeos. He stays with a guy named Miggie sometimes. Just hanging out."

"Miggie," Bob repeated. It sounded made up.

"Yeah, Uncle Miggie, they call him," Marco said.

"Who's he? What's he do?" Bob asked.

"He's a clown," Marco said. He swallowed harder than he meant to. "Like, a rodeo clown."

Again, Bob waited and watched Marco closely. So far, he knew Marco wasn't lying. There must really be a Miggie.

"So, Marco," he said, "what's the link between Jack, you, this Miggie clown, and that guy there?"

Bob pointed at Domingo's house across the street. Again, Marco's eyes darted around. He was horrible at concealing his emotions, and now, he was going to be forced to tell Jack's dad about what they had been up to or start with the untruths.

"I don't know," Marco said. "Miggie and that guy don't know each other," he followed, truthfully.

Bob sighed.

"Marco, I've known you since you were a little kid," he said as he put the truck into gear. "And I know you're a follower, not a leader. I know you know more than you're telling me, and if something bad happens to Jack, I'll make sure it happens to you. So, you think about what you need to tell me, and I'll be back this afternoon."

Marco's eyes widened. He'd never seen Mr. Buckhorn this way.

"I don't know anything," Marco said sadly. He looked down, giving away the lie.

"Yes, you do, Marco. I'm going out looking for him now, so, you remember what I said," Bob stated. "If it happens to Jack, and you could have warned me, it happens to you. As I live and breathe, Marco. As I live and breathe."

Bob smiled, nodded, and drove away. In the side mirror, he saw Marco put both hands over his face. That was not good. Whatever Marco knew, it was bad, but it was probably not something that, even if he told Bob everything, Bob could fix until Jack came home.

* * *

The district and state meets were big and had to be played at the schools with stadiums large enough to accommodate them. The biggest was at Pasadena High School. When Jennifer parked at school, she knew the day would be awkward, as awkward as practices had been. Lisa would barely look at her, David wouldn't stop looking at her.

She didn't ride in the back seat with Lisa on the way over, and instead sat in the front row by herself. This put both behind her, which meant she didn't have to worry about tracking their glances. They could both stare at the back of her head if they wanted, and she wouldn't know. Plus, no one wanted that seat, so she knew she'd be alone there.

In the days after the track party, she began to go to school with barely any make-up on. Towards the back of her closet were some shirts with pastel floral patterns that her mother had given her for Christmas that she had never worn. She found one that she liked and wore it with a short skirt and with her hair combed back and swirled into a relaxed bun. It felt good. It felt sexy in a more subtle way.

215

At track practice, she removed all her make up and pulled her hair into a tight ponytail. She wore no bracelets or rings or jewelry of any kind for the first time in years. It was so much faster to get ready, she thought, and she didn't really need the hassle of putting on her favored look right now. She was content to dress in a softer way. If anyone else noticed her altered appearance, they said nothing.

The warm-ups had gone the same way with Lisa avoiding her as much as possible. District championships were busy affairs, and Lisa was constantly conferring with the coaches and then running back to the team to issue instructions. She just referred to Jennifer as "Buckhorn," and gave no indication of any feelings one way or the other. After the first hour, Jennifer gained a new respect for Lisa's incredible focus and attention. She wasn't distracted, whatever she may have felt, and so neither was Jennifer. Early on, the Deer Park team racked up some victories and the hunt for first place was on.

When the hurdles came, Jennifer had warmed up, and she was focused and ready. She looked over the other girls and saw girls who were good at other events and had been forced into hurdles. They were shorter, heavier, and they looked miserable.

"These aren't hurdlers," Lisa said as she came along side.

"I was just thinking the same thing," Jennifer said.

"Don't get cocky," Lisa said as she looked them over. "You never know which one of these freaks just has a knack. Eyes down the track, don't glance over. Do what you do best, you'll win it."

"Got it," Jennifer said.

"Go get 'um," Lisa replied and slapped Jennifer on the ass. It was a gesture she had done before and she did to all the girls, but it came just as Jennifer was leaning over to stretch, and it was hard.

Lisa flinched.

"I'm sorry, I didn't mean to do it that hard," she said.

Jennifer stood up and smiled. Lisa had somehow become both strong and vulnerable and it was charming.

"It's okay," she said. "And thanks."

"For what?" Lisa asked warily.

"For being a good coach," Jennifer said. "I'm going to beat the pants off these bitches, and you're why. I didn't even want to do this. Now, I wouldn't be doing anything else."

Lisa looked down at her feet.

"You're welcome," she said, and added "You were already a winner. I just helped you find it."

Lisa turned to go to the finish line and Jennifer began to pull into herself. It was time to do what she knew and loved. She had learned to allow herself to burn with competitive fire. Her plan had been to glide along through her senior year, and now, she was coiled up inside and loving it.

She put her feet in the blocks and her palms on the dirty track. She could feel the eyes of the other girls on her, but she didn't give them even a glance. They got nothing. No one gets anything, all of this is mine and all mine and only mine. These were the thoughts that flashed through her mind in the fraction of an instant before the gun.

As she lifted off and took her steps toward the first hurdle, she saw a man standing on the first row. She knew it was her dad. He was standing, clutching a newspaper in one outstretched hand, the other curled into a fist. It was like he was there in a dream, and she changed nothing. She just observed.

It happened way too fast, she thought. The motion had gotten to be so automatic that now, rather than feel like an eternity or nerves, it felt more like what it was; a quarter of a minute of intense burning of energy and then a finish.

She looked up at the board and saw her time; 15.45. That was damn good. It was two full seconds ahead of second place. She thrust her arms into the air, triumphant, as Lisa and Marie ran over and hugged her. After a moment, Marie and Lisa ran off to get ready for the next event, and Jennifer looked at the stands to be sure she hadn't dreamt of her dad.

But it was no dream; he was standing and waving at her. She walked over to her dad, the confusion evident on her face.

"Wow! That was fantastic," Bob said. "You were like a machine! A hurdle jumping machine!"

"Thanks," she said, still panting and more confused than proud. "What are you doing here?"

"What do you mean? I came to watch you," he said, even though he knew what she meant.

"You've never done that before," she said, and then had a dark thought. "Is Jack okay?"

"I don't know," Bob said. He didn't want to talk about Jack. "Here, look."

Bob held up the newspaper he'd been clutching. His finger pointed at a Houston Chronicle article about Madonna. The headline in the Entertainment section read "Madonna Coming to Houston!'

Jennifer beamed and put her hands over her mouth. At a distance Lisa took note.

"No way!" Jennifer said. She let out a tight squeal.

"She's coming to the Astrodome. Tickets are on sale now," Bob said. "After this, let's go down and get you some."

"Oh, my God, yes!" she said. "Oh, my God! How did you even know I liked Madonna?

For a moment, in a way she couldn't have planned, the Daddy's Girl she once had been shown through.

"Honey," Bob said, "I may be blind, but I can still see. We'll get three tickets, and you take whoever you want.

"Thanks, Daddy," she said and reached out for him. He gripped her tiny hand in his and tried not to squeeze it too hard. After a moment he let go and she ran back towards her team, her ponytail swinging back and forth magically with her perfect gait.

Chapter 24

Jennifer was walking on air for the rest of the day. She did her high jumps and won that as well, but high jumps were never as exciting as the hurdles. She was okay with them, not great, and if the other teams had really focused on it, they could have beat her, but they didn't. The coaches always thought they could win in sprints, and they got nickel and dimed to death by the teams with a full squad, and Jennifer, with Lisa's help, made Deer Park a full squad.

When the relay finished, Deer Park was in second place, but that was enough to secure the trip to state. Lisa almost pulled a win out on the last leg, but she had to overcome a big deficiency. A half a step better start, and she would have won it. But the girls swarmed around her, and they treated it like a win. They were going to state.

The boys' team won outright, securing their own bid for state. David was their premiere middle-distance sprinter, and so all he did was run the 400 and 800 meters, which he did well. By the time they met at the buses an hour later, everyone was buzzing with excitement and hugging. The ride back to Deer Park was full of singing and yelling. Jennifer kept her position on the front seat but turned around to talk to the freshman girls behind her. She saw David steal a glance, and she smiled at him. Lisa was in the back seat as always, but she was leaning against the window and talking to Vonda.

When they got back to Deer Park, she saw her dad parked by her car. He was, of course, true to his word and they were going to get the Madonna tickets. It was then that she made up her mind about what she was going to do about David and Lisa.

She was first off the bus, and she put her big bag down on the ground and waited by the door. When David stepped off, she grabbed him by his shirt.

"Can you wait right here for a second?" she asked. There were a couple of snickers from his friends, but she didn't care, and he didn't either. He got out of the way of the other kids and was surprised when she turned back to see who was getting off next.

"So…" he said, "what are you doing?"

"You'll see," she said.

Then the girls started to get off the bus, and she saw Lisa reach the steps. When Lisa stepped down, Jennifer touched her arm.

"Hey, I want to talk to you," she said.

Lisa saw David standing behind her, and hesitated. What on earth, she thought, could be good about what was going to happen next?

Jennifer took them both by the arm and backed them up, out of earshot of the others. Lisa and David stood a few feet apart and didn't catch each other's eye.

"First, I want both of you to put the past behind you," she said. "What happened to make you two dislike each other so much?"

Lisa and David just stared for a moment.

"Come on," Jennifer continued. "I know you were friends at some point."

Lisa spoke first.

"Nothing happened," she said. "Our parents were friends. His family moved to a bigger house, and then we just didn't see each other anymore."

"Nothing happened," David confirmed.

"See? Then you two can be friends. Nothing happened that was so bad," she said.

She addressed Lisa.

"Lisa, I can't say it enough; thank you," she said. "I was going to let my senior year pass by just like I did the other years. I was going to let it be a big nothing, but you wouldn't let me. You made it interesting. You made it fun. You made me a winner."

Lisa had never done well with compliments. It wasn't common in her family.

"You're welcome," she mumbled.

Jennifer turned to David.

"I want you to know that I'm not mad at you. I think you're attractive. You're a nice guy. I don't care what you have with James. It's OK," she said.

David's eyes lit up.

"Okay, about that," he said defensively. "Look, I'm not gay."

Lisa snorted derisively.

"You're as queer as a three-dollar bill," she said.

"No, I'm not," David said. "James was an experiment. And it's over. I like girls."

"It doesn't matter," Jennifer said. "I'm glad you like girls. I'm a girl. She likes girls too. We all like girls. But what I want right now is friends. I like boys and girls, but I'm not going to have sex with anyone right now. And more than anything, I want you two as my friends. We only have four weeks before it's all over. Let's have fun. I'm not going to have sex with anyone before then, and after that, who knows. But right now, let's be the best friends we ever had. Okay? It's our time, right now. Let's live it."

David and Lisa look at the ground. Jennifer's proposition is not what they were used to. Neither were from families that placed any emphasis on fun.

"I could be friends," David mumbled. "But I'm not gay."

Lisa shrugged her shoulder.

"I've got a lot of friends that won't come out of the closet," she said. "If it will make you happy, I can have one more."

Jennifer grinned broadly and deeply.

"Madonna is coming to the Astrodome, and I'm going to go with my dad right now and get tickets. And both of you are coming with me!"

She grabbed them both into a hug.

"Now, let's give them all something to talk about," she said.

She took one of David's hands and one of Lisa's and started walking towards the locker rooms.

* * *

Bob and Jennifer were driving home. She held the three Madonna tickets in her hand. She was thinking about Lisa and David and their feelings around being gay. She accepted it and he did not. It was funny really. People were so complicated.

But, after a moment, her face grew serious.

"Daddy, Jack deals drugs," she said as she looked out the window. She didn't want to see his reaction.

"I figured as much," he said. "Do you know what and to who?"

"Coke, I think," she said, "but I don't know to who. What did Marco say?"

"He weaseled out of anything useful," Bob said.

They drive along in silence.

"I've never done it," she said. "I don't want to."

"You're a smart girl," he said. "You always have been."

She held up the Madonna tickets.

"You sure you don't want to go?" she asked with a sly smile. Bob felt his face make a broad grin, the kind he had not made in many years.

"I'm sure I'd love it, but it's going to be your night," he said.

She took his hand off the steering wheel, kissed it, and then placed it back on the wheel.

* * *

Jack popped up at the back fence, looked across the yard furtively, and then hopped over. He was exhausted. Days of hiding and living outside had worn him down. He walked cautiously up to the back door.

What he saw was Josie and Jennifer standing in the kitchen staring into the living room. Josie saw Jack walking up to the back door.

"Look who's back," he said to Jennifer who turned to look.

They watched as Jack came to the back door and entered. Immediately, he heard the yelling coming from the other room. It took him just a moment to realize that Bob and Carol were in a screaming, rage-fueled fight.

"Where have you been?" Jennifer asked. "You've had Daddy in a fit."

Jack heard more screaming and yelling.

"What in the hell is going on?" he asked.

"Mom and Dad are having a huge hissy fit," Josie said, his face contorted into a look of fear mixed with disgust.

Jack listened for a moment longer. This was not normal fighting; this was a verbal bloodletting. His mother's voice was far louder than he had ever heard, and his dad's voice was much higher.

"Over what?" he asked.

"Something to do with that guy Dave," Josie said. "I was upstairs, and mom and dad just started yelling. I saw Dave out my window, and he was leaving in a hurry."

Jack walked towards the living room.

Golden sunset light streamed in from the front window. A report from Chernobyl was on the TV, and the bluish TV light gave the room a sickly glow. It was sundown on this relationship, and it was ending with a nuclear meltdown.

Bob was on one side of the room, closest to the TV and Carol was on the other, pressed up against a bookcase. Jack slowly entered the room from the kitchen with Jennifer and Josie edged up behind him.

"I gave you everything you said you wanted," Bob yelled in a high pitch. "I gave you a home, I gave you three kids. I worked my ass off, and we went to the god damned moon!"

"Oh, you gave me those kids?" she retorted before he could finish. "Thanks! I thought I had a little something to do with it!"

"You know exactly what I mean," he said. "You wanted the American Dream, you as much as said so, and you got it. Now I guess you're ready to move on."

"I wanted to be a mom, but I didn't want to be a hostage the rest of my life," she said. "And how could I know what I want? I was a kid when you met me, and you took advantage. You were so much older."

"You were nineteen years old when I met you," Bob said, "and you were no kid. You had already been married and divorced by then."

"Whoa," Jack said involuntarily. He didn't know that.

"And how old were you?" Carol demanded to know of Bob.

"I was twenty-eight, Carol," he said. "There was nine years between us then just like there is now."

"I was still a child!" she stated. "And you took advantage of my insecurities. You talked so slick, giving me English books and telling me all you wanted us to do together. And then I was here, and then I was pregnant, you just paved the way for me. I didn't have any choice."

"You were pregnant with Jack when you got married?" Josie asked.

"No," Bob said. "We were married, we wanted a baby, and we had one. We did everything right."

"All of you, go outside!" Carol yelled at the three children, but they stayed stock still.

Bob continued; he didn't care what they heard.

"I paved the way for you, yes," he said. "I did, and now that's a bad thing? I brought you to the US, and made sure you had good medical care. I paid to get your mom and dad good health care."

"You cut me off from my own culture!" she carried on. "You and those NASA wives made me ashamed of being Mexican!"

"Mom," Jennifer interjected. "You never said anything about being ashamed of being Mexican."

"Carol, for the love of God, you aren't a Mexican. You're an American," Bob said flatly.

"See? See what he did?" Carol asked the children. "God forbid any other culture should be respected in this house. Mexicans are just nothing to you Texans."

This exasperated Bob further.

"Carol, I married a Mexican! In Mexico!" he yelled.

"You went shopping for a Mexican in Mexico! And you did it because of that bitch that broke your heart in California! She had an abortion, which was her right, and you were going to fix that problem!" she yelled back. "You just wanted a simple woman you could control!"

"Whoa," Jack said again.

"We made a home together here, in this country," Bob said. His appetite to continue was winding down "What difference does it make about what happened in California, or Mexico? We're here now."

"I don't want you to call me Carol anymore," she said. "My name is Karolina."

"I used to call you Karolita until you told me to stop," Bob said. He dropped down on the couch. "I'll call you whatever you want."

Even Carol was losing steam.

"You're an alcoholic, and you don't work anymore," she said. "This can't go on."

"Then get a lawyer, and let's get divorced," he said as he leaned his face into his hands. "But you can't have other men coming to this house."

In that statement, the whole ugly situation was summarized.

"He's doing something good for the world," she said quietly.

"He can do it elsewhere." Bob said and leaned back with his eyes closed.

After a moment, Carol headed upstairs. Bob finally looked over at Jack.

"Where have you been?" he demanded to know. "I've been out looking for you."

"I was at a rodeo," Jack responded with little conviction.

Jack wanted to tell the whole family what was going on and warn them the kind danger they were all in, but this didn't seem like the right time. He could not add to his dad's obvious burden now. For a moment, he thought about telling his mom, but she would just go to his dad. His dad was the last hope, and his dad was clearly broken.

Josie headed upstairs as well.

"This family is fucked," he said from the stairs.

Jennifer turned and went back to the kitchen. Jack could only watch as his dad lit a cigarette with shaking hands.

Chapter 25

Jack entered the bathroom he shared with Josie and locked both doors. He turned on the shower and pushed the water dial all the way to the left. He wanted the hottest water he could get.

As he showered, he felt a clock ticking in his mind. He knew there was a good chance the house was being watched, but there was also the chance that, since Ivan and Fernando had gotten the drugs back, they were gone. All he could do was go away and hope for the best.

He had walked back to Deer Park from Galveston which had taken over a full day. He stayed away from I-45 which would have been the fastest way back. Instead, he had walked along the shore, through neighborhoods, and even across the boundary of a refinery to get back to the part of the city he knew. When he was closer, he could see the big monument at the San Jacinto grounds. The Texas Star was at the top, and shortly after he could see that star, he began to recognize the roads where he was. He waited until dark to walk the last mile home.

When he stepped out of the shower, he was exhausted, fearful, and unsure, but he was clean. That counted for something. He had decided it was time to see the Northwest, and on the long walk home, he weighed out his options. Seattle was a big city, as was Portland.

In his bedroom, he packed up clothes in his high school book bag. It was all he had. The camping gear was in the garage and if he started to dig that out, he'd have to explain. His plan was to leave, tell no one, sleep somewhere hidden until morning, empty his bank account and call his dad from the road.

Then he heard the doorbell downstairs. His head snapped up in alarm.

Jack crept out of his bedroom and walked to the landing at the top of the stairs. He looked down at the front door where he saw his mom standing at the door, talking to someone, and when she walked forward, he saw her hug Dave, who'd come back to the house again. They were speaking in frantic tones, and Dave seemed foolishly devoted to whatever his plan was.

Jack turned away. As he was walking past Jennifer's room, he heard her talking. He noted the alarm in her voice.

"What are you doing here? How did you even get up there?"

Jack paused, and then cracked open Jennifer's door. He saw a girl at Jennifer's window hovering like a tracksuit-wearing vampire. Lisa had somehow climbed to the roof and was talking to Jennifer through the window.

"Who is that?" he said, more confused than alarmed.

Jennifer turned to look at Jack, and he saw exasperation on her face, but not fear.

"Just a girl on my track team," Jennifer said.

As Jack watched, Jennifer relented, and opened the window for Lisa, who stepped inside.

"Thanks," Lisa said as she stepped down to the floor. "I just wanted to talk to you for a few minutes."

"You okay?" Jack asked Jennifer.

"Yes, I'm fine," Jennifer said as she rolled her eyes so only Jack could see her.

Jack closed the door as Lisa gave Jennifer an awkward hug.

Jack's mind was still racing. He had never had to decide anything this big. He weighed the burden of asking for help and maybe saving the whole family from slaughter against his dad having the rest of the evening in peace, and he knew he was being stupid, but there was also the issue of admitting to his dad what he had done. What if his dad told him to call the police and Jack was implicated in Michael's murder? What if he fled, and they killed his family anyway, and only he survived? What would that feel like? His mother, he thought, had picked the exact wrong time to have this confrontation with his dad, in the moment when he needed his dad to be strong, to provide good advice, and help escape from the mess he had created.

He picked up the phone in the hallway and dialed. His stomach hurt and he was hungry, but he knew he couldn't eat. His head hurt, and his arms and legs felt heavy.

After three rings, Shannon, of course, picked up.

"Hello?" she said.

"I need to speak to Marco," Jack croaked.

"Why?" Shannon said. Was she being purposefully insolent and difficult? Jack suppressed the urge to yell.

"Shannon, put Marco on." he said a little louder.

"Jesus why don't you two love birds just get an apartment together?" she said. He could feel her smirking. "By the way, your sister has a lezbo in her room right now. I saw her climbing up a tree at your house."

Jack bit into his clenched fist.

"Shannon!" He burst out, then he calmed himself. He could not yell at her right now, he knew. "Just put him on, pretty, pretty please," he said.

He heard the phone handle hit the hall tabletop. There was a moment of silence, followed by Marco's footsteps padding up the stairs.

"Dude, where are you?" Marco whispered.

"I'm at home," Jack said. "I need you to go over and see if Domingo is home."

"I don't want to go over there," Marco said. Of course, he didn't, and Jack had a moment of renewed aggravation over getting Marco to do anything useful. "I don't think he's there anyway; the house has been dark for a while. Dude, what the fuck happened? I've been hearing really crazy things. I think that guy Michael is dead," Marco said.

"Marco, for Christ's sake!" Jack said. "Just go over there, and if he's home and if he's alone, come back to your house and call me. Do not call me from his house! Is he there and is he alone; that's all I want to know. Do that, and I promise, we don't ever even have to speak again."

"Well," Marco said, crestfallen. "that's not what I want, and not what I meant. I've been worried about you. I did what you asked and sent Shannon over to give him the money. He came to the front door, and she handed it to him. I still want to be friends."

Jack paused. He considered, for a moment, telling Marco what had happened and what he saw, then he realized Marco would not help in any way if he knew the truth.

"We can still be friends, but what I need you to do now is just go see if he's there," Jack said.

"Why don't you go?" Marco asked.

"Because he's really mad at me," Jack said.

"He's mad at me, too," Marco said.

228

"Not like he is at me," Jack responded calmly. "I'm trying to get us out of trouble, so please just do this for me."

"What kind of trouble?" Marco asked. "Oh my God, does this involve that Karlotta bitch?"

"Marco," Jack said, still controlling his urge to scream, "everything is going to be okay. And no, this does not involve that Karlotta bitch. I can get all this worked out, but I need you to go see if Domingo is there, and if he's alone, call me back. Just do this, and everything will be OK."

Jack waited for Marco to ask who else might be at Domingo's house, which would be the logical and smart thing to ask, but Marco took a big breath and relented.

"Okay, I'll call you back in a minute," Marco said, and hung up.

* * *

After hearing Jennifer declare that she was only interested in being friends, Lisa was deflated. She knew that Jennifer had said wonderful things about her, things that no one, in her entire life, including her parents, had ever said, but still, she felt the sting of rejection. All the reasons to fantasize about Jennifer were muted. It wasn't going to happen.

She turned to beer to help her cope, and she called Marie. They rode around Houston drinking beer until Lisa had convinced herself that it would be a wonderful surprise for Jennifer if she declared her love by showing up at Jennifer's house unannounced. Marie knew this was a bad idea, but she didn't offer much advice. She thought it would be funny to see Lisa pay a surprise visit to Jennifer's house, and Marie was still miffed by Lisa's determination to turn Jennifer, and not her, into the team track star. She had said nothing, but she burned with envy each time Jennifer won a race. After a few more minutes of drunk talk, Marie turned for Jennifer's house.

When they arrived, Lisa saw the tree to the side of the house and decided the best surprise would be to go to Jennifer's window.

"It's like that Romeo and Juliet song," she said to Marie.

"That's a play, stupid, not a song," Marie said.

229

"It's a song, it's that song by that band…" Lisa struggled to remember. "Just pick me up in an hour. No, two hours."

"I might fall asleep in two hours," Marie said as Lisa slammed the car door. Marie pulled away with no intention of returning.

Lisa crossed to the side of the house and with the dexterity of the true athlete, boosted herself up into the tree. Shannon had gone outside to smoke, and she observed from her front porch Lisa looking around the side of the house and then climbing the tree.

"The hell?" Shannon whispered.

From midway up the tree, Lisa could see the pink walls in Jennifer's room, and knew she was in luck. It was Jennifer's room right by where the tree would drop her off on the roof.

* * *

"What in the hell are you doing here?" Jennifer said, hands on hips. "It's late."

"I was thinking about you, and I was thinking about what you said," Lisa said.

Jennifer could see and hear that Lisa was sluggish.

"Are you drunk?" Jennifer asked.

"No," Lisa protested. "Okay, maybe a little."

Lisa plopped down on the edge of the bed and looked around. The room looked just like she had always imagined. She took the room in and sighed heavily.

"Wow. This room is awesome," she said.

"Thanks," Jennifer replied. She was amused at Lisa, who was not one to lose control physically, but she was also concerned that Lisa was too drunk to climb back down the tree.

"So, this is where you live," Lisa said dreamily.

"Yes, this is where I live," Jennifer said, unsure where this was going. "You could have just knocked on the front door."

"No, see…" Lisa said. "That wouldn't have been a surprise."

"Well, this is a surprise," Jennifer responded.

"Hey, so what you said," Lisa started. "I think it's really cool that you said you like boys and girls," Lisa said. "That's totally Madonna. I remember telling you that; that Madonna was bi, and now, you're bi."

"Okay, I'm bi, just like Madonna," Jennifer said. She had hoped to never have this kind of conversation with Lisa again.

"Don't you think that I, sort of, deserve some credit for making you realize this?" Lisa slurred.

"I guess, but…" Jennifer said hesitantly. The sequence of events that led her to Lisa, and then to David, was over. She didn't want to look back or explain. "What difference does it make now?"

"Okay…so," Lisa said, measuring her words carefully as she stood up. "So, we can have sex since you're bi?"

"No, I'm not bi in that way," Jennifer said.

"Okay…" Lisa said, unsure which track Jennifer's thought train had gone down. "So, what way are you bi?"

"I like guys, and I want to have sex with them," Jennifer said. "But I might have a three way."

Lisa sagged.

"So, if there are two dicks involved, that makes you bi?" Lisa asked. This had gone horrible wrong and the thought of Jennifer with two men was making Lisa lightheaded. "That's what you mean?"

"No," Jennifer said, realizing what she said sounded as ridiculous as Lisa made it sound. "I would have sex with a girl and a guy too. Under the right circumstances, I'd do it, which really means I'm sexually flexible. But, you know, it would have to be the right girl, and guy. It's the individual, really."

"Okay," Lisa said, her elation faded. "Am I one of those individuals?"

"Maybe," Jennifer responded.

Lisa flopped back on the bed.

"And I thought lesbians were complicated," she said.

* * *

Marco passed Shannon in the front hallway as he headed outside.

"Where are you going?" she asked, but he didn't respond. "Jennifer has that lesbian in her room. She climbed up a tree on the side of the house. Everyone over there is a freak."

"What?" Marco turned to ask. He was scared and not listening.

"Jennifer Buckhorn let that lesbian climb a tree to get up to her room," Shannon said, exasperated.

"Did you see anyone else over there?" he asked, trying to hide his alarm.

"That isn't enough?" she asked.

Marco started to say more, but his thoughts were muddled.

It was silent and still in the street. Marco stepped outside and looked across at Domingo's house, which was dark. He saw a car stop in front of the Buckhorn house, and a tall, blond man got out.

"What now?" Shannon said, seeing Dave walking towards the Buckhorn front door. "Something is up over there."

"Go inside, mind your own business," Marco said.

Marco crossed the street and headed down the side of Domingo's house. He came around the corner at the back of the house and walked up to the sliding glass door. He stepped up close and looked inside. He didn't see anyone, but then he saw a hand draw the door open.

"Hey, is Domingo here?" Marco said.

A long pistol connected to a dark hand answered his inquiry.

"Come in," a voice not Domingo's answered.

Marco entered this house, and the door was closed behind him. He was aware of two other people in the room, but what caught his attention was Domingo. The man was tied to a chair, and blood dripped from his chin.

* * *

Jack hadn't moved. He stood in the hallway and stared at the floor; his mind was racing but no power was getting to the wheels. He couldn't see the right plan, the perfect course of action. The phone rang and he picked it up.

"Hello?"

"Hey, it's me," Marco said. "Domingo's here, he wants you to come down."

Jack felt his stomach fall further. There was nothing but sure death at Domingo's house.

232

"I told you not to call me from his house!" Jack said, but then he froze. This was not just Marco's standard incompetence; this was death calling. "Put Domingo on."

There was an odd silence, and Jack heard the muffled sound of the phone being pushed into something to cover the sound.

"He says he's busy, so just come down," Marco said robotically. "He wants to talk to you. Here, at his house, I mean."

Jack hung up. Domingo was dead, they had Marco, and now they knew where he was.

He entered his room and finished pushing clothes into his backpack. His breathing was shallow, he was panting and sweating with fear. He couldn't think of which of his parents' cars to steal. Should he warn his family? Should he get one of his dad's guns? Or should he just flee. Fear decided for him; he was leaving right now. He'd take his dad's truck. The backpack went over his shoulder.

Jack entered the hallway and hustled to the top of the stairs. Carol was talking to Dave at the door, and Jack could see Dave and his blond mop of hair. Dave appeared to be pleading in some weird way, but for what, Jack couldn't imagine.

When Jack was three steps down the stairs, he saw past Dave to Marco who was walking across the lawn and up to the house. Ivan and Fernando were right behind Marco, not very carefully hiding their pistols. They seemed exaggeratedly large in Jack's reeling mind.

Jack ran down the stairs two at a time, hoping to get to the door first.

"Mom, shut the door! Shut the door!" he yelled.

His mother turned to him, softening and with sympathy in her eyes.

"Honey, Dave hasn't done anything to harm this family," she said.

Two quick mechanical cracks were issued from Fernando's pistol. Jack saw Fernando aim the pistol at the final moment and he ducked slightly. Both shots buzzed past Jack and hit the railing behind him.

Dave flinched and turned just in time to see Ivan raise his pistol. Ivan shot for Jack, but now Dave's big blond head was in the way.

Two cracks.

Dave's head exploded out of the back and bloody matter spewed across Carol. The force drove Dave's scattered skull pieces on her and dropped his big body across the threshold of the door. It couldn't be closed now.

Marco turned and fled back towards his house. Dave's dead body lay face up at Carol's feet. She turned and ran towards the kitchen and Jack headed back up the stairs.

Two more metallic cracks echoed across the neighborhood. Marco reached his front yard and turned back to look. He saw Ivan and Fernando stepping over Dave's body.

It was Fernando that had fired again as Jack reached the top step of the stairs. They were not well aimed shots, but the first hit Jack's backpack, and the other hit Jack in the left butt cheek. The bullet struck his pelvis and shattered it. The hot bullet stuck in the broken pelvis and cooked the tissue around it.

Jack felt the impact, and then the heat. His mind darkened, sure in the knowledge that he was going to die and that the men responsible for his death would kill his brother and sister, and probably his mom and dad. It was too late. He fell past the top of the stairs and crawled forward. He tried to stand but couldn't. Already his mind was starting to go blank. He knew he had seconds before Ivan and Fernando were at the top of the stairs. There was nothing to do except pray that they would leave the rest of his family alone.

"Run!" he called out to Josie and Jennifer. "Go out the windows and run!"

He looked at the end of the hall, where the door to his mom and dad's room was closed and the lights were off. But then to his horror, he saw Josie standing at his open bedroom door.

"Go back inside! Go out the window!" he said.

Josie's eyes grew big.

"Let me help you!" he said.

"No, just run!" Jack replied. Josie slammed his door shut.

After a moment, as expected, Ivan and Fernando crested the top of the stairs. Jack was on his side on the floor, his back turned against the wall.

"Puto, we waited for you," Ivan said.

Both men raised their massive pistols and Jack closed his eyes.

"I deserve this," he mumbled to himself. In some part of his spinning mind, the Catholic came out, and he confessed his culpability.

Jack then heard several loud blasts. They weren't the metallic clang of the executioner's pistols. These were more like explosions.

His hip throbbed but he felt little else, and the sound bounced off the hall walls, but it came from behind him, and not over him. He opened his eyes and saw Ivan staggering backwards. Jack turned his face back towards his parents' bedroom door and saw smoke coming from a long pistol barrel that was visible in the crack of the bedroom door.

In a split second, Jack saw the barrel retracted and the door closed. Ivan fell back on Fernando, and both men went down the staircase steps. When Ivan moaned loudly, Jack put the events together. His dad had shot that red-haired, foul-mouthed motherfucker.

Suddenly, Fernando popped up and fired back at the closed bedroom door.

The noise filled the hallway, and Jack covered his eyes and mouth. He smelled the smoke collecting in the hall, and it reminded him of going to the gun range with his dad years ago. He peaked through his hands and saw the bedroom door at the end of the hall had six big holes in it.

* * *

Jennifer was just about to ask Lisa to leave when they heard the first shots.

"What the fuck was that?" Lisa said as she sat up. She sobered up quickly.

Jennifer felt a cold hand grab her heart as she made the connection between the noise and Jack's drugs. She walked towards her door and then heard Jack calling for everyone to run.

"Go back out the window," she said to Lisa.

Lisa could see in Jennifer's face the terror and it spread to her. Even drunk, she knew the look of fear.

Lisa stepped out of Jennifer's window and onto the roof. She turned and held her hand out. She pulled Jennifer through the window and turned to take the tree limb that allowed her to reach the high second story.

"Just follow me!" Lisa said as she leaned forward to reach the limb. She would have reached the limb and held on to it while Jennifer put her sweet, strong arms around her neck, except her hand missed the limb by several inches. Lisa fell right off the house without a word. It happened silently and in an instant. Jennifer had just stood up, and suddenly, Lisa dropped from sight. She walked to the edge and looked down. Lisa was lying on her back, her mouth wide open, her eyes staring up, not moving.

"Okay, no thank you," Jennifer said. She backed up, clung to the rough edges of the dormer, and then climbed so she stood on top of it.

She heard gunshots and then a sound on the other side of the house. She saw Josie had gone out of his window and he climbed to the same position on top of his dormer. They looked at each other across the ridge vent of the big home.

"What is happening?" Josie said, panic in his voice. Jennifer wanted to walk over to him but dared not.

"Daddy will take care of it," she said as the next round of shots began. She and Josie felt the vibrations through their feet.

* * *

A few moments passed. Jack heard another moan from Ivan. Otherwise, it was quiet.

Fernando rose again with his weapon at the end of his arm.

Two loud shots rang through the hallway. More smoke filled the space.

But there was no return fire from the dark bedroom. The door hung at a crazy angle, partially open.

Jack looked back and forth from the door to the top of the stairs. Suddenly, he saw Ivan crawling to a standing position. Blood gushed down the front of Ivan's shirt. He knew Ivan wouldn't live, because there was no way they would go to a hospital, but this is why Ivan and Fernando were true killers, he thought. They were always ready to die.

"Don't. I can get the money," he said weakly.

Ivan was angry, his face nearly as red as his hair and blood.

"We come for your life, not your money," Ivan said. He no longer had a gun, but he pointed, and Fernando foolishly walked up the stairs and raised his pistol.

From his driveway, Marco heard the next sound. It was sustained and warlike. Shannon was coming out the front door when it started.

On the roof, Jennifer flinched and sat down so she wouldn't fall. Josie crouched down and put his hands over his ears. They could hear what they felt through their feet.

Carol had stopped in the kitchen and was staring at the blood dripping onto the kitchen floor from her hands, but the next sound drove her out the back door and running across the back yard.

Jack was in a dream and couldn't put together the sound with anything that made sense. He thought they had already killed his dad, and he was to be next. He hoped they would be satisfied and not go into Jennifer or Josie's rooms.

The door to Bob and Carol's room was shredded in an instant. The staccato of lead moving at 1700 miles per hour disassembled Fernando right where he stood. Jack felt the percussive effect in his ears, and he saw Fernando's broken remains bursting into bloody pieces. The mangled corpse was pushed off the landing and slipped down the stairs.

Jack watched as his would-be killer was mangled, but then the sheetrock, framing, and brick were blasted through, and a hole opened in the house. Through the smoke, Jack was looking at the oak tree in the front yard. The big caliber rounds had punched through the front wall of the house and opened a jagged window.

Finally, the ear-splitting rattle stopped. Marco and Shannon dropped their mouths open at the sight of the Buckhorn house burst open from the inside. Jennifer and Josie continued to cover their faces and ears.

Jack closed his eyes. Was it over? Out of the dark bedroom marched Bob Buckhorn in his underwear. He had the big Lewis Gun strapped across his chest. He marched to the top of the stairs.

Bob unloaded his remaining rounds on the bloody messes that was Fernando and Ivan. He blew the pieces to pieces, but he also blew away some of the stairs and the window and wall on the first level. More of the house fell away. Some of the rubble landed on Dave's inert blood-soaked corpse. Despite all the planning, Dave would not be walking on a peace march, not ever.

The Lewis Gun finally stopped barking just as the last of the brick on the front of the house fell off. Bob backed up and dropped the smoking Lewis Gun on the floor.

He knelt by Jack and pressed his hand on the bleeding wound.

"You've been shot in the ass, but I think you're going to make it," he said calmly.

Chapter 26

No one moves to Texas for the weather. No one in Texas moves to Houston for the scenery. The Comanche and the Mexicans knew better than to put a city along the bayous of what is now Houston because of the mud, mosquitoes, gators, and hurricanes.

But the people who founded first Galveston, then Houston, were a hardy bunch, and they could endure just about anything. They complained about the weather because everyone did it, but they also knew that it was annoying without being life threatening.

Occasionally, Houstonians were gifted a beautiful day, with bright skies and puffy clouds and not that much humidity, and those were the days that were worth living for. Bad weather made the good days precious.

Such was the day Jennifer Buckhorn graduated from high school. She had not been paying attention to the weather forecasts because she had been invited to a party, sometimes two, every night for the last three weeks of school, and she had gone to all of them. Sometimes she only stayed for a half hour and once she stayed until sunrise, but she decided after her reputation-making coming out misadventure at David's track party that anyone who wanted her to come to a party, just to see what she might do, she would go, and while she would keep her clothes on, she would put on a show, smile a lot, and let the boys and girls lean in and whisper their secrets to her. After what happened, that was the thing that surprised her most. Before, very few of the kids spoke to her, and afterwards, they wanted to tell her private things.

She had decided she would graduate high school as a virgin and push the final blossoming of her sexuality until college. There was no hurry. She had come to understand what it meant to be "like a virgin" finally, and it meant that no one thought she was a real virgin but treated her like one anyway. Nothing could be more perfect.

The morning of graduation, she woke up early and had showered, had gone to the gym, and was back in their hotel room before her mother had taken her eye shade off. It wasn't until she laid her gown on the bed that her mother seemed to remember that it was graduation day. Jennifer knew her mother was distracted and still weak from shock and fear. Carol made no mention of the final night at their former house, and all Jennifer knew was that she had gone to Dave's funeral, and then refused to speak any more about that night. She never even went to the floor of the hotel where Bob, Jack, and Josie shared a room.

Jennifer went to the room where the boys were every night before she left for a new party, and all three seemed to be happy, though Jack was in permanent pain. Jack was happy to be alive but in addition to the pain, he had a sharp limp and might walk with a cane for the rest of his life. Jack was not through with surgeries either. The bullet had done a lot of damage to his pelvis. Bob was happy to be alive, happy to not face any charges for killing two men and shooting off the front of his own house, and Josie was happy to be a real member of the group. Josie had started to say "fuck" a lot and no one cared. They had all survived an incredible wartime assault and lived to talk about it. The feeling of jubilation where the men were was in sharp contrast to the mourning around her mother.

She drove herself to school and met Lisa and David at her locker. True to his word, David had brought beer, and they drank two each and laughed at Lisa's impressions of everyone on the team. James had stopped by for a few minutes, and he drank a beer and left. He gave Jennifer a light hug just before she left.

"You doing okay?" he asked her.

"I'm fine, thanks," she replied and touched his hand. James, she discovered, could be quite charming.

Consistent with the school's indifference to the weather, graduation started at noon. The seniors assembled behind the stadium and hugged, and there were a few tears. Jennifer saw Shannon, but Shannon had dyed her hair black, and they didn't speak. The principal called out through a bull horn to get them all to listen and get in line.

Finally, they heard "Pomp and Circumstances" played by the freshman band, and everyone grew quiet. Kids who had known each other since first grade exchanged glances. After a moment, they began to walk out towards the folding chairs assembled on the fifty-yard line.

Jennifer sat and scanned the crowd. It only took a moment for her to find them. To her surprise, she saw them in the proper order, Bob, Carol, Jack, and Josie. Only Josie looked unhappy. Jack had given him his cane, and Josie was leaning his forehead upon it.

When the band started "The Star-Spangled Banner," everyone stood. Even the hippies in the class knew better than to stay seated and everyone took off their hats for the music.

Once everyone had settled, the principal, Mr. Wolf, came to the podium. Mr. Wolf wore thick glasses and many of the boys in the audience had developed a perfect impression of him over the years. He spoke in quick cadences with long pauses, and it was an easy style to imitate. Somehow everyone knew that Mr. Wolf had been a paratrooper in World War II and spoke perfect German. Exactly what he did in the war was less well known, but it was assumed to be something difficult and heroic.

Mr. Wolf greeted the parents and wasted no time getting things underway. He introduced the valedictorian, Susie Nguyen. Susie had come to the United States when she was six, and her parents pushed her relentlessly to learn English and study hard, and now, she had the chance to speak to the whole class.

Susie spoke first about the *Challenger* and Christie McAuliffe. She compared her many teachers to the now deceased astronaut and called them all heroes. The teachers stood and clapped but only a few of the students responded. They were watching Mr. Wolf, and he didn't stand. Susie went on to thank a few of her teachers, and then some of the students.

"The main thing I've been asked at school, over and over, is 'Is your name really Susie?',", she said towards the end of her speech. "And I've said yes, but it's not true. And now, that school is done, I'll tell you what my real name is."

This caused a hush to fall over the students. What the hell was Susie's real name? Susie was popular and there were a lot of nicknames for her that had traded around. "Susie Doosy" was popular with the boys. Most people pronounced her last name "new yen" and so she was called Susie New by some of her friends. A girl with Chinese parents tried to make 'Susie Gook' stick for a while but it didn't work; Susie was too nice for something that hateful to take root.

"The name on my birth certificate says Linh," she said, pronouncing it as 'Len.' "And even though everyone says my last name as 'New Yen' it's actually pronounced 'Win' and so all of you would know me as 'Len Win' if I had stuck with my birth name.

There was gentle laughter around the students.

"And here's something you don't know," she continued. "My mom, who is here today, her name is Dong."

There was a slight gasp in the crowd as the word 'Dong' echoed around the stadium.

"It means 'winter' in Vietnamese, and my mom was born in winter in a village in Vietnam," Susie said. "Dong Win; that's my mom."

In the stands, her mother covered her mouth. Her English was not good, but she knew her daughter had said her forbidden name and was talking about her.

"My mother's family was very poor, and they worked in the rice paddies day and night," Susie continued.

Bob glanced over at Carol to see if the story that was clearly coming would register. Carol looked down at her feet. She could see the story coming as well and didn't really want to hear it. Carol never thought a background of poverty was ennobling. She hated it.

"My dad was in the Army. He worked for the Americans as an intelligence officer, and if we had stayed in Vietnam, we would have been killed," Susie continued.

A perfect hush fell over everyone. Only the sound of the planes flying over made any noise at all. Many of the men in the stands had been in Vietnam, and they knew the ugly reality of what she was saying would have happened to her family and did happen to other families.

"We left Vietnam on a US Navy ship," she said. "My dad told us we needed to pick English names, and my mom picked 'Susie' for me. There had been a little girl on the base where we were refugees, she was the daughter of another American intelligence officer. Her name was Susie. My mother said that this little girl had blonde hair and frilly dresses, and she looked happy. So, she gave me this name. She wanted me to be happy, like that little girl. But my name is Linh, and my mother's name is Dong, and my father's name is Kai. We've made a life here in this country, and we're happy."

Bob watched Carol take some lip balm out of her purse and apply it absentmindedly.

"My dad isn't here because he had to work," she said, "but my mom is here, and so I want to say 'Mẹ ơi, con yêu mẹ' which means 'Mommy, I love you.'"

With that, Dong Nguyen covered her face and began to cry, but everyone else, including Mr. Wolf, stood, and clapped. The students stood and cheered for Susie and her mother. The moms and dads stood and clapped, but many, including Bob, knew that his broken family was not happy, and it was the easy lives they had lived relative to what had happened to the Nguyen family that made the difference. Adversity breeds commitment, and adversity had come too late for the Buckhorns to be happy.

Josie hadn't been listening and so was surprised when suddenly, everyone started cheering and standing. Jack struggled his way to a standing position without the cane and Josie stood up beside him.

"What happened?" he asked Jack.

"The valedictorian is talking about a happy family," Jack said.

With that, Josie sat back down and leaned his forehead on Jack's cane. He wasn't prepared to stand and clap for a happy family that was not his own.

Eventually, the school officials began the process of handing out diplomas. After Susie, the other speakers grew progressively longer, and Mr. Wolf started advising them to 'keep it short' as they came up to speak. And then finally, the seniors were instructed to line up by row.

Jennifer was in the second row, and she waited on the grass to the left of the stage. Senior after senior crossed as name after name was called out. There was Jessica Aaron, always first on every list. And then there was Michael Aaronson. There was Betty Antlers who had been on the receiving end of many jokes regarding her large bosom. There was Ben Applebaum, Paul Arnold, and Michael Axelrod who tried for years to get people to call him just 'Axe' Axelrod, but everyone called him Mike A, since there were so many other boys named Mike.

"Robert Bucharo," she heard as she placed one foot on the stairs. 'Bobby B' as they called him, had been in every home room, and he was reading most of the time. His mother was Mexican, too, and that was all she really knew about him.

"Jennifer Buckhorn," she heard and stepped up to the stage. The girls on the track team were cheering as Mr. Wolf handed her a case with her diploma inside.

"Congratulations, Jennifer," he said to her and looked to the boy lined up behind her.

"David Bucks," she heard as she stepped off the stage and went back to her seat.

Just like that, twelve years of school came to an end. Everything else she did, she got to choose.

When it was all done, she saw her family standing in a tight pod on the field. Already the future dynamic could be seen; Jack leaned on his cane beside Bob, Josie was right beside him. Her mother kept her distance from Bob. Lisa trailed behind her.

"Congratulations," Bob said as he hugged her.

She collected a polite hug from each and noticed once she was up close, her mother had been crying.

"Good job, honey," she said from behind her sunglasses.

"Okay, we're outta here," she said. "Lots of parties to go to."

"Home by two a.m., okay?" Carol said.

Jennifer nodded slightly, which was not a commitment.

"We'll be fine," she said.

"I'll make sure she gets back to the hotel," Lisa volunteered as they walked away.

An awkward moment passed as Jack hobbled away with Bob, Josie by his side. After a few steps, Josie turned around and looked at his mother who was headed in the opposite direction.

Chapter 27

The period after the shootings had been the most painful period of Carol's life. The picture in her head played itself over and over, in her dreams, and when she was awake, and when she was in the shower and when she stopped by the house to pick up more of her things. She'd see Marco coming across the grass and noticed that there were two men behind him. She'd feel the frustration that Marco was about to interrupt her efforts to get Dave to go away. She knew her marriage was over, and she wanted to go with Dave on the Peace March, but she couldn't just pack up and leave, which is what Dave was passionately asking her to do. Dave had no kids, and he didn't understand. He kept saying "You have to break free!" which was a message that appealed to her, but she wasn't ready to disappear for weeks with another man, or to lie about it.

Nothing she had seen in Mexico compared to seeing Dave's head explode in front of her. She had seen animals killed, she had seen traffic accidents, and she had seen a man in a ditch that had been murdered with an ice pick the night before. She had heard about other terrible things and of tortures from the Spanish Conquest and even before. She knew about human sacrifice, but she had never seen so much blood.

In her mental reenactments, she felt the hot blood and it was mixed with some kind of abrasive, which she didn't let herself place a name to. In her mind, Dave ceased to be Dave at that moment, and while it was Dave's blood that hit her, and other parts of what was Dave, in that instant, was gone. He was literally no more than forty-eight inches away when he took his final breath trying to convince her to leave with him. If she had said yes, maybe he'd still be alive, she thought. If she had let him in, maybe things would have been different.

After she saw Dave's head explode, she ran back through the kitchen and finally into the backyard where she hid behind the big fiscus in the back corner of the yard. When she heard the Lewis Gun, she had no idea what it was and thought for a moment that it was some kind of air attack on the house. She heard the front of the house fall off, and was sure, at that moment, that everyone inside was dead. She sat down on the wet ground and put her head in her hands and started

245

to pray. She was still there when Josie came outside looking for her. He sat beside her and hugged her, and they stayed there for a while, and he told her that Jack had been shot but was alive, that Jennifer was okay, and that the two men who shot Dave were dead.

"What happened to them?" she asked after a while.

"Dad shot them with a machine gun," Josie said. "He shot the front of the house off."

"That was your dad that did that?" she asked, incredulously.

"Yes," Josie said. "He killed those two guys, but everyone else is okay. Except that lesbian that fell off the house."

Carol started to ask but didn't. Some lesbian falling off the house was just a bridge too far, and she was glad enough to learn that Jack wasn't dead, and Jennifer wasn't dead, and Josie obviously wasn't dead, and she'd only have to mourn Dave. She hadn't seen the house yet and didn't realize it was dead too.

Josie walked with her to the kitchen and then thought about what was just around the corner. He knew she shouldn't see any of it, and so he took her hand and led her to sit down at the kitchen table. He knew where his dad's vodka bottle was, and so he took it down and placed it in front of her.

"Let's just stay right here for a while," he said. The house smelled like gun powder, and he wanted to get her out of it, but he stayed there with her, stroking her arm. She didn't move. Jennifer entered the kitchen eventually, crying hysterically. A police detective had put a blanket around her shoulders, and she sat down beside her mother.

"Oh my God, mom, they shot Jack," she said.

"Is he going to be okay?" she asked peacefully.

"I don't know," Jennifer said and started to sob.

The young police officer spoke up.

"He's been taken to the hospital, and we think he'll be okay," he said. "You are Mrs. Buckhorn?"

"Yes," she said robotically. "I speak Spanish," she added for reasons she later would not understand.

"Mom!" Jennifer said. "They don't speak Spanish! We need to go somewhere. Dad shot off the whole front of the house, and Lisa fell off the roof, and…there's blood everywhere!'

Jennifer put her head on her arms and sobbed. Carol just stared ahead. It couldn't get real.

"He's dead, for sure?" she asked the policeman.

"No, mom, he's at the hospital," Josie said, thinking she was referring to Jack. "Dad went with him."

"The man at the front door," Carol said. "He's dead?

"Yes, ma'am," the police officer said. The officer had seen many shootings, but this one was weird and different, and he suspected the man at the front door was the lynchpin of the whole case. "He was an associate of yours?"

"Yes," Carol said.

Even Josie could see what was about to happen.

"He wasn't an associate. He was just a guy she knew from the peace march stuff and the hippie café," he offered.

"I don't know how to call her parents," Jennifer sobbed. "She always called me."

"The young lady on the side of the house? You know her?" the officer asked Carol.

"They aren't related," Josie said. "The guy at the front door and the girl that fell off the roof, they aren't related to each other," he offered. "It was just a coincidence."

It occurred to Josie that he was now the only person in the house that wasn't broken by what happened, and he could see how the police might dig themselves into a hole. And he was worried that his dad might be implicated in something Jack had done.

"Can you take us to a hotel or something," Josie asked the officer.

"I need to pack first," Carol said.

"Take us somewhere, and I'll explain as much as I can," Josie said.

They let Josie go upstairs and gather some things for Carol and Jennifer. The stairs were crooked and broken and covered in blood and human remains. The police noted that he seemed like he was okay, so they let him walk right through the blood and guts and pack for his mother and sister. Josie came back to the kitchen with a gym bag full of clothes and they went out the back door, around the house and to a police station. At the police station, Josie called Uncle Bucky, who he found in the white pages, and Bucky and his wife came to pick them up.

Bucky moved the three of them into a hotel that night, and later Bob found them. He brought news of Jack, which was mostly good, but some bad. Jack would suffer some paralysis because of the severed nerves that went down his left leg, but he'd walk. His pelvis was shattered and would take a long time to heal. One of his legs would be a little shorter than the other, for the rest of his life.

Two days later, when it was okay to leave Jack, Bob looked at some rental houses near their house, and he took Jennifer and Josie to see them. They hated the houses he found, and he knew he couldn't share a bedroom with Carol anymore. Finally, he opted to pay for hotel space for a month. The hotel was near the hospital and two rooms, one for Jennifer and Carol, and one for he and Josie, worked out well, even if it was more expensive that way.

Lisa had been taken to a different hospital, and her parents had been called. When the police found her on the side of the house, she was still unable to catch her breath or get up, but once she was in an ambulance, she realized she was fine and wanted to go back to the house and check on Jennifer. They wouldn't turn the ambulance around and she began to yell at them. They thought her yelling was from the blow to her head, not her normal behavior, and she knew that and yelled louder. At the hospital, she was told Jennifer was okay and then her parents took her home.

For two days, her parents wouldn't let her leave the house, and so on the third day, she called Marie to come get her. Marie drove her to the hospital. Lisa walked the halls until she saw Josie sitting in a waiting room.

"Oh my God!" she said as she rushed to Josie and hugged him. "Oh my God, I'm so glad to see you!"

Josie recoiled a little and then gave in to her hug. When Lisa pulled back, he saw the genuine look of relief in her eyes.

"Where is your sister?" Lisa asked.

"She's at the hotel with my mom," he said.

"But she's okay? You're okay?" Lisa asked.

"Yes, she's okay, and so am I. Only my brother got shot," Josie said. "Are you okay? You fell off the roof."

"I was so drunk," she said. "I got knocked out when I hit the ground, and I don't remember much after that. I'm fine."

Josie went into Jack's room and got his dad to come out, and Bob drove Lisa to see Jennifer. When they met in the parking lot, they hugged for a long time. Josie saw a tear run down Lisa's cheek.

After that, Lisa found a way to the hospital or to the hotel every day. Sometimes, Jennifer was withdrawn and didn't want to talk, but Josie did and so she'd talk to him for hours. She made him laugh. Josie took her in to see Jack.

"I remember seeing you," Jack said weakly. "It's one of the last things I remember."

In the days after it all ended, and his home was destroyed forever, Josie found himself spending more time with his dad than he ever had. It made him happier than he'd ever been. They spoke at length about how both had reacted in the immediate aftermath of the shootings. Bob started calling for Josie as soon as he saw Jack's injuries. Josie heard him from up on the roof and began to climb down.

"Don't go back in the house!" Jennifer yelled across the rooftop.

But Josie went through his bedroom window and opened the door to the hallway. He saw Bob pressing a towel on Jack's bloody butt wound.

"Come do this," he called to Josie, and Josie used the towel to put pressure on Jack's wound. The pain had not really begun to register with Jack, so he just moaned.

Bob went back to the bedroom and called the police. When he returned to the hallway, he opened Jennifer's door, and he called her.

"She's up on the roof," Josie told him, so Bob called to her from her window. She came through the window and fell into his arms sobbing. It was later, after Bob left with Jack in the ambulance, and Lisa left in another, and he and his mother and sister were at a local police substation that he thought to look in the phone book and called Uncle Bucky. He couldn't think of anyone else to call and both his mom and Jennifer were sobbing wrecks. Bucky and his wife arrived about an hour later. Bucky met his niece, nephew, and soon to be ex-sister-in-law in the lobby of a police station.

Bob and Josie spoke about the whole sequence as they were eating breakfast at the hospital cafeteria.

"By the way," Josie said as he wolfed down his eggs. "I have cousins, and I want to meet them. Uncle Bucky has two kids. His wife told me. They live in Kingwood."

Bob's mouth dropped slightly open.

"You're kidding me," Bob said. "Bucky has kids?"

"Yep," Josie said. "A boy and a girl. And they're close to my age."

Bob sat in stunned silence. He had learned that Bucky had moved back to Houston a couple of years back. Bucky's wife had sent a Christmas card with no return address. The card had simply read "Merry Christmas from the Buckhorn Family" in a handwriting Bob knew was not Bucky's. The card looked to have been mailed in Houston. He hadn't seen Bucky in nearly two decades, and he knew the card was Bucky's wife's idea, and so he didn't invest the energy to track down Bucky again. He was, after all these years, still angry with his brother. After their mom died, Bob had made calls and found out that Bucky was still in Venezuela, but he never wrote or called. A Christmas card from a wife he had never met wasn't enough in Bob's mind to bridge the gap.

But that was then, and Bob had changed. He desperately wanted to forgive his brother for being from the same home and suffering the same consequences.

"Oh, yeah," Josie added. "I heard mom speak Spanish. Uncle Bucky's wife spoke to her in Spanish, and she said something back, and then they went on like that for a long time. His wife is really nice. And he was too, except maybe a little quiet. His hair is all white, and he has a beard. He looks like Santa Claus."

Bob smiled at the thought of additional family members, and of being an uncle himself.

"Your mom couldn't speak English when I met her," he said absently. He was thinking about how he was going to reconnect with his brother and this time, Bucky wasn't going to have a choice. They were going to be close. They were going to act like family. It was high time. Maybe he'd move to Kingwood, even though it was further away from NASA. If Bucky lived right down the street, he wouldn't be able to get away so easily.

"I didn't even know she could still speak Spanish," Josie said as he started in on his English muffin. "Signs and wonders."

Bob laughed at Josie's choice of expressions. Josie smiled back deep and broad.

"Signs and wonders," he repeated.

* * *

For the week following the shootings, Carol slept for prolonged periods. But one morning, she woke up to find her mind made up. She was going on the Peace March in Dave's place, she was getting divorced, and she was leaving Texas. Everything in Texas reminded her of when she arrived from Mexico, and the cartel executioners killing Dave and spraying his blood over her sealed, in her mind, that her path was the right one. She was going to be a good, well dressed, elevated American women with the highest standards, and Bob had served his purpose. She and Bob would, she decided, divorce. She was going to remake herself.

Two weeks later, when she told Bob that she was going on the Peace March and would be gone for six weeks, his response was "Good. I'll tell the kids." When she told him she intended to divorce when the march was over, he just nodded.

"We'll work it out when you get back," he said. "A little time between now and then would be a good thing."

Bob told Jack about his mother's plans a few days later, but Jack didn't say much. He already knew his parents had no future, and he was depressed about his own. The intense pain he had been feeling in his pelvis and legs was subsiding, but he knew he would have a limp for the rest of his life.

Initially, he had been distracted by the many police interviews he had to provide and then by the meetings with his lawyer. The police kept asking questions about the backpack, and Jack's lawyer insisted on being present when Jack answered their questions. The backpack had not been found at Domingo's house, and neither had a significant amount of money. It was only when the Midland PD found Miggie hiding at his sister's house that the story Jack told was corroborated, and the final pleading and legal settlement came into view. It was the police opinion that the backpack and cash had been returned to Mexico, and the chance of another hit squad tracking down Bob or his

251

family was low. The cartels had an unspoken rule about fighting back; they respected it. They mostly let survivors be.

After the police and lawyers left, Jack had lots of time to stare out the window. Bob saw him falling into a funk.

"People make mistakes, son," Bob said. "It doesn't have to define the rest of your life."

"Dad, I didn't just make a few bad choices. I got people killed," Jack said. "Michael's family, I led the killers to their door."

"When I was in Korea, I saw a man who had been shot," Bob said, "and I let him suffer. He was trapped on the perimeter fence, and he moaned all day, and then died. Maybe I could have saved him. I had the power to do something, but I didn't. I'm responsible for that. You couldn't act. They were armed. Every man I know, every Marine, would have done exactly what you did. I still think about that man sometimes, but Korea and the war didn't define me. I just went on, and I didn't know it, but the best years of my life were coming. So are yours."

"That night, I remember you and mom were fighting, and she said you had a girlfriend in California that had an abortion," Jack said. "That was right after the war?"

"Yes, it was," Bob said.

"That must have sucked," Jack said.

"It did, but after the Marines, I went to work, and I was too busy to think about what happened," Bob said. "Work was good for me. So was college after that. One foot in front of the other."

"That's when you were in the oilfield?" Jack asked.

"Yes," Bob said.

"And then you went to college?"

"Yes."

A big tear ran down Jack's face.

"Dad, I'm not a loser," he said. "I'm just stupid."

Bob had not expected this. Bob had no relationship with his father, and therefore, had never had to confess anything. Until recently, he had always reserved his emotions for Carol, and never with the kids, and he discouraged them from ever crying. Maybe, he thought, it was time for that to change. They all had it hard in some way.

252

"I know you aren't a loser, Jack," Bob said as he leaned closer and touched Jack's arm.

"I want to go to work," Jack said, his eyes already drying. "I don't deserve to go to college, not yet. But I want to work."

"We'll make it happen," Bob said. "We'll make it happen."

It was a few days later when Bob dropped by the lawyer's office to submit another check that he ran into Owen Williams. Williams had retained the same lawyers to defend him against a civil suit brought by Michael King's dad and was sitting in the lobby.

"They're wasting their time," Owen told Bob after they shook hands. The two men had worked together in Midland three decades back, and now, Owen admitted that he was finished as a rodeo promotor. "The rodeo is busted. I can handle a lot, but not drug deals gone bad."

Owen told Bob about his plan to go back to being a landman. Owen had maintained an interest in some leases, and he knew many of the biggest landholders in the state.

"What will Jack do next?" he asked Bob.

"He has to go to work somewhere," Bob said. "When he gets out of the hospital and off probation, he wants to do something honest and stay out of trouble,"

"You know," Owen said, "most rodeo cowboys are into something stupid or illegal. Jack wasn't the worst of them. He was respectful. If he wants to learn the land business, I might could use him to do some gophering and knock on some doors."

When Bob brought the opportunity up with Jack, he saw Jack laugh for the first time in weeks.

"Owen Williams would hire me to do something?" he asked incredulously.

"He says you were the least worst of the rodeo cowboys," Bob said. "Landman is a decent job, and it's not dangerous. You'd be a long way away from the drill bit. And you'd have a lot of time to think."

"Son of a bitch," Jack said. "Working for Owen Williams."

* * *

Later, when Jack made a deal with Owen to start work as soon as he was off probation, Carol had already left town for the march. Once she left Houston, she felt freer than she ever had. She marched with a group of people she really liked, and she fit in with them. They responded warmly to her, and she saw parts of Colorado, Kansas, Missouri, and Illinois she had never seen.

Along the way, as she marked off the steps across the United States, she had time to think. She thought a lot about her life in Mexico and tried to understand what she was running from. The two Mexicans who had murdered the man she thought she truly loved and shot her son had clarified things for her. Mexico was violent. Mexico had a violent past that offered human sacrifice to appease the gods, even before the Spanish showed up and imposed a different human sacrifice to a different God. It was blood and death all the way down. She had grown up afraid in Mexico, and Bob had offered her a path to safety. Bob was nothing like the men who wanted her when she turned thirteen, and the one man who had possessed her just two years later, in Mexico. Bob treated her as a person, someone who was interesting and worth listening to, and she had never experienced or even seen that in her native culture. It appealed to her.

But over the years, she grew used to that, and she saw Bob transfer his interest to his job. After they were married, all that really interested Bob was his job and the kids. Meanwhile, she saw the changes sweeping over her adopted country. She wanted to side with the people who stood for peace. If that was the hated hippies, and the peace marchers, then so be it. She was going to be her own person for the rest of her life. To the others she spoke to about her life, she said she had "graduated" and was ready to move on. They applauded her for it.

When she would call to check on the kids, Bob would find out where she was and wire her money, and she bought what she needed along the way. She stayed in Chicago for a few days and then flew to Washington to walk the final miles. In those days, she decided she wanted to live in Chicago, and she wondered if Josie would like it. When she told Josie on the phone that she wanted him to move to Chicago with her, she heard, for the first time, what the last couple of years, the past few months, and the recent days had done to him. Like his brother and sister, Josie had suddenly grown up.

254

"Mom, go fuck yourself," he said. "I'm not moving to Chicago."

It was Texas hot when Bob stopped his truck in the street at the former Buckhorn house. He and Jack stared silently at the now abandoned home. The front of the house was crumbled, and a giant canvas tarp covered the gaping hole.

A realtor sign in the front yard told the story. The dead house was for sale, the sign had a sticker on it that read Lot Available. The house was coming down, and a new home would be there one day.

Jack looked down the street and saw the For Sale sign in front of Domingo's house. He heard from Marco that the bloody carpet had been taken up and new carpet put in. He assumed the carpet had been taken up because of all the blood. Marco told him that a carpet crew had been at the house for a couple of days, and 'new carpet' was on the Chronicle listing for the house. That was enough to know.

Marco exited his house and saw the truck just as Jack saw him. Bob saw Marco as well, so he eased off the clutch and let the truck idle down to Marco who walked to the curb.

"Wow, look at this," Marco said.

"Hey, buddy," Jack said. He really didn't blame Marco for what happened. He knew others in his family did, but he thought that was just so they didn't have to think so poorly of him. Marco was a weasel, and weak, but he wasn't bad. Being passive wasn't that great a vice, all things considered. Sometimes, it's a real asset.

Bob leveled an icy glare at Marco.

"Wow, so you're selling the house," Marco said after an awkward pause. "Man, people in this neighborhood, they don't talk about anything else."

"Yeah, I bet," Jack said.

Marco continued to try and fill the void with something normal sounding.

"So," he said to Jack. "What are going to do now?"

"As soon as I'm off probation, I'm moving to Midland," Jack said. "Dad's going back to work for NASA. I'm going to be a landman."

"Great!" Marco said. It sounded like something great, but really, he didn't know what Jack would do or why, only that it seemed like something that made good money. He started to ask if Jack could work the oilfield with, you know, a limp, but then thought it was better not to ask questions. Marco also knew that Jack had plead guilty to some misdemeanor charges around the murders of Domingo, Michael King, Michael's sister, mother, and the two men in the trailer, and had never mentioned Marco even once. Jack's lawyer had counseled against bringing Marco into the case because of Marco's unreliability and the district attorney had gone along.

"What's Jennifer going to do??" Marco asked.

"A&M," Jack replied.

"Going to be an Aggie, far out," Marco said. "What about the little one?"

"He's transferring to Kingwood," Jack said.

"Great!" Marco said. "All the oil brats go there. And where is Mrs. Buckhorn?"

"Chicago," Jack offered.

Bob revved the truck to show the chitchat was over.

"You dodged a bullet, Marco," Bob said. He still thought Marco was a fool who evaded responsibility, and further, Bob knew Marco would always be that way. He'd inflict his weakness on some women eventually and then some poor kids. "A whole bunch of them."

"I know," Marco offered. It was a completely truthful statement. He did know. "We all did. Well, most of us."

Bob took his foot off the brake and the truck began to advance slowly, and Marco fell out of view.

"See you later?" Marco asked Jack, but Jack didn't respond.

He looked over at the crippled Buckhorn house and then went inside. Shannon had been looking out the window and saw the interaction.

"What did they want?" Shannon asked.

"See the house one more time, I guess," Marco said. "She's going to A&M, so you won't have to see that cunt ever again."

Shannon didn't take the bait. She knew it was time to leave childhood behind, and that included all the conflict that had marked her adolescence. She never told Marco, but the malevolent sound of the big Lewis gun was still in her dreams, and it scared her. She wanted to be a better person.

"That's too bad," she said, and left the room.

* * *

The Astrodome began construction in 1962. Bob learned of it in the newspaper. He wondered immediately how in the hell the grass would stay alive in a domed stadium, and sure enough, the grass died and so the stadium put down the first fake grass in the first closed sporting arena, dubbed 'Astroturf.' The grass made from synthetic fibers required lots of petroleum to create, which prompted Bob to claim that it was "the oil business giving back to nature."

Judy Garland was the first singer to play the Astrodome, and NASA purchased tickets for the engineers and their wives. Carol was extremely excited by the dome and the entertainer. When Judy Garland sang to the delight of all "Somewhere Over the Rainbow," he saw the tears in her eyes. He squeezed her hand, and she squeezed his back. Those were good days.

The intervening twenty-one years had defined him and put him on his path to happiness. He was happy to be getting divorced, and still taking care of his kids. He was happy they were all alive and still had a mother and father. Carol had been a few inches from the bullet that killed her boyfriend. Jack's backpack saved him from a wheelchair, or death. Bob knew they'd need him for years to come and he'd be there for them. He wondered, as he weaved through traffic and tried to get closer to the dome, if he didn't engineer the whole thing to get right where he was. As rude as Carol had been, he thought the divorce would be worth the expense. She needed to move on, and he understood that. He was more than willing to help her establish herself in whatever new life she wanted.

He was happy to be back at work. Arnold Aldritch had called him a few weeks after he had visited NASA and asked him to meet for dinner at Brennans. They sat in the bar and drank scotch, and eventually, after the third scotch, Aldritch brought up a job. He had the authority to hire who he needed to get the shuttle back in the air.

"You have to set aside, forever, whatever you think about the orbiter," he pointed out. "So do I."

Bob thought for a moment. He palpably wanted to go back to work, but he wanted to succeed.

257

"I don't know," he said. "Who works there now? Will I even fit in?"

"It's not the same crowd that came in after *Apollo*," Aldritch said. "There are a few of them, but the new engineers, they are less ideological. They want to accomplish things. If you give them a chance, they won't disappoint you. And frankly, I need old hands to steady the boat. We're under a tremendous amount of pressure."

Bob liked what he heard. While they waited for the valet to bring their cars, Arnold gave Bob a hug, and Bob realized he had a loyal friend. He is determined to make more

He also had a brother again. He bought a house two streets over from Bucky, and he walked to Bucky's house in the evenings. Bucky's second Venezuelan wife, Maribel, was much younger than Bucky and a chubby, happy woman who never seemed to leave the kitchen. Bucky's teenaged kids were wild and loud, and Bob marveled at how much Bucky had changed. The kids hung on him and teased him, and he just took it. After Maribel had fed them, he and Bucky would sit on the back porch and talk. Bucky told stories, things he remembered about being a kid, their dad, the war, Venezuela, his travels to the Middle East. Bob didn't dare ask anything about what had made Bucky change, for fear that the old Bucky would reemerge. And, he didn't care why Bucky had changed. It was none of his business. His business was to be a good kid brother, a role long denied him. He read enough into the things Bucky said to know that Bucky was sorry about what had happened, how he had acted, and wanted to be a good big brother. No more words were needed.

Mondays were when Bob was happiest to be back at work. The weeks went by quickly. Arnold had been right; the new engineers were a curious lot, eager to learn, eager to teach, and practical. They would get the shuttle back into the air quickly, and Bob was proud to be a part of it.

When Jennifer's big day came, he insisted on driving her, Lisa, and Josie, to the Astrodome to see Madonna. After graduation, David's parents decided he needed to go on a trip to Europe before college which kept him from going to the Madonna show. When he called to tell Jennifer, she heard James talking in the background. When she told Lisa, it was Lisa that said they should take Josie instead.

When Jennifer asked Josie if he wanted to go, he asked "Is Lisa going, too?" Jennifer saw again Lisa's intense ability to draw good things out of people. As a friend, Lisa was a keeper.

Bob listened in silence as the teens chatted frantically all the way from the Texas Tavern, where he dropped them off for dinner, to the Astrodome, and in that brief time, he picked up on Jennifer's glowing status with her friends. Lisa spoke of nothing else but who wanted to hang out with them that summer. Lisa hadn't gotten into A&M, but she was going to Blinn, a junior college, close by. Josie never stopped smiling and laughing. Lisa seemed more than a bit afraid of Bob, and he said nothing about that as well.

When he had gotten as close as traffic allowed, they got out of the car.

"I'll meet you right here, right at this corner, when the show is over," Bob said.

"How will you know when it's over?" Jennifer asked. She was decked out in her most glamorous Madonna gear and had her eyes made up dark and sultry and she glowed like a sparkling diamond.

"I'll be somewhere close and can figure it out," he said.

When Josie and Lisa were a few feet away, Jennifer got back in the car and grabbed his hand.

"Thank you," she said. Before she could stop herself, her throat constricted, and she let out a tiny sob. "You take care of everything and everybody."

"Go on," he said. He gripped her little hand hard. "It's your night. Go enjoy it. I'll never be that far away."

She smiled and started to wipe her eyes but remembered she couldn't without smearing her make-up. He stuck his arm out and she dabbed her eyes with his white sleeve.

After she got out, he drove away. She and Lisa and Josie linked arms and walked towards the giant dome where soon she'd see, in person, the woman she admired and tried to imitate the most. She heard someone calling her name and saw it was Susie Nguyen, and so she waved and the three of them ran to Susie and her friends. Josie saw some of the other new sophomores and they acknowledged him. Being seen with Lisa was doing something to his reputation as well, and it wasn't all bad. Lisa held him by the arm and whispered vulgar jokes into his ear which made him laugh.

Jennifer let the warm breeze and good feeling wash over her as traffic sped by. In her heart, she knew she had outgrown her mom, and one day would outgrow Madonna, Lisa, her dad, and even Houston, but that day wasn't this one, and she smiled deeply as she felt the warmth of her friend on one arm and her brother on the other, and she soaked in the glow of all those around her.

Jennifer felt as alive as she ever would and was as sure as she was of anything that she would never die. Life, sweet life, would carry on forever, and she'd somehow always be a part of it.

Tom Roush is a writer living in Houston, Texas and the author of several books, articles, and posts about subjects as diverse as movies to combat sports. He can be reached at thomasroush@gmail.com